"A funny, romantic, and memorable story."

—BOOKPAGE

"Utterly binge-worthy, this is a story about the theater, a girl, and her hilarious yet heartbreaking love life . . . Witty banter and endearing characters make this high school romance a delight to read."

—BRIGHTLY

"A contemporary romantic comedy with wit, heart, and spot-on pacing."

—FOREVER YOUNG ADULT

"Real-life romantic partners Wibberley (the Last Oracle series) and Siegemund-Broka (making his YA debut) collaborated in this theater-centered novel . . . The coauthors wisely balance out the romance with family drama, and Megan's commitment to a future life in the theater will please readers who share a similar love of Shakespeare and want a little romance to go with their drama."

—PUBLISHERS WEEKLY

"Megan and Owen's flirty, whip-smart banter is irresistible, and it's refreshing to see a swoonworthy Asian male love interest . . . Charming characters and an enchanting exploration of Shakespeare's romantic tragedy make this debut a must-read."

—KIRKUS REVIEWS

"A delightful, light romance readers won't be able to put down."

—SLJ

"It is refreshing to see a female character portrayed as fearless and comfortable with her own physicality . . . Supporting characters include a realistically diverse group of friends, and their interactions are authentic. Fans of Jenny Han and Kasie West will root for Megan's happiness."

—VOYA

OTHER BOOKS YOU MAY ENJOY

Always never yours

Always never yours

EMILY WIBBERLEY

AUSTIN SIEGEMUND-BROKA

PENGUIN BOOKS

PENGUIN BOOKS
An imprint of Penguin Random House LLC, New York

First published in the United States of America by Penguin Books,
an imprint of Penguin Random House LLC, 2018

Visit us online at penguinrandomhouse.com

LIBRARY OF CONGRESS CATALOGING-IN-PUBLICATION DATA
Names: Siegemund-Broka, Austin, author. | Wibberley, Emily, author.
Title: Always never yours / by Austin Siegemund-Broka and Emily Wibberley.
Description: New York, New York : Penguin Books, 2018. | Summary:
Between rehearsals for the school play and managing her divided family,
seventeen-year-old Megan meets aspiring playwright Owen Okita,
who agrees to help her attract the attention of a cute stagehand
in exchange for help writing his new script.
Identifiers: LCCN 2017058698| ISBN 9780451479846 (hardback)
Subjects: | CYAC: Dating (Social customs)—Fiction. | Theater—Fiction. |
Families—Fiction.
Classification: LCC PZ7.1.S535 Al 2018 | DDC [Fic]—dc23
LC record available at https://lccn.loc.gov/2017058698

Paperback ISBN 9780451478641

Printed in the United States of America

1 3 5 7 9 10 8 6 4 2

For our (respective) parents

Always never yours

ONE

ROMEO: *Is love a tender thing? It is too rough,*
Too rude, too boist'rous, and it pricks like thorn.

MERCUTIO: *If love be rough with you, be rough with love.*

I.iv.25–7

"ALL THE WORLD'S A STAGE . . ."

Brian Anderson's butchering the line. I listen for the posturing and borderline mania Shakespeare intended, but—nope. He's doing some sort of half English accent and throwing iambic pentameter out the window.

"How about we stop there for a second?" I interrupt, standing up and straightening my denim dress.

"Just once, Megan, could we get through the scene?" Brian groans.

I shoot him a look and walk into the middle of the "stage," which for today is the hill behind the drama room. Our drama teacher, Ms. Hewitt—who everyone calls Jody—sent us outside to rehearse whatever Shakespeare scene we wanted. And by "sent us," I mean kicked us out for being obnoxious. I picked the hill for our rehearsal space because I thought the pine trees nearby would evoke the forest in *As You Like It*.

Which was stupid, I now realize.

"I feel like we're not getting what's going on in the charac-

1

ters' heads," I say, ignoring Brian and speaking to the group. It's only the four of us out here in the middle of sixth period. Jeremy Handler wears a hopeless expression next to Brian while Courtney Greene texts disinterestedly. "Orlando"—I turn to Jeremy—"is fundamentally a nice guy. He only wants to steal from the Duke to help his friend. Now, Jacques—"

I falter. A glimpse of green catches my eye, a Stillmont High golf polo. Biceps I have to admire peek through the sleeves. A wave of brown hair, an ever-present smirk, and *wow* do I want to go over and flirt with Wyatt Rhodes.

He's twirling a hall pass, walking unhurriedly in the direction of the bathroom. He's chosen a good bathroom, I notice. Roomy, with plenty of privacy because it's not near the locker hall. Perfect for a brief make-out session. I could walk over, compliment his impressive upper arms, lead him into said bathroom—

Not right now. If there's *one* thing that could keep me from flirting, it's directing the hell out of Shakespeare.

"Now, Jacques," I repeat, regaining my directorial demeanor.

"Come on, Megan," Brian interjects. "This scene doesn't even count for our grade. Jody doesn't give a shit. She just wanted us out of the room. And you know everyone's distracted."

I'm opening my mouth to argue that every scene matters when I hear a voice. "Megan!"

I turn to find my best friend, Madeleine Hecht, jogging up the hill, her perfect red ponytail bouncing behind her, freckled cheeks flushed with excitement. "I just left the library," she continues, breathless—Madeleine volunteers in the text-book room during sixth period. "And when I walked past the drama room I saw Jody posting the cast list!"

Hearing that, my actors drop their scripts and disappear around the corner, obviously on their way to the bulletin board at the front of the Arts Center. Not suppressing a smile, I collect the scripts.

I'm a director, not an actress, so the cast list doesn't hold the same thrill and terror for me that it does for the rest of the class. But this year, I'll be making my Stillmont High stage debut in one of the smallest roles in *Romeo and Juliet*, the fall semester play. I'm guessing Lady Montague or Friar John.

I wouldn't be, except it's my dream to go to the Southern Oregon Theater Institute. It's the Juilliard of the west, with one of the best directing programs in the nation. For whatever reason, they require every drama student to have one acting credit on their résumé, a requirement I'm going to fulfill as painlessly as possible.

"Walk over with me?" I ask Madeleine.

"Duh." She quickly takes half the scripts off my stack, chronically unable to resist lending a hand.

Right then, Wyatt Rhodes emerges from the bathroom. I follow the lanky confidence of his walk, biting my lip. It's been six months since my last relationship. I'm due for my next boyfriend. Scratch that—*over*due.

"Wait here," I tell Madeleine.

"Megan—"

I ignore her, a boy-starved moth drawn to a polo-wearing flame. I'm grateful I spent the extra ten minutes brushing the inevitable knots out of my long brown hair this morning. I know I don't have Madeleine's effortless beauty, but I'm not *not* pretty. I guess I'm in the middle. I'm neither short nor long-legged. I have features not round, closer to round-*ish*. Mine isn't the body that comes with swearing off burgers or going running more often than every January 2.

Wyatt doesn't notice me, preoccupied with tossing his hall pass from hand to hand. I call out to him in a practiced and perfected come-hither voice.

"Hey, Wyatt." I gesture to his defined biceps. "Do the abs match the arms?"

Not my best work. I haven't flirted in too long. In fairness, it's kind of a high-school bucket-list item of mine to make out with a really, really nice six-pack, and the boy attached. Even in seven boyfriends, from athletes to drama kids, *nada*.

Wyatt grins broadly. I cannot believe I haven't hooked up with him yet. It's been obvious he's gorgeous for practically the entirety of high school, and this is far from the first time we've exchanged flirtations. He doesn't immediately come across as boyfriend material, but his hotness *must* bespeak a valuable interior. I can picture us now, having long, thought-ful conversations over cappuccinos . . .

"They do on the days I don't double up on breakfast bur-ritos," Wyatt crows.

Okay, *short* conversations over cappuccinos.

"Today's one of those days," he continues. "But don't take my word for it." He eyes me invitingly, his voice unsurprised.

Not just because he's Wyatt Rhodes and he knows he's gorgeous, either. It's because I have a reputation for being boldfaced like this. Unabashed. Unreserved. It's no secret I've had seven boyfriends, and I'm not ashamed. Class Flirt is a title I've enjoyed every minute of cultivating.

I'm about to take Wyatt up on his offer when I feel a hand on my elbow. "Bye, Wyatt," I hear Madeleine yell pointedly. "We have to go to class." She drags me away from him, and in a low if not entirely unamused voice, she says, "What've we talked about, Megan? Wyatt Rhodes is on the no-flirt list." She considers a moment, adding, "He's number *one* on the no-flirt list."

"No, he's not," I reply. "Principal Stone is."

Madeleine gives an exasperated grumble. "Point taken. Wyatt's definitely number two. You put him on the list yourself, remember? After he asked in sophomore English what book Jane Eyre wrote?"

I nod grudgingly. "And there was the time he said *Furious Seven* was his favorite book on the yearbook survey."

"You're going to find a guy way better than Wyatt. Just give it time," she reassures me as we walk down the hill toward the Arts Center. "You don't think Tyler has any competition for Romeo, do you?"

Tyler Dunning is Madeleine's boyfriend. He headed off with a group of guys to rehearse *Macbeth* when Jody banished us.

"Of course not," I answer easily.

Tyler's a leading man in every respect. Tall, broad shouldered, with dark wavy hair—he's undeniably hot. He plays baseball in spring and still manages to score the lead in every theater production. Between his charisma and Madeleine's

5

universal likability, they're the total "it" couple of Stillmont High.

"Who'd you audition for?" Madeleine asks.

"Lady Montague."

She wrinkles her nose. "Who even is that?"

"Exactly." I grin. "She's the smallest role in the play."

I'm expecting the crowd packed in around the bulletin board when we turn the corner. What I'm not expecting is how everyone goes silent. I feel eyes on me and hear whispers start to spread.

"You guys aren't being weird at all," I mutter, trying to sound sarcastic despite my mounting nerves. I know this silence. It's the silence of the un-cast, the scrutinized walk to the gallows of your play prospects. For the first time, I feel what my classmates must whenever a cast list goes up. My pulse pounds, nerves thinning my breath. I envision apologetic emails from SOTI, halfhearted tours of other colleges in winter. Even though I'm not an actress, I need this part.

I step up to the list, my pulse pounding, and intently search the bottom of the sheet where the smaller roles will be listed. *Lady Montague* . . .

I trace my finger to the corresponding name. *Alyssa Sanchez*. My heart drops. Alyssa was the obvious favorite for Juliet. Jody's not messing around. This was brutal casting.

Reading up the list, I don't find my name. *Friar John, the Nurse* . . . Unbelievable. Even after I explained my situation to Jody, she still screwed me over.

Then I reach the top of the list.

TWO

PRINCE: *For never was a story of more woe*
Than this of Juliet and her Romeo.

V.iii.320–1

"THIS IS A MISTAKE, RIGHT?" IN SECONDS I've fought through the crowd and thrown open the door to Jody's office. *"Juliet?"*

I hear something clatter to the floor. Jody's office looks like a yard sale of mementos she's kept from every Stillmont production. There are playbills, props, and even pieces of sets stuffed onto the shelves. What looks like a brass doorknob rolls in front of me.

Jody stands up from her desk, her chunky turquoise necklace rattling. "You're not happy," she muses, studying me through her bright red glasses. They stand out even brighter against her gray hair. "I thought you'd be happy."

I feel a heaviness settle on my shoulders. A nervous pit opens in my stomach. "This isn't a misunderstanding?" I ask weakly. "It's not Anthony pulling a prank or, I don't know, a typo from an incompetent freshman you asked to print out the list?"

"No, the incompetence is all mine," Jody says, a hint of humor in her voice.

"I auditioned for Lady Montague, not the lead of the play!" I barely keep myself from exploding.

She raises an eyebrow, unsmiling. "Well, you got the lead," she says, her voice level.

"Why? I don't want it. Can't I be someone else? Anyone else?" I know I sound pleading.

"You're just nervous, Megan." Jody crosses her arms, but her tone has softened. "Yours was the only audition other than Anthony Jenson's that demonstrated a true understanding of the material. I've seen you direct Shakespeare before, I know you understand the play. You're Juliet, whether you like it or not."

"Jody, please." Now I'm definitely pleading. "You know I only auditioned because SOTI has an acting requirement. I've never acted in my life."

"It's a learning experience. I'm not expecting you to win a Tony," Jody says.

"Well, are you expecting *Romeo and Juliet* to be a comedy? No? Then—"

"Megan," she cuts me off sternly. "You auditioned for the play. You got Juliet. You can take it or leave it, but I've cast every other role."

I know I have no choice—Jody knows it, too. It's already the end of September. This production's my last chance for an acting credit before college applications are due in December.

"This is not going to go well for you." I sigh in exasperation, reaching for the door.

♟

I've taken one step outside Jody's office when I run into something solid and flat.

"Whoa," I hear above me.

Of course. I step back to find Tyler grinning down from the imposing height of six foot whatever. "Hey, Juliet," he says, his deep voice working on me in ways I sincerely wish it didn't. "This could be awkward, huh?"

It hits me suddenly. Tyler's Romeo. And I'm Juliet.

I quickly recover. "Nothing could be more perfect than the two of us playing doomed lovers."

He laughs and turns to face Madeleine, who's come up beside him.

It's not a big deal, but Tyler and I dated last year. Now we don't. He's with Madeleine, but I'm not jealous or resentful. In a way, I was expecting it.

Honestly, hating acting isn't the only reason I don't want to play Juliet. The other reason is, I'm not a Juliet. I'm not the girl in the center of the stage at the end of a love story. I'm the girl before, the girl guys date right before they find their true love. Every one of my relationships ends exactly the same.

Take Tyler. He's the only guy I've ever felt myself close to falling in love with, and he dumped me six months ago to date my best friend. But I'm okay, really. Everyone knows Tyler and Madeleine are meant to be. Besides, I'm used to it.

It started when I was eleven. I'd just proclaimed to Lucy Regis my undying love for Ryan Reynolds with the intention to marry him. The next day we found out he'd married

Blake Lively. Not that that was a real example. Just an omen of things to come.

The first boy I kissed, in seventh grade, passed me a note in social studies the next day informing me he was going to ask Samantha Washington to the Hometown Fair. They've been together ever since. Freshman year, my first real boyfriend ended up cheating on me with the literal girl next door, who, it turned out, was Lucy Regis. They just celebrated their third anniversary.

It's happened time and time again. It's not a "curse" or something stupid like that—it's just more than a coincidence. And it's why I couldn't possibly get into the head of Juliet, western literature's icon of eternal love. If the world's a stage, like Shakespeare wrote, then I'm a supporting role. Or hidden in the wings.

"You're not going to steal my boyfriend, are you?" Madeleine teases, wrapping an arm around Tyler.

"No, that's your thing," I chide without thinking.

Madeleine's face immediately falls, and I'm afraid she's going to cry for the hundredth time. When Madeleine confessed to me her feelings for *my* then-boyfriend, it took two hours of hugs and reassurance before the guilty tears ended. It's not like they cheated—Madeleine's so ridiculously thoughtful that she told me before she even told him.

And it hurt. I won't pretend it didn't. But I knew the pattern. I knew what was going to happen with me and Tyler. And I understood I'd only get hurt worse trying to fight the inevitable. Better to let the relationship end before I fell for him for real.

I rush to put a hand on her arm. "It was just a dumb joke, Madeleine," I tell her. "You two are perfect."

She smiles, relieved, and leans into Tyler.

"You guys coming to the cast party?" Tyler asks.

"Where?" Cast parties are a Stillmont drama institution. Drama's sixth period, but rehearsal can extend until 5 or 6 in the evening. For every production, the cast and crew choose one location for post-rehearsal dinners and parties. I'm just hoping it's not Tyler's house.

"Verona, of course." He grins like this is amusing.

I groan. Stillmont's an hour from the Oregon Shakespeare Festival in Ashland. It's not a coincidence we're one of the strongest high-school drama programs in the state, probably the country. When I'm not being forced to play the most famous female role in theater, I feel pretty lucky to have a teacher like Jody, not to mention the departmental funding. Unfortunately, however, proximity to Ashland has its downsides. Namely, an inordinate amount of Shakespeare-themed establishments. Verona Pizza is one of the worst.

Tyler doesn't hear, or he pretends not to. He looks down at Madeleine. "I'll drive you home after."

"But I have—" she starts.

"I know," Tyler interrupts, tugging her ponytail affectionately. "Your sister's ballet recital. I'll have you home in time."

I roll my eyes. Watching them together was the quickest, if not necessarily easiest, way of extinguishing whatever lingering feelings I had for Tyler. Now when I look at him, I honestly can't imagine dating him—regardless of how his objective adherence to certain standards of male desirability might *occasionally* affect me.

They smile at each other for a moment, looking like the contented lovers in erectile-dysfunction ads.

I'd hate them if I weren't happy for them.

I walk to the restaurant while Tyler and Madeleine drive over together. Verona's just ten minutes from school—I'd probably go there every day if the place didn't repulse me. I'm hoping the easiest way to cure the cast's eagerness for Verona is a meal there followed by certain food poisoning.

In the parking lot, I glance up at the marquee, which today reads *To eat pizza or not to eat pizza? That is the question.* I shake my head. The Bard would be proud.

Inside, it's worse. The wood paneling of the booths gives way to kindergarten-quality murals of medieval towers and turrets, interposed awkwardly with out-of-context *Romeo and Juliet* quotes. *"What's in a name?"* is written in three different sizes over the soda machine, and I pass by *"Romeo, Romeo, where art thou, Romeo?"* over the door of the arcade. Yes, there's an arcade, and it's not even the correct quote. It's definitely *wherefore.*

The big booth in the back is packed with the usual theater crowd, but when I walk up, Anthony Jenson slides over to make room. He's holding a copy of the play, and when I sit down, he thumbs it open.

"This monologue is incredible," he says after a minute.

"Um, which?" I lean over. He's playing a lead, I'm certain of that. Ever since he transferred here freshman year, poached by Jody from a school district unwilling to cast a black actor in prominent roles, he's earned key parts in every production.

He glances up at me, mock-indignant. "You didn't check who I was playing?" He drops the script on the table in front of me. I read the open page. It's Mercutio's monologue about the fairy Queen Mab. "Everyone thinks Romeo's the best male role," he continues intently, "but Mercutio's way more challenging. He's got a long monologue, a death scene—" He breaks off suddenly. "What am I saying? I'm talking to Juliet!"

"Don't remind me," I grumble.

He eyes me sympathetically. "You'll be fine, Megan." He pats my shoulder. "In any case, it's a free trip to Ashland."

I blink. "Ashland?"

"The Shakespeare Festival—"

"I know what the Oregon Shakespeare Festival is," I cut him off. "What does it have to do with *our* play?"

"Nobody told you?" Anthony looks incredulous. "Stillmont got accepted to the high-school feature this year. We're performing *Romeo and Juliet* in Ashland in December."

A tightness takes hold of my chest. Jody just had to choose the most prestigious Shakespeare festival in the country to force me into the spotlight. "Learning experience, my ass," I mutter under my breath. I must look pale, because Anthony's watching me with an expression that's half concern, half distrust.

"You're going to be great. You *have* to be great. This production needs to stand out. Reps from Juilliard are going to be there, evaluating me—"

"I got it, Anthony!" I loudly interrupt. "I'm just nervous. I'll figure something out," I say.

Anthony's gone quiet. I glance over, guessing I'll find him with his head in his hands, weighing the devastation I'll wreak on his college chances.

But I notice he's no longer looking at me, and I follow his eye line—right to a blond and obnoxiously muscled busboy. He looks our age, but I definitely would have noticed someone like *him* at Stillmont. He must go to one of the private schools in the area.

"Oh my god," Anthony mutters, watching the busboy clear a table and head into the kitchen. I know what that look means. Like me, Anthony falls fast and falls often. The difference is, he falls hard. He believes every guy is the one, and he's devastated every time a relationship falls apart. Still, there's no use trying to stop him.

"Go," I say, standing up and letting him out of the booth. Wordlessly, he does.

I realize I'm left sitting next to a group of senior girls who I know all auditioned for Juliet. Alyssa Sanchez is looking at me like she wishes I would go full-Juliet and stab myself with a dagger right about now. Her entourage won't even make eye contact.

"I didn't audition for the part, you know," I say, hoping to defuse the tension. This kind of drama is yet another reason I prefer directing.

14

"Well, you got it," Alyssa replies icily.

"It's obviously going to be a disaster," I try to joke.

"Yes." She stands up. "It will."

A couple of her clique follow her out of the booth. I look around the room, feeling distinctly out of place—or out of context. I know everyone here from drama, where I watch and direct them, but never participate. Now I'm expected to act alongside them. I spot Tyler and Madeleine in the arcade, adorably tag-teaming a Whack-A-Mole game. Everyone else, I notice, is darting glances between Tyler and me. Between Romeo and Juliet.

Everyone except one boy, sitting by himself, writing feverishly in a notebook.

I recognize him as the new kid in drama this year. He's Asian, thin without looking underfed, with hair a little overdue for a haircut—which he's presently running his fingers through contemplatively—and wearing a well-fitting gray sweater. I'm not sure I've ever heard him talk, but he'd definitely be better company than Alyssa's minions giving me death glares. Without a second thought, I walk over and sit down in his empty booth.

"Owen Okita, right?" I remember his name from a class we had together once. Freshman math? I've seen him hanging out in the halls with Jordan Wood, the editor of the school paper who moved to Chicago this summer, but I've never really noticed him.

Owen blinks up at me.

"You weren't in drama last year," I continue.

"Don't I know it," he says, and his voice startles me. For a guy I've never heard speak, he sounds surprisingly sure of himself. "I'm completely out of my element."

"Who'd you audition for?" I ask, noticing he's fidgeting with his pen.

"I just wanted to play an extra. Instead, I'm Friar Lawrence. Like, I'm a character."

"Come on." I smile, relieved and sort of stunned to find someone else in my situation. "Friar Lawrence isn't an important character."

"Every character's important." He sounds slightly affronted.

I pause, curious. Owen signed up for drama in his senior year just to play an extra? "Well, why'd you audition, then?"

"*Romeo and Juliet*. It's, uh . . ." He looks embarrassed and drums his pen on the table. "It's my favorite play. When I saw drama was doing it I had to join, but I'm terrified on stage, and Friar Lawrence has a ton of lines."

I feel myself smile, respecting this boy who can admit to stage fright and appreciating *Romeo and Juliet*. "You think *you've* got it bad? Guess who I've got." I reach across the table and grab the pen out of his hand, putting an end to his nervous tapping. Owen's eyes follow it, his ears reddening.

"The Nurse?" he asks, stowing his hands under the table.

"The *Nurse*? Should I be offended?"

"I, sorry, I—" His ears flame brighter.

"Go higher," I instruct, enjoying how easy it is to fluster him.

Owen pauses. "Megan Harper," he says after a moment, like he's just recalled my name from the recesses of his memory.

I wonder if he remembers me from freshman math, too, or if he knows me for the reason everyone knows me—because I hang out with Madeleine and Tyler, homecoming queen- and king-to-be. I can practically see Owen connect my name to the cast list in his head. "You're Juliet . . ." He studies me. "And you're not excited."

"Nope." I return the pen in a gesture of goodwill.

"You must be the only girl in the history of high-school theater *not* thrilled to be Juliet."

"I don't think there's a girl alive who'd want to play Juliet opposite her ex," I reply.

His eyes widen. "Who's playing Romeo?"

Now it's my turn to be surprised. "You don't know?" I didn't think there was anyone left in Stillmont who hadn't heard in too much detail about Tyler and me breaking up. If he's unclear about my history, I guess he *does* remember me from freshman math.

"Uh. Should I?" Owen looks lost. I nod in Tyler's direction, and Owen's eyebrows shoot up once more.

"Seriously, I can't believe you haven't heard the story."

"My apologies for not being up-to-date on the drama-kid gossip," he says with a hint of a smile. I laugh, and his smile widens until it lights up his face. But before I can reply, Anthony's standing next to the booth.

"I got a job," he says, and without missing a beat, "Hey, Owen."

"You already have a job." I frown, looking up at Anthony. Then I notice the blond busboy collecting dishes across the room, and I realize what's happening here. "Anthony, tell me you didn't change career paths because you're hot on the busboy."

He rolls his eyes, but he's smiling. "Starbucks isn't a career path. And it's not for the busboy—it's for love. And the busboy has a name—Eric."

I'm about to complain about the loss of free Frappuccinos when my phone's alarm buzzes in my bag. "Shit," I say instead. I lost track of time. "I have to go."

"It's so early! You haven't even eaten!" Anthony protests. Then a moment later, his expression shifts. "Oh, right. It's five on Friday," he says, realizing.

I get up. "We'll talk about the busboy—"

"*Eric*," Anthony interrupts.

"—tomorrow," I finish, and give Owen a nod. "Talk to you later, Friar Lawrence."

I close the front door quietly when I get home. The house is silent, nothing short of a miracle these days. I head upstairs and hope my mom isn't frustrated. I'm a little late for our weekly video call.

Mom lives in Texas, where she moved when she and my dad divorced. When my dad divorced *her*, to be precise. I don't really understand why it happened. I know they married and had me when they were only twenty-three. People throw around things like *irreconcilable differences* and *too young* and *fell out of love*. I guess I don't really understand what it is to fall out of love. I *wouldn't* understand. I'm never given the chance.

But I remember the day my parents sat me down in the living room, my dad stony-faced and my mom trying to keep her composure, and told me it was over. The words *mutual decision* were repeated over and over. They began to ring false when Mom went to cry in the bathroom while Dad finished the conversation.

I didn't move with her to Texas because I couldn't pass up the Stillmont theater program, which she understood. I think it was good for her to get some distance from reminders of her ex-husband, me included. But I've spent every summer vacation at her condo in San Marcos since the split three years ago. While I could do without the 100-degree heat, it's nice helping out with the booth at the farmers' markets and fairs where she sells her jewelry.

I ease open the door to my room. It's a mess. Of course it's a mess. Three maxi dresses that didn't find their way to the closet are draped over my bedframe. It appears I launched a denim jacket at the green coat rack in the corner but missed, and it's heaped on the floor on top of my boots.

My laptop's buried under a tangle of jewelry—the remains of this morning's failed attempt to find a pair of earrings I'm pretty sure vanished in Tyler's couch. I sweep everything off and shove aside my wristband alarm clock. It was a "gift" from Dad, who was far too pleased with himself for thinking of it. I've worn industrial-strength earplugs at night since our house got noisier a year and a half ago but I have to wake up for school at 6, and the horrible wristband vibrates me awake.

I open FaceTime on my computer, taking a second to brush my fingers through my hair.

Mom's face appears on the screen. "Hey, I'm really sorry I'm late," I rush to say.

"If I expected you to be on time, I wouldn't be a very in-touch mother." She tucks a strand of wavy dark hair behind her ear. Mom has hair like mine, only much bigger. "What were you up to?"

"Just some unprotected sex with a guy I met on the Internet," I reply casually.

Mom blanches, then her expression flattens when she realizes I'm joking. "Don't terrify your mother, Megan. It's not nice."

Grinning, I continue. "I would've preferred unprotected sex with creepy Internet dude, honestly. I had to go to a cast party."

She studies me, confused. "For one of your scenes?"

"No," I groan. I explain about *Romeo and Juliet* and why I was forced to audition. "It turns out I'm . . . Juliet, or whatever."

Mom's eyebrows skyrocket. "You auditioned for a lead?"

"Of course I didn't! Jody's just being impossible. Believe me, I'd be anyone else if she'd let me."

Mom chuckles. "I'm just glad I wasn't in the dark about my daughter's newfound acting aspirations."

"No, there's nothing new with me," I say quietly.

20

Mom's watching me with something like concern when my bedroom door opens without warning.

"Megan, what did I—" My dad's voice comes through the door, followed by the rest of him. He stops when he catches sight of my mom. "Oh, right, sorry," he mutters, suddenly stiff. "Hi, Catherine," he says without stepping farther into my room. "How are you and Randall?"

"Fine," Mom replies in the pinched tone she always gets when talking to my dad. "How are you? And Rose?" she adds after a second.

"Tired." He gives what I think is supposed to be a smile, but it looks strained. "Rose is going to take leave soon."

"That's exciting." Mom nods.

Looking the opposite of excited to be having this conversation, Dad places his hand on the doorknob. "Well, I'll leave you guys to it. Megan, just keep the volume down."

I sigh, exasperated, and mumble about not being able to talk in my own bedroom.

Mom says gently after a moment, "You know, you're always welcome to move in with Randall and me."

I force a scoff. "And miss the opportunity to play Juliet opposite Tyler Dunning?"

Mom grimaces. "Oof, I'm sorry to hear that. But really," she continues, "if it's ever too chaotic there, we'd love to have you."

"Thanks, Mom," I say, softening, not wanting her generosity to go unacknowledged. She deserves a real answer. "It's just, I'm at the top of the drama program at Stillmont. I've built up my scene work here, I'm in charge of organizing the

Senior Scene Showcase, *Romeo and Juliet*'s even going to be featured in Ashland. I have to stay."

"Well . . . you can change your mind anytime," Mom says reluctantly. "What's this about Ashland, though?"

"It's nothing. Jody in her infinite wisdom put us up for a high-school feature at the Oregon Shakespeare Festival, and they took us," I say to the floor.

"That doesn't seem like nothing." Mom sounds excited. *Uh-oh*. "When is it? I'd love to come!"

"No, Mom, it's not a big deal, really," I hurriedly protest.

"Resistance is futile, Megan. If you won't tell me when it is, Dad will."

I'm rolling my eyes when from downstairs comes an ear-splitting wail.

"Sounds like you have to go," Mom speaks up over the screeching.

"What? You don't want to stick around? This will be going for the next twenty minutes," I say with half a grin, and she laughs. "I'll talk to you later, Mom."

I hang up and go downstairs. The source of the howling is sitting in her high chair in the kitchen. My nineteen-month-old half sister Erin is adorable, but she's got lungs that'd make her the envy of the spring musical cast. I stop in the doorway, wanting a final moment to myself.

My stepmom reaches for Erin. Rose is tall, blonde, and undeniably beautiful. If she looks like she just turned thirty, it's because she did. She and my dad have been married for two and a half years. I wasn't thrilled when I first met her. It was only months after the divorce, and I was still holding out childish hope my dad would change his mind and realize Mom really was his meant-to-be.

Rose ended that. When I learned my dad was dating a woman ten years younger, I had my doubts about his sincerity. I figured he was turning forty and having a midlife crisis, dating a pretty blonde who made him "feel young." He was a cliché.

Then I took one look at the two of them, and I finally understood what I didn't in two years witnessing my parents' crumbling marriage. He wasn't going through a midlife crisis. He wasn't chafing at the institution of marriage—he just wasn't in love with my mom. I saw the smile my dad gave Rose the day I met her, a smile I'd never remembered seeing on him, and I knew he could never really regret the divorce.

Because he'd fallen in love with Rose. It wasn't about her age, or about anything but the two of them together. He had become a cliché—only not the one I'd expected. He'd found his soulmate.

"Hey," Dad says from the stove, pointing a spatula at Rose. "I told you not to get up for anything." He glances back at her, his same adoring smile looking like a love-struck teenager's.

Rose also happens to be seven months pregnant.

She rolls her eyes but lays a hand on her stomach, her expression warming as she sits back down.

I should hate Rose. I should hate the very idea of her. Sometimes I even wish I did, but the truth is, I never have. It's not her fault my parents' relationship wasn't forever like I imagined. I don't blame her for my dad loving her in a way he never could my mom. Still, despite my inability to hate her, she and I are more like somewhat-awkward roommates than two people with the same last name.

Dad drops the spatula, wincing when Erin lets out a particularly shrill yell, and races to hand Erin her favorite stuffed elephant.

I give myself one more moment. I love Erin, and I don't dislike Rose, but it's hard sometimes. This is my senior year. I should be studying on weeknights and going to parties on Saturdays. Instead, I'm struggling to concentrate through my earplugs and babysitting. I should be figuring out my future and finding myself—instead, I'm figuring out a relationship with a new stepmother and finding baby food on my books.

It's not only that, though. What's hardest is watching my dad build a new life that I'm less a part of every day. Especially with Erin and the baby on the way, it's like they're just letting me live here for the year before I go to college. Before they have the family they want.

THREE

I RECOGNIZE HIS HAIR FROM A BLOCK behind him. Black, pushed in one direction like he's recently run his right hand through it a bunch. Which he probably has—I remember the way he fidgeted constantly in the Verona booth. As if when he's not writing in his notebook, his hands search incessantly for something to do.

Owen Okita walks by himself up to a corner, where a giant puddle's overtaken the curb, a remnant of yesterday's rainstorm. I spent the day watching and re-watching Olivia Hussey's performance in Zeffirelli's *Romeo and Juliet* for preparation, which only tightened the knots in my stomach. Today is Monday, the day of our first rehearsal.

I reach the stop sign and roll down my window in time to catch Owen crossing the street.

"Hey," I call. "You want a ride?" I'd welcome the conversation to keep my mind off the rehearsal.

He looks up, searching for the source of my voice. When

he finds me, his eyes a little surprised, he says, "I'm good. Thanks, though."

I wrinkle the corner of my mouth, putting on an offended pout. "I did shower, you know. I don't smell."

"That's not—" He shakes his head, cutting himself off. His eyebrows twitch in feigned inquisitiveness. "Do people often refuse rides with you because you smell?"

I can't help myself—I feel my eyes flit a little wider.

Owen looks satisfied when I have no reply. "I just like to walk," he explains. "It gives me time to think."

I shrug, recovering. "Your loss. For your information, I even used my coconut shower gel today. I smell *exceptional*." I drive past him, catching in the rearview mirror how he blinks once or twice, then takes a step forward directly into the puddle. He glances down sharply as if he's just remembered it's there.

Madeleine's waiting for me in the parking lot when I pull in ten minutes later.

Even though she's beloved by everyone and could have her pick of best friends, from the cheer captain to the future valedictorian, Madeleine's chosen me. For whatever reason. I wouldn't even call her popular, except in the dictionary sense of the word. I'm liked well enough, but mostly people know me because they know her.

It's part of the reason I don't mind being known as the school flirt. Because then I'm *something*. Something other than just the girl who's friends with Madeleine.

When I reach her by the bike racks, she greets me with a gushing recap of her weekend. She spent Saturday running a bake sale for charity and Sunday indoors while it rained, building card houses and drinking hot chocolate with her sister and Tyler. Tyler never hung out with my family while we were together—not that Erin's fun unless you enjoy wiping runny noses and repeatedly cleaning everything within reach of her admittedly adorable arms. But Tyler and Madeleine's relationship is different. I guess when you have a relationship like that it turns even the boring things beautiful.

We walk into the locker hall, and I'm distracted immediately by Wyatt Rhodes, who's admiring his hair in a mirror he's hung up in his locker. It's the vainest thing I've ever seen.

But I can't blame him. I'm admiring him, too, and it's really unfair he needs a mirror to enjoy the view the rest of us have.

"Megan." Madeleine's voice breaks my concentration. From her gently stern expression, I know I'm caught.

"What if he's a great guy on the inside? We need to give people a chance," I implore weakly.

Madeleine grabs my elbow with her perfect peach nails. "Number two. On the list," she admonishes. She steers me past Wyatt. I don't restrain myself from stealing a final look over my shoulder. When we've rounded a corner, leaving Wyatt and his arms behind, Madeleine plants us in the middle of the hall. She pulls me by the shoulders to face her.

"We're going to the football game this week," she says with finality.

"What? *Why?*" I have zero interest whatsoever in organized sports, especially in the high-school context. Unless the uniform's a Speedo.

"Because then I'll know you're nowhere near Wyatt Rhodes on Friday night."

I grimace. "You're worse than my mom. What's wrong with a hookup, even when it's . . . you know, Wyatt?"

A group of junior girls I'm sure Madeleine's hardly ever spoken to wave enthusiastically. She smiles back before her eyes return to me. "Nothing's wrong with a hookup with Wyatt," she replies with accusatory innocence. "What you want isn't a hookup, Megan. It never is. You want a boyfriend, and you're looking in desperate places because you've been single longer than usual. But Wyatt Rhodes wouldn't make you happy. You know that."

I fall silent, unable to argue. Of course she's right. She's Madeleine.

"I won't go for Wyatt," I grudgingly promise. "But I'm *not* going to the football game," I declare. Madeleine gives me a wry smile.

"We'll talk," she says, tipping her head forward in a *this-conversation's-not-over* gesture. She turns down the hallway to her first-period class.

Heading for the doorway to mine, I catch a glimpse of Owen down the hall. His sweater's askew, probably because he had to rush to get to school on time. He's putting a pile of papers into his locker. One falls to the floor, and I recognize an issue of the school newspaper. He must have two or three copies. It occurs to me he's probably sending them to Jordan, figuring he might like to have a copy.

It must be hard, having your closest friend move to a different state in your senior year. Even though Madeleine gives annoyingly perfect advice, I can't imagine how adrift I'd feel if she moved away one day and left me here. I have a feeling Owen didn't just join drama because he's really into *Romeo and Juliet*. He's probably trying to find new friends. I make a mental note to invite him to sit with the drama kids at lunch.

He hurriedly grabs his things from his locker and races to a classroom door, only to pause right outside. As if he can't control himself, he pulls out his notebook and jots down a quick—I don't know what. Observation? Idea? Reminder? The Fibonacci sequence? For the flash of a moment, I wish I knew.

I reach for the door to my class, weighing Madeleine's words. She wasn't wrong—not only about Wyatt. I have been single for a while. I *do* want a boyfriend. If I survive today, I'm going to put real thought into finding someone I could care about and who could care about me.

Hours before the first *Romeo and Juliet* rehearsal, I want to vomit. Or disappear. Or both.

Instead, I try to pretend nothing's bothering me as I sit down in one of the circles of drama kids decamped on the hill outside the drama room for lunch. Everyone's here except Anthony, who without fail uses lunch to get ahead in his classes. I once tried hanging out with him until the librarian ejected me for complaining too loudly and too often about how boring geometry is.

I usually enjoy sitting with the rest of the drama kids, running lines and planning cast parties. Not today. I don't like the way everyone's eyes turn to me when I sit down.

"You must be, like, totally excited," Jenna Cho says, beaming at me from across the circle. Her enthusiasm's as infectious as a headache, and no less uncomfortable.

"I'm . . . Yeah, definitely excited," I halfheartedly reply. *Ugh.* If my acting's this stiff in rehearsal, this play is screwed.

I notice Alyssa eyeing me. "You know, I played Juliet in a summer production at the community theater downtown. I'd be *happy* to sit down with you and show you my notes." She forces a saccharine smile.

I smile back at her, just as insincere. "Thanks, but I've got it, Alyssa."

Jenna reaches forward to hand me the plate of cookies they've been passing around. "I mean, it shouldn't be challenging playing opposite Tyler." Her grin widens.

"It wouldn't be the first time sparks fly between a Romeo and a Juliet," Cate Dawson chimes in, eyebrows raised. "You two even have a history."

Of course that's the moment Madeleine happens to walk up, arm in arm with Tyler. I see her smile fade, and I know she heard Cate's comment. Even worse, I'm not oblivious enough to figure she's not already worried about it.

I have to defuse. "I'm the last person who could have sparks with Tyler. Been there, done that, right?"

The girls laugh, and Madeleine gives me a grateful smile.

"Yeah, creating chemistry with Megan," Tyler starts, looking around the circle like he's on stage. "This will be the truest test of my acting prowess yet." He flashes the crowd his most charming grin, and I remember *Hamlet*—"one may smile, and smile, and be a villain."

Just because I'm over Tyler doesn't mean his insults don't hurt.

The sting of Tyler's words hasn't faded by the end of the day. But when I get to drama, Owen's sitting outside the class-room, writing in his notebook. Again. Everyone else has gone inside, and I decide to enjoy a couple more Tyler-less minutes.

I stop in front of his feet. "Ready to sell some drugs to underage girls?"

Owen looks up, his dark eyes going wide. "What?"

"You know"—I nudge his shoe with my boot—"Friar Law-rence?"

He pauses, then asks with feigned seriousness, "You ready to pursue an inappropriate relationship with an overemo-tional teenager that'll end terribly for everyone involved?" His features harden into an inquisitive challenge, underwrit-ten with humor.

"Sounds like a typical Monday," I reply.

Now he smiles, and it's the same smile from Verona, the one that brightens his entire face. He gets up and holds the door open for me.

Where on an ordinary day the drama room's just chaos—

improv games breaking out in the front of the room while the choir crossovers belt show tunes by the piano—today there's order to the commotion. Most of the *Romeo and Juliet* cast sits in a circle of chairs in the middle of the room. The senior girls have gathered around Alyssa, who's reading from Juliet's death scene. Anthony paces in the back of the room, doing vocal warm-ups. I'm hit with a new rush of nausea, remembering what he said on Friday, how much this means to him.

Jody comes in a second after I sit down with Owen. "We're doing a read-through of the scene where Romeo and Juliet meet," she announces, and shoves a stack of scripts into Anthony's hands.

I notice Tyler, seated opposite me in the circle, smirking when he finds his place in the scene. Once Anthony's handed out all the scripts, Tyler stands up and starts right in. "O, she doth teach the torches to burn bright!"

I poorly restrain an eye-roll. In every read-through I've been to, the actors didn't get out of their seats. Tyler's just grandstanding. But even I have to concede he's delivering it perfectly. If this is the truest test of his acting prowess, he's acing it.

"Forswear it, sight, for I ne'er saw true beauty till this night," Tyler continues, his eyes burning into me.

"Either he *is* good," Owen mutters beside me, "or he means it."

"He's acting. Definitely acting," I whisper, crossing my arms and sinking into my seat. I'm dimly aware of the scene progressing for the next couple minutes, but all I can think about is my impending first line.

Like he knows he's screwing with me, Tyler saunters from his seat to mine and stops in front of me. "If I profane with my unworthiest hand this holy shrine, the gentle sin is this." He reaches for my hand, and I snatch it away on instinct.

Tyler's eyes narrow. Whatever Juliet's supposed to do in this moment, it's not that. I feel the whole class staring at me. Tyler repeats the line, reaching for my hand once more. I force myself to let him take it. But when he leans down to brush his lips across my knuckles, I flinch and rip my hand from his. I hear Anthony groan.

"*Megan,*" Tyler whispers in a sigh of frustration.

I look at Jody. "It's a read-through, not a rehearsal. Can't we just read from our chairs?" I nod pointedly at Tyler's, which is empty.

"Don't be difficult," Jody says, hardly glancing up from her script.

"Fine," I murmur, even though it's not. "Um, could you go again?" I ask Tyler.

He takes a deep breath and delivers the line, impeccably concealing his irritation. I close my eyes as he takes my hand, but I know I'm not covering my grimace when I feel his breath on my skin. He's leaning down. I should bite my tongue, push myself to be Juliet.

But I can't. I jerk back for the third time, and Tyler's jaw tightens.

Wait, I realize, *this could work.*

"Good pilgrim," I begin, heaping sarcasm on the line before he can restart the scene. Tyler looks startled to hear me actually reading my part, and I hear the room holding its breath. "You do wrong your hand too much, which mannerly devotion shows in this"—I transform Juliet's lines from demure and cautious to combative and superior—"for saints have hands that pilgrims' hands do touch, and palm to palm is holy palmer's kiss."

Jody's gone still, pen pressed to her lips. But Tyler steps into the new dynamic without missing a beat. His delivers his lines flawlessly, making Romeo work twice as hard to impress my unimpressed Juliet.

"Saints do not move, though grant for prayers' sake," I say, sneering.

"Then move not while my prayer's effect I take." Tyler leans forward, lips puckered, and I dramatically turn my head to offer him my cheek.

I hear snickers around me, and Tyler and I banter the next couple lines. When I apply an extra dose of sarcasm to Juliet's final remark—"You kiss by th' book"—everyone laughs.

I feel my shoulders straighten. Everyone's eyes are still on me, but for the first time I don't feel the need to step out of the spotlight or deflect with a joke. Tyler bounds off to exchange lines with Jenna, the Nurse, and I'm left reflecting. If there was one thing I wasn't expecting from this rehearsal, it was to not hate every second of it.

The door opens in the middle of the scene, and a stagehand walks in holding a box of props. I'm following along with the dialogue when something tumbles from the box and loudly hits the floor. I glance up at the moment the stagehand bends down, and suddenly it's not just *a stagehand* picking up what he dropped.

It's a veritable hipster Adonis. I recognize his face, I just don't remember it being this, well—hot. It takes me a second to connect this stunning figure to Billy Caine, the scrawny stage manager I talked to a couple of times when I directed *Twelfth Night* last year. He's changed his hair to a slicked-back undercut, and from the way his black V-neck stretches across his chest, he looks like he went to the gym once or twice over the summer.

I realize the room's gone silent. Owen clears his throat next to me, and I remember—Juliet has more lines. I glance down at the page, but my brain won't form words out of the letters.

I splutter what I remember of Juliet's next line, "What is yond gentleman?" *What indeed?*

"That's enough," Jody interrupts, standing up and walking into the middle of the circle.

She's right. I've completely lost our momentum, not to mention how I reinterpreted the character in a huge, spur-of-the-moment decision. Jody pauses, gathering her thoughts, and I prepare for the worst.

"Megan . . . I like what you brought to Juliet's dialogue with Romeo," she finally says, and I let out a breath I hadn't realized I was holding. "But," she continues before I get too relaxed, "you lost focus, and the whole room felt it."

I hear a couple chuckles. *Great.* I guess it's not just my acting I have to worry about. It's my propensity to get distracted whenever a hot guy enters the room.

"I'm sorry," I get out.

Jody waves a heavily ringed hand. "Let's go again."

FOUR

ROMEO: *There is no world without Verona walls*
But purgatory, torture, hell itself.

III.iii.18–9

I FIND ANTHONY OUTSIDE THE DRAMA ROOM when rehearsal's over. I want nothing more than to get out of Juliet's head, even if I have to eat terrible pizza in a historically inaccurate restaurant. I didn't embarrass myself further following the Billy Caine incident, but I wasn't exactly a Juliet to die for.

"You're walking to Verona for your shift, right?" I elbow Anthony playfully. "I'm totally rehearsed-out."

"I don't know what you're complaining about," he says indignantly. "I spent three hours memorizing my Queen Mab monologue, and we didn't even do my scene today!"

"Um, you didn't have to suffer the lips of Tyler Dunning," I reply.

Anthony raises his eyebrow. "I don't know about *suffer . . .*" I swat his shoulder. "Yeah, I'm going to Verona," he says after he's pinned my hand. "But you sure you don't want to stick around?" He nods somewhere behind me, and I turn to follow his gaze—to Billy Caine talking intently to Owen.

"You noticed?" I ask dryly.

"Megan. Everyone noticed. I think William Shakespeare himself felt it in the grave." Now he elbows me. "It's about time for your next torrid whirlwind romance."

I take a second to study Billy's skinny jeans. "I'll meet you at Verona in twenty minutes."

I drift over to where Billy and Owen are talking and overhear a snippet of their conversation. It sounds like they're discussing poetry. Billy's praising the "forest imagery" but says the internal rhymes need work.

"I love it when guys talk internal rhyme," I remark, walking up next to them. "Hi, Owen. Hey, Billy." I smile.

Owen cuts in. "Uh, it's *Will* now."

Billy rolls his eyes, and I look from him to Owen. "I feel like I'm missing something."

"It's not a big deal," Billy—Will—says. "I just decided I prefer to go by Will."

Yes. Yes. We prefer Will. Everything about him works together perfectly. The blond hair, the fitted clothes, the elegant, understated name. I think I just might die.

"Cool," I say instead.

Will unleashes a dazzling smile. "Hey, I really liked your original interpretation of Juliet. You nailed that scene."

"Well"—I try to sound nonchalant—"I had to make her interesting somehow. It's hard for me to relate to someone so coy and hard to get." I see Owen's eyebrows shoot up, but I'm focused on Will's growing smile.

"It could be worse. You could be trying to get a guy to fall

37

in love with you while pretending to be a man." He crosses his arms, daring me to get the reference.

"*Twelfth Night*—or *As You Like It*. Yeah, I guess it's better than having my hands cut off by two lunatic brothers," I say, playing along.

Will raises an eyebrow. "I like *Titus Andronicus*! You know, it definitely beats having to get it on with a donkey."

"Well, Tyler *is* an ass," I mutter under my breath, knowing he's referring to *A Midsummer Night's Dream*.

"This is really cute," Owen interjects, "but, Will, did you want to give me your notes on the lyrics?"

"Lyrics?" I turn to Owen. I would be annoyed he interrupted my boldfaced flirting if I weren't intrigued.

"Owen writes lyrics for my band," Will says with the studied casualness of a guy who practices telling girls he's in a band.

My eyes widen. "*You're* in a band?" I ask Owen. Will I could believe, but shy Owen . . . ?

His ears go red. "I'm not. I just write the lyrics."

"I didn't know you were a writer." It would explain the ever-present pen and notebook.

"Are you kidding?" Will says, and I look back at him. With his debonair smile and incredible hair, I can't believe I ever looked away. "This kid does nothing *but* write. I can barely get through a conversation without him jotting down an idea for one of his plays."

"Will, the lyrics?" Owen holds out his hand, visibly uncomfortable.

Will hands Owen a folded sheet of paper from his pocket, and I go into conversational desperation mode. I'm not inclined to let Will leave before I procure a phone number. "Hey, you guys want to go to Verona for some undercooked pizza?"

"Alas," Will says, "I have to go over a scene diagram with Jody. But I'll see you Wednesday."

"What's happening Wednesday?" Not that it matters.

"It's the first run of your balcony scene. I'm head of the stage crew, so I have to be there. But besides"—he smiles a smile it's hard to believe occurs in nature—"I wouldn't miss it."

I wrinkle my nose. "You don't want to see—"

"Yes. I do." He looks me right in the eyes, and I swear my knees might give way. I guess I *won't* brainstorm boyfriend prospects tonight. Will could be exactly what I'm looking for. Even if I have to run the balcony scene a thousand times, suddenly Wednesday can't come soon enough.

Will walks off, treating me to a new perspective on his hotness.

"So, uh . . . pizza?" Owen's voice returns me to earth.

It takes me a second to realize I invited him, too. "Uh, yeah. Let's go."

The shortest walk from school to Verona is through the woods. It's not like Stillmont is encircled by trees—it's more like they intersperse the town, encroaching in surprising stretches. I like walking in the woods. I'm not one for Transcendentalist poetry and Bon Iver and stuff, but I've come to crave the quiet. Especially since Erin arrived.

I lead Owen onto a faintly defined path over the thick roots. "I didn't know you and Will were friends," I say.

"We're not," Owen replies, then corrects himself. "Well, we're not good friends. I'm friends with Jordan, and he was friends with Jordan. But now Jordan lives in Chicago, and he was—"

"The friend-glue," I finish the sentence. I know exactly what he's talking about. I've tried hanging out with Anthony's Math Olympiad friends while he wasn't present, and it did not go well. They glared when I confused the titles of *Star Trek: The Next Generation* and *Star Wars: A New Hope*.

"That's . . . exactly what it is," Owen says thoughtfully and with amusement. "But yeah, Will and I, we're friend-*ly*. I write him lyrics, and he gives me songwriting credit on their nonexistent recordings."

I grin. "He seems . . . different," I venture. "What's his deal?"

"Different?" I hear a nearly imperceptible edge in Owen's voice. As much I love the changes in Will, Owen evidently doesn't. "*Billy* went to a songwriting camp this summer. It was Will who returned. He kind of redefined himself."

I pause, hitching my bag up on my shoulder. "He got really hot."

Owen laughs shortly. "Well, don't tell him. He's been insufferable since he got back."

"I very much intend to tell him!" I glance over my shoulder to find Owen eyeing me skeptically.

"You're going to go for this guy after one conversation

swapping Shakespeare jokes and staring into each other's eyes?"

"Duh. I just said he was hot."

I turn back to the path and hear Owen laugh behind me. "I guess if it's love, one conversation's all you need. You'll make a fine Juliet yet."

"Love?" I snort, kicking a rock off the path. "When did I say love? I just think it'd be fun. I'm not really the love-at-first-sight, long-walks-on-the-beach, balcony-scene type." Not that I wouldn't be that type, if I believed those things weren't just a beautiful fiction. I want them just like every-body else. I'm just not holding my breath.

"What do you mean?" Owen sounds genuinely interested.

I don't usually talk about my unique pattern of breakups, but there's something about Owen that has me feeling like he'd understand. "Remember what I told you about Tyler? He dumped me for my best friend, Madeleine, and now they're, like, the perfect couple. The thing is, that's not the first time a guy's left me for the real deal. It's a perfect trend—everyone I date, it's right before they find exactly what they're looking for."

Owen is silent for a moment. I don't look back, worry-ing he's deciding I'm paranoid and self-pitying. But he only sounds sympathetic when he says, "Getting dumped sucks."

"I'm not dumped," I reply quickly, defensiveness creeping into my voice. "Guys don't leave me because of *me*. It's not like I scare them off," I add, needing to make this clear. "I'm just . . . the girl before."

"You're Rosaline," Owen says, and I stop. He's standing in

the middle of the path, hands in his pockets, looking out into the woods like he's lost in thought.

"The girl Romeo leaves for Juliet? That's not the most flattering comparison," I mutter. But in my head I know it fits.

He looks at me then, no longer contemplating—he's seeing me, giving me his full attention. I realize it's something I've never had from him in the past couple of days since we started talking. Whenever I've encountered Owen, he's been half-focused on his notebook or lost in thought.

He shakes his head. "I think Rosaline's really interesting. She's an underexplored part of the play. In a lot of ways, her story's probably more interesting than Juliet's. Or at least I think so."

The earnestness in his voice and the way he's looking at me have me turning back to the trail. I can't help feeling like he's seeing me for something I'm not. "First you say I'll make a fine Juliet, now I'm Rosaline"—I laugh, trying to bring the conversation back to casual—"I better be careful. If I keep talking, I'll turn into Tybalt."

I wait for Owen's reply. When I don't hear his footsteps behind me, I turn back around. He's climbed onto a rock and is holding his phone up toward the treetops in the universal human display of looking for cell service.

"Why do you need reception?" I ask. "We're five minutes from the restaurant."

"Cosima wants to FaceTime me," he says matter-of-factly.

"Cosima?" I stifle a laugh at Owen's woodland acrobatics.

"My girlfriend."

Owen has a girlfriend? *Interesting.* "What kind of name is that?" I ask, genuinely curious.

"It's Italian," he says, clambering down from his rock to find a new spot. "Like, she lives in Italy. We're in such different time zones, we have to video chat every chance we get."

An *Italian* girlfriend? Owen is full of surprises. I do a little mental math. "Isn't it like the middle of the night there?"

"Yeah, it's late." He's now standing between two giant pines. His expression even, he waves his phone with deliberate, unhurried movements. For someone who stopped suddenly to climb onto a boulder, he seems decidedly untroubled by his lack of success. "I'm trying to catch her before she goes to bed, but there's no service."

"We *are* in the middle of the forest," I point out unhelpfully. When Owen says nothing, I go on. "Well, I want pizza. Say *ciao* to Cosima, your Italian girlfriend who lives in Italy." Before I continue down the path, I catch the hint of a smile on Owen's lips.

In Verona, I find Jenna Cho and a couple of noblewomen from today's scene sitting in a booth by the soda fountain. Mercifully, Tyler and Alyssa are nowhere to be found. I could use a break from his smugness and her constant judgment. I slide into a seat as Anthony sidles up to take our orders.

"Wow, Anthony." I try not to laugh. "You look ravishing."

He's wearing a T-shirt printed to resemble a medieval tunic, and there's a Robin Hood–esque hat two sizes too small perched on his tight black curls. It's hideous, and wonderful.

"Megan, nothing you say can take this away from me," he says defiantly. He searches the room behind me. "Hey, where's Billy?"

"It's Will now," I correct. "He's not coming, but Owen's on his way. He's talking to his girlfriend right now."

"Cosima?" Jenna asks, something knowing in her smile. The rest of the table chuckles.

I feel like I'm missing the joke. "Yeah, why?"

"You know she's not real, right?" Courtney Greene answers with a conspiratorial smirk. "Owen's totally making her up. There's no proof."

Anthony clears his throat. "I have other tables, you guys. Would you like to, you know, order?" He pulls a quill out of his pocket. Unable to contain myself, I burst out laughing. We order a couple Benvolio's Banquets (pepperoni, sausage, and peppers, in what feels like a reach of textual interpretation), and Anthony gives me a final chastising look.

Owen shows up a few minutes later, looking out of sorts. He slides into the booth opposite me. Unhesitatingly, I smile and ask, "How was Cosima?"

"Blurry," he grumbles. The group exchanges glances. I know Owen notices because he turns to Jenna wearily. "You seriously don't still think she isn't real, do you?"

"There's no proof," Courtney repeats.

"Is this normal cast behavior?" Owen asks me, half-jokingly exasperated. "They've been interrogating me since my *first day* of drama about my real"—he levels Courtney a look— "genuinely human girlfriend."

"Better get used to it," I reply resolutely. The corners of his mouth curve upward. "Does she have a Facebook?" I try to give him a chance. I pull out my phone and open the app.

Owen frowns like he's heard the question before. "Cosima thinks social media's frivolous," he mutters.

Now I have to smile. "Awfully convenient." But before he can reply, I see I have an unread email. The subject line reads, "Your upcoming Southern Oregon Theater Institute interview!" I lose track of the Cosima discussion as my eyes scan the email. I've put off dwelling on the interview, but now it's in a couple days, and I'm having trouble thinking about anything else. The churning in my stomach only worsens when Anthony drops off the greasy pizzas.

"Hey, um, Megan," I hear him say quietly beside me. "Could I talk to you for a second?"

Eager for the distraction, I jump up and follow him to the salad bar—overwhelmingly the least crowded part of the restaurant. "What? Do you need me to go get you a change of clothes?" I ask when we've stopped.

Anthony cocks his head, not amused. "I'll have you know, I intend to wear this to your wedding. And your second wedding. And your third wedding."

I cross my arms, holding back a smile. "That's okay. It's the fifth wedding I have a good feeling about."

He laughs. "But really"—he drops his voice—"I need your wise counsel."

"Is it about boys?"

"Of course."

"Then you've come to the right place." I lean into the counter. "What's up?"

"Eric invited me to a party," Anthony explains. "But I'm not sure if the invitation was casual or potentially something more."

"Well, do you even know if Eric—" I break off when I notice the hostess walk by leading a family of five to a table. Anthony's hardly in the closet—everyone at school definitely knows he's gay. He just might not want his personal life publicized to his coworkers and random neighborhood families. "Do you know if Eric . . ." I try again, "enjoys sausage pizza?" I finish, wincing, and Anthony's eyes widen.

"That was *bad*," he admonishes.

"I know." I grimace. "But . . . does he?"

Anthony takes a deep breath, like he needs to prepare for what he's about to say. "I don't know, Megan. I've never seen him . . . order it. But I don't know if he enjoys it in private. If it were served to him, he might partake." Anthony rolls his eyes, halfway to a grin. "I just want to know what this kind of invitation means to guys. Is it definitely casual? Definitely a date?"

"It depends," I start. "Both have happened to me. When Charlie invited me to Courtney's birthday, I knew it was a date because he'd pursued me pretty obsessively for weeks before. When I went to a movie with Chris, I didn't really know. You know how Chris is. He barely has facial expressions. When Dean—"

"You're no help." Anthony sighs, frustrated, then looks behind me. "Hey, Okita, come over here for a second."

I turn to find Owen standing at the salad bar, understandably dissatisfied with the pizza. He squares his shoulders uneasily, uncomfortable to be singled out.

"I need a straight guy's perspective," Anthony continues. "The guy I like invited me to a party. Is it date, or is it just something straight guys do?"

Owen immediately turns endearingly thoughtful. His eyebrows go up, his eyes searching the room, bright like twin light bulbs. "I'll need to weigh several factors," he says finally. "How friendly is he? Did he invite other coworkers? What was his tone like?"

"Eric's not very social with people here," Anthony says, and I can hear him struggling to suppress the excitement in his voice. "I don't think he invited anyone else."

"This sounds good," I offer.

Anthony's excitement finally breaks through. "Good like, I should wear the navy blazer?"

"Whoa." I put a hand on his arm. "I think it's a bit early for the navy blazer."

"I wore it on our second date," Anthony fires back. "Remember? I cooked us carne asada—I seem to recall it going pretty well."

It did, I remember. It was the first time I really made out with a guy, and the last time Anthony made out with a girl. His cooking is legendary. It might be literally impossible for a guy Anthony's interested in—or girl, in the case of yours truly—to have his homemade carne asada and not fall for him. "You're right," I say. "That was an excellent date."

I notice Owen's startled expression. He's looking between Anthony and me, slowly putting the pieces together. He squints skeptically. "Wait, you . . . you guys dated?"

"It was years ago," I explain, watching Anthony, who looks lightly amused. "It was before Anthony admitted his love for sausage pizza." Anthony bursts out laughing, collapsing onto the salad counter.

"Wow." Owen's watching me intently again, like he did in the woods. There's endless depth to his dark eyes. "What you were telling me earlier, it's real."

"Oh, it's real," I say.

"We agree, then," Anthony announces, ignoring Owen and me. He pushes himself off the counter. "Blazer it is." The lady sitting in the booth behind him coughs pointedly, looking in our direction. "Shit," Anthony mutters, glancing over his shoulder. "I have, like, three tables I should be waiting on." He darts off, pulling out his ballpoint quill.

I walk with Owen back to the booth and sit down, taking out my phone to confirm the interview. Just reopening the email brings on a new wave of anxiety. I'm not the greatest student—I don't have a 4.0 and a résumé full of extracurriculars. I'm not like Madeleine, with her AP tests and her volunteer work, or Tyler, who's had recruiting scouts at his baseball games since sophomore year.

The only thing I *really* care about at school is directing, and when I think about college or the future, SOTI is pretty much everything. I wouldn't be doing *Romeo and Juliet* if it weren't. I know my directing credits put me up there with the best of applicants, but the interview is something else entirely—I'm not the most polished or poised conversationalist.

"Who're you texting?" Cate Dawson's voice interrupts my typing, and she winks when I look up.

"I bet it's Tyler." Courtney smiles suggestively.

"It's definitely Sexy Stagehand Will," Jenna chimes in.

"I'm not *always* texting a guy. I have real shit, too," I snap before I can stop myself. The table goes quiet, and I immediately feel bad. It's not like they said anything mean, and I do talk about guys constantly. I just wish they hadn't assumed.

I feel like everyone's waiting for me to elaborate, but I've never been one to talk about real-life things like college or the future. It's easier to be the Megan they expect me to be, to bear my disappointments in private. "I'll be texting Will *later*," I say, putting on a grin.

I watch them exchange glances, still too uncomfortable to laugh. I drop my eyes to my phone and try to pretend I don't notice their silence.

"What if I organize a group FaceTime with Cosima? Will you believe me then?" Owen interjects. The group's eyes light up. I release a relieved breath, glad the conversation's moved on. Not unaware Owen's brought back up a topic he dislikes in order to spare me, I gratefully give him a quick smile, then hit SEND on the email.

FIVE

JULIET: *It is an honor that I dream not of.*

I.iii.71

STILLMONT HIGH IS NOT A BIG PLACE. There's one main building, a gym in the back—one of my favorite places because PE's practically a flirting free-for-all—and an Arts Center that houses the drama room and a much cleaner orchestra room. Pines dot the quads in between the buildings, which aren't large. There's not a lot of ground to cover.

Paradoxically, the school gives us seven minutes to get from class to class. *Seven minutes.* That's enough time to hook up in the band closet, or to hit up the vending machine, eat your snack, then hit up the vending machine again and still make it to class. I spend most passing periods consoling Madeleine about her AP workload or, recently, hearing about the latest chapter in the ongoing romance of her and Tyler.

Today, we've taken a leisurely stroll to the second-floor bathroom. The only other girl in here leaves, and from outside the stall I hear Madeleine clear her throat. "Can I talk to you about something?" she asks, her voice unusually shy.

I'm mid-pee. "Uh." I fumble for the toilet paper. "Yeah."

"It's about Tyler and . . . sex," she says haltingly.

"I . . ." I can hardly restrain my laughter. "I might need a moment, Madeleine. To pull my pants up."

"Right. Of course." I practically hear her blush.

Once I've opened the stall door and stepped up to the sink, I turn to her. "Okay, hit me."

Her face grows brighter. "Tyler's planning something for this weekend. He wouldn't tell me what. But I'm getting, you know, that vibe from him." Her freckles have disappeared under the red in her cheeks.

I nod sagely. "The vibe." I wait for Madeleine to elaborate, but when she doesn't, I search her uncertain expression. "You've gotten the vibe before, though, right?"

"That's kind of the problem," she says quietly.

"Wait." I turn off the faucet as it dawns on me. "You two haven't had sex yet?"

"We've done other things," Madeleine rushes to say, like I've accused her of a crime. "And there's been a couple times when it seemed like he wanted more, but no, we haven't done it yet. I wanted to . . ."

She looks at me expectantly. I wait blankly for her to continue before I realize what she's saying.

"You haven't had sex because of *me*?" I splutter. She's just staring at me, growing redder. "You know," I continue more gently, "you don't need my permission to have sex with your own boyfriend."

"But it's a little weird. The last person Tyler had sex with is you," she points out.

"Don't think about that." I lay a hand on her arm. "Really, it doesn't bother me."

"I'm glad, but it's not that. . . . Well, it's not only that." She looks into the mirror, avoiding my eyes. "I just sometimes feel a little intimidated."

I raise my eyebrows. "Intimidated? Tyler can get the job done, but he's nothing to be intimidated by."

Madeleine gives me half a smile. "Watch it, that's my boyfriend you're talking about." But her voice drops when she continues. "No, it's not Tyler I'm intimidated by . . ."

I wait, uncomprehending. What she's suggesting—it's, well, it's crazy. "By *me*?" I get out. The idea that Madeleine, with her striking auburn hair and green eyes and her fairy-tale romance, could ever be intimidated by someone like me is laughable. It's not like the times Tyler and I did it were anything but a couple of virgins figuring things out together. It's a proven law of the universe that I'm not the girl who guys remember.

"Well, yeah," she says with a shrug. "What you and Tyler had, it was spontaneous, exciting, romantic. You were the kind of couple everyone watched. You burned bright—"

"And burned out," I interject.

"When you were together, what you had was passionate," Madeleine argues, sounding a little desperate. "I'm just afraid that after you, I won't be enough."

"Madeleine." I grab her hand and force her to look at me. "Tyler's into you now. You're just building this up."

"I hope." She still looks unconvinced. "But you and Tyler were each other's firsts. I can't compete with that."

"Firsts? What does that matter?" It's not like I chose Tyler to be my first because I thought he'd be "the one." I just knew

52

I felt something with him I hadn't with boyfriends before. I liked Tyler, and I guess I knew I could fall in love with him. I wanted to be closer to him. I'd hardly believed I'd found my soulmate—at Stillmont High, no less—but I wanted the physical aspects of the relationship. There's something about having that emotional connection made physical, the romantic rendered real, that's unique and impossibly enticing. Even though I knew the relationship would end, I felt in those moments of togetherness I could finally step out of the wings and into the center of our stage.

But none of that has to do with Tyler's position in the line of boyfriends with whom I'll one day have sex. He was my first because he was special—not special because he was my first.

"There's nothing extraordinary about Tyler being my first. Trust me," I tell Madeleine.

"Not to you, maybe," she says, looking at the floor.

But to Tyler? I'm caught off guard. If it had meant that much to him, we wouldn't have broken up. But I'm not going to tell Madeleine that. Still, some smaller voice in me wonders why Madeleine would believe otherwise unless Tyler said something.

The bell rings, and it takes me a second to realize we've somehow used up the entire passing period. Madeleine looks panicked—I'm certain she's never been late to class ever. I'd have to laugh if I weren't still reeling from what she just said.

But I don't want her to leave worried about my history with Tyler. "You and Tyler are perfect for each other, and you're going to have a perfect first time," I manage as Madeleine hurries to pick up her bag. "Speaking as the former authority on Tyler Dunning's sex life," I go on jokingly, "I have all the confidence in the world that you'll blow his mind."

"Thanks, Megan, really," she breathlessly says over her shoulder, and runs toward class. I follow her out, my mind lingering on what she said before.

It's not like I still have feelings for Tyler or even want him back. It's just unexpectedly nice to know what he and I had hasn't been entirely forgotten, even if he'll be giving a night of tender, fumbling, teenage love to my best friend this weekend.

Yet unfortunately, I'm the one in bed with Tyler after school.

In a prop bed, specifically. With the entire cast watching us. We're in the drama room, the plastic chairs arranged in rows in front of the open space we're using for a stage.

The bed's not even Juliet's, either. It's a leftover from the spring musical, *Rent*, and it's completely period-inappropriate —black and wrought-iron and unmistakably '90s. Will hasn't finished any of the set pieces, although I've taken every opportunity to admire his after-school shirtless construction process.

We're rehearsing Act III Scene v, the one where Romeo and Juliet wake up together after their own night of tender, (probably) fumbling, teenage love. We're both lying on our sides, Tyler behind me, pressed a little too tightly to my hips. The closeness combined with his Romeo eyes isn't helping me forget Madeleine's words from earlier. Not in a good way—it's just uncomfortable.

"Whenever you're ready," Jody tells us from the front row of seats.

Before I can start the scene, I feel Tyler brush my hair behind my ear. Then he kisses me on the temple. I jerk and nearly bust him in the lip.

"Good, Tyler," Jody calls. "I liked that."

I rush through my lines, knowing the sooner I finish the scene, the sooner I can get out of this bed. "Wilt thou be gone? It is not yet near day. It was the nightingale, and not the lark, that pierced the fearful hollow of thine ear. Nightly she sings on yond pomegranate tree—"

Jody interrupts me. "Juliet's trying to get Romeo to come back to bed. You sound like he couldn't leave fast enough." She's pursing her lips in a bit of a smile, like she knows just how true her appraisal is. Some of the cast laughs in the audience, and I catch Alyssa rolling her eyes in frustration.

"Well, I . . ." I start, searching for some interpretive explanation to defend my discomfort. "I'd like to play Juliet feistier. You know, modernize her." Honestly, if I were directing, I'd be into the approach.

Jody nods, considering. "Okay, but you still have to make the scene work," she says. "Go from the top."

I close my eyes and take a deep breath, trying to find my inner Juliet. When I open them, Tyler's gazing down at me with a teasingly longing look. "Wilt thou be gone!" I snap, knowing I'm throwing the scene out the window. But I just can't handle Tyler. His expression changes, and the amorous

Romeo fades from his features. He's just Tyler, irritated with his ex-girlfriend.

I sit up and face Jody. "Okay, I know that was too much, but—"

"Megan," she cuts me off. "Feisty Juliet works well for when she meets Romeo. It doesn't work here. We have to believe Juliet is so in love with Romeo she would die for him." I notice Alyssa watching me from the audience, smug. "You need to spend some time with the play," Jody continues. "Really learn how to get into Juliet's head."

I give Jody a look saying, *you knew this would happen.* "Okay," I reply even though I know it's impossible. The best I can hope for is faking it. But it doesn't matter if I pull this off, I remind myself. I'm not an actress, I'm not meant for the spotlight. I just have to get my acting credit and get through this play.

SIX

ROMEO: *Can I go forward when my heart is here?*

Turn back, dull earth, and find thy center out.

II.i.1–2

THE HOUSE IS A MESS WHEN I get home.

With rehearsal over, I can finally push Juliet out of my mind and focus on something important. I rush up to my room, where I throw on the most professional outfit I own— a tan dress I never wear in my daily life and a blazer I borrowed from Rose's closet. Trying to quell my nerves, I bound back downstairs.

I have to leave in ten minutes for my SOTI interview. But first, I search under piles of Dad's paperwork and Erin's sticky toys in the kitchen. I printed my arts résumé before school, and I know I left it on the kitchen counter, which I guess experienced a natural disaster in the last eight hours. I push aside one of Erin's arts and crafts projects and clumsily stick my hand into a glob of glitter glue. Even though it'd definitely make my application stand out, I'm going to have to have some stern words with my baby sister if she's turned my résumé into her latest sparkly impressionistic work.

My eyes fall on what's underneath Erin's finger-painting, and I stop.

It's a real estate magazine. But not one of the Oregon ones I've seen in some of my friends' houses—it's full of listings in New York.

I pick it up, dazed. *Why would my dad and Rose have a magazine of homes in New York?* But the moment the question forms in my head, I know the answer, and suddenly my worries about the interview feel distant.

"If you're looking for your résumé, I moved it to the table by the door." I hardly hear Rose's voice from the couch. She's taken to lying down for quick naps in the middle of the day.

I don't bother to thank her because I'm already climbing the stairs, magazine in hand. I check Dad's bedroom first. His desk is empty except for the stack of budgets for the middle school where he's vice principal. The obvious next stop is just down the hall. I hear his hushed voice reading *Runaway Bunny* as I push open the door to Erin's room.

"Dad." I try to pack urgency into my low whisper, noticing Erin nodding off in her crib.

Dad gives me an admonishing look and tiptoes out of the room. Only after he's quietly closed the door does he turn to me, still holding *Runaway Bunny*. "I just got her down, Megan. This better be important."

"We're moving to New York?" I hold up the magazine. "When were you going to tell me?"

The guilt that flashes in his eyes confirms what some part of me was still hoping wasn't true. "Nothing is final yet," he says after a moment. It doesn't matter how gentle and even his tone is, I can barely meet his eyes. He hid a life-changing family decision from me.

I try very hard to control the volume of my voice. "But you're looking at houses."

"With the baby coming and Erin growing up, we're going to need more space." He's speaking with the patience I've heard him use on overwrought seventh graders.

"So you're looking in *New York*?"

"Rose wants to be closer to her parents while the kids are young." I hear irritation creep into his tone.

"You weren't going to *tell* me we're moving to New York in—I don't know when?" I realize I've crumpled the magazine in my hand. "You expect me to just pack up my bags and move across the country with no warning whatsoever?"

His expressions shifts. Suddenly, he looks surprised, even a little apologetic. "Oh, no, Megan. None of this is happening until you're done with high school and settled in college."

Just like that it makes sense. It's not about us moving to New York. It's about *them* moving to New York.

In a way, it's the natural progression of what's been happening for the past three years. First my dad got remarried, then he had Erin and started a new family. Now they're going to leave the town where he raised me and start over somewhere else, finally closing the book on the last remaining chapter of my dad's former family.

I open my mouth to protest, and then I realize I just want out of this conversation. "I have to go to my interview," I mutter. "You know, so I can get into college and have somewhere to go when the rest of you move." I shove the crumpled magazine at him and fly down the stairs before he can call me back.

"Good luck," Rose wishes weakly as I run out the door.

Trying to force the conversation from my head, I get into my car and crank up the volume on the stereo, even though I'm in no mood for the Mumford & Sons CD well-intentioned Madeleine burned for me.

I drive to the Redwood Highway for the first time in months. The clouds hang low and heavy in the sky, and the rain patters my windows insistently—it's a constant presence this time of year. I don't get out of Stillmont often, because there's not much to do outside town. The all-ages club on Route 46 straight-up sucks, and I hardly ever drag Madeleine to concerts in Ashland. Her indie-folk playlists tend not to overlap with my Ramones and Nirvana.

The only other reason I have to take the highway up through the hundred-foot redwoods is SOTI. Specifically, the June and December Mainstage Productions. It hurt the first few times I went by myself after my mom moved. We used to go as a family before the divorce, but without my mom to persuade my dad to come, I weighed whether I wanted to go on my own. In the end, I decided the opportunity to watch the best student theater in Oregon was too important to pass up. I've gone to every production in the past three years, from *Othello* to *Chicago*.

Which is how I know the hour-long drive through the

forest by heart. With nothing but the trees to look at, my mind returns to the picture-perfect homes in the real-estate catalog, and I reach for my phone without a second thought to call Madeleine and tell her everything over speaker phone. She's the perfect listener—she doesn't sugarcoat or force advice on me, she just lets me talk. It helps a little, the way it always has.

When we hang up, the redwoods have given way to the strip malls and college-town shops of Ashland. I park in the visitor parking lot outside SOTI's geometric concrete buildings and take a moment to try to dispel the twin discouragements of rehearsal and my fight with Dad. *Not* how I want to feel before the most important interview of my life.

I'm not like most SOTI students, who go there because they love theater. I'm the opposite—I love theater because of SOTI. Before I cared or even knew I lived near one of the best drama schools in the country, I was being dragged to Mainstage Productions twice a year. I complained every time, but whenever I glumly questioned why we had to go, Mom would explain theater was important to our family. She loved to tell the story of how she and Dad fell in love when they both were stagehands in a college production of *My Fair Lady*.

I never cared about that until eighth grade, when everything changed. I could feel my family falling apart around me—every morning beginning with a whispered fight and every night ending with my dad sleeping on the couch. I know now that when Mom announced we were going to *A Midsummer Night's Dream*, it was a final effort to rekindle what they'd lost. It didn't work, obviously, but when the curtain closed, I realized I hadn't felt my family fracturing for three magical hours. My dad held my mom's hand, and at intermission they even laughed while trying to explain the story to thirteen-year-old me.

I didn't realize it until that *Midsummer Night's Dream* performance, but theater was never just an outing for my family. It was a time when we were a unit. No matter how briefly, no matter how ugly things were when we got home. There's something about theater, an immediacy that brings stories to life in a way nothing can tarnish. You can put down a book or pause a movie, but a play is breathing right in front of you—it refuses to be stopped. It's why I joined drama freshman year, and it's what I've held on to ever since.

I pull up a campus map on my phone and head toward the directing department. My interview is in Professor Salsbury's office, which looks like it's next to a black box theater, a small performance space with only a couple of rows of chairs and without a backstage. Once I step inside the building, I glance into the theater, where a couple students are putting blocking tape on the floor.

I hear them swapping notes on scenic interpretation in theater shorthand, and for a moment I feel like I'm exactly where I belong. It doesn't matter where my parents live. *This* is everything I need. This will be my home.

Feeling a rush of confidence, I knock on Professor Salsbury's door and walk in when he calls, "It's open!"

He's sitting at his desk, poring over a play. His rumpled gray oxford looks like he slept in it, and he doesn't seem much older than a student himself. "Hey, Megan, it's great to meet you!" he says with disarming enthusiasm.

"Uh, yeah, uh, thank you for having me." I take a seat opposite his desk. "I brought a résumé, if you want to have a look . . . ?"

"Prepared!" He reaches for the paper in my hand, his eyes lighting up. "I like that." He studies it for a moment, and I feel myself relax at his approving expression. "You've directed an impressive diversity of material. For someone your age, especially," he continues. "I notice you've met the lighting and set design requirements—great experiences to have."

"They were," I jump in. "They really helped me decide how to direct *Twelfth Night*."

He nods, briefly glancing up at me. His eyes return to the page. "You've done a musical—*West Side Story*, a favorite of mine—and a couple of experimental pieces, but it looks like a lot of your work has been in Shakespeare."

"He's the best," I say. "Really original opinion, I know."

He laughs and sets the résumé down. Then he looks me right in the eye. "So why directing, Megan?"

I'm ready for this question. "Because theater feels like home. It's the one place where I'm part of something that can bring people together or transport them," I finish decisively.

"It's clear you love theater." He studies me, his voice growing more serious. "But I want to know why you're a director."

"I'm really not a natural actor," I say. "I never feel comfortable or genuine or creative when I have an audience."

Salsbury gives me a gentle smile. "Well, you'll have to get

used to it to some degree. We do have an acting requirement, which I see you haven't fulfilled yet."

"Not to worry," I reply lightly. "I'm getting through it."

"Getting through it is one thing." His smile falters. "The requirement is there for a reason. Uncomfortable though it is to have an audience, learning how to inhabit a role will give you a deeper understanding of the emotions you'll need to bring out in every scene. It'll make you a better director. Even Shakespeare probably learned a thing or two from performing in his own plays."

My stomach sinks. Not just because Salsbury's eyeing me with a new uncertainty—because I know he's right. It seemed easy to brush off Jody's criticism in rehearsal and tell myself I don't care. But if I want to be a real director, I can't dismiss performing on stage just because it makes me uncomfortable.

"You wouldn't happen to be in Stillmont's *Romeo and Juliet*, would you?" His question surprises me. The professors here don't seriously keep tabs on every local high-school production, do they?

My hands start to sweat, and I fold them in my lap. "I'm, um . . ." *No point in hiding it.* "I'm Juliet."

Salsbury's eyes light up once more. "Well, I'm looking forward to seeing your performance."

"You—what?" I stutter.

"In December," he answers. "You know, the high-school feature at the Oregon Shakespeare Festival. A group of faculty members and I go every year."

Of course. Of. Course.

Just when I thought the Juliet situation couldn't possibly get worse. It was enough to play a lead in front of Jody, my entire school, and the ardent Shakespeare enthusiasts who attend the festival. Now I have to go on stage knowing I'm being evaluated by the faculty of my dream university. I remember Anthony telling me Juilliard people would be there, critiquing him, but acting is what Anthony's good at. It's what he's spent countless hours perfecting. I'm going to look ridiculous, and everyone there from SOTI will be watching.

I force a smile. "I . . . look forward to seeing you there," I manage.

SEVEN

CHORUS: *Now old desire doth in his deathbed lie,*
And young affection gapes to be his heir.
That fair for which love groaned for and would die,
With tender Juliet matched, is now not fair.

II.prologue.1–4

WHEN I WALK INTO REHEARSAL ON MONDAY, I notice the *Rent* bed's nowhere in sight. *Thank god.* The front of the room isn't set for a scene, and I know that can only mean one thing— Jody's doing a one-on-one with someone who has a monologue. I just hope it's not me. She comes out of her office, and I begin involuntarily fidgeting while the rest of the class files in. She watches silently until everyone's in their seats and the bell rings.

"Anthony," she calls, and I feel my shoulders sag in relief. "It's monologue time." Anthony fist-pumps in his seat, obviously excited for an hour of uninterrupted work on his part. "The rest of you," she continues, "pair up, work on memorizing."

My relief turns to irritation. Anthony would've been my partner. Without him, I search the room for a replacement. Everyone's pairing off. I notice Tyler looking at me with an inquisitive eyebrow raised. There's a certain logic to Romeo and Juliet working together, I know. But after Friday's bedroom scene and Madeleine's confusing intimations about Tyler's and my first time, I want space from him even more than usual.

I pointedly look elsewhere, and my eyes lock on to a familiar crop of black hair. Owen is talking to Alyssa. Before she can get her claws into him, I dart over and grab him by the sleeve. "I need you . . ." I say into his ear, pushing him forward.

He turns, his startled expression—his default, I've come to understand—returning, one long eyebrow curving upward questioningly. "Common sense dictates your partner's over there." He nods in Tyler's direction. "You know, Romeo?"

I make a face. "*Romeo* and Juliet? No, no, no," I scoff. "Friar Lawrence and Juliet, now *they* have a lot to work with."

Owen cracks up. He looks over his shoulder, where Tyler's dramatically proffering his hand to a group of sophomore girls. "He *is* being particularly obnoxious today."

We walk out into the hallway and toward the auditorium. Jody demands silence for her one-on-one rehearsals, and while we'd normally take the chance to rehearse outside, it's raining today. So instead, we're headed to the theater, which offers enough space for pairs to rehearse in corners of the room without overhearing each other's every word.

Still, the cavernous space sometimes echoes irritatingly. When the door swings shut behind us, I steer Owen down the aisle to the stage. "You want to run lines on stage?" He sounds incredulous.

"Of course not." I open the door to the left of the front

row. "We're going backstage. I have a key to the green room. It's quiet in there."

I lead him up the darkened staircase, through the empty wings, and to the locked room behind the stage. Owen follows me, his footfalls softly crunching on the cheap carpet of the stairs. I figure he's studying the cast-and-crew photos lining the wall from productions before my time. I know them by heart—2001's *Beauty and the Beast*, 2005's *Grease*, 2014's *Much Ado About Nothing*. I remember being crestfallen to learn they'd done *Much Ado* right before I started high school.

We reach the upper level. What passes for a green room at Stillmont is more of a hallway. It's long and narrow, with only a single couch covered in dubious stains.

Owen looks around when I close the door. "If Will comes by and you guys start making eyes at each other again, I'm out of here. This is way too intimate a setting." He drops onto the couch.

"If Will comes by, I'd *want* you out." I shrug. "The things we could do on this couch . . ."

Owen winces with exaggerated disgust. "Way more imagery than I wanted."

I collapse next to him. "If only it was more than imagery. It's not like he's made a move or anything," I say with more frustration than I intend to show.

I know he notices from the way his expression softens. "Don't read into it. Will . . . is new-hot."

I wrinkle my nose. "He's what?"

"You know, like new-money." Owen gestures in the air, his

knees jutting far over the edge of the couch. "Will's new-hot," he says. "He doesn't know the etiquette for these situations."

I raise an eyebrow. "These situations?"

"Like . . ." I catch him blushing. "Having a girl, um, interested in him."

"Interested would be putting it mildly," I declare. "You're his friend. Feel free to nudge him in my direction, or, you know, shove him forcibly," I say half-jokingly, pulling out my script and opening it to Act V. "You want to run your scene with Friar John?"

"Want would be putting it generously." His lips curl faintly, and I let out a laugh. *He's quick on his feet*, I find myself thinking, not for the first time. "But yeah, I guess," he adds.

I open to Scene ii and say loudly and clearly, "Holy Franciscan Friar, brother, ho!" Owen jerks back, and I point at the page. "No, really, that's Friar John's line."

He glances down. "Right." He looks up, trying not to read from the script. He swallows uncomfortably. "This same should be the voice of Friar John. Welcome"—his eyes flit to the page—"from Mantua," he finishes.

"That doesn't count," I cut in. "You haven't even started memorizing, have you?"

"I haven't had a lot of time," he grumbles, agitatedly bouncing his knee once or twice. "I had a breakthrough on my next play, and I spent the weekend outlining."

Curious, I set the script down. "Wait, really? Can I see it?"

"No!" he blurts out, then looks uncomfortable. "It's just, it's nowhere near ready," he says, rubbing his neck.

"What's it about?" I haven't exactly met very many teenage playwrights, and I guess I want to know what Owen Okita in particular writes about.

Owen turns his deepest-ever shade of red. "I got inspired by the conversation we had last week, actually."

"Wow." I put a hand on my chest, jokingly flattered. "I've always wanted to be immortalized in drama."

He smiles slightly. "It's about Rosaline. From *Romeo and Juliet*," he continues. "There's, like, nothing about her in the play, but in Shakespeare's Verona, she could have a life and a story of her own. She could be more than an early piece in someone else's love story."

His words deflate me. I'm a little more disappointed than I'd like to admit that this is the inspiration Owen drew from me. "Rosaline's story isn't as interesting as Juliet's," I say softly. "That's kind of the whole point."

"It could be interesting." Owen sounds defensive, and I don't blame him. I *did* just diss his play. "But I've been having trouble getting into Rosaline's head."

"Hence the weekend of not memorizing your lines," I say.

He shrugs. "There's just not that much about her in *Romeo and Juliet*, and it's hard to get into the mindset of this minor character who's left in a strange position from the events of the play." He folds the spine of the script in his lap, his thumb stained dark blue with ink. "I have to find her direction. Is she heartbroken? Or maybe she's embittered and pleased with Romeo's death."

"Or she knows fate won't give her some star-crossed love, and she's trying to convince herself it's a good thing." The

70

thought leaps to my lips before I know where it comes from. Hoping Owen doesn't read something more into my comment, I stand up sharply.

He only nods carefully. "That's really good," he says, his eyes going distant. He looks like he's in a different world, or just in his head. It's the look I saw in the woods and in the restaurant at the cast party—and on his sharp features it's entirely flattering.

Someone knocks on the green room door, and Owen blinks. I feel an unfamiliar disappointment when that faraway look disappears from his face. I drag myself to the door, hoping it's not Jody or someone else coming to yell at us—we're not actually supposed to be in the green room unsupervised.

Instead, I find Madeleine on the other side of the door, fussing with the strings on her Stillmont High sweatshirt and wearing a nervous, giddy smile. "Hey, Madeleine. Everyone doesn't know we're back here, right?" I quickly check behind her.

"What?" She looks thrown. "No, Tyler told me you guys were in the auditorium, and I figured you'd be in here . . ." She pauses, visibly uncomfortable. "Can I talk to you for a minute?"

"Yeah." I open the door wider. "What's up?"

"Um." She peers behind me to Owen sitting on the couch. "*Just* you?"

"Right. Of course," I say, remembering our talk in the bathroom and realizing exactly what's on her mind. I step into the wings and shut the green room door behind me. "This wouldn't have anything to do with the *extraordinarily* good mood Tyler's in today, would it?" I ask as Madeleine leads me out of Owen's earshot.

She turns to me with a tentative smile. "We had sex."

"You had sex this weekend and waited until the end of the school day to tell me? I demand details in reparations." I cross my arms with mock-sternness.

She chews her lip. "Really? I'd understand if—"

"Madeleine, stop," I tell her, dropping my arms to my sides and meeting her eyes. "I'm your best friend. I want to know as much as you want to share." Her smile returns, tingeing her cheeks light pink. "Was it perfect?" I press.

"He had it all planned out," she begins hesitantly, her voice wavering with excitement. Her words come more easily as she continues. "He drove us up to the cabin—you know, the one his family owns by the lake. He cooked dinner for the two of us, and he even had a bottle of his parents' champagne. Then when the sun went down, we went skinny-dipping. It was beautiful, there were stars and everything, like a movie or a postcard or something. And when we went inside . . ." Madeleine leaves the sentence unfinished.

I'm silent for a moment, because what I'm visualizing isn't a lake and a thousand stars. It's the couch in Tyler's basement, the sounds of the *Twelfth Night* cast party echoing down from upstairs. I enjoyed that experience with Tyler, feeling close to a guy I cared about, and feeling for once like *I* was important. Like *I* was the lead in a love story. But neither Tyler nor I imagined it to be this big, life-changing thing. And the décor, the timing—it wasn't exactly an experience someone would write poetry about.

Of course Madeleine had the perfect night. I'm *glad* it was perfect. I am. While Madeleine's watched me date a nearly constant stream of guys, I've watched her spend all her free time studying and volunteering and *not* having a boyfriend, and meanwhile becoming this incredible, beautiful person. It's nice to see her finally have the boyfriend piece, too.

"I told you you had nothing to worry about," I say finally.

"I guess." She tucks a loose curl behind her ear, smiling softly at her feet. "Anyway, I should get back to the library. I just wanted to tell you in person."

"I'm glad you did," I say, but an unexpected pit opens in my stomach. I walk her to the stairs. "Skinny-dipping under the stars at a beautiful lakeside cabin," I add, forcing a smile. "You give us mere mortals hope that true love is possible."

She laughs. "It is, Megan." She grins and practically bounds down the stairs.

I stand in the hallway, her words echoing in the small space. *It is.* I don't know why her confidence upsets me. Or why hearing about Madeleine's perfect night feels like a lump of lead under my lungs. I knew this was coming, and I wasn't lying when I told her I was fine with it. But I can hear the words Madeleine didn't say. Tyler gave her a night he never gave me because what they have is more real, more worthwhile than what we had. In his head, our night is forgotten, obliterated by something better.

Which it should be, I remind myself. They love each other.

But I guess I liked the idea that Tyler's and my first time meant something to him—that for one boyfriend I was worth remembering. Instead I'm realizing, however close I felt to the center of Tyler's and my stage, I was far off. Far from important. Far from extraordinary.

I try to push the feeling away. I open the door to the green room and find Owen reading lines under his breath. I remember what he was saying about Rosaline, how she doesn't have to be just a precursor to someone else's happy ending.

Madeleine and Tyler are perfect together—they're Romeo and Juliet without the tragedy. I've known their relationship was unique since the first time they sat together at lunch as a couple. Madeleine laughed at something Tyler said, and his eyes lit up like he'd never heard something so lovely before. It reminded me of the way my dad smiled at Rose. There are some things a person can't get in the way of.

But I'm not going to be just a bystander to their epic romance. I don't want Tyler, but I do want to be wanted.

"I need your help with Will." I interrupt Owen's reading and sit down next to him.

His head pops up. "Okay, first, you just made me lose my place," he says, sounding exasperated, but he shuts his book and gives me his attention. "Second, you don't need my help. You're doing fine on your own."

"No, I'm not," I admit. I've watched Will build sets after school three times, and still he hasn't said one word to me since we met. "What you were just telling me about Will being new-hot, that's the kind of insight I need. I don't know a lot about him, about what to expect, how to read him, what he's interested in. I like him," I say. "And I don't want to screw it up. You're his friend—you could help."

Owen doesn't say anything for a moment. He begins tapping his pen on his knee, and it takes everything in me to resist grabbing it out of his hand. "It could get uncomfortable if Will figures out I'm trying to set him up with someone," he finally replies.

I smile slightly, hopefully not enough for him to notice, because his answer wasn't a no. He knows I'm right.

He moves to drumming his pen on his notebook, and I realize how I can convince him. "I'll help you with your play." It comes out sounding like a statement, not an offer.

His pen stops, and he looks at me with curiosity, or hesitation. "I'm not really looking for a cowriter," he says gently.

"Not a cowriter." I shake my head. "I'll help you figure out Rosaline's character. You said you were having trouble getting into her head. Think about it. I *am* Rosaline." Owen blinks, his contemplative look returning. "You liked the idea I had about Rosaline convincing herself not to want what Romeo and Juliet had. I can give you more of that. I know what it's like to watch your ex fall for someone they'd die for, over and over," I go on. "I could tell you about first dates, last dates, breakups—oh, the breakups."

He's tempted, I can tell by the spark in his eyes. But he only asks, "Wouldn't that be kind of weird? Interviewing you about your romantic history?" His ears turn pink.

"It wouldn't be weird for me. I'm not embarrassed by it," I say with a shrug. But by the blush spreading to Owen's cheeks, I know it's not me he's worried about. I'm going to enjoy scandalizing him if he agrees. "Besides," I continue, "you said the play was inspired by me. You're a writer, Owen. How can you refuse the chance to get real, deep emotional insight into a character? That's what I'll give you," I finish triumphantly.

He thinks for a long second. I watch the wheels turning behind his dark eyes.

I stick out my hand. "Do we have a deal?"

When he puts his hand in mine, it's without a trace of hesitation. His fingers wrap all the way around my hand, and his palm is surprisingly rough. "Deal," he says.

"I am *not* going to regret this," I say, and withdraw my hand.

He narrows his eyes. "You . . . Don't you mean *I'm* not going to regret this?"

"Yeah, that too. But I *know* I'm not going to regret it," I reply, and Owen grins, a bit bashful. "What can I do?" I ask, ready to get down to business. "Do you want to start with my first boyfriend? My post-breakup ritual, what?"

He drops his *Romeo and Juliet* script in my lap. "You can read for Friar John. Jody's going to kick me out if I don't have something memorized by the end of the day."

EIGHT

ROMEO: . . . *all these woes shall serve*
For sweet discourses in our times to come.

III.v.52–3

OWEN LIVES ONLY TEN MINUTES FROM ME. Unlike my street, his is hemmed in by trees, and I think I see a trailhead down the block when I get out of the car. His house is a single story, and there's no car in the driveway. The lawn is brown, the leaves in dry piles by the sidewalk.

I knock on the door, and Owen opens it almost immediately. "Hey," he says with a smile.

"Wow." I peer past him into the living room. "Your house is *clean*." I hardly remember what a clean house looks like. I found some dried macaroni on my bag the other day.

"Is it?" He shrugs, but he looks a little pleased. "It's because my family's out right now."

He leads me down the hallway. The walls are sparsely decorated, only a couple of framed pictures of Owen and what must be his younger brother. Next to them hangs an enormous black-and-white photograph of a boyishly handsome Asian man in a seventies-style suit. I pause in front of it. "Is this your dad?" I ask.

Owen glances over his shoulder, puzzlement momentarily written in his brows. His eyes find the photograph, and his mouth twitches with contained laughter. "My mom *wishes* that were my dad. That's Yûjirô Ishihara," he says. "My mom grew up in Kyoto, and when she was a teenager, he was pretty much the biggest star in Japan. She was obsessed. *Is* obsessed," he adds, "even though he died thirty years ago."

"Damn. Your mom's a legit fangirl." I take a closer look, considering Yûjirô's eyebrows and jawline. "I get it, though."

"Great," Owen grumbles, pushing open the door to his room. "Not you, too." I follow him, grinning to his back.

The first thing I notice about Owen's room is the movie posters that line the walls. But they're not movies I know—half the titles are in French, and most of them feature surreal imagery I can't begin to decipher. "Whoa," I say, and look back at Owen, who's noticed my survey of the room.

"I have a bit of a thing for French cinema," he says casually.

"Oh? I hadn't noticed," I deadpan. "But seriously, how do these fit in with Shakespeare and Eugene O'Neill?"

He gives me a crooked grin and brushes his hand through his hair. "I'm a complicated man, Megan."

I step farther into the room. "English theater, French movies, *Italian* girlfriend . . ." I search for photos of Cosima on his cluttered dresser, his conspicuously clean desk, and his windowsill storing a set of encyclopedias. "She's not going to interrupt us on FaceTime, is she?"

"No, she already went to bed," he says, his voice neutral.

"*Of course* she did," I tease. I walk over to his desk and start opening drawers, finding only impressive stacks of note-books in each.

"Excuse me," I hear behind me. "What exactly are you do-ing with my personal possessions?"

I glance over my shoulder to find Owen leaning against the wall, his arms folded across his chest. He pushes him-self off the wall waist-first and crosses the room to shut the drawer I'm perusing.

"Looking for a picture of Cosima," I answer like it's obvi-ous. "She doesn't think being photographed is frivolous, too, does she?"

"No," Owen replies coolly. "I just don't have any pictures of her, is all."

"Where did you guys meet?" I ask, undeterred. I turn to the bookshelves by his bed. A small framed photo of Owen and Jordan from middle school sits between a beautiful hardcover of *The Great Gatsby* and a collection of Emily Dickinson poems.

"It was a summer theater program in New York." He sounds a little defensive. I can't see his face because I've walked be-hind him, but I'm certain he's blushing.

"Well, what's she like?" I press him.

"She's from a little outside Bologna. She writes dark, ex-perimental suburban stuff. Like David Mamet from Italy. Her parents are local politicians."

"You totally didn't answer my question."

He turns to face me, tilting his head and looking confused. "Yes, I did."

"No, what's she *like*?" I repeat. "You told me what she writes and where she lives, not who she is. If you're going to invent a girlfriend, you should flesh her out a little more." It's not that I definitely believe he made her up, it's just that I enjoy getting a rise out of him. "For someone who writes plays, Owen, you really should have a better command of character."

He frowns and raises an eyebrow at me. "She's social, she has a lot of friends. And a sarcastic sense of humor. Better?"

I grin. "Getting there," I toss back. "I'm still not convinced."

"Do you want help with Will or not?" he asks loudly. Without waiting for my answer he continues. "I thought we were here to work on my play."

"Fine," I say with a dramatic sigh, then take a seat on his bed and recline on his pillows. "Ask me anything."

Owen rolls his eyes at my posture before sitting down in his desk chair. He pulls a notebook from the top drawer, and suddenly his whole demeanor changes. His shoulders drop, he sits up straighter and fixes his eyes on me. I wait for him to ask about my thoughts on love or my feelings about myself, the kinds of things I'd imagine a playwright would want to know.

"How far do you and your boyfriends typically go? Like, sexually?" he clarifies.

My mouth drops open for a second, both at the question and at Owen's unexpected composure. Not about to let him think he's scandalized me, I give him a lazy grin. "You get right to it."

I expect Owen to blanch, but he doesn't. "It's important to the play."

"Well, if it's for the play." I smother a smirk. If he wants detail, it's detail he'll get. "Tyler was my first. We only did it a couple times, mostly on the couch in his basement in the middle of cast parties, with everyone upstairs." I ignore the lingering bite of comparing those memories with Madeleine's recent account, instead preoccupying myself with hoping I'll catch Owen's ears going red.

When he only continues writing, I deflate a little. I'll have to work harder. Which won't be a problem given the detail I could provide. "I wouldn't say it was amazing, but there *was* a reason we did it more than once . . ." I say suggestively, frowning when Owen only nods. I'm used to hushed laughter and gossip-glittering eyes when I provide details of my escapades—the consolation prize for their early, inevitable ends. Owen is . . . resisting. It's unexpected, and I'm uncertain what to make of it.

"I'm trying to get an idea of what Rosaline might feel if she'd slept with Romeo before the whole Juliet thing." His eyes remain fixed on his notebook. His hand moves with practiced speed, his pen in precise jolts. "Do you feel differently about Tyler than your other exes?"

"Not really." I shrug. "I did *plenty* with other guys."

For the first time, Owen's shoulders stiffen. I grin. *Everyone* has a sex-awkwardness pressure point, even young Shakespeare over here. I go on. "I went to third base with Chris behind the gym after homecoming sophomore year. Only hands were involved with Charlie because his mom was always coming home at inopportune times. Obviously nothing with Anthony—oh, third base with Dean, which took freaking forever. I had to—"

"That—that's enough, thanks," he cuts me off, completely crimson.

"Ha! *Finally*," I explode.

He looks up. "You were trying to make me uncomfortable?"

"Well, a little, yeah." I eye him playfully.

He lifts his pen, looking like he wants to say something, until he finally does. "Is this . . . how you are?"

"Is what how I am?"

"This, you know . . . forward. Provocative." I know it's not a criticism, or a joke. He watches me, his mouth a neutral line, his eyes searching. He really wants to know.

I laugh harshly. "I've earned the right. When you've had as many relationships as I have, you learn to find the humor in . . ." I reach for the right word.

"Heartbreak," Owen says.

"That's a bit more poetic than I would have gone with, but basically." He says nothing, and I pounce on the opportunity to change the subject. "Besides, teasing you is too much fun to resist." I reach toward the chair and pat him on the knee. "You're just so . . . sweet."

He shakes off my hand. "No, I'm not," he huffs.

He's looking at the floor, and I feel a sting of remorse. Owen *is* sweet. He's been nothing but kind to me, and I just turned that into something he feels self-conscious about. "You're right. I'm sorry."

"I have other questions, you know." Owen recovers his composure, returning to his notebook. "If you're ready to answer them like a mature human being." He flashes me a brief smile.

"Okaaaaay . . ." I drag out the syllables, relieved I'm for-given.

"Does how far you go with a guy affect your feelings in the breakup?"

I pause a second. He deserves a thoughtful answer this time. "The sex doesn't matter, per se. But if I've been with a guy long enough to have done things with him, I'm used to having him in my life, and it's worse when we break up. Even then, though, when I see him with someone else and they're perfect in every way he and I weren't, it's hard to stay upset."

Owen stops writing. "I would think it'd be the opposite—that it would hurt worse."

"Not when you're expecting it. My relationships end for something bigger. In the end, it's comforting."

He gives me a long look, like he's waiting for me to elab-orate, or to burst into tears or something. I don't know what he's thinking. When I do none of the above, he makes a couple more notes. "Do you believe in true love?" he asks out of nowhere.

"True love?" I scoff, not meeting his unfaltering eye con-tact. I don't know why the question throws me. Maybe it's the way he asked it, like true love is common and obvious enough to be brought up as easily as the weather. "I told you. I'm not really the romantic, love-at-first-sight type," I answer.

"You also said Tyler and Madeleine are perfect together."

"So?" I reply a little hotly.

"So," he repeats, his tone measured, "if two people are per-fect for each other, it suggests their connection is better than others. Deeper, truer."

"True love exists, like, in the world." I gesture vaguely to the air around me. I've witnessed true love too often to think otherwise. What Madeleine and Tyler have is true. Same with my dad and Rose. "But I'm certainly not holding out hope for it myself."

"Hmm," Owen muses, his eyes sparkling. He leans back, clearly confident about whatever he's going to say next. "It's interesting you think that."

"Think that? I *know* it. It's my own feelings." My skin itches down my arms. I roll my shoulders, trying to loosen the sudden tension in my back.

"And yet, when one relationship ends, you jump easily into another."

"Which, as the entire student body can tell you, means I'm flirtatious and boy-crazy. Two things I'm not ashamed of, by the way," I add, chin up.

"Of course." He nods quickly. "I'm not saying you should be. I just wonder why, if you're *only* flirtatious and boy-crazy, you go from relationship to relationship instead of hookup to hookup." His eyes bore into mine again.

I blink. I haven't known Owen very long, and somehow he's seen into the quietest, smallest corner of my heart. It's a wish I don't let out very often. Not everyone finds someone perfect for them. Or if they do, sometimes that person doesn't think *you're* perfect for *them*. My mom's lingering affection for my dad showed me that.

"I thought this was supposed to be play brainstorming, not psychotherapy or something."

Owen puts down his pen, his expression growing gentle.

"You're right. You've given me a lot of great stuff to work with."

The silence hangs in the air. I don't know what to do next. I guess I'm here to ask about Will, but would it be weird if I did? Or would it be weirder if I didn't? Would that just show I'm more rattled than I'd like to admit? I wish I could think of something to dispel the tension.

"Not amazing, huh?" Owen asks suddenly, and I'm thankful he's smiling. "Tyler, I mean."

I feel a grin spreading across my face. "His final performance didn't exactly live up to the acclaimed early previews."

Owen lets out a quick laugh. "Not a long run then?"

"Closed in minutes. Hoping Will lasts longer . . ." I raise an eyebrow.

"That's Sexy Stagehand Will to you," Owen says seriously.

"Of course." I lean forward. "Your turn. What's up with Sexy Stagehand Will? What's taking him so long? It's been days of me giving him my best bedroom eyes—and not like shitty, twin-bed bedroom eyes," I add. "Like four-poster, silk-draped, chateau bedroom eyes."

"Bedroom eyes?" Owen cocks his head skeptically. "Is that a thing?"

On the bed, I lean a little closer and look up at him through smoldering, half-lidded eyes.

"Ah," he says almost immediately. "Well, Will's not used to this kind of thing. He wouldn't make a move unless he knows you're interested."

"I'm not just going to march up to him in the middle of school or rehearsal and plant one on him. Not if he might not be into it. I do have *some* dignity."

"What if it's not at school?" Owen muses. "Will's band is playing a house party this weekend. It'll give you guys a chance to find some privacy."

Yes. In front of a crowd is one thing, but if I can get him alone, I'd definitely make a move. "Perfect," I say. "Sounds like I'll have a new boyfriend by Monday."

Owen looks at me curiously. I can read the question in his eyes.

I sigh with impatience, and maybe a little something else. "I told you, I'm not holding out hope for love. I like Will. I want Will to be my boyfriend. Even if I hope *someday, something* like . . . true love"—I almost can't get the words out—"is possible for me, I'm expecting nothing from him other than our relationship falling apart just like the rest."

"You're certain it'll fall apart," Owen asks, "and still you're eager to start a new relationship?" There's nothing judgmental in his tone.

It's not like I haven't asked myself the very same question. "What else can I do? Otherwise I'll just be watching everyone else." I get up off the bed and pick up my bag by his door. He's still watching me with the scrutiny of his interview, even though he's put his notebook down on his desk. "Besides," I add, throwing my bag over my shoulder, "it'll be fun while it lasts."

NINE

JULIET: *Give me my Romeo, and when I shall die,*
Take him and cut him out in little stars,
And he will make the face of heaven so fine
That all the world will be in love with night
And pay no worship to the garish sun.

III.ii.23–7

EVER SINCE MY DAD TOLD ME ABOUT the move, just being home puts me in a bad mood. I've spent afternoons this week doing homework in the drama room or, when Jody goes home for the night, in the corner booth in Verona eating half-baked pizza and watching Anthony watch Eric. But on Friday night, I'm home early to talk to Mom.

I head downstairs to hydrate before the party. I'm in luck— Dad's at a school board meeting, and the house is quiet. In the kitchen I walk past Erin in her high chair contemplating the universe over a tiny bowl of applesauce. When I grab a bottle of water and close the fridge, something splatters on the wall next to me. I spin to find Erin regarding me, pink plastic spoon in hand and a big grin on her face. She lets out a giggle, and I notice there's applesauce in her ear.

I sigh. "Rose?" I call. There's no answer. Seeing no other choice, I turn back to Erin. "You can't go around looking like that," I chide. Gingerly, I scoop her out of her high chair, careful to avoid the applesauce sliding down her cheek. She shrieks in delight.

I leave the water running while I wet a paper towel and wipe down Erin's face. Clearly thinking this is the best thing in the world, Erin flings her hand through the stream, splashing water on the halter dress I've chosen to catch Will's eye. I put my hand on my hip and adopt an indignant tone. "You did *not* just do that." I flick a drop of water at her in return, and she explodes into giggles.

"Megan?" I hear Rose from the hall before she steps into the kitchen, her eyes jumping from me to Erin. "Sorry, I walked away for a second to pee for the twentieth time today." She smiles. "You two look like you're having fun."

I was. But when Rose lays a hand on her swollen stomach, I'm reminded of why my dad's moving across the country. "You left her with applesauce. I had to clean her up," I tell Rose, working to keep my voice unemotional.

"Thanks, Megan," she says gently as she walks forward to pick up Erin. "Erin would thank you, too, if only she could pronounce your name," Rose adds, smiling. "The hard *G*, you know?"

I only shrug before I head upstairs.

When I get on FaceTime with Mom five minutes late—as usual—I must still look out of sorts, because she immediately studies me, concerned. "What's wrong?"

"Did you know Dad and Rose are planning to move to New York?" I blurt out.

Mom looks taken aback, but she quickly recovers. "They . . . haven't told me about that, no."

"Well, they're looking at houses," I charge on. "I only found out because they left a real-estate catalog in the kitchen."

I watch her fuss with the mug of tea she's holding, one I realize I don't recognize. It wasn't one of the things she packed into cardboard boxes before she left Oregon, and her marriage, to find a new home in Texas. I've never known how that felt to her, but now I'm beginning to understand. I'm beginning to know the disconnection from home she must've felt, even though I'm staying put in Oregon for college—hopefully—and she moved halfway across the country.

I blamed her the night they told me she was moving. I didn't understand why she'd decided to leave. When I caught her hours later forlornly staring at the family photos in the hall, I realized she hadn't. Not really.

"Megan, I'm sure they were going to tell you," Mom says softly. "You know your father. He never lets anyone into his plans until he's figured the details out himself."

"Yeah. I guess," I mutter.

"If this bothers you, you should talk to your dad." Her voice is still sympathetic, but there's a patented Mom firmness to it. "He'd want to know you're upset."

"Why bother? It's not like they'd listen to my opinion."

Mom says nothing for a second, her eyes flitting downward. I know we're both remembering some of the worst fights of her and Dad's final months together. Shouting matches about Dad's tendency to make decisions for the whole family without listening to her, or even talking to her. There's a motorcycle in the garage to prove it.

"You know, New York might not be the worst," she says with a hesitant smile. "You could go to shows in the city when you're home from school."

She's trying, like she must've when she unpacked in her new home. She must've searched for what was exciting and worth looking forward to where she'd be living. Not wanting to worry her, I nod.

"You *could* come to Texas," she adds in a quietly hopeful voice.

"Maybe," I say. I don't tell her moving to Texas wouldn't fix the real problems. It wouldn't keep my dad and Rose from building a new life without me. It wouldn't keep them from erasing the only home I've ever known, consigning my childhood memories to the past.

"How's the play going?" Mom asks, and I know she's trying to distract me.

"It's going okay," I mumble. "We're mostly just working on memorizing. I haven't done a lot of real performing yet."

She sets down her tea, a worrisome gleam in her eye. "Well . . . Randall and I have gotten tickets to come to the Ashland showcase."

Shit. "Wow," I say instead. "Sounds great, Mom."

"It'll be Randall's first trip to Oregon," she goes on excitedly. "I was thinking the three of us could go to the lake. I finally get to show him where you grew up, and I know

Randall's looking forward to spending more time with you."

"That—would be really nice," I get out.

Mom cranes her neck to look behind her. "He's in the other room if you have time for a quick hello."

"Um, sorry. I have a party to get to. How about next time?"

"A party?" Her eyebrows lift. "You'll tell me about the new boyfriend tomorrow, I expect?"

I roll my eyes. "There's no boyfriend." *Yet*.

Mom gives me a look that says she knows better. "Be careful, Megan."

"Bye, Mom," I say loudly before I disconnect.

I shut the computer and put on my burgundy lipstick in front of the mirror. The thought of both parents and their significant others in Stillmont puts me on edge. It's hard to watch Mom and Randall next to Dad and Rose, the perfect couple Mom and her boyfriend will never be. Mom met Randall online after two years of blind dates and setups in Texas. Dad met Rose months after the divorce. They were married within the year, and with their second kid on the way, they still have Friday date nights and can't keep their hands off each other.

Because of course Dad bounced back. It's easier to be the one letting go.

I park at the end of Derek Denton's driveway, an impossibly long path to where his house perches on a bluff. Cars are parked the whole way up like it's Coachella and not a high-school house party. It's dark here, without streetlights among the trees. This is one of the priciest neighborhoods in southern Oregon, and I can see why. When I look up there's nothing but treetops and endless stars.

It takes ten minutes to walk up to the door, though my heels are partly to blame. It's a chilly October night, and I gratefully pull my jacket tight. When I get inside, I'm surprised I don't recognize everyone here. Stillmont is a small school, and I've only been to a couple of parties where the invites reached into other towns nearby, but Derek's living room is filled with people I've never seen before. The house is even bigger than it looked from the outside, with a wide oak staircase up to an indoor balcony where a group of girls lean on the railing, nodding along to the music. I look over the heads of the already inebriated crowd to the double doors that open onto an illuminated azure pool, where a few brave souls have jumped in despite the weather.

But next to the pool I spot what I'm looking for, a cleared space with a drum kit and a couple of amps. Setting up a microphone in front of the drums is the tall, leather-jacketed, gorgeous reason I'm here tonight.

I plunge into the crowd, stepping past the coffee table where Jeremy Handler is presently passed out. Courtney Greene shoves a red Solo cup in my direction. "I'm good!" I yell, not to be deterred.

"Megan!" someone shouts in my ear, and I turn. There are only a couple of voices that could stop me right now, and one of them is Anthony's, especially when I know tonight's the night he's supposed to be out with Eric. He looks no less surprised to see me than I am him.

"Wait." I recover first. "Wasn't Eric's party—" Then I realize. "*This* is the party Eric invited you to?"

"Yeah," he says. I notice he's wearing one of his best outfits—his caramel chinos and the iconic navy blazer over an oxford with the top two buttons undone. "What are you doing here? I didn't know you were coming out tonight."

I throw a glance toward the makeshift stage where Will's now tuning a guitar. *Be still my heart*.

"I see." Anthony nods slowly.

"How's it going with you?" I search the crowd. "Where's Eric?"

Anthony seizes my arm. "It's going *great*. Eric picked me up, and we drove over here together. Which means he's driving me home." He gives me a smile I recognize from years of being front row to his flirtations. "High hopes for the night."

Behind him, I catch sight of Eric in a neon frat tank, holding up two Solo cups and heading our way. Anthony grins, and I gently shove him in Eric's direction. The screech of an amp cuts through the shitty dance music inside, and I take it as my cue to press on to the back door.

Finally, I reach the stage. "Will!" I shout from a couple feet away, trying to sound like I'm surprised to run into him—not like he's my single objective for the night and hopefully the next couple months.

"Megan, hey!" Will faces me, looking genuinely surprised. "I didn't know you'd be coming." He sets his guitar down and gives me a grin that has me rethinking the whole privacy premise of tonight.

"This house is crazy, right?" I nonchalantly toss my hair. "I heard there's a path to a bluff with an incredible view."

"Really?" He looks interested, and my stomach somersaults. He crouches down next to an amp to plug something in. "Give me a—"

"Hey, Will!" The voice comes from what must be one of Will's bandmates, who's standing on the other end of the stage. "The PA's broken again. I've tried plugging shit in everywhere and—nothing. We need that stagehand magic."

Will sighs, frustrated, and looks at me apologetically. "I have to—" he starts.

"No worries," I cut him off, hoping he doesn't hear my disappointment. "The show must go on. I'm looking forward to it."

His devastating grin returns. "Find me after, okay?"

"Definitely." Like he has to tell me. Even though it physically hurts to pull myself away, I retreat into the crowd growing on the edge of the stage.

Will must be a genius with PAs, because it's only five minutes later that he steps up to the mic while the rest of the band take to their instruments behind him. Without introduction, Will counts them off and strikes the first chord. He's incredible. I am dead. They're playing a kind of alternative punk that I'd probably enjoy even without the hot singer.

I try to move up, but I'm blocked by Dean Singh, my ex from two years ago. He's dancing overeagerly with Amanda

Cohen, whom he left me for when she transferred to our school three months into our relationship. I watch him smash a sloppy kiss on her lips in front of me.

I hesitate, wrestling with the warring desires to get a better view and to avoid Dean. I didn't exactly exit the relationship gracefully. I wasn't completely used to being dumped yet, and I let Dean know I was pissed. There might have been defiling of his locker involved. We haven't spoken since, and I'm not looking to break the streak. In a moment of panic, I spin and search for a new vantage point to watch the band. My eyes find Anthony on the outdoor balcony.

I quickly go inside and step over a worrisome bikini top on my way up the stairs. It's less crowded up here with everyone on the dance floor. When I walk out onto the balcony, Anthony's draped on the railing, his eyes fixed on the crowd below. Immediately, I know something's wrong. In no typical party would Anthony be by himself while everyone else is having fun.

"What's up, Anthony?" I hesitantly ask when I reach the railing.

He wordlessly points to the edge of the dance floor, where I glimpse a flash of neon. Eric.

He's dancing—with a girl, the sort of girl someone like Eric would be expected to attract. Bleach-blonde hair, tall, curvaceous.

"They could just be friends," I say, watching the girl press her butt into Eric's front. "Besides, you said things were going great. I bet it's nothing."

Anthony turns to me, his eyes combative. "Does she *look*

like just a friend?" He nods to where Eric's now running his hands down the girl's sides.

I have to admit, it doesn't look good. A guy in a Saint Margaret's School lacrosse jersey walks past Eric and thumps him on the back. That's where Eric goes to school, I have to guess. He exchanges bro-nods with the lacrosse guy, then returns to his concentrated grinding.

"I don't get it," Anthony mutters. "I really felt like we connected in the car."

"I'm sure you—" I hear my name shouted up from the lower level. Anthony and I both turn, startled, to peer over the railing.

Owen's standing under the balcony. He must be the only person in the entire party not dancing or watching the band. He's wearing a gray sweater and black jeans, and even though I know I've seen the outfit before, it looks somehow better tonight. When our eyes meet, he grins.

"What're you doing up there?" he calls.

I gesture in the direction of Will and the band, who've finished their first song to drunken cheers. "Better view!" I shout.

"How Juliet of you." Owen nods at the balcony, his grin widening. I have no choice but to roll my eyes. Beside me Anthony groans, and I glance to Eric—whose hands have risen perilously close to Blondie's chest.

Anthony's head drops into his hands. But he jerks upright when I take him by both shoulders and spin him to look me in the eye. "Anthony," I say urgently. "This?" I gesture to him crumpled on the railing. "Isn't how you get guys interested.

Especially not when you're wearing the blazer and button-down you *know* leave people breathless." He gives me a weak smile. "Pull yourself together. Get down there," I continue. "Talk to him. Dance with him."

My monologue doesn't exactly leave Anthony looking like a virile sex god, but some of the despondency's gone out of his expression. He straightens his blazer and walks inside, and I lean over the balcony's edge.

"Owen," I shout. "This is ridiculous. Come up here."

Will counts off the second song, and I take special note of the way he pushes his slightly sweaty hair out of his eyes. Sometime between the hair push and Will gripping the mic with both hands in a way that makes me wish it were my face, Owen comes out onto the balcony.

"Did you bring a date?" I ask him when he joins me by the railing.

He frowns, but I can tell he's trying to hide a smile. "No, Megan. I didn't bring a date. I have a girlfriend."

"Oh, *right*. I keep forgetting."

He scrutinizes me for a second. "Is there . . . applesauce in your hair?"

"What?" I quickly try to hide my head from Owen and grab my hair, mortified when I feel something sticky. "It was—a crazy pregame," I mutter, furiously trying to brush it out.

Owen turns back to the band. It feels like he's giving me a moment to collect myself, and I'm grateful. "They sound okay tonight," he says.

"They sound *amazing*. They're probably the best band I've ever heard."

"You mean seen," he says with the hint of a smile.

"Seen, heard . . . What's the difference?"

Owen laughs. "Remind me to take you to a real concert sometime."

It's a tossed-off comment, but for a moment my mind lingers on the idea of Owen Okita taking me to concerts, to other places on nights out . . . But I lose my train of thought when I hear Will sing, *"Come on, baby, touch me and feel me burning for you!"*

I can't stop listening. Hot lead singer notwithstanding, they *are* good. *"You're a fire in the night, crimson in the trees,"* Will sings. *"If you do nothing else for me, baby, burn me down, please."*

"Wow . . . Will, these lyrics, it's working for me," I say in a low voice.

Owen rubs the back of his neck, looking uncomfortable.

"Wait." I grab his arm. "Owen. Did *you* write these?"

The blood rushes from his face. "Yes, I did."

"No wonder you're with your fair Cosima if she inspires lyrics like these. A few weeks of theater camp and you two really got down to business."

He shakes his head sharply. "The lyrics weren't inspired by anything. I was just trying to channel Neruda's love poetry in a modern context. It was a poetical exercise."

I raise an eyebrow. "Is that what the kids are calling it these days?"

"I swear," he insists. "They're completely innocent."

"Sure, Owen."

I feel my phone buzz. Pulling it out of my purse, I find a text from Anthony. **YOU NEED TO COME DOWN HERE,** it reads. Anthony texts entirely in capitals. When I asked him why, years ago, he told me "the world won't wait for men who write in lowercase."

y, I send back.

I WANT TO DANCE WITH ERIC. TOO SCARED. NEED BACKUP.

I look down into the crowd and spot Anthony awkwardly hovering near Eric and the girl. I notice the Saint Margaret's lacrosse boys have moved away from the dance floor to the keg by the doors. Smiling, I stow my phone and grab Owen's arm again. "Come on," I command. "We've got to go dance."

He looks startled. I swear, one of these days that expression's going to stick. "Us? Now?"

"It's a group thing. For Anthony." I walk backward while tugging him toward the door. "It's nothing to make Cosima jealous."

Owen breaks into a grin. "So you admit she's real?"

"You're impossible." I roll my eyes, leading him down the stairs. "Come on, lover boy."

I keep hold of his arm as we make our way through our drunken classmates. The crowd hasn't thinned out, and I'm nearly elbowed in the face by a couple baseball guys I recognize from Tyler's games. I let go of Owen when we reach Anthony, who's worked up the courage to move closer to Eric. Luckily, Eric and the blonde have separated long enough for us to join them and form a lopsided dance circle.

I reach for Anthony's hand and playfully grind up on him, and he places his hands on my hips. Anthony's a good dancer once he's been loosened up.

As soon as the blonde walks off to join the group of girls beckoning her over, I nudge Anthony in Eric's direction and face Owen, who's making a good effort at dancing. I watch him bob his head for a couple beats before I take his hands and dance lazily with my fingers entwined in his. I feel him hesitate for a second, but then I exaggeratedly flip my hair, and he relaxes, grinning.

When the band starts a faster number, Owen cranes his neck to look over my shoulder. Following his eyes, I turn and catch sight of Anthony and Eric swaying near each other, holding hands below their waists.

I whip to face Owen. "Oh my god," I mouth. He nods slowly, eyebrows arched. I laugh and pull him closer, our bodies just barely touching. He stiffens, but still he doesn't pull away. By the time the song ends, he's gripping my hands tightly and we move faster in rhythm through the next couple songs.

"That's our set. Thanks, Stillmont," I hear Will's voice coming over the mic. "You've been a beautiful audience."

I step back from Owen and wipe the sweat from my fore-head, catching my breath. He gives me a shy smile, a smile in which I see a different Owen than the one hunched over his notebook in Verona. An Owen willing to follow me onto a dance floor and match my every move with one of his own. Just when I think I have him figured out, he keeps finding ways to surprise me.

The thought hangs in my head for only a moment because,

out of the corner of my eye, I glimpse the blonde girl from earlier heading our way, followed by two Saint Margaret boys. Eric drops Anthony's hand—and while Anthony watches in stunned silence, Eric grabs the girl and presses his lips to hers, folding her into a shameless kiss.

I lock eyes with Anthony.

Horror, heartbreak, and anger collide on his face. I open my mouth, trying to think of something to say—of what I could possibly say—but he's storming off before I've even gotten his name out. The crowd's breaking up, staggering back into the house. I push aside exhausted couples clinging to each other on the patio, following Anthony.

I finally reach him by the pool, but he holds up a hand. "Please, Megan," he says in a low, uneven voice. "I just need to be alone right now."

"Let me drive you home at least," I say, because it's the only thing I have to offer.

"No, go back inside. Find Will. I'll be fine, really. I'll get a ride with Jenna." He irons a little of the waver out of his voice.

I stand there and watch him slowly walk into the house with everyone else, wondering if I'd be a shittier friend to let him leave or try to follow. Before I've decided, Owen steps up beside me.

"Is he okay?" Owen asks.

"Not really. But Anthony's tough."

He nods. "Well, I wanted to catch you because the band's packing up. Now's your shot with Will."

He's right. I'm here for a reason, and I can't leave without trying. I look to the stage, where Will's drummer and guitarist are hauling equipment toward an open van parked in the back. But Will's caught in a circle of girls near the mic stand, each of them leaning in a little closer than what could be considered friendly. I'm not surprised to find Alyssa's among them.

Part of me irrationally hopes he'll look for me over the heads of his new groupies. But of course he doesn't.

"Are you going?" Owen sounds expectant.

I gesture to the girls encircling Will. "I'm not interested in playing that game." And I definitely don't want to stick around and watch him notice someone else. "I'll just wait until everyone's leaving and talk to him then."

With nothing better to do, I follow Owen into the enormous, trashed living room, where inexplicably he begins picking up beer cans and Solo cups and throwing them into the black Hefty bag taped to the wall. Feeling guilty next to Mr. Party Samaritan, I grab a towel and wipe up a salsa spill on the chip table.

"You're his friend. What has Will said about me?" I ask after a couple minutes.

Owen drops a can into the trash bag, then stops, seemingly weighing his words. "He said you're hot in a deep way."

I straighten up. "What does *that* mean? No, wait, it doesn't matter. It sounds promising." I take a seat on the stairs and smile to myself, until curiosity gets the better of me. "But what does that mean?"

Owen laughs at my change of heart. He leans on the banister, his eyes becoming contemplative. His words come slowly at first, but they gather momentum while he speaks. "It means you're, like, this unafraid force of being. You know exactly who you want to be, and you never pretend to be someone you're not. It's inspiring. Being around you—" He looks up sharply, then shakes his head. "This trash bag's going to break," he says abruptly, tying off the bag beside him, eyes averted from mine. "Would you hand me another?" He points to the box of bags on the table.

Judging from the limp outline of the one he's tying shut, it's nowhere near full. But I grab a new bag anyway.

I hand it to him, saying nothing. I don't know what *to* say. Owen tapes the new bag to the wall, then straightens his sweater like he's desperately searching for a distraction. I feel something I hardly recognize—a blush rising in my cheeks.

No one's ever said anything like that to me. I've never thought of myself as a force of . . . anything.

"No wonder you write the lyrics," I say lightly before the silence gets too awkward.

Owen's laugh sounds relieved, but he stuffs his hands into his pockets.

"Will didn't say all that, did he?" My voice comes out soft, and at first I think he didn't hear me over the music pounding through the walls. No one's turned the iPod off even though the party's dying down.

"Not exactly," Owen says after a long moment. He glances sideways, and I want to ask him what he was going to say next, before he cut himself off to ask for the trash bag, when I hear someone's footsteps coming from the now nearly empty patio.

"Hey," Will says when he sees us.

"Good set tonight." Owen sounds casual, none of the gentle sincerity of a couple seconds ago lingering in his voice. "I should head home," he continues, tossing a pointed look in my direction. I know he's purposefully giving me time with Will. "I'll see you guys for rehearsal on Monday."

He leaves us by the stairs. I waste no time in getting up and smoothing my dress. Without saying a word, we drift back outside. There's a certain charge in the air, like we both know where this is headed.

Will pauses under the strings of small, dim lights strung over the patio. "I looked for you after the show, but I couldn't find you."

"I knew you were getting mobbed." I shrug, not wanting to think about Alyssa and the groupies right now. "Hot lead singer and whatnot."

He laughs, his voice rough and raspy from an hour of singing, and I wish we'd skipped the small talk. "You get right to the point. I like that," he says, eyeing me like he's wishing the same thing.

I'm leaning forward to kiss him when there's a horrible retching sound next to us. We both startle back to find Jeremy Handler, head between his knees, spewing an acrid beige outpouring onto the grass. "Wow . . ." Will mumbles.

"Yeah. We have to find a better place for this."

"What was it you said about a bluff with a view?" he asks, a smile returning to his eyes.

"*Yes.*" I grab his hand. "Perfect."

The path begins behind the pool, and it's startling how quickly the backyard full of beer cans—and now vomit—disappears on our way up. Hardly a five-minute walk up the trail, it feels like Will and I have stepped into a starlit night completely our own. I lead him to the rocky edge of the bluff. The view is unbelievable, sweeping over the sparse lights of Stillmont and the moon reflected in Hudson Lake.

"I don't want to be the kind of guy who fishes for compliments," Will speaks up after a moment of looking out on the view, "but what'd you think of the band?"

I grin and face him, my hand still in his. "I think you're a great vocalist," I say not untruthfully. I take a step closer. "And Sexy Stagehand Will is an understatement."

His eyebrows nearly reach his hairline. "Is that what people call me?"

I close the distance between us. "Certain people," I say in a hushed voice. Then my lips are on his. He stills and pulls back after a second, looking at me questioningly. "You said you liked that I got right to the point," I whisper. "This was the point, wasn't it?"

Will's uncertainty fades, replaced by something that stops my breath. "Yes. It definitely was."

For a single heartbeat, I look into Will's eyes and wonder if I'm doing this right. If I shouldn't slow down and get to know him before beginning this. The whisper of an idea slips into my mind. *Maybe I shouldn't begin every relationship with the expectation it'll end. Maybe it could last if*— I bury the thought.

I don't have time to waste. I'm going to enjoy every second I have with Will before it's over.

He pulls me in this time and kisses me hard. Even though we're a long way from the ocean, it feels like waves crashing.

I glance in the mirror once I've gotten back in my car, and *holy shit, is my hair messed up*. It's fifteen minutes past my curfew, but there's someone I have to text before I go home and have my phone taken away for the weekend. I haven't texted Owen before, but we exchanged numbers after our first play-brainstorming session.

went gr8. Thx ur the best, I send him with a kissy emoji.

Who is this? he replies.

u didnt put my # in ur phone??? megan, I shoot back.

It's a couple moments before my phone buzzes again.

> **Forgive me for not recognizing you through the grammar of a sixth grader from 2001. Is this how you write everything, or are you very drunk?**

Smiling to myself, I return, **NOT drunk. who do U usually text w/? david foster wallace?**

> **David Foster Wallace is dead, Megan. I WISH I texted with David Foster Wallace.**

I find I'm grinning wider.

back 2 point: Will!!! (RIP david foster wallace)

My phone buzzes seconds after I've hit SEND.

Punctuation! Like rain in the desert!

keep it in ur pants, Owen, I fire back.
I watch the typing bubble for a half minute before I receive his reply.

**I'm happy for you about Will. I hope you still want
advice, though, because my play's nowhere near done.**

I know this is probably just Owen being a Serious Writer,
but still I'm touched he wants to hang out. I send back, **dnt
worry, Im not going anywhere.**

TEN

WILL'S WAITING FOR ME OUTSIDE ENGLISH WHEN lunch begins. I wasn't expecting him, and I beam when I notice him leaning on the lockers. It's nearly been a week, and we haven't had the conversation where we "define the relationship." But it doesn't matter if we're dating, or hooking up, or just friends with benefits, even if it's only PG for now. Whatever we are, I'm enjoying it.

He reaches for my hand as we walk down the hallway. Momentarily surprised, I jerk to face him. "Handholding? I'll take it," I say coyly. In the past couple days, we've jumped straight to the more physical, more private forms of contact, skipping over the simple stuff like holding hands.

"I'm not moving too fast, right?" He flashes me his irresistible smile.

I play along. "I don't know, Will. It's bold of you."

"Megan Harper talking to *me* about being bold?" He releases my hand and spins to walk backward facing me.

I laugh. "I haven't a clue what you're implying."

"Oh really?" He cocks an eyebrow. "Even with what happened yesterday after rehearsal?"

My stomach clenches deliciously at the memory of a Grade-A make-out session in the green room, complete with a costume rack knocked over and a shattered prop lamp.

"You raise an excellent point," I concede. Still thinking about yesterday, I grab his hand and stop him outside the art closet. His eyes light up. Wasting no time, he follows me inside and closes the door.

Twenty-two minutes later, I straighten my skirt and step out into the hall. Will places a hand low on my back, and we head to the quad. We find Tyler and Madeleine, Owen, Jenna, and a few juniors I know on the hill outside the drama room. Without warning, Will sweeps his arm behind my back, dips me slightly, and kisses me. With tongue.

When he pulls back, he's grinning. "Too bold?"

I place a hand on his chest. "It's Megan Harper you're talking to, remember?"

He laughs and follows it up with a quick kiss. "I'll see you after rehearsal."

"You better," I warn. I sit down between Madeleine and Jenna, my eyes on Will as he walks into the Arts Center.

"Where's Will going?" Madeleine asks next to me. I notice she looks genuinely disappointed. One of the things I love about her is, not only does she comfort me through every breakup, but she's excited every time I date someone new—no matter how often that is.

"He had to finish some set design." I give her a fake pouty look, which she returns.

"You mean we *don't* get to watch you make out for the rest of lunch?" Owen dryly laments. "How will we survive?"

I grab one of Madeleine's celery sticks and chuck it at Owen. He catches it to his chest and promptly eats it. Madeleine, looking mildly indignant, moves her celery farther from me. "Have you guys talked about it yet?" she asks. "You and Will? Walking you from class, that looked like boyfriend stuff."

I shrug. "Not yet. We're taking it slow."

I hear a low chuckle from Tyler, and I'm surprised to notice Owen shoot him a look, his expression hardening. "What did *that* mean?" Owen asks flatly.

Tyler glances between Madeleine and me, recognizing the indelicate position he's put himself in. "I've just never known Megan to take it slow," he finally says haltingly.

I hardly have time to be offended before Madeleine puts a hand on my knee. "With a guy who looks like Will, I know *I* wouldn't." It's a remark aimed to irritate Tyler, and from the way he stiffens and crosses his arms, I know it worked. "What's he like?" she continues in a gossipy tone.

"He's funny, and he's confident . . ." I begin, only too happy to brag about my new boy-*whatever*. "And he's the best kisser *ever*." I don't look at Tyler, but he knows I'm talking to him.

"Sounds like this one might last out the month," he sneers.

Madeleine whacks his shoulder, staring daggers at him.

It's sweet of her, but the damage is done. It's one thing for me to joke about my short-lived romances—it's something else for people like Tyler to think *I'm* the flighty one in my relationships. I might enjoy the flings, the fooling around, the green-room make-outs, but I'm never the one to keep them from developing into meaningful relationships. I get up to leave, no longer in the mood to talk about Will, and catch sight of Owen watching Tyler furiously.

I throw my bag onto my shoulder. "Don't be a dick," I overhear Madeleine hiss. I ponder where exactly I'm going to go, but the bell rings, deciding for me.

"Why, that same pale hard-hearted wench, that Rosaline, torments him so that he will sure run mad."

Anthony's strutting across the small stage in the drama room, delivering his lines with his characteristic panache. I'm sitting in the front row, next to Owen, the play open on my lap in a feeble effort to look like I'm memorizing my lines. Tyler's a couple of rows behind me, obnoxiously rehearsing for a group of enraptured sophomores, but I'm trying not to dwell on what he said during lunch. Instead, I'm determined to sort out something else bothering me.

Anthony's been avoiding me since the party. Every day, he rushes out of rehearsal before I have the chance to talk to him, and he hasn't replied to a single one of my texts. I have no idea why. I know he's hurt about Eric, but it feels like he's upset with me, too.

"Farewell, lady, lady, lady." Anthony says his final line, and Jody waves him off stage, dismissing him. I sit up straighter and try to catch his eye. It works—for a moment. But then his eyes dart from mine, and he ducks out the side door.

"We'll do Act Two Scene three next," Jody declares, breaking my concentration. It's not one of mine, but even though I'm dying to follow Anthony, I can't leave until Jody dismisses me. Owen gets up and walks to the front of the room, where Tyler's waiting on stage. I realize it's a Friar Lawrence scene, and immediately I feel for Owen. Every week, he's the only person who gets more nervous than I do on stage.

Today, something's different.

Owen's script doesn't shake in his hands, and he's not fidgeting with his sweater the way I know he sometimes does. *Good for him*, I think to myself. I remember dancing with him at the party—when Owen dives into something, he's kind of inspiring.

I pull out my phone. I'll have to redouble my efforts with Anthony. I work on composing yet another hopeless text, but it's next to impossible when I don't know why he's dodging me.

"What a change is here!" I jerk my head up, surprised by the unusual fire in Owen's voice. "Is Rosaline, that thou didst love so dear, so soon forsaken? Young men's love then lies not truly in their hearts, but in their eyes." Owen's face is red, not in embarrassment this time, but in what looks like genuine anger.

He's really busting Romeo's balls, I think before Jody waves her hand and steps onto the stage. Even when Owen drops his script to his side, he's glaring at Romeo. Or maybe it's Tyler.

"Tell me about your interpretation here, Owen," Jody says, pen to her lips. "Why did you read Friar Lawrence that way?"

"Romeo's a jerk, honestly," Owen grimly replies. "Friar Lawrence criticizes him for being thoughtless and disloyal to the girl he was in love with two days ago, and he's right."

Jody considers for a moment. "That's a good reading, but Friar Lawrence is a friar, a man of the cloth. He wouldn't come on quite that strong." Owen grudgingly nods, and Jody tells them to take it from the top.

They begin the scene again, and I watch closer this time, intrigued now. Owen tempers his voice, but I know him well enough to detect the concealed anger in his rigid posture and his clenched jaw. *He's pissed at Tyler . . . for what he said today*, I realize. *For me*. I feel a rush of gratitude. Even if I'm only doing this play for an acting credit, I'm glad it's brought Owen and me together.

Out of the corner of my eye, I notice Will stop in front of the window in the drama room door. He makes no move to come in, and I consider incurring Jody's wrath to cross the stage and drag him in here. Then he laughs, and I realize he's talking to someone. He takes a step to the side, revealing Alyssa right at the moment she's not-so-casually reaching out to touch his arm.

"Wast thou with Rosaline?" I hear Owen say from the stage.

"With Rosaline, my ghostly Father? No. I have forgot that name and that name's woe," Tyler replies.

It's happening again, I realize, watching Alyssa laugh uncomfortably close to Will. He and I didn't even get to define our relationship before it began falling apart. First the groupies at Derek's party, now this. I wish I could ignore it and return to my script, but for some masochistic reason, my eyes linger on them in the hall.

Whatever Will and I are, we won't be much longer.

I walk out of rehearsal an hour later determined to find Will. He never came inside, and even though we'd planned to meet afterward, he's not waiting in the hall like he was yesterday. Figuring he might be working on the set in the woodshop, I round the corner and nearly collide with a red-haired someone.

"Megan," Madeleine says, and places a hand on my shoulder to steady me. "Hey, I'm sorry about lunch today." I hear guilt in her voice.

"Oh, uh—it's fine, really. Have you seen Will?" I move to step past her. Tyler and lunch feel distant now, and it's not like what he said is Madeleine's fault.

But Madeleine doesn't release my shoulder. "No, it's not fine. What he said was *not* okay. I have half a mind to break up with him for it."

That stops me. I'm not Tyler's biggest fan, but I wouldn't want to come between him and Madeleine. I look right into her contrite expression. "You guys can't break up. You're perfect together," I say gently.

Her eyes soften. "It doesn't give him the right to dump on my best friend. I'm going to talk to him."

"Only if you want to. Owen already laid into him during rehearsal. Don't feel like you have to withhold sex from him or something."

I'm expecting her widened eyes and scandalized smile. "Megan!"

"Never mind," I tease, "I know you couldn't hold out for long anyway." She tries to swat me, but I dodge and spin out of her reach to continue down the hall. "I have to find Will," I call over my shoulder.

"Hey, what are you doing the Saturday after next?" I hear behind me.

I turn to face her. "I don't know. Why?"

"I'm organizing a tree-planting day," she begins. Madeleine's not content to restrict her volunteerism to school days. Since sophomore year, she's spent weekends working with something called the Oregon Forester Society, planting trees and holding Earth Day fairs. The sick thing is, I don't even think she does it for college. I think she *enjoys* it. "I wondered if you wanted to come and hang out?" she continues. "I know I've spent a lot of time with Tyler, and I miss you. It'll be time for just us."

"And some freshly planted trees," I shoot back with a grin.

"It'll be fun! Promise."

Madeleine's never invited me to one of her community service projects, probably because she rightly knows digging holes in the forest isn't my thing. But time with my best friend is. "Of course I'll go."

I turn to continue my search for Will, but then I pause. I'll see him tomorrow. Besides, the idea of finding him in the woodshop or pulling him into the art closet suddenly doesn't seem quite so important.

ELEVEN

FRIAR LAWRENCE: *They stumble that run fast.*

II.iii.101

I'M UPSTAIRS IN MY ROOM A WEEK later, thrilled to be working on a script that's not *Romeo and Juliet,* when Dad comes in without knocking.

He sits down on the bed. "What's that you're reading?" He sounds like he's uncomfortable, which would make two of us.

I could give him the long answer. I'd tell him I'm planning the blocking for Act I Scene xi of *Death of a Salesman* for the drama department's Senior Showcase in November. I'm in charge of the whole event this year after three years of directing scenes for it despite not being a senior—I won the esteem of the upperclassmen when I directed the freshmen drama production of *The Crucible,* and I've been invited into the Showcase ever since. This year, I couldn't co-direct the winter production with Jody—because I'm the lead—so I'm especially eager to work on the Showcase.

But I know Dad's not here because he's genuinely interested. I give him the short answer. *"Death of a Salesman."*

"I hope Tyler Dunning's not playing Willy Loman," Dad grumbles sarcastically.

"What, you're not a fan of Tyler's work?"

"I had enough of Tyler's acting when he promised to bring you home by ten on Halloween," he replies with the hint of a smile. I can't suppress one of my own. Sometimes Dad's funny even when I don't want him to be.

"That *was* one of his finer performances."

Maybe he *did* come in here just to talk. I look up from the book, waiting for his reply. But his eyes have shifted to somewhere near the bottom of my coat rack, and the humor of a couple seconds ago dissipates.

"There's something I wanted to talk to you about," he says.

Great. The line that begins every unpleasant conversation with a parent.

"Rose and I have continued to make some inquiries into homes outside New York City," he goes on, "and we've narrowed it down to a few."

"Cool," I reply flatly.

"We have to fly out and look at the houses with a realtor." He sounds unfazed by what I thought was a pretty obvious display of disinterest. "This weekend."

"What?" I hear my voice go up. "*This* weekend? I thought the move wasn't happening until I went to college. Or is there something else you haven't told me?"

"It's not happening until then." Dad puts a hand on my knee, as if *that'll* make everything better. "But we have to visit soon because I don't want Rose to travel too close to her due date."

"Of course," I mutter.

"While we're gone, you and Erin will stay at Aunt Charlotte's."

I sit up in surprise, letting my book fall shut. "Why do *I* have to stay with Charlotte? It's far from school, and I'm seventeen years old, Dad. I'm not going to burn the house down."

"Megan . . ." He rubs a crease in his forehead.

"What?" I snap. "Next year you'll be in New York, and I'll be here on my own anyway. We should just get used to it now."

He glances up at me. He's silent for a moment, and I think I see a shadow of hurt in his eyes. Or maybe he's just tired of arguing with me. It's hard to tell.

When he does speak, I'm glad he's not using his patronizing middle-school-principal voice. "You're calling me every night," he says softly.

"Text. I'll *text* you."

He gets up and walks to the door, and I think he's going to leave without saying anything else. But he stops and turns back, smiling slightly. "Please try to text like a fully functioning adult. If I suspect you've been drinking, Charlotte's coming over."

"Whatever you say," I mumble, in no mood to joke. I pick up my copy of *Death of a Salesman* and wait for him to leave.

Today, I decide when I get to school the next morning, *is the day I force Anthony to talk to me.*

I don't want to think about the conversation with my dad or the upcoming trip, and I'm hoping to distract myself. I send Anthony one more text from the parking lot, which he doesn't answer, and when I go to find him in the library at lunch, he's nowhere to be found, like he knew I'd look for him here. In rehearsal, I'm too busy sucking at Juliet's death scene to keep an eye on him, and he slips out before I stab myself on stage for the hundredth time today.

I have no choice but to drive over to Verona after rehearsal. I park in the gravel lot under the marquee, which today declares, *A pizza by any other name would taste as gr8.*

The jukebox is playing Dire Straits's "Romeo and Juliet." This is too much. But before I can dig out a nickel to change it to something non-Shakespearean, a clamor from the corner booth distracts me. I glance over to see Anthony pouring orange soda for ten eight-year-olds in soccer uniforms, half of whom are standing on the booth.

"Anthony," I say from the jukebox. His eyes find mine, and he blinks. Without a word, he sets down the last drink and darts directly toward the kitchen.

But he's too slow. I intercept him by the soda machine and block his path. "Why're you hiding from me?"

"I'm busy, Megan. I'm on my shift." He steps past me with some impressive footwork.

I follow him into the kitchen. It's a slow-moving hubbub of white-aproned employees placing pizza pans in the ovens and dishes into the dishwasher. "I think it's because of the Eric thing," I tell him over the noise.

He pales, a horrified expression crossing his face, and I know exactly why. Eric's washing dishes at the sink, potentially within earshot. Anthony fixes me with a glare and grabs me by the arm, pulling me to the other end of the kitchen and into the ingredients locker. Only once I'm inside, leaning against a wire shelf stocked with bags of flour, does he let go of my arm.

"I don't want to talk about it, okay? Not with him, not with you," he says urgently. But what catches me is the tremor in his expression. He doesn't look angry—he looks nervous.

"Have you even asked him where you guys stand since the party?" I lower my voice.

"Why bother?" he fires back. "I saw enough."

His shoulders sag. He sounds like he's given up. It's nothing new—Anthony's always burying his feelings at the first sign of something falling apart. But I know he really likes Eric. He's just too insecure to fight for what he wants, which means he needs me to do it for him.

"Stay here," I tell him. Leaving the ingredients locker, I walk directly to the sink.

"Eric," I say over the running water. He turns, plate in hand, but he doesn't exactly look surprised that I'm in the kitchen, where I'm definitely not supposed to be. It's like he watched Anthony and me walk into the kitchen. Like he's aware of Anthony's whereabouts, like he keeps track of him. It's what I do when someone I like is nearby.

"What's the deal with you and that girl from the party?" I ask abruptly.

His eyes widen for a split second, then he resumes scrubbing the plate, and his voice is casual when he replies. "You mean Melissa? She's . . . a friend. I go to Saint Margaret's, and she goes to our sister school. I know her from school dances and stuff. I don't know—we hooked up." He's playing it cool. If I weren't a director, I wouldn't know he's acting.

"Are you guys, like, a thing now?"

For a brief moment, I think I see his eyes flit to somewhere behind me—to the ingredients locker. "It was nothing serious," he says slowly, his eyes returning to mine.

"Do you *want* it to be a thing?" I press him.

Now I know he glances to where Anthony's waiting. But then he shrugs. "She's not really my type, but who knows?" he says coolly. "I wasn't expecting to hook up with her that night. I only knew about the party because I overheard a couple of Stillmont guys who came in here talking about it. I didn't figure people from *my* school would be there."

He fixes me with an indicative glance, and what he's really saying fits into place in my head.

I remember how he danced with Melissa every time the Saint Margaret's guys were nearby, and how he danced with Anthony only when they weren't. He's not out to his school. He did invite Anthony with a purpose, but it was ruined when people he knew showed up.

I nod, hoping my expression tells him I understand. Wordlessly, Eric peels off his gloves and takes a water pitcher out into the restaurant.

I return to Anthony, who's exactly where I left him, hanging out with the flour and canned tomatoes. "It's safe to come out now," I tell him. Expressionless, he walks out into the kitchen and picks up an order of breadsticks off the counter. "But you should know," I continue, "Eric's not dating Melissa, he said she's not his type, *and* he looked at you twice. I think he got cold feet at the party because he's in the closet. If I were you, I'd ask him out on a more private date."

But Anthony doesn't meet my eyes. "Thanks, Megan. I have work."

He goes into the dining room, and I'm left in the kitchen, confused and a little hurt. I just served up the guy Anthony likes for him with a side of breadsticks. Instead of going for it, Anthony chose to walk away. Brusquely, I shove open the door in the back of the kitchen and kick the gravel as I walk to my car.

I'm getting out my keys when I hear Anthony call my name. He's still wearing his frilly hat, which only makes me laugh a little inside because whatever fear was in his eyes earlier has disappeared. Now he's angry.

"This is why I was avoiding you." He strides toward me but halts suddenly in the middle of the parking lot, like he doesn't want to come too close. "I knew you'd do something like this. You can*not* keep interfering with my relationships. I know *you* come into any hint of a romantic situation guns blazing, but I'm not like you. I can't just rush into things."

I'm in no mood to be lectured. "Why not? You like him. I think he likes you, but you'll never know until you try."

"He's had every opportunity to talk to me," Anthony

123

replies darkly, "to explain what you're only guessing. If he wants this, he would've come to me."

"It doesn't work that way," I almost yell. "It'd be nice if it did, but getting the boyfriend you want is hard work. You can't expect anything to happen if you don't make a move. If you want him, do something about it." I know I struck a nerve because his expression clouds over. "Don't be afraid of this," I go on, gentler. "The only way this definitely doesn't work is if you do nothing."

He stays silent. I've done my best. "I have to go home," I say, pulling out my keys.

I get in the car and twist the key in the ignition. With the windows rolled up, I barely hear the muffled, "Did he really look at me twice?"

I roll down my window. "Forlornly." I nod.

"I guess . . ." He puts his hands in his pockets. "I could invite him over for carne asada."

My lips begin to form a smile. *"What?"*

Anthony returns the hint of a grin and nods in the direction of Verona.

"Break a leg," I tell him.

When I pull onto the highway, for once I'm grateful for Dad and Rose's trip to New York, because I know what I'm going to do tomorrow night. I'm taking my own advice.

TWELVE

ROMEO: *Thou canst not teach me to forget.*

I.i.246

I WORKED HARD ON THIS OUTFIT.

I hunted for nearly an hour in my closet for a dress, but nothing felt quite right. It was only when I got the brilliant idea to take apart the bridesmaid dress from Dad and Rose's wedding that I found the perfect thing—a pale pink shift with lacy detailing in the neckline. It hits me mid-thigh, and I've paired it with studded black ankle boots and feather earrings to keep from looking too girly.

Because tonight, I have a plan. Will's coming over, and we're going to have sex for the first time. I'm not going to wait around for him to define our relationship. I want to enjoy every part of whatever this is with him while I can, and though I haven't fallen for him yet—though our relationship's much younger than Tyler's and mine was—I'm not letting that get in my way. Why would I? I'm practically an adult. I'm a non-virgin, a sex-having person. This relationship's quickly expiring under a ticking clock named Alyssa, and I want to feel that closeness with Will. So what if I have to rush a few steps?

By eight, I'm downstairs in my bronze eye shadow doing what every girl dreams of on a Friday night—reading *Romeo and Juliet* on the couch. Dad and Rose went to the airport this morning, Erin's at my aunt's, and I have the house to myself.

I roll my eyes at Juliet's latest oversentimental proclamation. *This bud of love, by summer's ripening breath, may prove a beauteous flower when next we meet.* The play's a terrible distraction while I wait.

The doorbell rescues me from Juliet's pining. I leap off the couch, then take a second to rearrange my hair. When I reach the door, I know I look amazing. I pull it open, and Will stands before me.

Never mind. He just redefined amazing.

He's wearing a faded denim jacket over a plain white V-neck, and he's cuffed his tight black pants above his Timberland boots. He rests his hands lightly in his pockets, and it takes everything in me not to attack him right there on the doorstep.

"Hey," he says, and my pulse pounds. "I thought you might need a break from *Romeo and Juliet*"—he holds up a copy of *Shakespeare in Love*—"with some Romeo and Juliet."

I laugh and shut the door behind him. "Two sexy Williams in one night? I think I'm blushing."

He raises an incredulous eyebrow. "I've *never* seen you blush."

"Then you're not trying hard enough," I say over my shoulder, walking farther into the living room. I reach the stairs and look back to find he's sitting on the couch. Instead of following me. *Owen was right, he is clueless.* I remind myself he's probably never done this before. "Oh," I say nonchalantly, "I thought we'd watch on my laptop upstairs."

"Why?" Will looks puzzled. "We've got the bigger screen down here."

Oh my god. "I thought we'd watch on my bed," I clarify with a meaningful look.

It takes him a second, but then the light goes on in his eyes and he jumps off the couch. "Oh. Yeah. Of course. Good thinking. *Great* thinking."

Finally! Smiling to myself, I lead him upstairs. He's quiet the whole way. As I'm putting the movie into my laptop, I notice he's standing aimlessly in the middle of the room. Hands back in his pockets, he meanders over to my bookcase—on the opposite side of the room from my bed.

"That's from *The Crucible*," I say, nodding to the cast photo on the shelf he's studying. "Freshman spring. It's the first show I ever assistant-directed."

"I remember," he says, his back still to me. "I was in the crew."

"No way." I put the laptop down, surprised I don't remember him and never noticed him in the photo. I walk over to the shelf beside him. Searching the photo, the first thing I notice is Tyler in the middle of the group, putting on his not-yet-perfected Tyler Dunning grin. There's Anthony, a couple of rows behind him, his hair grown into something resembling an Afro and his arm around me. We were dating at the time. I lean in and inspect the back rows, and—

"*No*," I gasp. Because there's Will—or Billy, actually—rail-thin and with the awkwardly stringy hair of freshman boys everywhere.

"Don't say a word," Will says through his teeth.

I round on him teasingly. "But your *hair*." It's a sharp contrast from the perfect, gelled sweep of blond hair he's presently running his hand through.

He steps back from the bookcase, a flush of red rising up his neck. "I know, I know," he mutters. "It's the reason I've never had a girlfriend."

I wait for the "until now," but it doesn't come. Will continues to look at the other shelves in my room, and I'm left once again wondering what he considers me. I told myself it didn't matter if I'm his girlfriend or just his hookup buddy, but I kind of want to know. Before I get the chance to ask, he turns back to me, the confident glint back in his eyes.

"Not everyone can be like you," he says, nodding to the photo. "Beautiful then, too."

His words push the question from my mind. We're obviously on the same page, because he wraps an arm around my waist and pulls me to his lips. The kiss somehow feels different, charged with both of our expectations. For the first time, it's the first step to something else.

Breaking off, I lead him to the bed and slide off his jacket, my lips still stinging. I lightly push him onto the mattress and close my laptop on my desk. "I don't think we'll need the pretense," I say, kicking off my boots and climbing on top of him.

"We wouldn't have watched much anyway," he breathes before I grab him and kiss him again.

His hands slide down to my waist, and I feel his fingers pressing into the small of my back. I run my hands down his chest when he moves to kiss my neck, his hand inching up the hem of my dress. Then I'm pulling off his shirt. Then I'm lifting my arms over my head, and my dress hits the floor. Then his fingers glide up my back.

Then my phone buzzes.

"Shit." I jump off the bed. The phone vibrates a couple more times, and I know Dad's upset. The rule was me texting him, not him texting me. "Give me a second," I tell Will. "I forgot to do something."

Dad's sent exactly the same text three times—**Where are you, Megan?**—and then an accusatory line of question marks.

im home, I shoot back.

I set down the phone and start to climb back into Will's lap. Just as we're picking up where we left off, my phone rattles from my desk once more. I sigh angrily and scramble off Will again. "Sorry . . ."

It takes me a second to make sense of what my dad's sent. The first message reads, **What do you think?** and below it are three images too small to discern on my phone's lock screen. I slide it open, and my heart plummets.

Three photos, each a different angle of a badly lit sidewalk view of a house. *Chesapeake Lane*, reads the sign on the street corner.

What do I think? Like it matters what the house looks like.

Whatever house they choose, it'll be a perfectly nice place for Erin and the baby to grow up, and for me to stop by on holidays to sleep uncomfortably in an impersonal spare bedroom.

looks fine, I send back.

I toss my phone not gently onto my desk and turn back to Will, eager to put Chesapeake Lane out of my mind. I crash into him again, and he's pulling me closer, and I'm reaching for my bra. But I can't bring myself to do what I wanted to. He's sitting underneath me, and he's gorgeous, but I feel hollow.

He's noticed my hesitation and caught the look on my face. "What is it?" he asks.

"It's nothing," I say, because there's no reason to tell him more.

I clamber off him and pick up my dress off the floor. I'm pulling it over my head when I hear him say, "Wait, what?"

"I'm sorry," I say in a flat, unconvincing voice. "I'm just not in the mood right now."

"Okay . . ." He sounds skeptical, even indignant. I watch him get dressed. "Guess we'll do this another time."

If he even wants another time, a familiar voice says in the back of my head. With the way Alyssa's been acting around him, and how I just totally screwed tonight up, I'd understand if he didn't want to give me a second chance.

He walks out of my room, and I don't bother seeing him to the front door. I pause uncertainly in the middle of my room, wishing I could have ignored my dad and just focused on Will.

But even now, I find myself staring at the photo Will and I were looking at minutes earlier. I survey the plays on my bookshelves, the coat rack in the corner, the playbills pinned to my bulletin board. In a matter of months, everything will be packed into cardboard boxes and shipped to New York, and the room I grew up in will be empty.

I collapse onto my bed, where a hard corner digs into my back. I reach under me and pull out the DVD case of *Shakespeare in Love*.

My plans for the night come back in an uncomfortable rush. I feel unsteady. And I know it's not only because of the impending New York thing. I run a hand through my hair impulsively, trying to iron the tremble from my fingertips. What was I doing with Will? What felt promising and exhilarating and *right* an hour ago feels upside down now.

I thought I could do this. I thought our relationship status wouldn't make a difference. I thought I could have sex with Will right now and capture the connection, the closeness that I'm desperate for—a little too desperate, I guess. Part of me wonders if I didn't know deep down it wouldn't work.

Part of me wonders if the texts from Dad weren't the only reason I stopped things.

I'm glad Will and I didn't go further, I decide. But everything's in limbo now. My relationship's not a relationship. My home won't be for much longer. Everything's lurching out of reach, and I'm in territory I don't recognize.

I force myself upright. I can't look at Will's DVD right now. I can't be reminded of how tonight could have gone, and how fractured we left things. I shove *Shakespeare in Love* into a drawer and out of my mind.

Owen's on my doorstep the next morning.

When I woke up after three hours of fitful sleep, I threw on the first things I found in my room. Now I've parked myself on the couch in the living room once more, and I'm reading the same scene of *Romeo and Juliet* I was last night. It still sounds ridiculous, and while I'm finally beginning to memorize the lines, it's not helping me to picture myself saying them on stage at Ashland.

I open the door to find Owen wearing a dark blue button-down with his hair neatly combed, and for a moment I regret my old jeans and hole-ridden The Clash T-shirt.

He holds up a crisp white paper bag, beaming. "I brought coffee and bagels."

"Oh. Wow, thanks," I say, stepping aside to let him in. We'd planned a couple days ago that he'd come over this morning for our second play/Will-information session. What we hadn't planned on was him bringing me breakfast.

He turns to give me a knowing smile. "I figure you probably had a late night."

He means Will. "Something like that," I say.

I grab a couple of plates from the kitchen and set them out in the living room. But when I look up at Owen, I see his eyes flit into the kitchen, and a strange combination of expressions crosses his face. "Does a baby live here?" he asks abruptly.

I follow his gaze to Erin's high chair, which, I realize, Will probably didn't even notice. "Oh, yeah. But she's at my aunt's."

Owen looks pale. "Whose . . . baby is it?" he ventures gently.

"Oh my *god*," I explode. "You do *not* think I had Tyler Dunning's love-baby." It's too ridiculous for me to be offended, honestly.

He looks briefly relieved, until he winces in obvious mortification. "I'm— I didn't—" he stutters.

I have to laugh. "Erin's my half sister," I explain. "My dad and my stepmom's kid."

He nods understandingly. "I have a ten-year-old brother. You can hardly go five feet in my house without stepping on a LEGO." He winces again.

"I was in your house." I take a sip of the still-too-hot coffee. "There wasn't a LEGO in sight."

"Yeah, because I cleaned for two hours before you got there."

He says it casually, like it's something he'd do for anyone. And who knows? He might. Still, it's sweet. I almost tell him that, and then I remember it didn't exactly go over well last time I called him sweet. "Hey, I'd trade LEGO for applesauce in my hair any day," I say instead.

His eyes widen. "It *was* applesauce!"

I nod grimly.

Owen sets the bagels down on the coffee table in the living room. I reach in and grab a cinnamon raisin. He takes the other and drops into the armchair next to the couch. "You probably don't need my help, what with last night," he preempts me, crossing a foot onto his knee. He's dashed lines of familiar blue ink on the white rubber edges of his Converse. "Will told me when you invited him over yesterday."

I don't reply right away, spreading cream cheese on my bagel. "He didn't text you afterward, I guess."

Owen's eyebrows go up. "Guys don't really do that, Megan."

"Do what? Text?"

"No . . ." he says slowly, looking a little amused. "Text about . . . certain topics."

"My mistake." I return a faint smile. "Well, I kind of hoped he'd texted you. Things ended . . . weird."

Owen frowns, concern creasing his forehead. "Weird like he didn't want to?"

"Owen. Please."

He goes red. "I— Of course, he wanted to," he stutters.

Wait, what? Was that Owen calling me hot? Or hook-up-with-able, or whatever? Part of me wants to press him on the subject further, but I'm not sure if Owen's the type to handle my flirtatiousness. He might think I'm genuinely coming onto him. "He did want to," I say, "and we did, or started to. Then when we . . . didn't, he seemed kind of pissed, and I don't know where we stand now."

Owen's blush hasn't entirely faded, but his voice is even when he tells me, "Will's not pissed. He's a better guy than that. What happened?" He clears his throat, and the blush comes raging back. "I mean, why didn't you guys do it?"

"I got a text from my dad." The words come out before I've even thought about how I'm bringing up my family. But once they're out there, I realize how much I do want to talk about it with someone. Before I know it, I'm telling him more. About the hookup, about the photos from my dad. About New York.

"You're moving?" Owen sounds startled.

"*They* are," I quickly reply, "when I graduate. Rose, my stepmom, is pregnant again and wants to raise her kids in New York."

He nods, considering for a long second. For someone who's only really known me a few weeks, he looks unexpectedly relieved to hear I'm not going anywhere. "I can see why that would kill the mood," he finally says.

I let out a rueful laugh. "Yeah."

"Did you tell Will all of that?" Owen watches me as he takes a hesitant sip of his coffee.

"I wasn't sure if I should. I mean, that's the other thing. He said something about never having a girlfriend, and it sounded like he didn't think of me that way. I didn't want to, like, unload my personal shit on him if he doesn't see us as having that kind of relationship."

"I have to say," Owen begins, "if you just shut down a hookup without an explanation, I'd understand if Will was a little confused. Remember, he's pretty inexperienced. I don't know how many conversations with girls he's even had. It might not occur to him to ask what's wrong."

He has a point. Will's so gorgeous, it's easy to forget that everything's new to him. "I guess," I tell Owen. If Will's that inexperienced, he might not even know how to bring up the question of a relationship with me. "What do *you* think? Do you think he considers me his girlfriend? Has he said anything?"

He takes another sip of coffee, clearly stalling. "I don't . . . know, Megan," he says delicately, or uncomfortably.

"Well, could you please ask?"

He gives me an uncomprehending look. "Yeah, in the midst of our next slumber party, after the pillow fight. When we're exchanging our deepest, most tender secrets over a flashlight, I'll be sure to bring you up."

"That'd be great, Owen. Thanks," I say dryly.

"I was just—"

"*I know.*" I roll my eyes. "Just, the next time you talk to him about Cosima, bring the conversation around to Will and me."

"Evidently I'm not saying this right," Owen says with forced patience. "The conversations you're imagining, they don't happen. Especially between . . . me and Will. We're not that close. No friend-glue, remember?"

"*Please, Owen,*" I implore, batting my eyelashes and knowing damn well it'll work.

He sighs, dropping his head back over the chair. When he returns his eyes to me, I can tell he's hiding a smile. "Fine. For you."

"That wasn't so hard, was it?" I stand to collect our dishes. "Now, what do you want to know for your play?" I call over my shoulder as I carry the plates into the kitchen. *Wow*, I catch myself realizing, *I'm glad Owen didn't look past the high chair.* The kitchen is a mess, and not just an Erin mess. There's the box

136

of microwave macaroni I left out from yesterday's dinner, a pile of Rose's paralegal paperwork on the counter, and a piece of scratch paper from the Trig assignment I didn't finish next to the toaster. Mental note—clean the house before the next time Owen comes over.

He's taken his notebook out by the time I walk back into the living room. "I'm working on Rosaline's relationships with characters other than Romeo," he says while reviewing his notes. "Would she have known Mercutio or Tybalt or Romeo's family?" He looks up from his notebook, fixing his eyes on me. "I was even toying with the idea she might've known Juliet."

I know where he's going with this. "You want to talk about me and Madeleine."

"Why are you friends with her?" he blurts.

I guess I'm not the only one who gets right to the point. Still, the transparent way he said it makes me laugh. "What's not to like?"

"Stealing your boyfriend."

"It's more complicated than that," I say. "We've been friends forever. She moved to Stillmont a month before the end of freshman year, right around when my dad remarried. Even though she hardly knew me, she immediately invited me to stay over while my dad was on his honeymoon. She spent twenty hours with me in the hospital while Erin was being born, she baked brownies for me every day I missed my mom, she's come to every one of my shows, she's been there for me after every breakup—"

"Except for one," Owen interrupts.

137

"It's not like she decided to steal my boyfriend." I shrug. He looks skeptical. "Well . . ."

"She fell in love with a guy who I *happened* to be dating, and he fell in love with her. I didn't exactly imagine kids and a white picket fence with Tyler Dunning, and you can't help who you fall in love with."

"I suppose not," he says softly, his eyes averted almost pointedly, as if he wants them anywhere but on me.

I go on, feeling like it's important I defend Madeleine. "When she realized she had feelings for Tyler, she told me. They both did. It's not like I didn't see it coming. Tyler has his faults, but he treated me decently, better than Romeo did Rosaline."

Owen determinedly taps his pen on his knee. "There's really no bad blood between you and Madeleine? The whole best-friend thing isn't some passive-aggressive act?"

"Wow. Devious, Owen." I give him a half smile. "No, everyone figures that. But I'm honestly happy for my best friend. Love is inconvenient sometimes. I mean, *you* know. It's probably not ideal to have a girlfriend in Italy."

Owen's stopped writing. He's staring down at the notebook, and he's got that contemplative look I'm realizing I quite like. "Yeah," he says. "It's inconvenient."

"How often do you guys even talk? What with her strict bedtime—"

"She doesn't have a strict bedtime," Owen cuts in. "It's just the nine-hour time difference."

"Whatever. It doesn't look like cross-continent FaceTime is the easiest thing in the world, either."

"We talk every weekend," Owen says grandly, like this is something to be proud of.

I make sure to look aghast. "Every *weekend*? What about the other *five* days of the week? Already we're only talking about phone sex here, I don't know how you—"

"Oh my god, Megan." He hangs his head in his hands.

"What?" I say, laughing. "I tell you everything about Will and me!" My face hurts from grinning. Which . . . is unexpected, after last night.

"Not because I ask about it!" Owen fires back, but he's definitely on the verge of laughing himself.

"Wait, *do* you guys have phone sex?" I drop my voice seriously.

"You have no idea." He quirks an eyebrow, and he's almost got me convinced, until he doubles over laughing.

"You actually *can* act!" I say, enjoying the way his hair has gotten ruffled.

He catches his breath. "What were we doing here again?" he asks with a rhetorical air, pen to his lips. "Oh yeah, helping me on my play."

"Fine . . ." I hold my hands up in surrender. "Ask away, Shakespeare."

By Sunday night, I've surprised myself in two ways. I've memorized Juliet's long scene with the Nurse, even the monologue and my cues from Romeo, and honestly . . . I'm proud. It's the first time working on *Romeo and Juliet* that I feel like I've accomplished something. Even if I can't pull off a convincing Juliet performance, at least I won't lose my shit and forget my lines in front of a huge audience.

I'm in the kitchen, reading the balcony scene over a dinner of macaroni—which I remembered to return to the cupboard this time—when I hear my phone vibrate on the table.

I glance down at the screen. Anthony's texted, **NEXT FRIDAY NIGHT. YOU'RE COMING OVER.**

I take a bite and type with one hand, **anthony, if i didnt kno sum things id think u were propositioning me**

CARNE ASADA. ERIC, he replies. Immediately, I drop my fork and snatch my phone off the table.

omg omg omg omg, I send back.

Either Anthony's in a hurry or he expected my enthusiasm, because he replies simply, **BRING A CASUAL DATE. WANT EVERYTHING TO BE CHILL.**

roger, I confirm.

Anthony's typing bubble reappears, and a second later I receive, **UM WHO'S ROGER??**

meant yes!! I send, then follow up with, **ugh id never date a "roger," def not a sexy name**

BEG TO DIFFER, Anthony replies.

Smiling, I send him, **what happened w eric??? call me**

SORRY. SHIFT STARTING.

I open the NEW MESSAGE window, but before I type Will's name, I hesitate. Inviting him to be my "chill date" would kind of implicitly dismiss the questions I still have concerning yesterday. If only Owen could've shed some light on things between my possibly-boyfriend-but-who-knows and me.

I just have to talk to Will in person, I decide. Tomorrow I'll find him between classes.

I poke my fork into my macaroni container only to discover it's empty, so I walk to the other side of the kitchen and drop it in the trash. The echo of plastic on plastic is surprisingly loud.

It's stupid, but it makes me feel lonely. The house feels stiflingly empty. I thought I'd be relieved to have peace and quiet with Erin out of the house—I had epic plans for today of napping on the couch and blasting music in my room— but I'm surprised to find the solitude is starting to bother me. I even slept with my industrial-strength earplugs in because I felt weird without them.

I study *Romeo and Juliet* for two hours before I hear keys in the front door and my heart does an unfamiliar leap. Not bothering to play the cool, independent teenager, I jump up to meet my family at the door. The first face I find is Erin's. She's held over my dad's shoulder, eye-level with me, and she breaks into a tiny-toothed smile when she sees me.

"Menan!" she squeals.

Rose, walking in behind my dad with a hand on her stomach, notices Erin's delight. "Looks like somebody missed her sister."

Somebodies, I think. I lift Erin off Dad's shoulder, and he immediately turns back to get the luggage out of the car. Erin reaches for one of my earrings, and I coo to her uncompre-hending grin, "Let's try to go twenty-four hours without get-ting your food in my hair, okay?"

"How was your weekend?" Rose asks from the doorway.

"Good. Quiet," I say. But she's looking at me like she wants to hear more, and I feel unexpectedly grateful after a day of nothing but texting by way of social interaction. "It's nice to have everyone home," I add.

Dad walks back through the door, wheeling two suitcases behind him. He briefly smiles at the sight of me with Erin, but when his eyes land on Rose, a look of horror crosses his face. "You weren't supposed to carry anything!"

"Oh, come on," she says, smiling and shrugging the small diaper bag off her shoulder. "It's nothing."

But Dad's halfway to her by the time she says it. He quickly seizes the diaper bag and kisses her on the temple.

"Henry," she chastises like she's exasperated, but the blush coloring her cheeks gives her away. She meets my eyes when Dad's walked out of the room. "He's ridiculous sometimes," she says, fighting a smile and losing.

"Just sometimes?" I ask, half-sarcastic, and Rose chuckles.

"Did you eat? Or can I make you something?" Rose quickly returns to mom mode.

I set Erin down in her playpen. "I'm good. But thanks," I reply, wishing now I hadn't already had dinner.

I head up the stairs to my room while Dad unpacks and Rose watches Erin. I plug my headphones back into my computer—Erin will be going to bed soon, and my dad's strict about hearing music from my room after nine—but it doesn't bother me. For a moment, I'm just happy to have everyone back home.

Until I remember why they left in the first place. I've always assumed I'd go to college near home, near my family. I'd pictured coming home on weekends, being there for Erin's milestones and the new baby growing up. If they're in New York and I'm at SOTI, none of that will happen. I'll visit them for Christmas and summer, and that's it. It's not just the house I'm going to lose when they move, not just my childhood bedroom. It's the thought of this family, however new it is, being nearby.

THIRTEEN

ROMEO: *Why then, O brawling love, O loving hate,*

O anything of nothing first create!

I.i.181–2

I DON'T GET THE CHANCE TO TALK to Will until Wednesday. He hasn't met me between classes this week, which isn't a good omen for the conversation I'm hoping to have. I couldn't at lunch due to a forgotten Gov exam I had to study for, and when I walk into the drama room, I notice the stage crew is nowhere to be found.

Rehearsal is demoralizing. Whatever confidence I had from memorizing the monologue flies out the window when Jody criticizes my "level of enthusiasm" in Act II, Scene vi. Apparently, I didn't sound convincing in my portrayal of a thirteen-year-old eager to marry the boy she met a week ago. So it's not in the best of spirits that I walk down to the parking lot after school to find Will.

I round the corner and, for a moment, every one of my worries vanishes. Because there's Will, shirtless, nailing together the pieces of a wooden staircase. Now I'm *certain* he's hit the gym over the summer. My mouth goes dry, which is a good thing, because what jumps into my mind is a joke about how big of a tool he's working with.

But when I walk over to him, I say only, "Hey."

"Megan, hey." He straightens up and grabs his shirt from the stairs, wiping the sweat from his forehead. "How was rehearsal?" he asks like he's searching for something to say.

"It was fine." I sound no less stiff. "I just, uh— I wanted to apologize for what happened Friday. I hope you know it wasn't you."

He looks surprised. "Oh, it's . . . all right," he finally says.

"Is it? Because we haven't talked or texted since then."

"It's fine, really. I've just been busy." He nods to the sets behind him. "Besides, it kind of seems like you have other stuff on your mind." I can't tell if his tone is concerned or frustrated.

"I did, but . . ." I take a breath, remembering Owen's advice. "I figured I should probably tell you what was going on with me."

"You don't have to do that," he says quickly.

"Oh." Well, now I'm really confused. Is he trying to be considerate, or does he not care? "Yeah, it's whatever," I say, trying to sound like it is indeed *whatever*.

He nods, then smiles. "So do you want to see the balcony set I'm—" he starts, but he's interrupted by the ding of a text from his pocket. Before I can reply, he pulls his phone out and glances at the screen. "Shit. I told Alyssa we would figure out a time when I could help her memorize lines."

"Alyssa?" It's on the tip of my tongue to point out that Alyssa hasn't missed a chance to remind everyone how well she knows *Romeo and Juliet*. She doesn't need help.

145

Will's phone starts to ring. "Yeah. And now she's calling me. I'm sorry, Megan." He sounds genuinely apologetic.

"It's cool. We'll just talk later," I say, but he's already picking up the phone.

With nothing else to do, I walk toward my car. The parking lot is carpeted in pine needles. I take out my phone, weighing my options. I need a date for Anthony's carne asada, but this conversation's only made me more reluctant to invite Will.

I get in the car and open a message to Owen. **U busy fri nite? Need platonic date 4 carne asada**

I smile when Owen's reply comes in before I've even turned on the car. **I love carne asada. I'm in.**

Owen's waiting under the giant fir tree that towers over his house when I pull up on Friday. Instantly, I notice what he's wearing—a dark blue button-down, slacks, and leather shoes with just the right amount of scuff.

"Whoa." I nod to his outfit. "It's not a real date."

"Of course it's not, Megan." He furrows his brow quizzically and gets in the car. "Wait, why do you say . . . ?" He smiles wryly at me. "Are you saying I look nice?"

"Nicer than I'd want *my* boyfriend to on a not-date with another girl." I turn around in Owen's driveway.

"Sounds like you're implying something, but I don't really know why when I could say the same thing about you." He gestures to my close-fitting, black velvet dress.

"Touché." Part of me is glad he noticed, the part that chose this dress wondering what he'd say. Not that I'm the kind of girl who'd go for a guy with a girlfriend—not that Owen's the kind of guy I'd go for in the first place—but I won't say I don't enjoy a little harmless flirting with him. "Seriously though, thanks for coming with me tonight," I say as we're passing Verona on our way to the other side of town.

"No problem. But, why exactly did you invite me? Why does carne asada require a platonic date?" He's idly tapping on the armrest, and I know it's because he doesn't have his pen in his hand.

I realize he signed on for tonight without hesitation, without me even explaining the plan. "Remember Eric, the guy from the party? Anthony wants to have him over for carne asada. It's Anthony's best move. It always works."

Owen raises his eyebrow. "What exactly do you mean by 'works'?"

"Let's just say, when he used it on me, we only got fifteen minutes into *West Side Story* before I decided there were things I'd rather do. Anthony, now that I'm thinking about it, probably just wanted to watch the movie," I say, considering.

Owen laughs. "Sounds like Anthony should just have Eric over alone then."

"Anthony's afraid Eric won't be into it. He wants me there in case Eric comes over not wanting tonight to be romantic, and I *guess* there's the possibility Eric's not gay. But if he is, and if things do go well, Anthony doesn't want to have unintentionally created a group-hang vibe. That's why he wants me to have a platonic date. It could be a casual hang, but it could also be a double date."

"Wow, complicated." Owen looks impressed, then thinks for a minute. "What if it *does* turn into a double date? What are we supposed to do?"

"Sex on the table sound good to you?" I promptly reply, unable to restrain myself.

We've pulled into Anthony's driveway—and thank god, because I burst out laughing when I see Owen's face. His eyes are blown wide, like he's very earnestly trying to figure out if I'm joking. "Jesus, Owen. I was kidding. We'll FaceTime Cosima or something. It'll be fine."

Eric's not here yet. Ours is the only car in front of Anthony's house. Anthony told me his parents are at an engagement party for one of his twenty-two cousins. I lead Owen up to the front door, positive he's blushing a shade previously unknown to man. He's silent, and, feeling guilty, I figure I must have gone too far with that sex-on-the-table comment. I should probably ease up on him.

I knock on the door, hearing Anthony's go-to cooking music, the Black Eyed Peas, from inside. While we're waiting, Owen leans on the wall in front of me. "Cosima went to bed hours ago. We'll have to think of something *better* to do," he says slowly.

There's a suggestive look in his eyes, and I feel my jaw drop open. I know I'm joking when I flirt, but Owen?

He breaks into a grin. "Jesus, Megan. I was kidding." His voice is playful, and he shakes his head. "Your face, I swear. I never thought I'd see Megan Harper stunned into silence."

Anthony opens the door, and Owen walks in past him, leaving me impressed and even a little disappointed. He obviously was thinking of that comeback the whole walk up the driveway, and I find myself half wishing it wasn't just a comeback. Which then has me thoroughly wondering why I'd wish that, even fractionally. This is Owen.

We're overtaken by the smell of chili and lime inside. Anthony rushes back to the grill, and I follow him and Owen in, passing Anthony's mom's intimidating crucifix in the hallway. Mrs. Jenson is Mexican and was raised Catholic, though on Sundays she goes to the gospel services at Anthony's dad's Baptist church.

"This is a bad idea," Anthony mutters behind the grill. "He doesn't like me—"

"Shut up. You look amazing," I reassure him. He does, too. "The vest, the rolled-up sleeves, the hair . . . it's really working for you." He meets my eyes and lets out a breath, looking like he's regained some of his confidence.

Then the doorbell rings. Anthony's panic returns, and he thrusts the grilling tongs he's holding into Owen's hands. While Owen, surprised, steps behind the grill, Anthony takes a hesitant couple of paces toward the door.

I stop him and reach for his apron. "Here." I untie it, pull it over his head, and push his curls back into place. He gives me a grateful look, and I lightly shove him in the direction of the door.

When I join Owen by the grill, he's deftly turning over the strips of beef. I guess he notices me studying him, because he shrugs. "I cook sometimes," he says simply.

I hear the front door open and glance over at Anthony. Eric walks in, and it's clear he's come from some practice or game. He's wearing a green and white jersey with ROGERS written on the back. I grin. *Of course Anthony thinks Roger is a sexy name.* He and Eric exchange quick heys before Eric tilts his head in the direction of the kitchen. "Smells awesome. I'm pumped for some carne asada."

I watch Anthony to gauge his reaction. "Yeah, man. It'll be . . . tight," he says, wincing. I wince with him. He's trying, but the nerdy thespian in him can't pull off bro-talk.

They head onto the deck outside the kitchen, and the four of us congregate awkwardly around the grill. "Hey, Eric," I say, mostly to break the silence. "You remember Owen from the party, right?"

Anthony's obviously just recalled that Owen's presently cooking dinner and darts over to take back the tongs.

"Yeah," Eric says. "What's up?"

"Nothing much," Owen starts. "Good to see you again," he adds like he's trying to keep the conversation going. Eric nods, and the silence returns. I try to think of everything I know about Eric, searching for possible conversation topics. *Busboy, possibly gay, not into Melissa from the party . . .* and that's it. Not exactly the greatest pre-dinner topics.

Eric fortunately saves us. He glances toward the table, then calls to Anthony, "Could I help with anything?"

"Drinks," Anthony gets out. "There's soda in the garage you could go grab." He sounds as relieved as I feel to have something to say.

I make a split-second decision. "I'll show you where," I say, leading Eric into the living room and toward the garage.

We find a couple two-liter bottles of root beer on the wire

shelves next to a bicycle hanging on hooks from the ceiling. While Eric's hefting the bottles down, I nervously wait by the door, weighing my words. I have no idea how to broach this topic.

"You know, whatever might happen tonight, Owen and I won't say a word to anyone," I blurt, and immediately I wince, regretting how presumptuous and insensitive that came out. What if I've crossed into territory he didn't want to tread? I wonder for a horrible moment if I'm completely wrong about him and I've misinterpreted his comments, his interactions with Anthony.

Eric falters, hand on one bottle, then gradually places it on the floor. "I appreciate that, Megan," he says finally. "There are things about me I wouldn't want my all-boys, Catholic school to know."

I nod, relieved. "Which, by the way," I venture with half a smile, leaning an elbow on the shelves, "an all-boys school? That's got to be either a dream come true for you, or a complete nightmare."

Eric laughs, his posture relaxing a little. "It's a nightmare, trust me. I've never really ..." his voice grows quieter, heavier. "I've never had the chance to do this before."

I stand up straighter. The comment catches me, and it takes me a moment to figure out why. I can't imagine going to Eric's school, balancing everything he has to every day, and I know I'd be eager to experience this side of myself if I were in his position. But Anthony's not just some boy-shaped experience to be had. I won't let him be used or get hurt. "If you're only interested in Anthony because you've never had a boyfriend," I begin, "and he's an easy secret to keep from your friends—"

Eric cuts me off. "It's not that," he says decisively. "It's about him."

I permit him a smile. "Well, then I have to give you the obligatory best-friend speech," I go on. "Anthony's serious when it comes to relationships, and he's been hurt before. He really likes you." Eric's expression softens. "Don't screw this up," I finish.

I pick up the root beer and walk out without waiting for him to reply.

"Dinner's about ready," Anthony calls when I'm back in the kitchen. "Everyone should sit, and I'll bring it out."

We head to the round dinner table where I've helped Anthony memorize countless monologues and cues over the years. Anthony follows with the sizzling platter of carne asada.

Nobody's saying a word. Owen, next to me, is giving an inordinate amount of attention to pouring his root beer. Anthony appears to be dutifully avoiding Eric's eyes, while Eric looks at me imploringly.

I don't understand what's going on here. I've given Anthony plenty of encouragement to go for Eric, and I just straight-up told Eric how Anthony feels. What else could they *possibly* be waiting for?

I glance at Eric and notice he's wearing a lacrosse jersey, like the guys at Derek's party. Trying to jumpstart the conversation, I ask, "What, uh, lacrosse position do you play?"

"I'm a midfielder," he answers unhelpfully.

I try to catch Anthony's eye to signal that this is where he should jump into the conversation. But he's only determinedly stuffing strips of steak into a tortilla. Unbelievable. I look back at Eric, struggling to recollect even the first thing I know about lacrosse. I'm pretty sure there's a ball but . . .

"This is crazy good, man," Eric says to Anthony through his first mouthful.

Anthony looks up—*thank god*—and gives Eric a stilted smile. I know he's thrown by the level of jock-bro that Eric's exuding. Otherwise he would never go catatonic like this under pressure.

"My brother plays lacrosse—" Owen says suddenly, and I could kiss him.

Wait, did I just think that? I blink. Obviously I didn't mean literally.

"—but he's ten, so when I say 'plays lacrosse' I really mean he hits me with his stick." Eric cracks up, and before I get the chance to shoot Owen a grateful look, he and Eric are having a full-on conversation about the great sport of lacrosse. While they're occupied, I nudge Anthony's foot under the table with a get-your-head-in-the-game glance.

"Hey," Eric says suddenly, interrupting his conversation with Owen, "looks like we're out of salsa."

Anthony blinks, his eyes flitting to the jar of his mom's homemade salsa on the counter, then back to the table. "Oh, um," Anthony stammers. "I'll get it." He starts to stand.

"Let me," Eric says. But as he gets out of his seat, my eyes go wide because in one innocuous motion Eric's placed his hand over Anthony's. I watch Anthony straighten like there's an electric current running through him.

When Eric's back is turned, I find Anthony's eyes. Where there was defeat just seconds ago, now there's the kind of exhilarated determination I've only seen when he's walking off stage after nailing a performance. "Oh my god," he mouths at me. Eric returns with the refilled bowl, and I watch Anthony expectantly, waiting for his next move.

I don't even know how it happens. But the next moment, I feel Owen's hand in my hair. I jerk to face him as he withdraws his hand, removing—a clump of guacamole. The only possible explanation is I was so focused on Anthony, I absentmindedly ran a dirty hand through my hair.

"First applesauce, now guacamole." Owen grins, wiping his fingers on his napkin. "Your baby sister's not here to blame this time."

"Are you saying I'm messy, Owen?" I pull a scandalized expression.

"I didn't say it. You did," he replies.

I open my mouth with a comeback, but Eric preempts me. "You guys are cute," he says. "How long have you been dating?"

It takes a moment for me to realize he means me.

And Owen.

Me and Owen.

I look at Owen, and it's impossible to read his expression. Somewhere between bemusement and indignation, probably.

I don't know what Eric finds cute about Owen pulling guacamole out of my hair, but I'm thrown. "We're, uh . . ." I begin, not sure what Anthony wants me to say, or what Owen wants me to say. He was supposed to be my flex date for the night, but I wasn't anticipating actually having to lie about our relationship status.

"Oh, my mistake," Eric quickly amends, picking up on my hesitation. "I thought this was a double date."

It's not a second later that Anthony blurts, "They've been together for a month!"

I cut Anthony a glance, but I have to smile. It's one thing for me to lie about dating Owen, but if someone else does it for me, I guess I'll just *have* to play along. I spare Owen an apologetic look before I lay my hand on his. He stares down at it like it's radioactive, but he doesn't move. His hand is warm under mine.

"We met at auditions for our school's *Romeo and Juliet* production," I tell Eric, then fix my eyes lovingly on Owen. Weeks of playing Juliet have given me an aptitude for playing the doting girlfriend, it turns out. Owen looks like a deer in the headlights. "I promised myself I wouldn't date within the cast, but Owen was unrelenting." I catch Owen roll his eyes. "He even wrote lyrics about me for his friend's band, and let me tell you, they were . . . steamy."

Owen turns to me, and there's a spark in his eyes. "It's pretty impossible to resist Megan. She's an *outstanding* actress."

I bite my cheek to keep from laughing. "Eventually I

stopped objecting. He makes a really hot friar." I stare at him, daring him to keep the act going, and he stares back at me, undoubtedly considering his next line.

"Is this the play you're in?"

I've been so preoccupied with Owen, I didn't notice how Eric's eyes have shifted to Anthony.

"I have a role, yes," Anthony says smoothly.

"He's being modest," I cut in. "He's the best actor at Stillmont. He has a huge part—you should see his monologue."

"I'd like to." Eric's voice softens.

"I could give you a preview . . ." Anthony offers. When he's on, his flirting game is downright inspiring.

"Right now?" Eric smiles. "At the table? In the middle of dinner?"

"In private," Anthony says simply, and I have to restrain myself from giving him a standing ovation.

Eric pauses, and I know he's enticed by the invite. "I'd like that. But I'd like to see the real thing, too."

I'm pretty certain everyone's picked up on the definite charge in the room by now. I spring out of my seat and grab Anthony's plate. "Let me clear the table," I quickly offer. "Anthony, this was incredible, per usual. Owen and I have the dishes covered since you cooked."

Of course, it's not like I needed to say anything. Anthony and Eric are halfway to the hall by the time I've finished speaking.

I carry the plates to the sink and turn on the faucet. Owen comes up next to me with a couple more dishes. He hands them to me, then stops beside the sink, like he's trying to decide whether to say something. "A really hot friar?" he finally asks way too nonchalantly.

I shake a spoon at him, splashing water on his face. "I didn't know I was impossible to resist, either."

Owen swats me with a towel, grinning. "Yes you did, Megan." I laugh, noticing how he didn't deny it.

Only once we've finished the dishes do I realize we haven't heard anything from down the hallway in a suspiciously long time—no, a promisingly long time. Like he's just read my mind, Owen glances in the direction Anthony led Eric. "What do you think is going on in there?" he asks softly.

"How about you go check?"

He whirls, eyes wide. "No. No way."

"Fine." I shrug. "You wait here." I throw my towel at his face and tiptoe down the hall. Anthony's bedroom is on the left, next to a very realistic portrait of Jesus. I only know where his room is from the study sessions where he helped me not fail my finals—definitely not from when we were dating. His door is ajar, spilling light into the darkened hallway. First I see one pair of knees jutting off of Anthony's bed, then I adjust my angle to get a better view of . . . Anthony and Eric kissing to their hearts' content.

I feel a rush of vindication. I linger only long enough to see Anthony push Eric down onto the bed. Quietly, I return to the kitchen, where Owen's waiting. I beam at him. "They're totally making out," I whisper, and start cleaning off the counters, looking for dessert. I know Anthony made something.

"This is kind of weird. We're just going to hang out here while they . . . uh . . . while things progress?" Owen stands stiffly to the side.

I move a giant bag of flour to reveal a golden apple pie. "Uh, yeah," I say over my shoulder. "I'm not going to let this pie get cold." I pass Owen on my way into the living room and notice his skeptical look. "Anthony's fine with us having pie *while things progress,*" I promise. "Believe me. I've done this before."

I drop onto the couch and hold a fork out to Owen while digging into the center of the pie, not bothering to slice it. I think it's my moan of pie-induced ecstasy that persuades Owen to grab the fork and sit down next to me.

"Howv da play gumpf?" I ask through a mouthful.

"What?" Owen studies me.

I swallow. "How's the play going? Can I read it?"

He shakes his head with surprising vehemence. "It's nowhere near ready. I'm still deep in outlining."

"*Outlining?* I've given you so much material."

He stabs the pie with a little less enthusiasm. "I haven't had a lot of time."

"Because of *Romeo and Juliet*?"

"Yeah, and home stuff." He doesn't lift his fork, and it remains in the center of the pie. "You know, picking up my brother, making him dinner, helping him with his homework."

There's something serious in his eyes, his squared shoulders. I set my fork down. "You do a lot for your brother," I say after a second.

158

Owen shrugs. "It's not so bad. It's my mom who works night shifts and two jobs."

He falls silent, but I don't want to interrupt in case he's going to say more. Besides, I wouldn't know how to respond. I wish I did—I'm even a little embarrassed I don't—but while I've bared family problems to him, I've never heard his. Instead, I poke at the pie.

He does go on. "My dad walked out on us the year my brother was born. My mom works really hard to make things possible for us, like the theater camp I did last summer—it wasn't cheap. It's nothing to take care of Sam in return."

"I had no idea," I say, hearing how inadequate it sounds.

He gives me a quick smile. "Yeah, I'm not exactly the oversharing type. I'm more comfortable writing in my notebook than talking to most people."

"You don't seem to have a problem talking to me." I nudge his shoulder with mine.

"You're not most people."

He's looking at me intently, and there's a hum in the air I wasn't expecting. One I don't know what to do with. I look down. "No," I say, trying to sound undisturbed, "I'm loud, sarcastic, boy-crazy—"

"—thoughtful, perceptive, witty," Owen finishes. He doesn't look away, and I lift my gaze to meet his. The truth is, I could say the same thing about him. He's quiet and patient enough for me to talk while he listens, and yet he keeps surprising me by making me laugh. I nearly do tell him. Instead, in the silence that follows his comment, I inch closer to him on the couch and take his hand, entwining my fingers with his.

Owen doesn't move. I watch him look down at our hands and then up at me. There's possibility in his eyes. I lean forward, but before I reach him, he quietly says, "You like Will."

I pull back just a bit. I definitely felt like Owen wanted this. Why would he bring up Will? I tell him what I haven't wanted to admit before now is the truth. "It's not going to happen with Will."

He blinks. "What? Why?"

"It's run its course. Trust me. I've been here before. I know what happens next."

"But you still like him." His eyes are guarded.

I drop his hand. What brought us this close on the couch was how easily I felt I could like Owen one day. I could use him to get over Will or even fall for him for real, even though I know he's right—in this moment, I do still like Will. "Yeah," I say bitterly, "like that ever means anything."

"Why do you do that?" I'm surprised to hear he sounds accusing.

"What?"

"You sell yourself short," he says, softer this time. "You give up. It's what you're doing with Juliet and the play. I think you did it with your and Tyler's relationship, too. If you like Will, then don't write it off. I know you, Megan. Don't undervalue yourself."

His speech momentarily stuns me. It's charged with conviction, and the words linger in the air while I search for what to say.

It's on the tip of my tongue to point out that even if I like Will, I can't force him to like me, when Anthony's door bangs open. Eric storms down the hall, his hair disheveled. He startles when he sees us and stops for a moment. "It was good to see you guys," he mutters distractedly. "I've got to go." Before we have time to react, he throws open the front door, and he's gone.

Anthony trails into the room, looking dazed. I'm on my feet and rushing to his side. "What happened? It looked like it was going great," I say, realizing a second late I just let it slip I'd spied on them.

If he notices, he doesn't care. "It was. Everything was perfect," he says emptily. "And then his dad called, and he got weird and distant and just left."

"Was there a family emergency or something?" I ask.

"Of course there wasn't a family emergency," he snaps, finally whipping his gaze to me. "This was just a terrible idea."

"A terrible idea? You just hooked up with the guy you've been obsessed with."

"Which is everything I could have hoped for, right?" he fires back. "It doesn't matter he's obviously in the closet with no intention of having a relationship with me—or that he's definitely never going to talk to me again." He's yelling now, and there are tears in his eyes. "Because it's enough I got to hook up with him, right? It might be for you, Megan. But not for me."

I fumble for words. "I didn't mean . . . I'm not— You don't have the first clue what's *enough* for me," I fire back, finding my voice. "Or how much I did to help you. If it wasn't for me, you wouldn't have had what you did have. Which wasn't nothing."

"I didn't ask for your help. Whatever you did, whatever you said to him—you pushed him. You pushed us both. Not everyone wants to take things at your pace. Relationships aren't a race against the clock." I flinch, but Anthony blazes on. "I've never even had a real boyfriend. I thought Eric would be different. I thought he got me. It's hard enough meeting guys in high school. It's not like I've got endless relationships and hookups around the corner to console myself with—hard though it might be for *you* to understand."

"That's not fair," I say, stung.

"Not fair?" He steps closer to me, and I can see he's shaking. "Not fair is having to move schools because you're too black and too gay to get lead roles. Not fair is dreading every school trip because you know no guy wants to be your roommate. Not fair is worrying every time you flirt with a guy if he's going to laugh in your face."

His words have me looking past the malice in his voice. Anthony hardly ever talks about this stuff, but I'm not unaware of the toll it takes on him. And I know tonight meant a lot to him. Of course he's heartbroken. "I'm sorry. I think you'll have another chance with Eric," I say gently.

"I know you do. You don't get it. It's easy to tell yourself everything is going to be okay when really, inside, you've already resigned yourself to failure."

I feel tears of hot anger in my eyes. I don't have the words to deny what Anthony's saying. Maybe I am resigned, and maybe it's unhealthy. But right now, I don't know how not to be.

"Fuck this." I hear my voice waver. "I'm trying to be here for you. I'm trying to help. But forget it. You don't want to talk. You only want to take your ruined night out on me."

Grabbing my bag, I remember Owen behind me. "Come on, Owen," I tell him, walking to the door. I think I catch him give Anthony an apologetic glance before I follow in Eric's footsteps.

We drive home in silence, wrapped in too many layers of things left unsaid. Owen's not meeting my eyes, and we exchange muted good-byes when I drop him off in front of his house.

The windows of my house are dark when I pull into the driveway. I walk in the front door, past the remnants of what looks like a family craft night, and up to my room. It takes everything I have not to slam the door behind me. It's not just thoughts of Anthony and Owen that torment me. It's something more selfish, too—that I teared up in front of them, and I'm not the kind of girl who cries.

I don't even bother turning on the lights. I head straight for my bed. But once I've buried myself under the covers, I can't sleep. I dwell on the words Anthony flung at me. He said things a person shouldn't say to a friend even when angry.

Nevertheless, they rang painfully true. Anthony might be right. I've always thought my relationships give up on me.

It's easier, in a way. They're out of my control—comfortably predictable. Inevitability has become my coping mechanism.

Except what if it's become more than that? The question comes with a queasy rush. What if somewhere along the way, a coping mechanism became a chain around my neck, pulling me in directions I didn't want to go? I'm beginning to feel like whatever happens to my relationships, my negativity can't be helping. What if they don't give up on me—what if I give up on them?

I turn over to face the wall, fighting to calm my racing thoughts. This time of night, fresh from what happened with Anthony, is not the time to fray the edges of those questions, hard though I'm finding it to force them down.

There's one thing I do need to do tonight. I have no business going for a guy who has a girlfriend while I have feelings for someone else, no matter how thoughtful, perceptive, and witty he is. I reach for my phone on my nightstand and type out a text to Owen.

sry for earlier. b4 anthony

He doesn't reply, and I can't help remembering how quickly he did when I invited him to Anthony's. He could just be putting his brother to bed, I tell myself. I try to let it go, but twenty minutes go by and I'm still awake, still worrying I lost two friends in one night.

i hope i didnt mess stuff up btwn us, I type before I can stop myself, then a second later I add, **ur a good friend.** I hit SEND.

This time, it's only a couple minutes before his reply comes.

> You're a good friend too. You don't need to
> apologize . . .

I feel myself let out a relieved breath. Then I receive a second text.

> I get it. I know I'm a really hot friar.

I laugh, hurting a little less. I send him my reply.

> the hawtest. can't wait to c u in ur frock

FOURTEEN

JULIET: *Was ever book containing such vile matter*

So fairly bound? O, that deceit should dwell

In such a gorgeous palace!

III.ii.89–91

IT'S DAWN, AND I'M DRIVING UP THE dirt road to where Madeleine texted me to find her for tree planting. It's thickly forested on both sides, and my mom's old Volkswagen skips over the loose rocks. I crest the hill, and spreading out below me is the horizon painted pink by the rising sun.

It's beautiful. And I hate it.

I take one hand off the wheel to rub sleep out of my eyes. Only for Madeleine would I get up at five in the morning on a Saturday and venture into nature. I spot her car on the side of the road, where she told me it would be, and pull in behind it.

Walking into the woods, I pull my scarf over my very messy ponytail. October's giving way to November, and it is *cold*. In the crisp morning light my breath is depressingly visible. I hear rustling up ahead, and voices drift to me a second later. I can't believe Madeleine actually convinced other people to come to this.

When I enter a clearing in the forest, I find a handful of volunteers working with shovels, among them Madeleine, whose head is bent over the hole she's digging. She looks better than anyone has the right to at this ungodly hour in the middle of the forest, wearing a blue bandana with perfect carelessness over her tidy bun and a baggy Windbreaker that somehow still flatters her frame. She doesn't notice when I come up next to her.

"You know," I say, and Madeleine's head pops up, "this is awesome. Whenever I look into the woods, what I find myself thinking is, *needs more trees.*"

She rolls her eyes. Grinning, she grabs the small sapling beside the hole and drops it in. "They're to replace the foliage lost when a couple of drunken idiots on a camping trip started a fire." Now that she mentions it, the ground here does look ashy. "Besides," she continues, patting the dirt around her tree, "it looks great for college."

She straightens up and produces a trowel from her back pocket. Holding it out to me, she gives me an expectant look. *Is she serious?*

I pull a fake pout.

She's not amused. One eyebrow arches, and she waves the trowel in the air, flinging dirt at me.

"Okay, okay," I grumble. We walk to the next sapling, a few feet over. Following Madeleine's lead, I kneel and shove my trowel into the earth, no idea what I'm doing. Far away, I hear the chattering of some indiscernible woodland creature. Madeleine, however, knows exactly what she's doing, and she confidently removes a shovelful of dirt in one even motion.

"Doesn't it ever get tiring being perfect?" I ask, watching her.

I meant it half-jokingly, but she wrinkles her nose. "Perfect?"

"I mean, saving the forests, volunteering at the library, perfect GPA, perfect boyfriend. It's a lot to keep up. Don't you ever just want to screw something up?" I got two hours of sleep after somehow ruining one of my closest friendships, and here Madeleine is, saving the planet.

She stops digging and stabs her shovel into the ground. "What's with you today? You're snarkier than normal."

I shrug. She's not wrong. With last night weighing on me, of course I'm snarkier than normal. "This is just me at six a.m.," I mumble. I feel her scrutinizing me, but after a second she resumes digging with a little more force than before.

"Do you think I give up too easily?" I ask abruptly. The thought's been burning in my head since Owen and I talked on Anthony's couch. Madeleine's been my friend for a lot longer than Owen. She'd have perspective he doesn't.

She straightens up once more, this time pausing with one foot planted on her shovel. "Give up on what?"

"On everything. You know . . ." I hesitate, reconsidering. It's not *everything*, really. I haven't given up on SOTI, haven't given up on Anthony or Madeleine herself, even when we fight. "On relationships," I finish.

"This is about Will," Madeleine says knowingly.

"Yeah, Will, and everyone, I guess," I go on. "I've had a ton of boyfriends, but I've never been in a relationship longer than four months." I'd never thought anything of it before, but pondering Owen's words in bed at 2 a.m., it began to depress me.

"Well, you shouldn't waste your time when a relationship's not working." She pulls off her bandana and wipes her face with it.

"But what if I'm too quick to think a relationship's not working? I was ready to give up on Will after one awkward night and seeing Alyssa flirt with him. Which, you know, Alyssa flirts with everyone. Everything."

Madeleine doesn't laugh. She puts a hand on her hip. "Why are we talking about this?" She sounds slightly exasperated. God forbid I disturb her community-service time.

"I don't know. Just looking back, it feels like I was too quick to . . . write some of them off." I'm using Owen's exact phrasing, I realize.

"But . . . Tyler was different," she says slowly.

I point my trowel into the soil and shovel out more dirt. The motion comes easier this time, like I'm finding a rhythm. It feels good, even. "I guess. I mean—" I stop myself, realizing who I'm talking to. "It's not like I want him back," I quickly reassure her. "It's just, maybe I let things fall apart with Tyler and with my other boyfriends, too."

From the look on her face, I know my reassurance didn't work. Blood has started to color her alabaster cheeks in uneven splotches, and her downturned mouth is twitching. Her eyes are narrowed and fixed on me. It's a look reserved for instances like unfair grades and jocks pushing the yearbook staff into lockers.

"It wouldn't have made a difference with Tyler, okay?" she says quietly.

I shake my head. "I just mean hypothetically. What if it would have—"

"We were together before you even broke up," she nearly shouts.

My mouth drops open, my trowel into the dirt.

"You . . . *What?*"

"He kissed me the closing night of *Twelfth Night*."

I stand there, blinking in the brightening day, my thoughts chasing each other in circles. I remember the closing night of *Twelfth Night*, the final cast party of the season at Tyler's house. It was one of the rare instances of Anthony getting drunk, and Jenna and I watched him recite a version of Hamlet's soliloquy. *To beer or not to beer.*

I remember how Tyler and I had had sex for the first time just weeks earlier, and we would go on to break up about a month later. I remember them both coming over to my house a few weeks after the breakup, asking if it was okay with me for them to date and promising they'd done nothing together at that point.

I remember believing them.

All the anger drains out of Madeleine's face. Her eyes fill with tears, her face goes pale, and she rubs the bridge of her nose. I can't believe she has the nerve to drop this on me and then cry about it. Wanting *me* to take care of *her*.

"I shouldn't have said that," she says weakly, her voice pinched.

"No, you *should* have said it six months ago." I can't even look at her.

"I know. I'm *so* sorry, Megan. I should have," she blurts out through her tears, but there's exasperation or even frustration behind her remorse. "I know things have been weird between us, it's why I wanted today to—"

"I *defended* you," I cut her off. "Everyone thought you and Tyler cheated, and I played the best friend because I trusted you. You told me nothing had happened while we were still dating."

"I know, I know." Tears are streaming down her face, and a couple volunteers' heads have turned in our direction. "Please, let's go to my car, let me explain . . ."

Some of my anger has ebbed away. I take a step toward her, my instinct kicking in to forgive and be there for her. But before I reach out to her, I remember what Owen told me. *Don't undervalue yourself.* I shouldn't sweep my hurt under the rug so Madeleine doesn't have to feel bad. My feelings matter, too. I'm tired of pretending they don't.

I turn on my heel and walk back to my car, leaving Madeleine to her tears.

I wake up to six missed calls from Madeleine after sleeping for the rest of the morning. I delete the voicemails without listening to them.

Surprisingly, I feel good about how I handled the fight.

Not about the reason for the fight, obviously—I feel really betrayed. I honestly believed my best friend when she promised she hadn't hooked up with my boyfriend behind my back. Even if they are the perfect couple, what they did fucking sucks. But I'm genuinely proud that I stood up for myself and didn't just let something go instead of meeting it head-on.

Which has me thinking about Will.

Yeah, Alyssa flirtatiously touched his arm and wanted to "read lines" with him—the oldest trick in the book. But it was just a week ago he was in my room telling me I'm beautiful. I'm done waiting for him to drop some hint about how he sees our relationship. I'm going to find out.

I grab my phone off my desk. u busy? I text him.

Not right now. Why? he replies.

I text him a location and, 30 min!!! And I don't let myself worry about whether he'll be there.

Thirty minutes later, the bell chimes on the front door of the place I told him to meet me. Will's head of immaculately slicked hair appears in the doorway. His eyes flit over the shelves, and I signal to him with a wave from my small table in the back.

He sits down across from me, looking quizzical. I push the almond blueberry coffee cake I ordered toward him. "You want something to drink?" I ask.

He stares down at the cake, then looks up at me, lightly amused. "What's happening here?"

I take a deep breath. "A date." I turn one of the forks so it faces him. "Coffee cake?"

"A date," he repeats, reaching for the fork. He doesn't look entirely convinced.

I begin reciting the speech I prepared in my head on the drive over. "I feel like we've been off ever since the night we hooked up at my house. I have a tendency to rush things, but I don't want to do that anymore. Which, I guess, means I'm not ready to have sex with you"—I pause—"yet. It's definitely a yet." Will smiles. Encouraged, I continue. "I like you. I want to be with you. I want to date."

He puts down the fork. For a horrible moment, every doubt I've had about this plan floods my mind. *He's not interested. He likes Alyssa. I came on way too strong. He wants to have sex now.* And worst of all, *Owen was wrong—I don't give up too easily. People give up on me.*

Instead of saying any of those things, Will puts his hand over mine on the table. "I . . . have to tell you, I was a little intimidated when we started hooking up. Everyone knows you're hot, and funny, and talented. It was hard to measure up to."

I blink. I didn't know "everyone" thought that. To the rest of the school, I thought I was just Madeleine's flirty friend. Madeleine's perpetually dumped friend.

Will goes on. "I didn't know how to handle it, but I want to be with you, too, Megan," he says with a growing smile.

Muscles I didn't realize were tensed relax, and I feel unbelievably relieved. But I'm not done yet. It's now or never. "Okay, then I want a straight answer," I say. "Boyfriend?"

Will nods once, definite and unmistakable. "Boyfriend."

"Well," I say, beaming, "great."

"I guess that makes this our first date. And we are . . ." He looks around the room. "Where, exactly?"

I let my eyes wander over the familiar surroundings. In the front of the shop, antique books, foreign titles, and bestsellers vie for space on wooden shelves that look on the verge of collapse. Posters of long-dead literary figures curl away from the walls over the register. A spindly staircase in the center of the room winds up to an alcove overcrowded with Shakespeare paraphernalia. The smell of what must be the strongest espresso in Oregon wafts from the coffee counter in the back, where Will and I are sitting. It's dimly lit, dusty, and perfect.

"It's Birnam Wood Books," I tell him. "I first came here to annotate *Macbeth* for a scene workshop. I found it because of the reference. Ever since, it's been pretty much my favorite spot."

Will sniffs the air. "Kind of musty."

"It's great, isn't it?"

He takes a bite of the coffee cake and shrugs. "It's definitely the first time I've gone on a date to a bookstore. But then," he adds, almost like an afterthought, "it's the first time I've gone on a date." It's not as if I'm surprised, but it's sort of endearing to hear him admit it. "How's *Romeo and Juliet* going? I notice the balcony scene's on the schedule again this week."

"Don't remind me." The last rehearsal went terribly. I'm hopeless on the lines where Juliet declares her love for Romeo, no matter how much emotion Tyler puts into it or how often Jody stops us to repeat it. "Right now, I'm more focused on the Senior Showcase and the scene I'm directing," I say.

"But that's one scene," Will says slowly.

"I'm *directing* one scene," I quickly counter. "I'm organizing the entire showcase."

"I just don't get why you'd focus on that." His tone's light, but underneath it there's something nearly judgmental. "*Romeo and Juliet*'s going to Ashland. Come on," he says, the grin I once found dazzling losing a little of its luster, "you're the lead in a professional-level performance. That's way bigger than Stillmont's Senior Showcase."

I shrug, trying not to be annoyed that he doesn't get it, or offended by the way he said *Senior Showcase.* "It's my senior year. I've been a part of the showcase since I started high school. I want it to be perfect, you know?" Will nods, but his eyes remain skeptical like, no, he doesn't know. "Besides, I'm not going to let the showcase interfere with Ashland."

"Do you have a cast yet?" he asks after a second, and I'm relieved he's taking an interest.

"No, why?" I raise an eyebrow flirtatiously. "You interested?"

"I might be," he says slowly. "If I'm promised special attention from the director."

"I think that could be arranged."

He grins. Then without warning, he takes my hand and pulls me toward the front of the shop. "A first date merits a first gift. Don't you think?" he asks over his shoulder.

Butterflies I haven't felt in a while flutter in my chest. "You don't have to," I half protest, enjoying Will's affection if a bit thrown by the gesture.

"I insist," he says unhesitatingly. He doesn't slow his steps, and I follow him.

Near the front, I find my eyes drifting to the shelf of leather-bound notebooks on one side of the door. I admired them the past couple times I was here, and—

"This." Will holds up a black bracelet. "This is perfect."

Oh. "It's beautiful," I'm quick to say.

He gives me a pleased smile. When he places it on the glass counter by the register, I notice there's a word engraved on the inside. Or—a name.

"Ophelia?" I ask.

Will hands a twenty to the cashier while turning to me. "Yeah!" he says enthusiastically. "Isn't *Hamlet* the best? Or, like, definitely"—he holds up a hand, correcting himself—"*one* of the best."

He takes the bracelet out of its packaging and hands it to me. I slip it on with a grateful smile, choosing to overlook that Ophelia does nothing for the entire play except obsess over her boyfriend until she goes crazy. And it gives me a quiet, familiar thrill. I appreciate Will's eagerness, his affection, and what it represents—togetherness. It doesn't matter what the bracelet says. It's a gift from my boyfriend.

FIFTEEN

MERCUTIO: *A plague o' both your houses!*

III.i.111

DESPITE THE SUCCESS OF WILL'S AND MY date, I get to school on Monday in not exactly the greatest of moods. When I went home on Saturday, two hours and one torrid make-out session in the Shakespeare section later, I overheard my dad on the phone. It was on speaker, and I only stuck around long enough to figure out he and Rose were talking to a realtor whom they'd hired to appraise the house. To put a price tag on seventeen years of homemade dinners, birthday parties, fights, tears, and memories.

For the first time ever, I stopped myself before instinctively texting Madeleine. There's a part of me, a very big part, that wanted to tell her what I'd overheard. But then I remembered that I'm not talking to her. That she's not the friend I thought she was.

I ignore her during English and pass her without looking at her between classes. Eventually, I notice Anthony's giving me the same treatment. But I have Will to distract me, a task he accomplishes with impressive tongue work, and the day goes pretty much okay. Until lunch.

I walk to the hill outside the drama room, knowing Madeleine's going to be there. I'm not going to talk to her. Not a chance. But I've decided I won't be the one to run from her. She's not going to steal my boyfriend *and* my lunch spot.

I march right into the middle of the group and sit down next to Owen. I can feel Madeleine looking imploringly at me. "Hey, Megan," she pleads. "Can we talk? I tried calling you this weekend."

Without looking at her, I unwrap the chicken-salad sandwich Rose insisted on packing for me. "There's a reason I didn't pick up." Not wanting this conversation to go any further, I pointedly turn to Kasey Markowitz, the junior who played Olivia in *Twelfth Night*. "Kasey, I know you're a junior, but I want you to sign up for my senior scene. I'm doing a gender-flipped Happy Loman, and I think you'd be great."

She flushes, obviously flattered, but Madeleine interrupts. "You're seriously just ignoring me right now?" Her tone's gone from pleading to pissed.

I finally whip my head in her direction. "I'm sorry, I'm not in the mood to talk to my former best friend who was screwing around with my boyfriend behind my back." Next to her, Tyler's eyes widen, and I briefly wonder if she even told him that I know.

Everyone falls silent, and Madeleine's cheeks ignite. Hurriedly, she drops her Thermos into her bag and gets to her feet, smoothing her skirt with trembling hands. Tyler tosses me an apologetic look. "I have to . . ." He gestures in her direction. "I'm sorry, Megan," he says before leaving to follow Madeleine. I don't know if he's apologizing for walking away from the conversation or for betraying me while we were dating. Either way, I'm not ready to deal with how furious I am with Tyler.

Everyone gradually resumes their conversations, occasionally stealing glances in my direction. Everyone except Owen, who leans into me. "I'm getting the sense something... changed since we talked about Tyler and Madeleine."

Seriously? Now? "Get your notebook out, Owen. I've got some *great* material for you," I snap.

He jerks back. "What? No." He sounds stunned, even hurt. "I'm not trying to get material. I'm trying to be your friend."

I feel a stab of guilt. Of course Owen's just trying to be my friend. It's what he's been doing since the day we met. I exhale. "It turns out I was an idiot for not believing what *everyone* told me. Madeleine let it slip this weekend she and Tyler hooked up a month before he and I broke up."

"That ..." Owen reaches for words. "Definitely sucks."

"I'm not surprised on Tyler's end, honestly. But Madeleine ... She's the one person I couldn't believe would do that to me." I stare at the ground and absently rip out blades of grass. "The messed-up thing is, part of me wants to pretend it didn't happen. There's more stuff going on with my dad, and I wish I could talk to her, have her sleep over, like we did when my parents were splitting up."

He nods. "What are you going to do?" he asks evenly.

"Do? I'm not the one who has to *do* anything. I want her to ... I don't know. Figure out a way to make it right."

"She will," Owen says without hesitation.

I shoot him an incredulous look. "How do you know?"

He glances down like he's considering the question. "I don't," he admits. "But she will if she's the kind of friend worth having."

I don't know what to say to that. I want to believe Madeleine's the kind of friend who would want to fix things between us. And I do believe it. I'd forgive her if she showed me that I mean more to her than how she treated me.

I feel my stomach sink. I'm not the only one who deserves to feel that way. Anthony means more to me than the way I've been rushing him, too. He should take his relationship—or flirtation, or whatever it is—with Eric at whatever pace he wants.

"You know," Owen says, and I realize he's been waiting patiently during my lengthy introspection, "I'm not Madeleine—sleepovers with me might be a bit weird—but I'm here for you if you need."

I look up into his dark, thoughtful eyes. "Sleepovers with you wouldn't be *weird*, Owen . . . unless you're into 'weird.'" I wink. Before he begins to blush, I lower my voice and say sincerely, "But really, thanks."

I have Trig after lunch. Outside Mr. Patton's door, I decide I'm going to skip class. I know it'll be boring, and besides, I have urgent business. I turn and walk against hallway traffic until I reach the science wing, where I wait for the next fifteen minutes after the bell rings and the hallway empties.

When Ms. Howell leaves the AP Physics room, I hover by

the bathroom door and try to look like I have total permission to be here. I know where Howell's headed. I had Intro Physics with her last year, and without fail she goes to the parking lot for a smoke break fifteen minutes into each of her afternoon classes.

I slip into the room behind her. It's a scene of utter chaos. The AP students are armed with fluorescent purple Nerf crossbows. Foam darts fly across the room trailed by students with measuring tapes and notebooks. A dart hits me in the back of the head, and I hear a whiny voice complain that I'm interrupting the data-collection process.

I don't bother to apologize. I'm here for one reason, and he's in the back of the room.

Anthony's head is bent over his notebook. He doesn't look up when I lean on the counter next to him. "I'm in the middle of class, Megan," he says flatly.

"I know. It'll only take a second."

He drags his eyes from his paper and glares at me. "What, you haven't messed with my life enough already?"

I flinch. "I'm sorry," I hurriedly continue, knowing I won't have long before he shuts me out again. "I shouldn't have rushed you. You were right, even though you said some shit that really hurt."

Anthony looks away, but he doesn't ignore me. "Why are you here, Megan?"

"I want to be a good friend. The kind of friend worth having. You've been a good friend to me, and I want to make things right." I take a deep breath. "I'm sorry I forced you to take things faster than you wanted to."

"It's not just about being sorry," he replies immediately, his voice harsh. "You don't understand how not like you I am. I know you wanted to help, but you never bothered to consider what kind of help or encouragement or friendship *I* wanted. I don't have your no-holds-barred attitude toward relationships, and I never will. You're fearless, and that's awesome," he goes on, something somber entering his eyes. "But it's painful and honestly frustrating when you push me to date the way you do."

"I understand," I reply. "Or I'm trying to understand. I'm going to keep trying, if you'll let me. To be fair, though, I didn't exactly force you and Eric into your bedroom together," I point out, and Anthony's eyes flicker. "You're hardly timid when it comes to guys. But I know I went about this wrong," I rush to add. "I'm sorry I screwed everything up with Eric. I won't intrude in your relationships from now on. Promise."

His expression begins to soften. "You didn't screw everything up," he says gently. "It's my fault, and Eric's, not yours. I'm sorry, too. I took some low blows at your relationship history, and I didn't mean what I said."

I smile tentatively. "They weren't entirely undeserved, but thanks. I'm not going to tell you what to do, but you know, I'm here for you."

"I want to hit pause on the Eric situation," he says after a long second. I know from his hunched shoulders and the waver in his voice that it's not something he's pleased to admit.

"I understand," I say quickly.

"But for the record," he continues, beginning to smile, "the *entire* night wasn't terrible."

"No night with your unbelievable carne asada could be."

He laughs. "Stuff with Eric . . . wasn't the worst."

"It didn't look it."

Anthony's eyes slowly widen with realization. "You did *not*."

I give him a close-lipped smile. "Just for a second."

He shakes his head admonishingly, but he's grinning. "Well, watching you and Owen concoct your fake relationship story . . . It was *almost* the highlight of the night." He fixes me with an indicative stare. "You know, you two would actually make a cute couple."

I say nothing. I won't pretend the thought's never flitted through my head, but he's . . . Owen. No way would a guy who's never without his notebook, whose current relationship consists of blurry video chats twice a week, who's quiet and reserved, go for someone who's brash and forward like me. No. I'd be better off sticking to guys who want to get to the point. Guys like Will.

Instead of saying all that to Anthony, I seize the crossbow from the counter and shoot a dart into his chest. He rolls his eyes. "Why are you even talking to me?" I ask with joking indignation. "You're in the middle of class."

SIXTEEN

JULIET: *O Romeo, Romeo, wherefore art thou Romeo?*

II.ii.36

"DENY THY FATHER AND REFUSE THY NAME, or, if thou wilt not, be but sworn my love—"

"Nope!" Jody's voice rings sharply to where I'm standing on the balcony set. It's the first day of rehearsal with the half-painted wooden structure Will built—a single-story tower with a staircase down the back and a trellis with plastic ivy winding up the front. I think Jody expected performing on the set would awaken my inner Juliet. No such luck.

I hear Tyler sigh from the stage below. I don't blame him, really. It's the sixth time Jody's interrupted us before we've even finished the scene. On the other hand, I'm not exactly overflowing with sympathy for Tyler Dunning at the moment. It's been a week since Madeleine's confession, and I haven't forgiven either one of them. Not even close.

Jody climbs onto the stage. "This isn't working," she says, her eyes on me. "I know you're trying to find the softer Juliet, Megan, but it's not coming through. No one is buying this romance."

"It's partly my fault," Tyler butts in before I have the chance to reply. He glances over at me pityingly, and I feel my blood heat with anger. He's got some nerve, implying my performance is falling apart because of personal stuff between him and me. It's not just patronizing, it's wrong.

"I feel like I'm playing Romeo's opening lines too comedic," Tyler continues. "It's probably throwing Megan off."

Wow. Even worse. Tyler never criticizes his own work. He must think I'm on the verge of having a meltdown in the middle of rehearsal over something he did to me half a year ago.

Jody rubs her eyes. "No, Tyler, it's not just on you," she mutters. Putting her glasses back on, she looks from Tyler to me. "I think the two of you need to take a couple minutes to talk through the scene dynamics. Regroup backstage, and we'll pick up in five."

I literally would rather change a thousand of Erin's diapers. Clenching my script, I head down the narrow stairs. Tyler's waiting for me backstage, rubbing his neck, looking uncharacteristically nervous.

"Jody's on the warpath today. I actually think the scene's going pretty well," he says in a rush and way too casually.

I stare at him hard. "Why are you doing that? First you try to take the fall. Now it's Jody's fault? I can handle getting critiqued."

"I guess I feel bad." He shuffles his feet uncomfortably. "You know, for my part in what happened. I never meant to cheat on you."

Is he for real? "Oh, well, if you never *meant* to, then it's fine."

He pulls a remorseful expression—one I've seen too

many times on stage. "I'm trying to apologize, Megan."

"Then I should fall over myself forgiving you, right? What you did was shitty, and I'm not just going to be cool with it because you feel bad." I hear Anthony hurling insults at Jason Mitchum on the other side of the curtain, rehearsing Mercutio and Tybalt's fight sequence. At least everyone's not just listening to Tyler and me.

"Huh." He rubs his jaw. "I didn't think you had it in you."

I narrow my eyes. "What?"

"You just never seem to really care about, well, anything."

I blink a couple times, his words setting in. First Anthony telling me I'm resigned to failure, now Tyler thinking there's nothing I care about? Is *that* who everyone thinks I am? Just a girl who flits through life without trying, without hurting, without caring about anything except the next guy?

"Well, I do care," I fire back. And I want to prove it. I glance down at the script in my hand. "Right now I care about figuring out this scene."

He stares at me disbelievingly for a moment, then scoffs. "I don't know what to tell you, because honestly I'm killing it out there while my Juliet can't even be bothered to look impressed at my flawless intonation. You have no idea the nights I've spent perfecting iambic pentameter—"

"Tyler, shut up for a second." Surprisingly, he does, and I realize in an unexpected rush of inspiration what's wrong with the scene. "This is exactly the problem. If you read the lines, Juliet is not impressed by Romeo's wordiness. But there's a point in the scene where something has to change, because by the end Juliet's professing her love to him. I feel like we haven't figured out that point." I notice Tyler's actually listening. "We need a moment where something softens her—where she falls head over heels."

"What do you propose?" he asks.

"We need something genuine, where Romeo's words get out of the way."

He nods slowly, but his eyes are bright, and I can tell he's with me. "Something physical?" he offers.

"Exactly." I'm liking this interpretation. I only need to figure out how to fit it into the script. Looking past Tyler, my eyes catch the wooden stairs leading up to the balcony. I nod toward the set, the idea coming together in my head. "This is what we're going to do. My genius boyfriend built the set so you can climb the trellis."

Tyler starts to grin.

I find the page in my script and point. "Here."

"Deny thy father and refuse thy name, or, if thou wilt not, be but sworn my love, and I'll no longer be a Capulet." I'm back on the balcony, doing my utmost to look like a teenage girl in the throes of irresponsible love.

This time, I'm not just trudging through the lines. I'm excited, and it's making the dialogue come easier, more naturally. When Juliet asks, *Wherefore art thou Romeo?* into the night, she's not flush with passion, not yet. It's more like she's trying the feeling out.

"What's Montague? It is nor hand, nor foot," I continue

reciting, "nor arm, nor face, nor any other part belonging to a man." I allow Juliet a smirk, knowing what part she has in mind. "That which we call a rose by any other name would smell as sweet."

When I finish my speech, Romeo leaps out of the bushes, and I immediately turn Juliet skeptical. I'm downright stand-offish by the time she proclaims, "I have no joy of this contract tonight. It is too rash, too unadvised, too sudden, too like the lightning, which doth cease to be ere one can say 'it lightens.'" I'm *enjoying* delivering the lines, capturing the inflection. It's almost better than watching actors navigate their lines when I'm directing.

"O, wilt thou leave me so unsatisfied?" Tyler moans, and the rest of the cast laughs from the audience.

I haughtily raise my chin and ask him challengingly, "What satisfaction canst thou have tonight?"

I catch Tyler's eye. He's turned toward me, and the audience can't see his face when he flashes me a quick grin. I hold my breath as he executes a running leap onto the trellis. In two graceful steps, he's scaled up to my level, and out of the corner of my eye I notice Jody lean forward in what I hope is interest.

"Th' exchange of thy love's faithful vow for mine," Tyler utters in a stage whisper.

Then for the first time in six months, Tyler Dunning's lips meet mine. I give Juliet a moment of stunned recoil before I melt into the kiss. He smells the way I remember, but it's not weird like I expected it to be. I don't feel like Megan Harper kissing her cheating ex. I feel like Juliet falling in love.

Maybe it's because I'm getting better at getting into character. Or maybe it's because he's not kissing me like Tyler Dunning, not reaching for my bra and parting my lips with too much tongue. He's kissing me like I imagine Romeo would, his hands remaining on the balcony while he gently presses his lips to mine.

"I gave thee mine before thou didst request it, and yet I would it were to give again," I breathe when he pulls back.

"Okay"—Jody's voice cuts between us—"stop there."

I turn to where she's standing. Every ounce of excitement I just felt for the scene drains out of me, and doubt rushes in. The cast is hushed like I've never heard them during notes—except for Alyssa, who's whispering in Courtney's ear and sneering at me. I search Jody's expression for any indication of what's coming, whether she's going to tell us to rethink the scene again or whether I'm finally kicked out of the role for good. I figure it's one of the two.

But it's not me she speaks to first. "Tyler, what could have possibly compelled you to climb the set and kiss your co-star?" I hear nervous laughter from the audience. "Last time I checked, that wasn't in the script or the blocking we discussed. When I told you to step through the scene in private, I didn't mean come up with an entirely new, entirely dangerous staging."

"It was Megan's idea," Tyler says unhesitatingly, jumping off the trellis. *Well, so much for trying to take the fall for me.*

Jody turns her attention to me. "You're an actor here, Megan. Not a director. You need to remember your role." It's an agonizing few moments before she continues, like she's

189

torturing me on purpose. "But . . . I'm impressed," she finally says with a slight smile. "That's the Juliet I've been waiting for."

I breathe a sigh of relief without entirely meaning to, hearing Owen's words in my head. *Don't undervalue yourself.*

"Me too," I reply.

I walk out of rehearsal half an hour later, still grinning stupidly from nailing the scene, and go directly to the bulletin board in the front of the Arts Center. The campus is quiet this time in the afternoon, the sun beginning to dip below the trees and paint the pavement. There's only a scattering of cars left in the parking lot, those belonging to the cast and the athletes here for afternoon practices.

Today was the deadline to sign up for the Senior Showcase scenes, and while I really should head home—Dad told me if I was late to dinner one more time there would be ill-defined "consequences"—I have to know who signed up. The exhilaration of the showcase beginning to come together, combined with the *Romeo and Juliet* rehearsal, is nearly enough for me to forget how messed up things are with Madeleine.

I fold back the open-mic night poster on the bulletin board to find the flier I printed out with *Death of a Salesman* at the top. I left four lines for the four actors I need. I'll sort out who plays who later. The first name I spot is Tyler's. Yeah, he'll be a perfect Willy Loman. Sorry, Dad.

I read down to *Kasey Markowitz*, who I'm glad took my advice and signed up, and *Jenna Cho*, written in her exaggeratedly loopy handwriting.

Then at the bottom of the list, *Owen Okita*.

He's written his name in the deep blue ink I recognize from the endless scrawl in his notebook. I feel my chest warm with gratitude. He didn't even tell me he'd be signing up, and I wonder why stage-shy Owen would volunteer before it occurs to me, of course he would. He's a good friend like that.

But the feeling only lasts a moment because I realize there's one name unaccounted for, one I was really hoping to see. Will made it sound like he wanted to sign up.

The door to the drama room swings open, and Owen walks out, backpack slung over his shoulder and notebook in his hand. "Owen!" I shout. "You signed up for my scene!"

He spins to face me, his eyes finding mine. "You're right. I did," he says, looking amused. "I wanted to experience Megan Harper directing firsthand."

"Was that before or after you watched me *direct* an actor into kissing me?" I had to. I can't help it.

But Owen doesn't blush this time. Instead, he rolls his eyes. "Before, Megan. Cosima, remember?"

"Come on, Owen. If it's on stage, it doesn't count."

"Good to know," he says, and I swear there's a sparkle in his eyes. He comes up to read over my shoulder. "Who else is on there? I didn't really check before, I was in a rush."

"Tyler, obviously . . ." I say under my breath. I'm hyperconscious of Owen behind me, his face next to mine.

He takes a step back, and he's frowning when I turn to face him. "Why's that obvious?" he asks.

"Well, it's just, my scenes have a reputation for stealing the show . . ." I know how full of myself that sounds, but whatever. It's the truth.

Owen grins. "Right. Obviously." But he must notice I don't return his smile, because quickly his face turns concerned. "Hey, what's up? You seem upset."

"It's stupid, but I thought Will would sign up," I mutter. It's not Owen's problem, I realize as I tell him. I pull out my phone and write a message to Will.

senior scene signups?? I send, and look up at Owen.

"Death of a Salesman doesn't feel like Will's kind of thing," he ventures.

"I guess," I reply. A second later, my phone vibrates. I glance down and read Will's text.

Shit, I forgot!! I'll make it up to you later? ;)

"He forgot," I say emptily, returning my phone to my pocket. Owen bites his lip like he's trying to figure out what to say. Before he does, my phone starts vibrating repeatedly. "Someone's calling me," I say, pulling my phone back out.

"Is it Will?"

I check the screen. "Uh, no," I say, surprised. "It's my mom's boyfriend. I guess I should answer."

"Oh, of course." He nods. "I'll talk to you later."

I start to raise the phone to my ear, but watching Owen push open the Arts Center door, I call after him. "Hey." I hold up the signup sheet. "Thanks. You'll make a perfect Biff Loman."

He breaks into a wide smile before he turns and leaves me to my phone call.

I hit ANSWER. "Hey, Randall," I say.

On the other end, I hear a clattering sound and then Randall's voice. "Megan, hi! I'm not getting you at a bad time, I hope?" He sounds surprised, like he wasn't certain I'd pick up. "Your mom told me you have rehearsals after school, and I didn't know if you'd be done, and there's the time difference—"

"It's not a bad time," I cut him off.

In the background, I hear an unexpectedly loud voice. "Randall, buddy! We need you! Epps just bowled spare number two. We need the Strike Master."

I have to smile. *The Strike Master?* "Are you at a bowling alley?" I ask Randall.

"I'm, oh, I'm sorry," he stutters. "I, the team I'm on, we're in the second bracket of a regional tourney. I ducked out a bit early. I wanted a quick word with you."

"Okay . . ." I've never been able to figure out how to talk to Randall. I don't know how my mom does it. Honestly, Randall's kind of an incongruity in the life of my mom, the former experimental visual artist who never fails to meet my sarcasm with some of her own. Randall is an accountant and painfully awkward. When I met him, he was wearing toe-shoes—those goofy shoes that look like gloves for your feet, which he wore around the house even though I'm fairly certain they're meant for running—and he excessively complimented everything my mom cooked that first night like he was afraid she'd kick him out if he didn't. He keeps unveiling odd new hobbies, first pottery and now this. How does my mom go to bed next to a guy who spends weeknights in regional bowling tournaments?

"What's up?" I ask when he says nothing.

"I'll be in Stillmont in a couple weeks," he says a little too loudly. "I hoped you might be available to get coffee?"

"Yeah. Um. Okay." I don't know why Mom didn't ask me herself. Then a worrisome thought occurs to me. "Wait, is Mom coming with you?"

"No! I'm, uh, no, it's a business trip," he clarifies. "I'm only going to be in Oregon for a day or two, but I'd kick myself if I didn't spend time with my—with you. But your mom's very excited to be coming in December for the festival!"

"Right . . ." If this phone call's any indication, a one-on-one coffee date with Randall is going to redefine stilted small talk. But I should give him the benefit of the doubt. He's nice, and he must make my mom happy somehow. "Okay, yeah," I say with more conviction. "Text me when you're in town, and we'll figure it out."

"Perfect! I'll—I'll just text you," Randall exclaims like the idea had never occurred to him.

"Cool." I'm about to hang up. But instead I add, "Break a leg. You know, with the tournament."

"Thanks for the *warning*, Mom."

It's Friday, 5:13 p.m. In the grainy FaceTime window on

my computer, Mom's eyebrows go up. "Warning?" she chides with half a frown. "You need a *warning* before you talk to Randall? I never got a warning when I'd come home to find the newest boyfriend making out with my daughter on the couch. I get to have a love life, too, Megan."

Damn, Mom. "I didn't mean it like that," I say, chagrined. "Like, what do we even have in common? It's going to be so awkward!"

"You have me in common!"

I roll my eyes. "Not exactly the subject I want to discuss with my mom's boyfriend. I guess I'll have to brush up on my professional bowling news if I'm going to have something to say to the Strike Master."

"Be nice to the poor man," Mom orders, not amused. "He's not used to talking to seventeen-year-old girls."

"I should hope not." I adopt a scandalized tone, and Mom laughs. There's a knock on the door, and per usual, Dad infuriatingly walks in without waiting for my permission.

"Hi, Catherine." He nods to the computer, and instantly my anger dissipates. I'm struck by how congenial he sounds. There's none of the tension or reserve that typically characterizes my parents' conversations.

"I hope I'm not too early?" Dad asks.

"No, now's fine," Mom replies, and I whip to face her.

"Fine for what?" I look between them, trying to figure out what could possibly compel my mom and dad to talk in my bedroom like old friends.

They exchange a look, and I know whatever this is about,

it's something serious. "We wanted to discuss something with you," Dad says in his vice-principal's-office voice, sitting down on my bed.

"*We?*" I repeat.

He goes on, making more eye contact than I'm used to. "Rose and I put in an offer on the house in New York, and it looks like the seller's going to accept."

Without a word to Dad, I turn to Mom. "You knew and didn't tell me?" I don't try to hide the hurt in my voice.

She meets my eyes unwaveringly. "We wanted to have the conversation with you together." Her voice is even, but there's something placating in it, like she's trying to urge me to take this in stride.

Not going to happen. "What else have you decided in these conversations I didn't know were happening?" I ask bitterly.

"Megan, we're grown people who have a daughter together. Occasionally, we talk," she replies.

No, you don't, I think to myself, knowing better than to say it out loud. How many times have they told me to check with each other about who'll pay for my summer programs and plane tickets, to convey happy birthdays, to figure out separating their iCals and the family iTunes library? *Now* they're talking again?

"There's something else we've discussed, actually," Dad says next to me, his eyes shifting back to my mom. "Catherine, you want to, uh . . . ?"

"Your father and I have talked quite a bit more lately," Mom says gently, "and what with your festival, Randall and I have decided we're going to extend our visit a couple weeks. We'd like to be there for the birth of your sister."

I suck in a breath. Already the idea of a couple of dinners with both my parents and their respective significant others had me nervous. But this? Watching my dad be the perfect loving spouse to Rose and father to the new baby? Waiting for my mom to finally realize just how little she—or I—belong in Dad's new family?

"Sounds . . . weird," I say. It's the understatement of the century.

The corners of Mom's lips begin to curl, and there's a knowing gleam in Dad's eyes, like they're sharing a joke. It's the kind of look I remember from years ago, when they were always stealing glances they thought I couldn't see after I'd pushed them to their parenting limits. It's almost too painful to watch.

"Maybe a little." It's Mom who speaks up. "But it's exciting. For you, for your father. . . . And while your dad's in the hospital with Rose, it'll be a chance for you and me to hang out. Do mother-daughter things."

"With everyone here? It's still weird." I won't look at either of them.

"We'll get to spend time together, the seven of us," Dad chimes in.

The seven of us. It sounds impossibly strange. Erin's birth was jarring enough, but with every new step my dad takes, his family gets further and further from me. And while I enjoy every Friday-night video chat with my mom, I can't deny that she's changing, too, that I understand less and less about this person who takes pottery classes and dates someone like

Randall. It doesn't feel like seven of us. It feels like four and two, and me fitting nowhere in the middle.

I'm spared having to reply because there's a huge clatter from downstairs followed by a tiny voice bellowing, *"Noo-noos!"* It's Erin-speak for noodles.

"That didn't sound good," Mom says, a smile in her voice.

"Erin's taken to throwing her dishes. I have to go clean Spaghetti-O's off the wall. Third time this week." Dad heaves himself off the bed with a resigned sigh, then glances at my mom in the FaceTime window. "I'm looking forward to having you guys in town. It'll be a chance to welcome in the new shape of our family."

He lays a hand on my shoulder before leaving the room, and even though I didn't think it possible, my heart plummets even lower. I don't let it show on my face because I know Mom's still watching me, still hoping her efforts to make this sound positive might have worked.

But I hate the feeling of a "new shape" of my family. To me, that shape feels like the pieces of *my* family broken apart, held together only by memories everyone's trying to forget.

Everyone except me.

SEVENTEEN

JULIET: *I should have been more strange, I must confess,*

But that thou overheard'st ere I was ware

My true-love passion.

II.ii.107–9

I LOVE SHAKESPEARE, BUT I'VE HAD JULIET'S dialogue and cues running through my head for a month now, and it's a breath of fresh air to rehearse a scene without the words *anon* or *forsooth*.

"Give my best to Bill Oliver—he may remember me," Tyler says in the voice of a defeated Willy Loman, ending the scene I chose for my piece in the Senior Showcase. He gazes wistfully into the distance like he's looking into the past, and then his shoulders relax. He and the other three members of my cast turn to me from the drama room stage, waiting for directions.

It's been two weeks of Senior Scene preparations. Two busy weeks. Outside of *Romeo and Juliet* rehearsals, I've worked every night on directing my scene *and* organizing the entire event. I've had to rehearse my actors, book the auditorium, arrange the ads for the programs, figure out the lighting with the theater-tech kids, and keep the other directors on schedule for the performance.

Honestly, I love it.

Checking on everyone's scenes isn't too hard, and it's fun seeing what they're working on. Anthony's doing Samuel L. Jackson's final monologue from *Pulp Fiction*, which includes a level of profanity I had to push the teachers to permit. Brian Anderson, I'll grudgingly admit, is doing a pretty nice job directing and starring in a scene from *Rosencrantz and Guildenstern Are Dead*. The only possible problem is Courtney, who's putting on something from *Cats*. Why. Just why.

With the showcase at the end of the week, I'm pleased with the progress on my own scene. Today's rehearsal went well. My instincts were right in casting Kasey, and I have a hunch that after seeing her performance, Jody will give her the lead in the fall play next year. Tyler's obviously stepped into the role like he was born to play Willy, and he and Jenna pair really well. Even Owen's holding his own—and I have a feeling he'll cut a nice figure in a 1940s suit.

"Perfect, guys," I yell from the back of the room. "See you all tomorrow."

They shuffle off the stage while I walk forward to collect the few props we're working with. I reach down to pick up a briefcase Tyler's knocked over, and out of the corner of my eye I notice Madeleine hovering by the door. I figure she's waiting for Tyler, and I take an extra-long time returning to my seat and packing my bag, busying myself in the hope she'll leave before I have to pass her. I know Madeleine feels horrible, and I don't enjoy that she's suffering, but I'm not ready to face her. I can't help the hurt I feel whenever I think of what she confessed to me.

"Megan?" I hear her voice right behind me, and I fumble the pen I was stuffing into my bag.

I straighten up, glancing around the room to find everyone else gone except Owen. He's standing near the back door, watching me warily. I silently plead with him not to leave me here to deal with this conversation on my own. Not answering Madeleine, I brush past her and head for the door.

She's undeterred. "Can we talk?" she says to my back.

"I'm busy right now," I get out. I hear her footsteps trailing after mine, and I realize if I go to my car right now, she'll just follow me. Madeleine is nothing if not persistent. Time to take action.

Instead of going to the door, I course-correct toward the stage. "Owen," I say urgently, coming up with a bullshit theatrical criticism on the spot. "We need to—rethink Biff's emotional progression in the end of the scene."

Owen, whom I internally thank for waiting by the door this whole time, hesitates uncertainly. I give him a pointed look and glance at Madeleine. His face softens as he understands. "Yeah, do you want me to run the lines, and you can tell me where it goes wrong?" he asks, dropping his bag and walking to the stage.

"That'd be great," I practically sigh in relief.

Madeleine rolls her eyes, understanding what's going on here. I should've known I'm not a good enough actress to sell this excuse. "Please? It'll only take a second," she begs while Owen climbs onto the stage, looking thoroughly uncomfortable.

I ignore her. "Whenever you're ready, Owen."

"He did like me. Always liked—" he begins before Madeleine cuts him off.

"Enough, Megan." She walks up to the stage. "This is so typically you. Something goes wrong, and you're ready to move on like our friendship was never important to you." The sudden fire in her voice stops me. It's not something I hear often from poised, polished Madeleine. Not something anyone hears often. "I'm your best friend," she continues, "and I made a mistake."

"Forgetting to return a library book is a mistake," I scoff. "And yeah, you were my best friend, but—Owen, where do you think you're going?" He's inching toward the side door, trying to escape. He turns back, his expression pained.

"I'm *still* your best friend," Madeleine returns. "I'm still the girl who was there for you when your stepmom moved in, who pulled all-nighters blocking scenes with you in your room, who picked you up from a hundred rehearsals when you didn't have a car. You remember when you asked me if being perfect was exhausting?" She pauses, but she doesn't sound like she's waiting for an answer. Her anger has faded, and her eyes fill with tears. "Well, now you know I'm not. What's exhausting is having to look like I am, having to live up to everyone's expectations. Sometimes I feel like if even one person figures out the truth, I'll—disappear. I know lying to you was worse than kissing Tyler, but I couldn't tell you. I couldn't watch the person who means the most to me realize I'm not who she thought I was."

I say nothing, weighing her words. I want to forgive

her because it's obvious how terrible she feels, and I'm no stranger to forgiving people who've hurt me. I really liked Anthony, but I forgave him for dating me when he knew he had a thing for guys. He wasn't out and wanted to keep up appearances, and I sympathized with his situation. I even forgave Tyler for dumping me for my best friend, and I guess I've already forgiven him again for cheating on me.

But Madeleine hurt me worse than any boyfriend, because almost every boyfriend isn't supposed to be forever. Madeleine and I were.

She wipes her eyes, her 4.0-GPA, after-school-volunteer composure returning. "That's what I wanted to say. If it's worth anything, I'm sorry and I miss you."

With that, she walks toward the door.

Owen shifts uncomfortably on his feet. I watch his eyes flit from me to her and back.

I don't want to give up on Madeleine. I don't know if she's made this right or not—I don't know if she could ever make this right—but sometimes not giving up on somebody means forgiving them even when it feels like the hardest thing in the world. If I want Madeleine and me to be forever, I can't let her leave feeling like her apology was worth nothing.

"Wait," I call after her.

She stops just short of the door. Slowly she turns, her eyes expectant but guarded, like she's not daring to hope. I walk off the stage to where she's standing, and despite how she's crossed her arms, I step forward and wrap her in a hug. She stiffens, startled for a second, before wriggling her arms free and hugging me back.

"I get it," I say over her shoulder. "You could never disappear." She hugs me tighter, and I hear her sniffle. I hold her for a minute longer until her breathing comes more evenly. "You even had the perfect apology, stupid," I add with a chuckle.

I feel her laugh into my shoulder.

Madeleine and I take a detour to the bathroom so we don't look like emotional wrecks when we get home. She's a renowned ugly crier, a reputation earned amid the A-minus-in-AP-Euro debacle of sophomore year. I'm not faring much better, my mascara streaking black lines down my face like I'm in an emo music video.

We part ways in the hallway after we've put ourselves together. Walking back to the drama room, I run into Owen, who's coming out the door in the opposite direction.

"Owen!" I say, surprised. "You're still here."

"Uh, yeah. You left your stuff in there." He holds up my bag and jacket.

"Thanks. You didn't have to wait for me." I take my things from his outstretched hand. "You want to go get pizza? I was going to drop in on Anthony."

"That depends." Owen grins. "Do you have a tearful reconciliation with him scheduled for today, too?"

I laugh. "Nope, I got that one done a couple weeks ago." We walk toward the front of the Arts Center, and I pull out my phone. "I'll text Will. He should come, too. I know how much you love to watch us flirt."

"It's practically an extracurricular activity," Owen returns, giving me a sideways glance. "I could probably put it on my college applications by now."

I roll my eyes. When I begin typing the message, he reaches over and covers the screen with his hand.

"Please," he says with mock desperation. "Call him. By the time he deciphers your mangled stream of abbreviations and dropped punctuation, we'll be there."

"Will understands me just fine," I say indignantly, shoving him lightly. But the idea of getting Will on the phone does sound good. I hit the CALL icon, pointedly ignoring Owen's triumphant smirk. It's a couple rings before Will picks up.

"Oh. Hey, Megan?" Will's voice sounds distracted.

"Hey. Owen and I are going to Verona. Meet us there in fifteen?" Owen holds the door for me, and we walk out into the quad.

"Now?" Will says in my ear. "I'm, um, kind of busy. I have to run some errands for set crew."

"It's seven at night, Will," I say more softly.

"Yeah, we're really behind." I think I hear his voice take on a bit of a defensive edge.

I want to be the cool girlfriend who doesn't mind stuff like this, who doesn't blink when her boyfriend has other plans, who doesn't overanalyze whether he's avoiding her. But I can't hide how much the brush-off deflates me. "You've been kind of busy a lot lately," I hear myself say.

He exhales over the line. "I know. I'm sorry. We'll do something this weekend," he promises. "Once the showcase is over."

I hear the sincerity in his tone, and the idea of a real date this weekend replaces my worry about his reluctance tonight. I glance at Owen walking beside me. "Okay. I'm going to make Owen help me come up with something awesome for us to do."

Owen looks back at me, his eyes wide and horrified. "I am *not* helping Will get laid."

I cover the mic on the bottom of my phone. "What about *me*?" I ask Owen, batting my eyes. "Will you help me get laid?" His ears redden, and he speeds into the parking lot a couple steps ahead of me.

"Huh?" Will's voice pulls me back to the phone. "Uh. Yeah. Okay. I'll talk to you tomorrow."

"Sounds good." I drop my phone into my bag and catch up to Owen. It's night, and the parking lot's single light casts the pavement in orange. "Meet you over there," I half shout to him in the fog now rolling through the trees.

"Or you could give me a ride?" He's stopped next to the light pole.

The moment he says it, I notice mine is the only car in the school lot. "Yeah, of course." I remember the time I saw him walking to school and he refused the ride I offered him. "Do you walk every day?" I contemplate the distances. From Owen's house to mine and mine to school . . . "Isn't your house, like, four miles from here?" I open my car door.

He goes to the passenger door and gets in next to me.

"Yeah, my mom usually needs the car. One of her jobs is on one end of town, the other on . . . the other." He shrugs. "I do like the time to think. It's why I don't take the bus."

Impressed and feeling very lucky for my old Volkswagen, I say nothing. We pull out of the parking lot and drive the rest of the way in silence. Past a certain time of day, the roads in Stillmont get eerily quiet. There aren't many restaurants in town, and most people eat at home, which is why there's not much of a dinner rush—and why we end up at places like Verona Pizza when we do dine out.

Shall I compare thee to a $4.99 breadsticks platter? reads the sign lit on a backdrop of the forest when we pull up.

Inside, Anthony catches sight of Owen and me and escorts us to one of the booths lining the far wall. We pass Eric wiping a table, and I tap Anthony on the shoulder from behind. "Hey, how's—" I catch myself before I say his name. "Nope, not going to mention you-know-who."

"Voldemort?" Owen asks, grinning unhelpfully.

"Knock it off, Owen." I smack him on the shoulder, and we take our seats on opposite sides of the booth.

Anthony smiles at me. "It's okay." Glancing over his shoulder in Eric's direction, he drops his voice. "He's been giving me weird looks today, actually." I stay silent but raise my eyebrows knowingly. Catching the look and rolling his eyes, Anthony says, "I have to get your drinks."

I turn to Owen, who's been watching our conversation with writerly interest. "Okay, date ideas," I say, opening the Notes app on my phone. "Let's go."

"Do we have to?" he groans.

"Please, Owen? I need your help." I smile at him coquettishly.

"*My* help? Girlfriend who lives in Italy, remember?" His brow rises with wry incredulity. "I don't exactly have dating experience. And definitely none in Stillmont."

Okay, he has a point. Anthony drops off two Sprites, then leaves before we have the chance to order. "But you know Will," I say to Owen, taking a sip of flat soda. *Fuck this place. Really.*

"Yet somehow I've never taken Will out on a date," he replies, sounding amused.

"Come on. If Cosima suddenly came to town, where would be the first place you'd take her? Besides your bedroom, of course." I try for my usual provocative nonchalance. But to my genuine surprise, the joke tastes bitter on my tongue. The idea of some beautiful, foreign girl in Owen's bedroom isn't exactly hilarious.

Owen, however, doesn't seem fazed. His eyes have gone distant while he considers. "I'd take her to Birnam Wood Books," he announces after a second.

I flush despite myself. "I love that place!"

Owen's eyes find mine, and I can tell he's pleased. "But it's not Will's thing."

"Oh." I push aside my disappointment. *I* thought he liked it. "What about the old movie theater downtown?"

"The Constantine?" he says immediately.

"Do you think he'd like that?"

He pauses and finally shakes his head. "I tried to convince

him to go once to a Jean-Luc Godard screening, but he wasn't into it."

"Well, what *does* he like?" I ask, exasperated. "Paintball? Thai food? Strip clubs? Please let it not be strip clubs."

"Concerts?" Owen sounds like he's guessing. "He's mentioned the all-ages club on Route 46. You know, the one where college students pretend they're DJs on the weekend."

I wince. "I hate that place. Why is this so hard?" I open the Internet on my phone and search "best date spots in Stillmont." Before the page loads, Anthony swings by and drops a tray of pizza on our table. Or—*pizzas*. There's a whole pie's worth of slices on the platter, but each appears to have come from the remnants of a different table's meal.

"What the hell is this?" I ask, pushing apart two of the obviously disparate slices with a tentative finger.

"It looks like free pizza." Anthony shoots me a reproving look. Owen swallows a smile.

"From *other people's tables*?"

Owen reaches for a slice. "It looks delicious." He piles enthusiasm on the word. I watch in horror as he takes a bite of what I vaguely recognize was once a Benvolio's Banquet.

Anthony glances at me as if to say *told you so* before he walks away, presumably to check on his other tables. Since I'm definitely going nowhere near the undoubtedly plague-ridden pizza, I pick up my phone to find that the search results have loaded. I tap the top one, which looks promising. It's a list of "Ten Places to Date in Stillmont" from the *Josephine County Courier*.

"Owen, come over here." I slide to make room on my side of the booth.

He doesn't move. "But I'm eating," he protests through a mouthful.

"Well, bring your reject pizza with you." I pat the seat next to me. With an exasperated grunt I know he doesn't mean, Owen carries his plate and pizza with him, and sits down next to me. His elbow brushes mine, and just like that I'm very aware of how short this bench is. It's probably meant to hold nine-year-olds.

I scroll down the list, feeling him looking over my shoulder. Birnam Wood Books, the Constantine, and the club on Route 46 go by. With Stillmont's size, I guess I shouldn't be surprised there's not a ton of places for this sort of thing.

Owen stops me in the middle of one final halfhearted scroll, his hand grazing mine. "I've been there," he says, setting his pizza down and pointing to an entry called Bishop's Peak.

"Where's there?" I study the photo. It's of a campground on a mountain overlooking a forest. The view is ridiculous, honestly. Judging by how much higher it is than the dense greenery below it, it must take hours to hike there.

"It's the end of this trail," he says, his shoulder pressing against mine. "It's beautiful and quiet. It would be the perfect place to take someone if you want to be alone with them."

I tilt my head to look at him. "It sounds like you're speaking from experience." I raise an eyebrow.

He laughs, and I realize I feel him shaking all down the

length of my side. "No, I was just there to write. I definitely did not get lucky up there."

"Well, we should do something about that." It's out of my mouth before I fully realize what it sounds like I'm implying. Owen stiffens.

But he's not the only one. The flirtatious stuff I say is always designed to put guys on edge and intrigue them, to make them think about me in a way they might not have. But this time, it backfired. *This* time, I'm unable to think about anything but where my skin touches Owen's below my sleeve. My face gets hot, and I realize I'm blushing at my own joke.

I feel an unfamiliar urge to put distance between the two of us, but I'm penned in by the wall. Instead, I settle for clearing the air. "It sounds like it would be a great date spot," I say haltingly. I uncomfortably rub the Ophelia bracelet from Will.

"It's where I'd take you," Owen replies quickly. Realizing what he's said, he stutters, "I mean, where I'd—where'd you—where Will should take you."

Well, now we've both gone and said way too much. I have to smile. Nudging his shoulder, I watch his ears go that delightful, familiar shade of red. "You and I *should* go there." His eyes widen. "To brainstorm for your play," I add with a wink.

I lean farther into him, and it feels like giving in to how much I like the sound of the things we've suggested. I don't exactly know why, but I'm drawn to Owen. I probably have been for a while. I guess the reason my flirtatious joke backfired is that it wasn't a joke at all.

Except I have a boyfriend. Having to remind myself of that is as unexpected as everything else tonight. In all of my relationships, I'm never the one to forget her commitment.

Will. I want to go to Bishop's Peak with Will. I'm going there with Will.

Owen's face is still close to mine, our shoulders still pressed tightly together. And when I lift my gaze to meet his, I find him watching me with inevitability in his eyes, like he knows exactly what I was close to doing because he's been waiting for it.

Which is why I blurt out, "I need to pee."

He pulls back, looking confused. "Oh," he says.

"So I need to get out," I say heatedly, beginning to step over him. My lingering confusion has given way to frustration with myself, frustration about not knowing what I want. Or worse, worrying that I might know exactly what I want.

"*Oh.*" He stumbles out of the booth. "Were you just going to climb over me?"

I slide down and straighten up. "You say that like it'd be a bad thing," I say, stepping past him, attempting to force my voice into its old flirty flippancy. I don't think it works. Not wanting to hear Owen's reply, I dart in the direction of the bathroom, nearly colliding with a group of middle-school girls.

I barrel through the swinging door. Like every other inch of this restaurant, the bathroom's walls are covered in Shakespeare verses. I face the mirror and ignore them, the way I always do.

I turn on the faucet and splash cold water on my face.

"This is ridiculous," I tell myself out loud in the mirror. *I do not like Owen Okita. He's a great friend, but he's not my type. Tyler, Dean, Will, they're my type. Owen's bookish, quiet, and constantly preoccupied with his journal,* I remind myself.

Okay, he's kind of cute, with his startled smile and the way his ears redden every time I—

"Stop," I order myself. "I have a boyfriend." He's overcommitted, but my boyfriend nonetheless. Owen has an imaginary girlfriend. We're friends. Nothing else.

I turn and head for the stall. But one word written in several places jumps out at me from the quotes on the wall. "LOVE is merely a madness." "I know no ways to mince it in LOVE, but directly to say, 'I LOVE you.'" "LOVE comforteth like sunshine after rain." "The course of true LOVE never did run smooth." Whoever bothered to paint them there used obnoxiously iridescent colors everywhere they wrote *love*.

I slam the stall door behind me.

As I'm about to sit down, I hear the bathroom door open and close, followed by a low voice asking, "Megan?"

"Eric?" I nearly stumble. That could have been tragic.

"I—I know," he rushes to reply. "This is bad."

"Why— What are you doing in here?" Why does this keep happening? Why do people get the impression cornering me in a stall is a good time to start a conversation? I pull up my pants.

"It's about Anthony." Eric walks farther into the bathroom. Grudgingly, I unlock the stall and step out to face him. "I didn't want him to overhear. He's pissed, isn't he?" he asks nervously. I open my mouth to answer, but he continues. "Of course he is. He probably hates me. You probably hate me, too. I promise I wasn't using Anthony because I can keep him a secret. I don't *want* to keep him a secret, it's just— My dad called. He wanted to know where I was. I think he guessed, and— He doesn't— And Anthony— He's, you know—"

I interrupt him. "Eric, I feel like you should be saying this to"—I glance toward the door—"someone else?"

He vehemently shakes his head, and he looks defeated. "Not while he's avoiding me. If he doesn't want to talk to me, I don't want to force him. I just want him to know what happened." He raises his gaze from the floor and looks at me. "If you could just—"

"Eric, it's not my place to get between the two of you," I say firmly. What Anthony told me was that he wanted to hit pause on things with Eric, and I promised him I wouldn't meddle or rush him along. Telling Eric anything about Anthony's feelings would undermine his wishes and break my word.

"But—" Eric starts.

"No buts. I'm rooting for you, Eric, but you have to talk to him yourself," I say with finality.

Eric nods forlornly. "I just really like him," he says after a moment's pause. Knocking his knuckles once on the sink, he turns to leave.

"Eric," I call him back. "Give me your phone."

"Why?" Confusion narrows his eyes, but he holds out his phone.

"For when it goes well with Anthony," I tell him while I type my number into his contacts. "I'll want to hear about it

214

without you cornering me in the bathroom." I pass the phone back to Eric, whose expression has lifted into a smile.

He gives me a nod and pushes open the door. Briefly, I wonder if anyone notices him exiting the girls' bathroom before I go back into the stall to do what I came here for. I follow Eric out a couple minutes later.

I start to return to our table, but I stop when I see Owen's back on his side of his booth, writing in his journal. I don't know if I wanted him to have moved or not, but it doesn't seem like what a guy would do if he was into whatever was happening between us before.

It hurts a little. I consider dropping into the seat next to him, our shoulders touching like they were minutes ago. Out of an impulse that's part instinct and part something deeper, I want to recapture the way it felt to be pressed against him while he looked at me with guarded anticipation. To—

No. Owen moved for a reason. I should respect that. It felt good to honor what Anthony wanted regarding Eric, and Owen deserves the same consideration. Even if I did like him—which I *probably* don't, not really, not in a way that could last—I wouldn't want to push him into something he obviously doesn't want. Not to mention the fact *he has a girlfriend*.

I slide into the booth opposite him. Feeling bold bordering on reckless, I grab a slice of lukewarm Montague Meat Lovers. Owen doesn't look up from whatever he's writing.

"I'm going to take Will to the club of the college DJs," I nonchalantly announce.

"Wait, why?" Owen's head pops up. Blue ink stains his

throat just beneath the corner of his jaw, and I wonder what he was mulling over while he rubbed his neck. "What happened to Bishop's Peak?" he asks tentatively, either relieved or disappointed.

I'm not going to bother wondering which it is—I just want things back to normal. "You should have it. If you call it quits with the imaginary girlfriend and settle for a humble Stillmont girl, you're going to need a place to get it on."

He says nothing, but he gives his startled smile, and his ears redden.

EIGHTEEN

BENVOLIO: *Alas that love, so gentle in his view,*

Should be so tyrannous and rough in proof!

ROMEO: *Alas that love, whose view is muffled still,*

Should without eyes see pathways to his will!

I.i.174–7

IT'S THE FINAL MOMENTS OF BRIAN ANDERSON and Jason Mitchum's *Rosencrantz and Guildenstern Are Dead* scene. It never fails to surprise me how tranquil everything seems on stage, how measured and quiet. The actors are the only moving pieces on the fixed world of the set, in front of the audience watching in hushed stillness.

Backstage, it's chaos. But I'm not complaining. Despite the nonstop commotion in the wings of the theater, the Senior Showcase is going beautifully, and I love the frenzy of the minutes before a performance.

In the girls' dressing room, I step over piles of midcentury coats and medieval dresses in search of a tie. I spot it sticking out underneath someone's bright purple bra. I pull the tie out and rush for the door. But before I reach it, I glance into the mirror and have to stop.

Jenna Cho, aka my Linda Loman, is smoothing her hair,

seemingly oblivious to the fact she's wearing only one eye-lash.

"Jenna!" I hiss, and she looks at me in the mirror. "Check your eyes. I think you're missing something."

"Ohmygod," she gasps, fumbling for her makeup bag.

I dart from the room and duck into the green room down the hall. It's wall-to-wall insanity. With everyone else's scenes done, the rest of the actors have begun sneaking drinks from the flasks some of the guys smuggled in, still dressed in a wild array of half-costumes and stage makeup. My eyes quickly find Kasey Markowitz in the corner, muttering to herself, re-hearsing her lines.

"Kasey. Here." I hand her the tie. She's dressed in a suit, her hair tucked up under a fedora. She grabs the tie without pausing in her line. "You need help with that?" I ask, the syl-lables stringing together so they sound like one word.

"Nope." Effortlessly, she wraps the tie around her collar and winds it into a perfect knot.

I don't have time to be surprised before a stagehand taps me on the shoulder. "The briefcase prop," he says breathless-ly. It's little Andrew Mehta, a sophomore.

I wait for him to say more. "What about it?" I fire back when he doesn't.

"It's not on the props table."

I sigh. *Of course it isn't.* "Try the guys' dressing room. Tyler keeps forgetting to return it to props." Andrew rushes off, and I find Owen near the door. He's frantically fiddling with his collar, and I have to laugh.

"Need a hand?" I gently tease, coming up beside him and

wrapping my fingers in the tie he's mangled into nothing resembling a proper knot.

He won't meet my eyes. "Uh, thanks." He fidgets with his cuffs like he can hardly stand still while I undo the damage.

"You're going to be great," I reassure him, knowing stage fright when I see it. I begin the knot and find Owen's now looking down at me—I guess I never noticed he's about six feet tall, much taller than I am—a distracted, unconvincing smile on his face.

"*We* will be, the whole cast. You've done an incredible job pulling this together."

I feel warmth spread through me, but I focus on evening out the ends of the tie. "Hey, have you seen Will?"

He looks away again. "He said he might be a little late."

"What?" I pause in mid-knot. Will didn't tell me he'd be late. Once more I hear the vicious voice in my head telling me to be the cool girlfriend, but this isn't just a trip to Verona. "This is the showcase. This is, like, important . . ."

Owen reaches up to his collar and places a hand on mine. Gently, he squeezes my fingers. His wrist is dotted with familiar blue ink, and even though he's in costume I know his notebook and pen aren't far away. The observation relaxes me somehow. When I look up, his eyes have returned to me. "He knows. Don't worry about him," he says delicately. "The show will go perfectly."

His hand is still on mine, and I should pull away, but I'm having a hard time remembering why I like Will and not Owen. I rub the stain on his wrist. "Did no one teach you how to use a pen?"

219

He blinks once, then his eyes find my finger wiping ineffectually at the blue spot. "I press down on them too hard," he says, his voice a controlled murmur. He doesn't remove his hand. "I can wash it off if you want."

"No, I like it," I say, but I don't stop kneading my thumb across his wrist. Distantly, the applause for the previous scene sounds through the wall. I drop my hand. "That's our cue."

Owen's eyes flicker, like he's just remembered where he is. "Right."

I usher him in the direction of the stage right stairs, then sweep my eyes over the green room for inattentive cast members. Finding no one, I make my own way backstage, noticing faint blue smudges now coloring my fingertips. I smile even as my chest constricts with the mixture of excitement and nerves that begin every performance.

My actors have lined up in the wings, and I watch them file on, Tyler with his briefcase. Peering around the curtain, I look into the audience. But the stage lights are on, and I can only make out the first couple rows. I search the faces of drama underclassmen, proud grandparents, and the occasional teacher.

Nowhere do I find Will.

Fighting disappointment, I turn my attention back to my scene. "Call out the name Willy Loman and see what happens! Big shot!" Tyler proclaims with desperate bravado.

"All right, Pop," Owen replies, placating.

Somebody sneezes in one of the front rows, and I whip my head back to the audience to find a mortified-looking, allergy-stricken freshman sitting next to—*Rose?*

She's by herself, Erin nowhere in sight, and she's put herself together annoyingly perfectly for a woman eight months pregnant. Her hair's done up in a neat bun, and she's wearing the dangly earrings she can't around Erin and a long-sleeve dress that highlights just how little weight she's gained.

Dad's in New York, doing something house-related. I guess Rose would have had to drop Erin off at Aunt Charlotte's, and she came without Dad bringing her. I want to be grateful—she was kind to even look up when the showcase was, let alone make arrangements to come. Yet instead, what I feel is guilty, even a little bitter.

If not for the divorce, it would've been my mom in the front row. She was the one to drag my dad and me to SOTI performances, and she even brought me to the occasional Stillmont High School production when I was younger. She would have loved to be here. Somehow Rose showing up tonight feels like she's encroaching on my mom's and my relationship in a way Rose living under our roof doesn't.

"Don't yell at her, Pop, will ya?" Owen's incensed voice pulls my focus back to the stage. In the moment, because of the way I've blocked the scene and the way Owen's squaring his shoulders, he actually looks bigger than Tyler on the stage. He's bringing an intensity to the final lines that he hadn't in rehearsals, and I'm impressed.

Tyler hunches over and drops his voice to deliver Willy's final line. "Give my best to Bill Oliver—he may remember me." A couple of people in the audience covertly try to wipe their eyes in the heavy pause that follows.

221

The lights come back on, and the audience applauds as my actors take their bows. Feeling the heady rush of a perfect performance, I begin to step back from the curtain—but then I catch Tyler beckoning me on stage, wearing the ridiculous grin he gets every time he's in front of an adoring audience.

"No way," I mouth while Tyler continues to wave me on.

I watch him—unbelievably—exchange a knowing glance with Owen, who darts to where I'm hiding behind the curtain and, before I know it, hauls me by the elbow onto the stage. He holds me firmly in place under the spotlight.

"Could we give an extra-loud round of applause for Megan Harper," Tyler shouts to the crowd. "Who's probably going to kill me because of this, but not right now. Too many witnesses." The audience laughs, still under Tyler's spell. I can't blame them. Even if he's right and I will kill him after this.

"Not only is Megan an extraordinary director, she put together the entire Senior Showcase," he continues. "She's done amazing work in four years of bringing drama to life on this stage—and giving me more opportunities than I deserve to make a fool of myself in front of you guys." He unleashes his cockiest grin for the span of a second before his features settle into something sincere. "It's been an honor working with her."

Nothing in my history with Tyler prepares me for the way he looks at me then—with genuine respect. A stagehand comes out of the wings bearing a ridiculous bouquet of white orchids, and Owen gives my arm a reassuring squeeze. I turn to look at him, but he's already releasing me and stepping back out of the spotlight. Leaving me alone at the center of everything.

Heat rises in my cheeks. I must have taken the flowers from Andrew Mehta's hands, because distantly I'm aware of the petals pressed against my shoulder while the audience applauds me.

By choosing to be a director, I've tried to avoid moments like these—moments where everyone's eyes are on me, where my classmates' cheers and Rose's loving smile are for me. I thought this would feel like an unwelcome reminder of what I'll inevitably lose when everyone moves on. But it doesn't.

It feels like everything I've missed out on.

I hear someone backstage shout, "Get it!" and I know without a shred of doubt it's Anthony, whose *Pulp Fiction* monologue was, for the record, amazing. Jenna and Kasey laugh behind me, and in the moments that follow, the applause gradually dies down. Everyone begins to shuffle out of the auditorium, everyone except Madeleine. She pushes through the crowd to reach the stage, her smile lit up with pride.

I jump down off the stage next to her. "You on your way to meet Tyler in the boys' dressing room?" I ask, waiting for her to flush.

Which she does. *"No,"* she protests. "I'm waiting for my incredibly talented, gorgeous, director-extraordinaire best friend." She sweeps me up in a crushing hug.

"You're the best for coming," I say into her sweatshirt. "Now seriously, I saw Tyler go backstage."

Madeleine releases me from the hug and glances behind me, hesitating.

"I have to go talk to Rose," I reassure her. "You should congratulate Tyler. I'll find you later." She squeezes me in a final hug, but it's all the encouragement she needs, and she bounces to the stairs up to the stage. I join the crush of people filing into the quad. Hoping to find Will—I figure he has to be here somewhere—I do a quick sweep of the crowd outside. I frown when I don't find him, but then again, it's nearly impossible to tell who all's here.

Rose, however, stands out. She's waiting next to the refreshments table, and despite how packed the courtyard is, everyone's giving her pregnant stomach a three-foot radius. She looks lost. I understand why—she's never done this kind of thing before.

I walk over to her, not really knowing what I'm going to say. I want to thank her for coming, but we don't often talk one-on-one. It's not like I have a script for this sort of thing. Besides, I still feel like I'm betraying my mom by being happy Rose is here.

Her eyes light up when she spots me coming out of the crowd. Instead of telling her something appreciative, what ends up coming out when I reach her is, "Where's Erin?"

Rose blinks, then her composure returns. "I figured we should wait until she's three before we expose her to *Death of a Salesman*'s suburban nihilism," she replies, and despite myself, I laugh. Encouraged, she smiles gently. "It was wonderful to watch your scene. The whole thing, really. You put on quite an event. I loved your staging—how Willy was increasingly isolated from the rest of the actors as his advice grew more delusional."

I reach for words, surprised. It's precisely what I was going for. "You—know the play?"

"I was an English major in college," she says with a smile. Betrayal of Mom or not, I feel guilty I didn't know that about Rose. There's probably a lot I don't know about her, I realize. Where she grew up, her favorite movie, whether she's ever been in a play herself, why she chose to be a paralegal.

"It was really nice of you to come," I finally say, knowing I should've just done so earlier.

"I'm glad I could." She nods to something behind me, her smile turning knowing and playful. "Looks like Biff Loman wants to talk to you, which I think is my cue. I'll see you at home."

"Yeah. See you there."

"You want me to take your flowers?" She points to the bouquet I forgot I was holding.

"Oh." I hold them out to her awkwardly. "Probably a good idea. Thanks," I say, then turn to find Owen a few feet behind me, fidgeting with his tie.

I walk up to him and tug it out of his hands. "You were incredible," I tell him, meaning it. He smiles for only a second before his nervousness returns. He looks just like he did in the green room, wracked with stage anxiety. Except the scene's over. "What's wrong?"

His eyes drop. "Could we, uh, talk somewhere?"

"Definitely, but give me a second. I haven't found Will yet. I should let him know before I disappear on him." I look past Owen to search the quad, where there's still no sign of Will, but Owen takes my hand. My eyes latch on to his.

"That's what I wanted to talk to you about." His voice is lower, urgent now. I feel a tremor tighten my chest.

"Owen, what's going on?"

"We should talk somewhere private."

He gently leads me by the hand back into the auditorium, up the stairs to the vacant backstage, and toward the green room. It's empty except for Brian Anderson, who nods with a smile I'm too wound-up to return. "Kickass job, Megan," he says, stepping over the ears from Courtney's cat costume on his way out.

"Thanks," I say distractedly. "Your Rosencrantz was kickass too, Brian."

"Totally, right?" He shuts the door behind him.

Without a moment's hesitation, I round on Owen. "You've been acting weird today." A horrible explanation drops onto my heart like a lead weight. "Is this about the other day at Verona?"

"No, it's not— Wait, what?" His eyes betray no impression he's bothered by our possibly flirtatious, definitely awkward discussion of Bishop's Peak.

"Never mind," I say, relieved.

Owen goes on, his words coming in a rush. "Will texted before the performance telling me he wasn't going to make it. I should have told you then, but I didn't want you to worry about him instead of watching your scene. You've put so much work into tonight." He looks off into a corner of the room. I watch his jaw clench and the tendons in his neck tense visibly. He's not nervous, he's angry. "I hate Will for doing this. You're my friend, and I don't want to hide stuff from you—"

"Owen," I cut him off, wanting him to just get it over with. "What is it?"

He produces his phone from his pocket, and I catch a glimpse of a photo of the Brooklyn Bridge on the screen—probably a place he took Cosima when they were in New York together for the theater program. Wordlessly, he opens the Messages app and passes me the phone.

The conversation on the screen is with Will. My eyes land on his text reading, **Hey Owen . . . Cover for me, k? I don't think I'm going to make it.** It's time-stamped twenty minutes before we went on stage. Before I fixed Owen's tie and he told me Will would be late.

I scroll down. Owen instantly texted him back. **What the hell?? What could you possibly be doing besides going to your girlfriend's show?**

Will didn't reply until ten minutes ago. **I'm at Alyssa's man! Not leaving anytime soon ;)**

A winky face. It's stunning how hard the semicolon and parenthesis knock the wind out of me.

I return Owen's phone, unable to read the screen a second longer. Will's words repeat in my head like a broken record. Utterly broken. *At Alyssa's. Not leaving anytime soon.* I expected this. I expected this. Didn't I? Even if I'd begun to wonder about . . . someone else, I put away those questions because I cared about Will. Or convinced myself to care. Why was I stupid enough to believe he cared about me?

Owen's watching me with concerned eyes. "I'm sorry, Megan. He's an asshole," he says, and I can tell he means it. I'm not ready to reply. "This is the first I've ever heard of him and Alyssa," he goes on. "I had no idea. Otherwise, I would have said something."

"It's fine," I get out, hearing how hollow my voice sounds. "It's not like I haven't been through this before."

"Don't do that." He frowns. "Don't pretend it's fine, because I know it's not. What Will did was messed up, and you *should* be pissed at him."

The empty ache fills with anger. But not at Will. "I know how to handle a breakup, Owen," I snap, knowing he doesn't deserve my resentment but not bothering to control it. "Don't tell me what I *should be* feeling."

He flinches. "It's not— What I mean is you deserve better."

As quickly as it flared up, my anger collapses. "My boyfriend didn't think so." I feel tears choking my voice, and my eyes start to burn. *Damn it*, I thought I was past being hurt by this kind of thing.

"Will is a moron," Owen says gently. "I'm definitely not giving him any more lyrics for his stupid band." A tearful laugh escapes me, and Owen smiles. "What you deserve is to go out and celebrate this incredible show you put together. Everyone's going to Verona. I'll buy you a real pizza—you know, one we ordered, not someone's leftovers."

I smile weakly. "But what about your costume? Don't you need to change?" I nod to the gray suit and pinstriped tie he's still wearing.

"I'm not worried about it." He shrugs. "Besides, I won't look any more ridiculous than the employees." He holds the door open for me.

"Thanks," I say. He wraps an arm around my shoulder, and I know he understands I don't just mean the door.

Walking into the empty auditorium, I remember every time I've joked with Madeleine, Anthony, and even Owen about my "curse," my "whirlwind romances," my endless stream of breakups. It's less funny now. It's easier to joke when I'm not feeling this, when I'm not feeling replaceable. But the truth is, I have no reason to hope I won't be playing this role forever. To hope one day I'll be the one chosen and not just the girl before.

NINETEEN

FRIAR LAWRENCE: *Confusion's cure lives not*

In these confusions.

IV.v.71–2

I KNOW ABOUT ALYSSA. WE'RE DONE, I text Will the following day. I silence my phone, not wanting to read whatever he replies, and in a final moment of closure, I slide off Will's Ophelia bracelet and throw it behind me.

I'm sitting in my car in front of Luna's Coffee Company, the only coffee shop in town other than Birnam Wood Books and the Starbucks in the mall. It's in the nicer part of Stillmont, up the street from the salon where Madeleine and I had our hair done before junior prom last year. I proposed Randall and I meet here when we coordinated this morning.

It's a testament to the awfulness of my weekend that the prospect of coffee with Randall doesn't sound terrible. I'm here early, but I decide I don't need to spend more time sitting in my car dwelling on Will. I walk in and begin to head for the line, but I stop when I realize Randall's already sitting at a table, giving me a tentative wave. I suppose I shouldn't be surprised he's here early. He sounded especially enthusiastic on the phone this morning.

For whatever reason, he stands up when I reach the table. I try to take a seat, but before I have the chance, he's bending forward for one of those uncomfortable one-armed hugs. "Oh, uh . . ." I stutter, returning his hug.

We sit. It's only then that I notice Randall looks . . . better somehow. He's trimmed his usually overlong curly hair, and it's possible he's lost a couple pounds. He's not wearing one of his customary short-sleeve button-downs and opted for a navy polo instead. His mustache remains, however.

"Thanks for sparing the time to meet me, Megan," he says, grinning bashfully. "I ordered your favorite. Unless your favorite's changed since you visited over the summer." He gestures to the solitary cappuccino on the table.

"Thanks," I say. Despite whatever questions I have about Randall, I can't deny he's thoughtful.

I wait for him to say something. The burden of conversation is on the inviter, right? When a few moments go by and he doesn't, I try the only question coming to mind. "How was the flight?"

He looks startled, like he didn't expect us to talk during this coffee date. "It flew by. I had a full binder of spreadsheets to review," he says as if the one relates in any way to the other.

With no response to that, I wrack my brain for other Randall-related topics while the conversation descends into silence. Finally, one comes. "How's your and Mom's pottery class?" I know I'm fidgeting with the handle on my mug.

"It is terrific," Randall replies unhesitatingly. "Your mother's nearly finished a complete set of bowls for the house."

My mother, finisher of bowls.

"Cool," I say because I have literally no other way to contend with that statement.

"How's *Romeo and Juliet* going?" Randall asks.

I know he's trying. But right now, I'm in no mood to remind myself of playing Juliet on Will's sets, in front of Alyssa whispering behind my back. "It's good," I reply shortly.

He says nothing, and faced with the prospect of having to come up with a third conversation starter, I consider faking a call from my Dad or a forgotten obligation. But I decide to try one final question first. "Why'd your firm send you out to middle-of-nowhere Oregon?"

Randall's demeanor changes visibly. He shifts in his seat, his shoulders rising, and he reaches for a napkin and begins anxiously folding it in his lap. "They, uh, they didn't," he finally says. "It's what I wanted to talk to you about."

If his firm didn't send him to Stillmont, why is he here? "Does Mom know?"

"She doesn't," he replies haltingly, "and I, well, I need you to keep it that way."

"Okay, now you're making me nervous. I don't—"

"I want to propose to your mother," he interrupts.

My hand clenches on the cup of lukewarm cappuccino. "Oh." My mind empties. I'm unable to process what he said. "Um, okay."

Randall's face breaks into a grin. "Okay?"

"Yeah, uh . . . Wait, what?" He's looking at me like I've just done him a huge favor, but I don't know what it is.

"I wanted your permission." His grin falters when he realizes I haven't exactly given it. "You're the most important person in your mother's life, and of course you knew her before I did. I wouldn't feel right trying to build a family with her without your blessing."

The word *family* from Randall flips me upside down and shakes out my thoughts like the pieces of a puzzle. *Family.* Mom and Randall. It's the kind of thought that on most days would have me asking myself all the questions I have for months. If they start a family like Dad and Rose did, where will I fit in? Who will I be except the bump in the road before my parents found the families they wanted?

But today, something's different. My eyes find the place on my wrist where Will's bracelet no longer rests. I know none of my relationships can even begin to compare to what my parents had—years and decades of marriage, of messy effort, of memories stinging and sweet. I've never fallen for someone the way my mom fell for my dad.

Yet I know a piece of her pain. I know what it's like to watch the people you care about replace you and never look back. I've gone through it eight times now. In the hardest moments, when I face my mom and find my reflection, I can't help feeling convinced we'll end up the same in love, forever cast to play the Rosaline in real life. If Randall changes that for her, if he heals even a fraction of the wounds my dad inflicted . . . she should be with him, even if it means starting her own family without me.

I lift my gaze back to Randall. "I think you should definitely propose to my mom. It would make her really happy," I say softly, ignoring how the words ache.

He lets out a breath of relief. "I'm delighted to hear it!" He grins broadly. "I want to do it when the three of us are together. I thought . . . the trip when we're here for your performance in December might be the right time?"

Numb, I force myself to nod. "It sounds perfect."

When I get back to my car, I stupidly check my phone. Force of habit. Six unread messages from Will stare up at me.

Wait, what??

I think you might have heard something and gotten the wrong idea . . . Call me, and I'll explain.

You can't just ignore me, Megan. We at least have to talk.

Fine. You're acting really immature, but if this is what you want, then fine.

I scroll through the first couple, then delete the thread without reading the rest. I delete his number, too, just for good measure.

He and I were supposed to go on our date tonight to the shitty club on Route 46. That won't be happening, which at least spares me from a night amid sweaty, gyrating teenagers and throbbing techno music. With my weekend now pretty much unscheduled, my first thought is to text Madeleine. It's a post-breakup ritual to go to her house, bake homemade Pop-Tarts, and break out the middle-school yearbooks to mock the pictures of the boy in question.

But I hesitate. Madeleine spent the majority of her time with Tyler while I was pursuing Will. I love her, and talking to her would be a comfort, but she's not the one who knows every detail of the relationship. Instead, I find myself remembering the hours spent with Owen discussing even the most insignificant facets of my interactions with Will.

Owen. He's the one who's been there for me through the whole relationship. It's only right he help me with its end.

I drive to his neighborhood on the other end of town. It's nearing nighttime, and the streets are empty. The couple of people out walking are wrapped in coats and scarves, their breath visible under the streetlights. I crank the heat up in my car to compensate for winter settling in.

I park under one of the trees on Owen's street, a couple of houses up from his. Realizing I should probably check if he's busy before arriving on his doorstep, I pull out my phone and send, **hey**, testing the waters.

Hey. You doing okay? he replies a moment later.

my mom's getting married, I watch my thumbs type out and send, not fully knowing why.

It takes Owen longer to respond this time. A couple minutes go by. **Is that good or bad?** he sends.

good i guess. dont want her to be alone. I rub my bracelet-free wrist. It crosses my mind that I drove over here to talk about Will. Yet here I am, talking about my mom after one sentence.

You're not alone either, Megan. Do you want to come over for dinner? It takes him only a few seconds to reply, which is nearly as surprising as what he's said.

i wasnt talking abt me. Once I've sent that, I type out a second text. **but yes i wud thx.**

I'm reasonably certain you were.

I let that one lie, but I'm smiling to myself as I step out of the car. **im outside,** I send, walking up his driveway. He replies a second later.

Outside where?

TWENTY

ROMEO: *Thus with a kiss I die.*

V.iii.120

INSTEAD OF REPLYING, I RING THE DOORBELL. In my billowy floral dress, tights, and a denim jacket, I'm hardly dressed for the weather, and I hug myself while I wait. Running footsteps sound from the other side of the door, followed by Owen's voice.

"Sam, what's the rule about the door?" I hear him yell sternly.

The footsteps stop, and the voice that answers Owen sounds about ten years old. "No opening it without checking who it is first," the voice glumly replies. I step back, smoothing my dress, expecting scrutiny through the small peephole. "It's some girl . . . wearing grandma clothes." I cross my arms, affronted if not a little amused.

"She's pretty," the voice—Sam—continues, redeeming himself. "Prettier than Cosmo."

Ha! I'm going to like Sam.

"It's Cosima," I hear Owen exasperatedly correct him. The door swings open, revealing Owen, his ears their natural shade of red, and a small boy with spiked hair, Owen-y features, and a *Minecraft* T-shirt. *"Very* sorry about my brother," Owen says emphatically, then glances behind me, his lips forming a light smile. "You hang out outside my house often?"

I stride inside, refusing to be embarrassed. "Hey, this is a nice street. Good lighting, great, um—trees."

His grin widens knowingly. "If I'd known how much you liked the *trees*, I would have invited you over more often." He leads me toward the kitchen. "You know you're welcome whenever," he adds after a moment, his voice gentler this time.

In the kitchen, he grabs a striped apron and throws it over his head.

"You're making dinner?" I don't hide my surprise.

He stirs something on a pot on the stove. "Yeah, spaghetti. It's Sam's favorite."

"No, it's not!" Sam bellows from the other room.

Owen chuckles, and I realize they've had this conversation before. "It's his favorite of the things I can make," he explains to me, "which consists of spaghetti and spaghetti." Sam wanders into the kitchen, and Owen points the spoon at me. "Sam, this is my friend Megan. She's going to have dinner with us."

I face Sam, about to give him a wave hello, but he marches right up to me and sticks his hand out. "Nice to meet you," he says formally, shaking my hand in a small but impressive death grip.

"It's nice to meet you, too," I reply. "For your information, no grandmas have ever worn my clothes."

He squints at me. "You sure about that?"

"Sam," Owen warns.

"It's okay." I laugh. "He said I'm prettier than *Cosmo*, so we're cool." I glance at Owen, waiting to see how he'll contend with that, whether he'll defend his girlfriend or put his guest down. I consider it a victory when he wordlessly turns back to the stove and spoons pasta onto the plates.

He carries one into the dining room and places it on the small, scuffed table. Sam clambers into his seat, and I sit down opposite him while Owen returns with the other two plates.

"You're in Owen's play, right?" Sam asks between bites.

My mouth full, Owen replies for me. "Megan's the lead. She's the main character," he clarifies.

Sam's eyes widen, and he looks at me with new respect. "*You're* Juliet?"

"You know *Romeo and Juliet*?" I ask, intrigued. Apparently, a penchant for theater is an Okita family trait.

"Owen told me," Sam answers proudly. "He said it's about this girl who's like the coolest, most beautiful girl everyone's ever seen, and blah blah blah, and she likes some guy, and then everybody dies."

I smile at Owen, not overlooking the adjectives in Sam's summary. "What a deft Shakespearean commentary," I say, still looking at Owen. Then I raise an eyebrow at Sam. "Do *you* think I'll be a good Juliet?"

Sam shrugs. "Owen says you're, like, perfect."

I turn back to Owen, unable to restrain myself from wondering what else he's said about . . . my performance. But before I have the chance to ask, he's leaning over to ruffle his brother's hair. Sam yelps and swats him away, indignant that Owen's messing up his gelled spikes.

"How'd your spelling test go?" Owen asks, withdrawing his hand.

Sam groans, clearly having already forgotten his brother's infraction. "Ninety-eight percent," he mutters resentfully.

"What word did you get wrong?" Owen sounds playfully admonishing.

"Lead, the metal!" Sam pounds an emphatic hand on the table.

Owen laughs. "That one really gives you trouble, huh?"

"Well, Owen," I cut in, "lead's, like, the hardest word ever."

The two Okitas face me, Owen's expression skeptical. "Does that word stump you on your spelling tests, too, Megan?" He's not quite smirking, but the corner of his mouth is upturned.

"Don't be a smartass," I shoot back, then notice Sam's eyes widen. "Sorry," I tell him. "For your information, *Owen*"— I turn back to him—"lead is an inhumanly difficult word. Lead, the metal, is spelled like lead, the verb, which is the present tense of a verb of which the past tense is spelled L-E-D, pronounced led, like the metal, lead," I finish triumphantly.

Owen's smiling now, his mouth half-open in an expression of stunned amusement I don't bother to keep myself from noticing is cute.

"*She* gets it," Sam exclaims, throwing out a hand in my direction.

"I stand reeducated," Owen pronounces, then reaches over

to jostle his brother's shoulder. "Hey, buddy, ninety-eight percent is great. Mom's going to be really proud."

Sam straightens up in his seat, and I realize he's somehow finished all of his spaghetti. "Can I stay up tonight to tell her?"

"*That* depends on if you finish your homework. Quietly, *and* in your room," Owen tells him.

Sam hops off his chair and brings his dish into the kitchen. While he's out of the room, I gesture to where his spotless plate was. "How did he . . . ?" I whisper to Owen.

"He inhales it. I don't know. It's insane," he replies, taking a bite of his own nearly finished dinner.

Sam stomps into the doorway. "You guys aren't going to go *kiss* now, right?" he asks, like the question's a bomb he's been waiting to drop since I got here.

I laugh and dart a glance at Owen, who just points a finger into the hall. "I'm not going to dignify that with a response," he says, doing an impressive job of covering any embarrassment he might be feeling. "Homework. Now." Sam trudges into the hallway wearing a mischievous smirk he definitely didn't learn from Owen.

I spin a forkful of spaghetti. "Sounds like you do this kind of thing often," I say to Owen. "Sweep girls off their feet with the perfect-brother routine, then take them to your room for some *kissing*."

Owen scoffs, obviously playing dumb. "What perfect-brother routine?"

"Oh, please," I say through pasta. "The home-cooked dinner, the helping with his homework. Girls love that."

He feigns surprise. "I had no idea. I've had the perfect chick magnet right here the entire time." He picks up my plate, ever the gentleman, and brings both of our dishes into the kitchen. I walk over to help him. Usually now is when I'd nettle him about Cosima or keep teasing him about Sam's "kissing" remark, but for some indiscernible reason, I don't. Instead, we wash dishes in silence for a couple minutes before he speaks up. "Hey, uh, how are you . . ."

"Since your asshole friend cheated on me?" I supply.

"*Former* asshole friend," he quickly corrects, and I have to smile, knowing I was right when I figured he'd be the one who could lift my spirits.

"I'm okay," I say, and for the first time today I feel it's true. "I sent him a breakup text this afternoon. More than he deserves. Honestly, I'm happier eating spaghetti with you— and Sam, of course—than going to Club Trying-Too-Hard with him." He laughs, and I shrug. "It's for the best. I have a thousand lines to memorize by Monday, and I'm way behind because of the Senior Showcase."

Owen pauses. He takes the towel out of my hand. "You want to stay? I could help," he offers, his voice casual but something searching in his eyes.

I meet them. "It's the Capulet Manor scene. Don't tell Sam, but there's definitely some, uh—kissing involved." *Hm.* I've never known myself to be the kind of girl to stumble over the word *kissing*.

"I'm no Tyler, but I think I'll get the job done." He flashes me a smile, but his phrasing leaves me wordless. *He doesn't mean . . .* No. He's talking about the lines. Definitely the lines.

Like he doesn't know what he's just done to me, he points his thumb over his shoulder. "I have to check on Sam. He plays *Minecraft* if I leave him unsupervised. You want to wait for me in my bedroom?" He looks coy.

And god help me, I blush. "You—your bedroom?"

"Well, where else would we do it?" He walks past me, brushing his shoulder against mine in a move I know is intentional. "Read lines, I mean," he clarifies with a cocked eyebrow.

Wait a second. I follow him into the hall. "I don't believe this," I say to his back. His—*since when?*—well-shouldered, strokeable back.

"Believe what?" he says over his shoulder.

"You're Megan-ing me!"

He throws his head back and laughs. It echoes in the narrow hallway. "Am I?"

I grab his arm and spin him to face me. "You *definitely* are. This is terrible!" How does he expect me to decipher what's for real and what's for fun?

He's grinning, but his voice holds none of the teasing it did before. "Now you know how the rest of us feel. We mere mortals never dare to hope your insinuations are anything but a pastime."

"Wow, you're such a writer sometimes." I don't know what else to say.

He pushes back his hair. "You never told me how fun it is," he says, the humor returning to his voice. He leans a shoulder on the wall pointedly, his eyes inviting—demanding—a reply.

This will not stand. *I* do the Megan-ing around here! I put a hand on my hip and level him a goading stare. "You think *this* is fun? You haven't seen anything yet."

Now his eyes widen, jumping to his door and back. "I have to check on Sam." His voice comes out low and furtive. "I'll only be a second."

I toss my hair over my shoulder and strut past the Yûjirô portrait into Owen's room. "I'll be waiting," I reply.

His room is dark and as orderly as I remember. My hand shakes as I flip on the lights. I force my racing heart to slow down, reminding myself I have no idea what's going to happen when Owen comes in here. I know better than anyone that flirtatious remarks, winks, and nudges don't need to go any further. And how much further do I think they're going to go with *Owen*? He has a girlfriend. *He has a girlfriend.*

I walk around the room, wondering where I should be when he comes in, and my eyes fall on his notebook, half-open on his desk. He's never shown it to me, but he's never told me *not* to read it either. I know I shouldn't. I'd be crossing a line, invading his privacy, and violating his trust. I pause in front of the notebook, willing myself to walk away.

But Owen's writing about Rosaline. About *me*. Part of me—*all* of me—has to know how he sees her.

The sound of Owen's and Sam's muffled voices drifts down the hall, and before I know it, I've picked up the notebook. The open page is covered mostly in illegible and crossed-out half sentences, but I can make out a few lines jammed in between the others.

It's a monologue for Rosaline, and she's . . . a force of nature. She's fierce and honest, her words passionate and heart-breaking. But she isn't tragic, not the way Owen writes her.

"I don't know how far we're taking this but—" I hear his voice from the doorway. I turn, holding the notebook, and his face goes rigid. He crosses the room in a split second. "That's nowhere close to ready." He grabs the notebook from my hands, his voice hard.

"Why? What you've written is good," I protest. It *is* good. It's ringing in my ears, everything he's written about Rosaline.

"It's not good *enough*." He closes the cover and shoves the notebook in a drawer. The subtle shift in his voice weakens my resistance. For the first time, I didn't mean to make him blush.

"When do you think I'll get to read it?" I ask, gentler.

He won't meet my eyes. "I don't know. I haven't exactly made a lot of progress."

"You need more Rosaline insights from the expert?" I want to help him. He's drifting into the shy version of Owen, one I haven't seen in a long time. One it hurts to see.

He smiles slightly. "No. You've been great."

"What then? Is Rosaline just not interesting enough?" I thought he'd written a Rosaline worthy of the page, but I'm beginning to wonder if he disagrees. "You can't say I didn't warn you," I continue, an involuntary edge entering my voice. "There's a reason she never comes on stage."

"No." He shakes his head, intensity in his eyes when they return to mine. "There's *not* a reason except that this play is Romeo and Juliet's. Rosaline could be the central character of her own story. Just because Romeo didn't want her doesn't mean no one else will." He gestures to the drawer. "You read what I wrote. Isn't it obvious how I feel about her?"

There's a pressing current of passion in his voice, passion I don't think was solely pulled from defending his play's premise. I drop my eyes, feeling my neck grow hot. Not wanting to argue with him, to convince him that no, Rosaline is in fact nothing more than the castoff she is in Shakespeare's pages, I mutter, "It sounds like you know exactly what to write."

"Maybe I do." Owen's answer sounds somehow far away, and when I dare to glance up at him, he has that pensive, concentrated look. The look I now recognize as the same one he wore the very first time I admitted he was cute. I hadn't thought anything of it at the time.

"You said you had a thousand lines to memorize," he says suddenly, breaking my reverie, the distance gone from his expression. He bites the corner of his lip in a way that is entirely unfair and holds out a worn copy of *Romeo and Juliet*.

I nod and take the play from him, careful not to brush his hand. Folding the book back against its spine, I find the right scene. For a moment, the words dance in front of me. Not because I don't know these lines, but because I can't get Rosaline out of my head. I need to be Juliet. Just for an hour. *Please can't I be her for just an hour?*

Deep breath in, deep breath out. I let my posture soften, then turn to face my Romeo. He's leaning against his desk, hair falling across his forehead, his hands still ink-stained even after washing the dishes. I offer him my hand, and he stares at it, uncomprehending.

"I believe you are to take my hand, good gentleman," I say in my best Juliet voice. But it still just sounds like me.

Owen's fingers find mine, and all my focus narrows in on the pleasant warmth against my palm. "If I profane with my unworthiest hand—" he begins.

"Wait, what?" I interrupt with a brusqueness Juliet never would.

He drops my hand, eyes uncertain. "What? Did I start at the wrong place? I thought we were doing their meeting."

"No. I mean, yes, we are, but where's your script?"

"Um, you're holding it, Megan." A grin slides across his features.

"You're telling me you know Romeo's lines for this scene?" He nods, and I know he's holding in a laugh. "But you're not Romeo!" I say because it feels like a fact that's been forgotten.

"No. I'm not."

"Then . . . you just happen to have the scene memorized even though it's one without Friar Lawrence?"

"The scene, the play," he says with a wave of his hand as if his words are easily dismissed.

"Oh my god," I groan. "What happened to no time to memorize your lines?"

Owen shrugs. "I ended up reading and rereading it enough times to write my play—and because I love it, honestly. Memorizing everything just kind of . . . happened."

I do my best to look unimpressed. "You're such a showoff."

"Megan, are you maybe procrastinating a little?" Now he isn't bothering to hold in his laugh.

"Ugh, fine." I stick my hand back out, knowing I've completely lost any chance I may have had of being Juliet tonight.

Owen clears his throat theatrically and takes my hand. "If I profane with my unworthiest hand this holy shrine, the gentle sin is this: my lips, two blushing pilgrims, ready stand to smooth that rough touch with a tender kiss." He bends over, his lips hovering close to my hand, and he's about to kiss me—

"I'm sorry, Romeo is *ridiculous*. I mean, comparing his lips to *two blushing pilgrims*?" I blurt for some indefensible reason, and Owen blinks and straightens up. And I want to kick myself. *It's just a kiss on the hand. It doesn't mean anything.* But I can't explain why it makes me nervous like I haven't felt in I don't know how long.

"I think Shakespeare deserves a little credit for poetic language," he says, no hint of nerves in his easy smile.

I consider telling him to run the scene from the top, giving me a second chance at that kiss. But I don't. I'm kicking myself again when I jump right into my line. "Good pilgrim, you do wrong your hand too much, which mannerly devotion . . ." I say the rest of my lines trying to muster the impatient sarcasm that's come easily in every rehearsal. But it's not working, and I know why. It's because I don't really want to turn Owen's advances down, even if they're scripted.

Which is what has me nervous. If this goes further, I *wouldn't* turn him down. But I have to. Because without Will to focus on when I sense my feelings shifting, I'm now forced to confront how much I want to be with Owen.

So much, I know it would destroy me when things collapse between us the way they inevitably would.

Before I'm prepared for it, we've reached the line where Owen's supposed to kiss me. Not on the hand this time. "Then move not while my prayer's effect I take," he says, his voice low. He's not delivering the lines like Tyler, but his speech doesn't sound tight or hesitant like I would have expected. He sounds like Romeo, and I feel myself closer than ever before to the precipice of becoming Juliet. I feel like I could close my eyes and fall in.

But I don't close my eyes. I keep them on Owen. Even though I know in the rational part of my brain he's definitely not going to kiss me just because it's the stage direction, it . . . kind of looks like he's leaning in.

"Romeo might have terrible pick-up lines, but I have to give him credit for going for it," I say abruptly, ending the leaning-in question right there. I walk to the other side of the room, not really having a theatrical explanation for the distance. We recite the lines before their second kiss from opposite ends of the room. When the moment for the kiss comes, I wait for Owen's eyes to find mine, or his voice to waver, or something. But he does nothing.

"You kiss by th' book," I say, and exhale, relieved that's the final line, wanting this pointless, poorly written, totally not-romantic scene to be over.

"Does that mean Romeo's a good kisser or a bad kisser?" Owen wonders aloud, clearly not understanding we *need* to move on to a different scene.

"Bad, definitely bad," I say. He wanders over to the dresser and leans on it, closing some of the distance between us. "Juliet's saying his kisses feel studied and boring," I inform him.

Maybe it's the way he smiles then, or maybe it's how much he loves this play—how he's memorized the entire thing and wants to pull apart its lines and figure out how they work. But I find myself leaning on the dresser too, my nervousness fading.

It'll destroy me to lose Owen after having him. I know that. But it'll destroy me now to never have him at all.

"Okay, then," he says teasingly. "Tell me, kiss expert Megan, what does Juliet think Romeo should do better?"

I pretend to consider, giving in. "It's a fine line. Too stiff or too repetitive and it feels like you're not interested. Too enthusiastic and you're overeager. The key is a lot of passion and a little creativity. You want each brush of lips to feel like the first time, like you don't know where it could lead—"

He kisses me.

Owen Okita kisses *me*, drawing my face in with his hands like it's not enough for only our lips to touch. He hits me with such force that we flatten against the dresser, the script held between us. If I'd ever let myself wonder about kissing Owen, I couldn't have imagined the way his lips draw the breath from mine or the way he guides my head, tilting me to deepen the kiss. It's like nothing I've ever felt. This kiss isn't just one moment—it holds the possibility of innumerable kisses to come. It's extraordinary, and precarious.

It feels real.

He pulls back just an inch, his eyes searching mine. "Is this—"

"Yes," I breathe. I tug his collar to bring us back together. The second kiss—or perhaps it's the second act in one long kiss—is slower, more measured, like he's taking the time to savor every touch. His body becomes flush with mine, and the script falls to the floor.

"By the book or not?" he whispers with a faint smile.

"*Not* by the book. It's like you've never heard of the book. It's like you're illiterate."

Owen's smile widens. "Well, I've thought about doing that for long enough."

I run a hand down his chest in answer. I know a thing or two about kissing, and when I bring my lips to his, I hold none of it back, walking him to the other end of the room and pressing him to the edge of the desk. I know it works, because he withdraws a moment later, his eyes wide. "Whoa," he exhales.

I shush him. "Let's not talk, Owen."

He complies, instead lowering his hands to my waist and spinning us so I'm the one pinned to the desk. The back of my leg hits a drawer with an unexpected bang, causing us both to break apart and laugh at the interruption.

"What about Sam?" I whisper.

"He's fine." Owen pushes a strand of hair behind my ear. "He's probably playing *Minecraft* with the volume up."

He kisses me again, but I pull back a moment later. I don't know how much time we'll have before Sam interrupts us, before everything falls apart and Owen changes his mind. I won't waste a single second. "Should we move to . . . somewhere quieter?" I glance toward the bed.

He swallows, but his eyes say he's not opposed to the idea. I slide out from in front of the desk and take his hand, leading him to the bed. He watches me recline first onto one elbow, then both on top of the comforter. Without hesitating, he joins me, his body held as if by a thread over mine.

He brings his face to mine, and—he blinks. "What are we doing?" The intensity in his eyes goes distant. He recoils, rolling off me, and onto his knees on the bed. His voice is low with uncertainty.

I sit up. "Hooking up, I thought." I try to say it lightly, but his expression unnerves me. I can feel whatever I have with Owen—whatever I could have—falling apart already.

"You and Will broke up just this afternoon." He runs a hand through his hair.

"So?"

"So . . . what is this, your next fling?"

I jerk back, stunned. Studying his face in the silent seconds that follow, I try to work out where this is coming from. How could Owen, who knows me so well, *not* know this— right now—is like nothing I've felt before?

He must notice the way my expression flares with anger, because his face falls. "I didn't mean it like that. It's just, I don't know what to expect because you tend to move from one relationship to the next pretty quickly."

I flush with anger and embarrassment, and like that, I've found my voice. "Hey, *you're* the one who kissed me," I seethe, "while you supposedly still have a girlfriend."

He looks stricken, like he's just remembered her. He hurriedly climbs off the bed, then fixes me with a narrow stare. "Why do you say 'supposedly'?"

"Because she isn't a real girlfriend, Owen." I slide to sit on the edge of the bed.

"Enough with that, Megan," he snaps. "Now is *not* the time. Cosima's not a joke."

"I'm not joking," I reply coolly. "I know she's real. But your relationship's not. You hardly ever talk to her. I asked you to tell me what she's like, and you told me where she lives. Your entire relationship is based on one summer camp together. You even forgot about her long enough to hook up with me. I think you're only with her because it's easier, or safer or something. You can't get hurt by someone you don't really know, someone you keep at a distance of five thousand miles."

He's clenching his jaw like he did the other times I've seen him really mad, when Tyler insulted me and when Will cheated. "What would you know about my relationship?"

"I watch you, Owen. I watch you delay and hedge and keep your distance with Cosima, and I watch you do the very same with your play." I gesture to his notebook, stuffed in the drawer. "You're scared to finish. You're scared to put yourself out there because the more you do, the worse you might get hurt."

I half expect him to fall silent, but he doesn't even glance at the notebook. "Just because I didn't tell you everything about my girlfriend doesn't mean I don't know her," he shoots back. "She's not just some placeholder."

Of course she's not. I fight to push down tears. *Cosima's not the placeholder. I am. I'm always the placeholder.* I shouldn't have expected anything else, not even with Owen. Owen, who would prefer to be with someone he talks to twice a week than with me.

"Well, if you're in love with her," I say, getting off the bed and crossing my arms, "you shouldn't have kissed me. But whatever. It's not like this meant much to me either."

He flinches. "Then you shouldn't have flirted with me. But I guess that's just what you do. I should have known you never mean it."

"You know me, Owen." My voice is ugly, bitter with resentment. Not only for him, of course. Why did I ever imagine something like this could happen for *me*, the girl who's the punch line of a hundred oh-she's-boy-crazy jokes? I push past Owen to the door, my vision glassy. "I'm going to go."

"Megan—" I hear the regret in his voice, like he knows he went too far. But I don't turn back, knowing there's nothing he could possibly say to fix this—and not wanting him to see the red in my eyes. I slam his front door behind me.

I get into my car and drive up his street. When I know there's no chance of him following me outside, I pull over and do something I haven't in years.

I cry. Really cry, not the couple stray tears and sniffles that follow fights or breakups. I press my forehead to the steering wheel, and my shoulders shake for everything I'm worth.

TWENTY-ONE

BENVOLIO: . . . *one fire burns out another's burning;*

One pain is lessened by another's anguish.

Turn giddy, and be helped by backward turning.

One desperate grief cures with another's languish.

I.ii.47–50

I POINT TO JEREMY HANDLER, BRINGING REHEARSAL to a halt. "Jeremy," I call out from the front row of the auditorium. He pauses on stage, in front of three girls from the cast sitting on a bench. "You're telling those noblewomen that if they don't dance with you, it's because you think they have blisters on their feet. But because you *want* them to dance with you, you shouldn't stand that far from them. You could even try taking one of their hands."

"Okay." Jeremy nervously steps closer to Cate Dawson and gently grabs her hand. "Like this?"

"Perfect." I notice the way Cate's face has lit up, and she's sitting a little straighter. "If Lord Capulet is going to be a creepy old man to his guests, he might as well go the extra mile," I finish.

In the two weeks since my fight with Owen, I've had nothing but a small, stilted Thanksgiving with Dad and Rose—and

Erin, who threw her cranberry sauce on the floor gleefully—and rehearsal to keep me busy. I didn't think it possible, but I hate Juliet more than ever before. It's not getting in the way of my performance. I'm good, to be honest, better than I ever thought I'd be. I never thought I'd say it, but I feel lucky to have Tyler. His loving gazes and passionate delivery smooth over my rougher lines. Which is fortunate, because the Oregon Shakespeare Festival is in a week. We're driving to Ashland two days early and checking into a cheap hotel—Jody wanted time to rehearse in the performance space.

But none of that has me feeling relieved or excited. I just feel empty.

What keeps me going is the thirty minutes a day Jody allows me to direct *Romeo and Juliet*. I guess she noticed my mood lately, or maybe she took pity on my general lack of enthusiasm and wanted to give me something to look forward to.

The only scene I passed up directing was one of Friar Lawrence's. I haven't talked to Owen since I left his house. Nor Will, not that I would have wanted to if he'd tried. But where Will's and my breakup feels distant, like someone else's life, what I lost with Owen—and what I never had—hurts like the day it happened.

It's a sign of my desperation that I spend a lot of time outside of school at Verona. Verona is Will- and Owen-free, and better, I know it's where I'll find Anthony. He and I are both heartbroken, and we spend afternoons and evenings in between his shifts commiserating over old, free pizza. While Madeleine drops by sometimes and tries to join in, it's not like she has a lot of experience with heartbreak. Or any. And Anthony and I have more to do than mope. With his Juilliard audition coming up, I've been helping him narrow down his monologue choices.

I've probably watched him deliver a thousand recitations of a dozen different monologues to the men's bathroom mirror by the time I convince him to choose based on the feedback of a live audience at an open-mic night.

I'm grateful for the distraction. As long as I'm focused on getting Anthony to pick the perfect monologue, I don't have to replay Owen's words in my head or remember the way it felt to be in his arms for one crushing moment. He should be easy to move on from. We were only together for minutes. But those minutes were more than months with Tyler and weeks with Will. I don't know how to move on from something I thought was real.

So I don't. I stay exactly where I am.

I walk into Luna's Coffee Company Thursday evening, and I'm not surprised to find the rest of the drama class already there. Even though he's not as flashy as Tyler, Anthony is looked up to as the undisputed best actor in school. Everyone's tightly packed into the front room, sitting on wooden tables, burgundy leather couches and the rugs on the floor—every inch of space is taken.

"This seat's open," someone says to my left. I spin and find Wyatt Rhodes smirking up at me from one of the built-in benches under the windows. I'm stunned for a moment. I would not have taken Wyatt for an open-mic-night kind of guy. He's not wearing his golf polo—instead, he has on a millennial-pink button-down, the top three buttons undone. It's completely over the top and exactly the kind of outfit that would have had me drooling months ago.

Wyatt nods toward the seat beside him. It's hardly big enough for two, but judging from the look in his eyes, that's probably the point.

"What are you here for?" I ask. He blinks, obviously thrown by the total lack of flirtatiousness in my response.

"Open-mic night. Reading poems has been known to impress the ladies." I notice the Neruda collection on his lap and remember Owen telling me about trying to channel Neruda in his lyric writing.

I flinch, pushing the memory away. This is the point where I say something suggestive, ask Wyatt who he's planning to impress tonight. He's as gorgeous as ever, and he's materialized out of thin air right when I'm in need of someone new.

I say nothing.

"What's up, Megan? I feel like we haven't hung out in a while," he says, a flicker of confusion crossing his face.

"Sorry, Wyatt. I can't," I tell him. I can't flirt with you anymore, because I don't only want flirting. I want everything. I had it for just a moment, and I can't lie to myself any longer. Flirting was never enough. "Good luck with your poems," I say instead, and walk away.

In the middle of the room, I spot Jenna waving me over from a couch. I make my way through the tangle of people seated on every surface possible, and she moves her arm, giving me a place to sit on the armrest right as Anthony steps up to the mic.

"Okay, I know there's often a kind of sharing-is-caring spirit with open mics, but I'm going to hold this shit down for the next half hour." He's dressed in the charcoal suit I know he bought for his audition in New York. "I'm testing monologues. Stomp if you hate it, cheer if you love it. Sound good?"

I cheer with the rest of the drama group, earning eye rolls from the only other open-mic participants I can pick out—two bearded guys with mandolins in the corner.

Anthony extravagantly clears his throat. The rest of us hold our breath, and except for the hiss of the cappuccino machine the room is silent. "About three things I was absolutely positive," Anthony begins. I frown. This isn't one of the monologues we prepped. Chekhov? Ibsen? Beckett?

"First, Edward was a vampire. Second, there was part of him—"

The room erupts into stomping punctuated by a few exuberant cheers. I whoop from the armrest, recognizing Stephenie Meyer's iconic declaration of love from *Twilight*. Anthony collapses onto the mic stand, laughing.

"Okay, for real this time," Anthony promises, straightening his tie. He closes his eyes, taking a beat to find his composure. When he looks back up at us, he's transformed. "Because you can't handle it, son. You can't handle the truth. You can't handle . . ."

He continues the speech, and I watch my classmates' ex-

259

pressions for reactions. He's doing Shakespeare for both the classical monologues Juilliard requires and Chekhov for one of the contemporary, but he needs one more contemporary. I've been trying for weeks to dissuade him from the famous speech from the play version of Aaron Sorkin's *A Few Good Men*. It invites inevitable Jack Nicholson comparisons, and Anthony's talents are better suited to the subtle than the overexpressive. Sure enough, I notice skeptical looks and pursed lips on the faces of the crowd, and while I hear the occasional cheer, the stomping builds slowly until Anthony stops in mid-line.

"Really? You're not feeling Sorkin?" he says, breaking character and rubbing his neck.

The stomping continues, even louder. Anthony shakes his head ruefully.

I call out from my seat. "Scorpius!" I'm expecting the exasperated sigh Anthony heaves when he recognizes my voice. Every time he'd begin the *Few Good Men* speech in the Verona bathroom, I'd cut him off and insist on Scorpius Malfoy's monologue from *Harry Potter and the Cursed Child*. Anthony's been adamantly resisting—he protests that it's too commercial to command respect. But it doesn't matter. He's brilliant at it. He switches seamlessly from righteous anger to wounded vulnerability and captures a world of sorrows in just a few lines.

"Can you even slightly imagine what that's like?" Anthony begins, his voice aching. "Have you even ever tried? No. Because you can't see beyond the end of your nose. Because you can't see beyond the end of your stupid thing with your dad."

Immediately, I'm proven right. The crowd goes quiet, this time watching Anthony with unconcealed interest. Even the baristas stop pouring drinks and listen from the counter. Anthony's eyes dance, and I know he feels the energy in the room. I get up and toss him an I-told-you-so glance. He sees me but doesn't break character. He'll definitely be performing this one in New York. Taking advantage of the lull in the line, I step up to the register, where one of the baristas looks annoyed to be handling my order.

I walk to the other end of the counter to wait for my cappuccino, watching Anthony from behind the coffee machines. When it's been a couple minutes with no cappuccino, I turn to check who's waiting in front of me and—

"Eric?"

He whirls, looking panicked. When he realizes it's me, he relaxes.

"What are you doing here?" I ask.

"I'm, uh—" he stutters like he's searching for an explanation, then stops himself. With a soft smile, he nods toward the stage. "I'm here for Anthony's monologues."

"Thought so." I smile. "Have you two . . . figured things out?" In all the time I've spent at Verona, Anthony's never mentioned Eric, but I haven't wanted to press. It's possible they've talked.

"We haven't," Eric says stiffly, his smile fading. "And we're not going to. I know I'm not the type of guy Anthony wants or deserves to be with. But I wanted to watch the monologues because Anthony told me a lot about the audition before . . ." He looks away. "I heard about tonight and had to come."

I have to give Eric credit. For someone whose wardrobe consists of only lacrosse jerseys, he's pretty emotionally insightful. "But it's clear you still care about him," I say.

"Yeah, I do." Eric's eyes drift to Anthony. "When I'm with him, I feel like there are a million reasons why we should be together. I feel like I'm . . . my entire self, not just . . ."

While he's talking, I notice a familiar head of black hair framed in the doorway. "Playing who you're supposed to be," I finish Eric's sentence as I watch Owen walk into the front and take my seat on the couch.

"But sometimes it doesn't matter," Eric continues. "I'd just mess things up for Anthony—there's too much in the way."

The applause from the other end of the room tells me Anthony's finished his monologue, and I pull my gaze from Owen to find Eric putting on his jacket. "I think I should go," he says.

"Eric. You definitely don't want to talk to him?"

He shakes his head, his eyes pointedly avoiding where Anthony's bowing by the mic. "I don't want to interrupt his night. It's better if he doesn't see me." He nods once before brushing past me to the door.

"Cappuccino," the tattooed barista calls out.

"Thanks," I mutter, taking the ceramic cup and gingerly carrying it back to where Anthony's joined Jenna and everyone on the couches. The room's beginning to clear out, and no one's listening to the folk musicians' gentle Iron & Wine cover. I sit on the edge of the table, putting plenty of distance between myself and Owen.

Jenna drapes her arm around Anthony. "Which one's it

262

going to be?" she asks, flopping her head on his shoulder.

"*Harry Potter*." Anthony sighs and gives me a grudging smile. "Definitely *Harry Potter*."

"It's a really cool pick," Owen speaks up. "You're great at capturing subtler dynamics. Seems like this is definitely your best option."

I scowl. It's enough he's here—he didn't have to go and have the exact same opinion as me.

"You only saw the one!" Jenna straightens up and slaps Owen on the knee. I scowl again. "Where were you? We said we'd meet here an hour ago."

Owen stiffens. "I, uh . . ." His eyes flit to mine for the first time in weeks. It's a glance so quick I nearly miss it, but I know exactly how to read it.

"Talking to Cosima?" I guess loudly.

Now he levels his gaze with mine. "Yeah. I was."

"On a Thursday? Wow," I say with unrestrained bitterness. "What, is she helping you run lines?"

"What's it to you?" Owen's eyes are unreadable.

"Nothing," I say, ignoring the confused expressions on Anthony's and Jenna's faces. "It's nothing to me, Owen." I get up, cappuccino unfinished. "I'm going to get—a muffin," I finish, painfully conscious of how undramatic that sounded.

But turning toward the counter, I freeze in place. Will and Alyssa are stepping up to the line, her hands in his back pockets, and they're kissing for the whole world to see. *Well, perfect.*

"Actually, I'm just going to head out," I tell the group.

I walk past Owen on my way to the door, and out of the

corner of my eye, I see him start to stand. He looks torn, like the part of him that wants to comfort me for what he obviously just saw happen with Will is wrestling with the part of him that remembers we're in a huge fight.

He looks like he wants to follow me, right up until he sits back down.

TWENTY-TWO

PARIS: *Venus smiles not in a house of tears.*

IV.i.8

OWEN AND I DON'T TALK FOR ANOTHER WEEK.

It's December, and Ashland is this weekend. I'm running late for the first full run-through before we leave tomorrow. Not helping matters, it's a dress rehearsal, and right now I'm struggling to stuff a full medieval gown into my bag. I forgot to bring my costume to school—to Jody's open-mouthed horror—because I had a twenty-minute discussion with my dad this morning about dinner plans for when my mom and Randall fly in tonight. Jody had me run home the instant school let out. Apparently, the world will end if the costume designer doesn't have one final opportunity to make alterations before we leave town for the performance.

I rush into the auditorium, nearly colliding with an irate Jody. "Why aren't you *dressed*?" she shouts in the shrill voice she inevitably gets in the final days before a show.

I know how to handle her. "You told me I had to be back in ten minutes. Here I am. Now let me go change," I return over my shoulder, pushing past Tybalt and Benvolio engaged in a duel with their wooden swords.

"Five minutes, Megan!" I hear behind me. "We're doing the Nurse's scene before we take it from the top."

I dash up the stairs to the stage and dart behind the curtain. Everyone's waiting in the wings in full costume, and I have to elbow past lords and ladies and an apothecary on my way to the dressing rooms. Pulling off my scarf and unzipping my jacket, I pass through the green room, where three crewmembers are bent over a mic pack. I open the door to the girls' dressing room, but I'm brought to a halt in the doorway. Cate Dawson's making out sloppily with Jeremy Handler in between racks of clothes, his hand unmistakably up her shirt.

Not a chance I'm going in there.

I hit the stairs to the boys' dressing room two at a time. It's markedly smaller than the girls', but it'll have to do. Ignoring the thick stench of boy clothes, I do a quick sweep of the space, afraid of another uncomfortable walk-in. I drop my bag on the counter, closing the door behind me. Not a minute to waste, I rip the costume out of my bag and fling it onto a hanger, then undo my belt and shimmy out of my jeans.

I peel off my shirt next and throw it over my head. But when I open my eyes—Owen's staring right at me.

Not into my eyes.

My mouth won't work for a couple terrifying seconds. The thought crosses my mind this was a regrettable day to wear my red boy-shorts with "Super Sexy" printed on them.

"What the hell, man?" I yell after what feels like an eternity.

Owen blinks and blushes furiously in his friar's frock. Like he's just remembered his decency, he looks away, then turns a full one hundred and eighty degrees. I guess averting his eyes wasn't enough. "This—this is the guys' dressing room," he stammers.

Remembering he's right, I hastily pull the dress over my head. "Jeremy and Cate were doing something decidedly off-script in the girls'," I mutter by way of explanation. Eager like I've never been for anything to extricate myself from this situation, I yank my dress down and—it gets caught.

I can't figure out on what. I have one arm halfway in a sleeve and the other sticking out what I suspect is the neck hole. The other sleeve is tangled in the straps of my yellow pushup bra. "Fucking shitty costume," I gasp, pirouetting feverishly and trying to fix the problem.

"Is— Um, what's going on?" Owen's voice sounds pinched.

"My fucking costume is stuck." I whack my arm on the counter and swear again.

"Uh, where?" He still doesn't turn.

"If I knew, *Owen*, I'd fix it," I snap. "Just give me a hand."

I hear his voice after a couple more frantic seconds of pulling on the sleeve. "It looks, um, stuck on your bra." He clears his throat, like the effort of keeping his voice level was too much to bear. "I'll go get someone," he offers.

"There's not enough time. Jody's going to kill me if I'm not down in, like, negative-one minutes."

"But, the green room—" he protests.

"The only girl up here is Cate. If you'd really rather interrupt *that* than help me with my bra, then go right ahead."

He looks to the door like he's considering it. But a moment later, I feel his hands on my back, twisting the fabric to unfurl the sleeves.

"Just, pull the collar—" I prompt.

"Move your—"

"Now my arm's stuck."

"How did you—? Have you ever put on a dress before?"

"Have you, Owen?"

"Stay still," he orders me. I feel him struggling with the bra. *This is hopeless.* He circles me to try from the front.

"Just take it off!"

Owen's hands still. "What?"

"Unhook the bra."

He looks up at me, expressionless. "I am *not* taking off your bra right now, Megan."

I let out a short, rattling sigh. "Okay, I will." I reach behind me. But right then, Owen gives the dress a final yank, and mercifully it comes free.

He instantly steps back and turns around again, like he wasn't just nose-deep in my décolletage. Ten hurried seconds later, I've pulled on both sleeves and straightened the bodice over the guilty bra. I'm reaching for the door when I hear, "Wait."

I do, not entirely knowing why. I'm not expecting the fervor of the past few minutes to have prompted him into an apology or a declaration of love, like this is some stupid rom-com.

I feel Owen's hands on my back once more. He sweeps my hair out from under the dress, his fingers brushing the nape of my neck. It's impossible to ignore how I shiver under his touch, try though I might.

"Thanks," I say, a bit breathless.

"No problem." His reply is short and distant. He edges past me to the door.

I follow him, unsteady on my feet, unsure what just happened. Owen's been cold to me for weeks, and he practically told me he's devoted to his girlfriend. But the way he gently touched my neck felt—well, intimate.

Rehearsal keeps my mind from wandering. First full run-throughs never go smoothly, and between remembering my lines and hitting my cues, I have no time to talk to Owen—other than the brief scene in which Friar Lawrence sells Juliet poison, which isn't exactly brimming with sexual tension.

Rehearsal ends twenty minutes behind schedule, and I roll through stop signs on the way home. Dad's waiting impatiently in the driveway. He hustles me into his car with only a "Come on, Megan. We have to go."

It's an hour to the Medford Airport, and I anxiously listen to Dad list off dinner plans and travel arrangements for Ashland while the redwoods fly by in the window. I keep waiting to hear strain in his voice at the prospect of being around his ex-wife again, but it hasn't crept in yet.

We pull up to the terminal, and I'm startled by the little leap my heart does when I catch sight of Mom. Before Dad's even put the car in park, I'm jumping out of my seat and running to give her a hug.

"I wasn't expecting this treatment from my seventeen-year-old daughter," Mom tries to joke, but the lopsided smile on her face betrays how pleased she is. "Shouldn't you be re-bellious or something?"

"I missed you," I say into her shoulder. "I'll resume stan-dard operating rebelliousness tomorrow."

Randall's holding the suitcases behind her. He gives me a conspiratorial wink over her shoulder, and my heart sinks a little. In just under a week, my mom's going to be engaged.

I hear the trunk pop, and Dad walks around the car and wraps my mom in a delicate hug. "Catherine, it's great to see you."

Mom gives a small smile in reply, and I notice a faint blush on her cheeks. Dad turns to Randall and reaches for a suit-case, but inevitably Randall insists on carrying it himself. The two of them end up awkwardly walking the suitcase be-tween them the entire way to the trunk.

Mom and I exchange a glance. I follow her into the back of Dad's Rav-4, not ready to give up Mom proximity just yet. "You haven't traded this thing in by now, Henry?" she asks with a laugh while Dad and Randall get in the front. Randall slides his chair back to fit his six-foot-four frame, plowing the back of the seat into my knees.

"No," my dad answers, grinning. "You'd be surprised how long a car can hold out when *someone's* not riding the brakes to every stop."

Mom holds up a hand in defense. "I do not—"

"She does. She really does," Randall confirms, making Dad laugh.

I say nothing, not believing what's happening. I didn't

dare expect this drive would be anything but small talk and long silences, and here we are, laughing already. But this trip's far from over.

Dad and Randall fight over the suitcases the entire walk up to the porch. The house smells like sweet potatoes when I open the front door, and Mom heads straight for Erin, who's shouting *noo-noos* in her playpen.

"Look how big you've gotten," Mom coos, earning a giggle from Erin.

Rose emerges from the kitchen, holding an assortment of silverware, her other hand on her back. I watch my mom for the death glares she gave Rose the last time they were in the same room, and I'm stunned when Mom pulls Rose into a one-armed hug. From the look on Rose's face, she's stunned, too. I can't decipher my mom's unexpected warmth toward her. It could be the years since the divorce, the distance, the fact my mom has a boyfriend, soon-to-be fiancé.

Or it could be an act.

"Megan," Rose says, withdrawing from the hug, "would you finish setting the table?" In mute surprise, I take the silverware from her and walk into the dining room, over-hearing Mom and Rose begin to chat about baby names and nurseries.

We sit down once Dad and Randall have dropped off the suitcases in my bedroom, where Mom and Randall will sleep before everyone drives up to Ashland.

271

"The whole meal is nut-free, per Randall," Rose proudly announces as the guys file into the room.

"Well, I'll be." Randall grins, sitting down. "So thoughtful of you, Rose. Wow."

As the plates of potatoes and roast chicken are passed around the table, I watch Mom and Dad for signs of strain. They're perfectly normal, Dad serving Mom a spoonful of the potatoes while she chides him for not doing any of the cooking. I chew quietly and listen to Randall recount his victory at the regional bowling tournament. The other three jump in with questions every now and then like they're old friends.

"What time are you guys leaving tomorrow?" Dad asks me when Randall goes into the kitchen to pour everyone refills.

"After rehearsal," I say in between bites.

"And who are you rooming with?" Mom has a knowing smile.

"I don't know, Mom."

"Not Tyler, I hope," she replies teasingly.

I can't keep myself from rolling my eyes. "The rooming is same-sex."

"It's going to stay that way, too," Dad warns, his brows flat.

"Like there's anyone I'd want to invite over." Owen won't talk to me except in the direst of circumstances, and considering the things he said to me in his bedroom, I'm not exactly keen to talk to him either. No matter how good of a kisser he is or how I felt when his fingers brushed my neck. It'll be my first drama trip in years without a hookup.

I catch the look my parents don't even try to hide. "We're not falling for that," Mom says dryly. "This is a class of your

272

drama friends. Even in Texas, where you didn't know a soul, you still had one crush by the end of the summer. One that we know of," she adds a second later.

"Wait, what?" Dad looks up from his plate, startled.

Before I have the chance to defend myself, Randall chimes in. "I caught the neighbor's kid loitering in the backyard one night—"

"Michael was harmless," I interject.

"—the week *after* you left Texas," Randall finishes.

I'd forgotten I ghosted on Michael, honestly. He texted me a couple times after I got home and then promptly found himself a blonde cheerleader. I wonder if they're still together. I bet they are—shit, they're probably engaged. It's Texas.

"Like that kid on the roof," Dad interrupts my train of thought.

I feel the blood rush to my cheeks. "Oh, Jesus."

Mom folds her lips inward, trying not to smile. Rose looks between the two of them, eyebrows arched. "On the *roof*?" she repeats.

I try to nip this in the bud. "We really don't need to relive that. It's . . . It's in the past. There's . . ." I gesture to Erin in her high chair. " . . . a child present."

"Erin's not too young to start learning from her sister's misadventures," Dad says, then nods to Mom. "You tell it, Catherine. You're the one who found him."

I shake my head. But for a moment, it feels like it's four years ago, my parents are together, and Rose and Randall are just a couple we're having over for dinner.

"We were in bed watching some horrible movie . . ." Mom

begins, looking to Dad. "What was it? You really wanted to watch it."

Dad leans back in his chair and crosses his arms. "Hey, *Snakes on a Plane* is a classic of American cinema."

Mom waves off his unsolicited review. "I thought I heard thudding on the roof," she continues. "*Henry* tried to tell me it was just in the movie."

"In my defense, I knew she was looking for every reason to pause the film," Dad cuts in.

"The third time it happened, I went outside to see for myself. Lo and behold, there's somebody standing on the roof over the garage."

"The next thing I know," Dad takes over, "Catherine's running back inside, looking pale, telling me there's some guy trying to break into the house. Not an overreaction *at all*."

Mom laughs into her hand, blushing now, and through my mounting mortification I realize what's happening here. My parents are rediscovering their friendship over what they have in common—embarrassing me.

"I obviously pause *Snakes on a Plane*," Dad goes on, "grab a baseball bat, and go downstairs. We get outside, I take one look at the guy on the roof, turn to Catherine, and say, 'That's a fourteen-year-old boy. Why is there—?' and then I realize he's there to get into Megan's room." He levels me an accusatory look.

"I ask if he's sure." Mom jumps back in. "He just says, 'Believe me, I'm sure.' Then he yells up at the poor kid, and the kid trips and falls on his butt. Henry orders him to get off the roof, but the kid just sits there, looking like he's about to throw up. I take Henry by the arm and tell him I think the kid's stuck."

Rose and Randall shake with laughter. Even I have to admit the situation was kind of funny.

"I get the ladder and climb halfway up. But the kid doesn't move. I hear the upstairs window open, and Megan sticks her head out." Dad looks at me. "Megan, why don't you tell everyone what happened next?"

"Okay, what was I supposed to do?" I protest.

"Not invite the boy on the roof into your room," Dad says.

"You did what?" Rose gasps.

"He was stuck!" I defend myself. "My window was closer than the ladder. I didn't want Charlie to fall!"

"I swear to god, Megan yells down to him, 'Come on up! Just come in here,'" Dad confirms, and I collapse my head into my hands. "Needless to say, that wasn't going to happen."

"Falling wouldn't have even been the worst of Charlie's worries," Mom mutters. "He finally opens his mouth and explains he's *not good with heights*. Let's just say, Henry made it very clear Charlie had to come down *right* then."

"What did you say to the poor kid?" Randall shares a grin with my dad.

"I might have told him . . . I'd throw him off if he didn't," Dad says with a shrug.

"That worked?" Randall returns incredulously.

"Not exactly." Dad bashfully massages the back of his neck. "Catherine coaxed him down eventually." He looks up at Mom. "I'm just glad you were there. I honestly might've killed the kid. You were always the even-tempered one."

It happens so fast, I nearly don't notice. But Mom's eyes flicker, and her smile falters just a touch.

When we finish dinner, I stack dishes to carry into the kitchen while Rose gets dessert ready. Erin begins the frustrated whimper that means we've overtired her, and a tiny spoon clatters to the ground. I hear Dad get up, mumbling about Erin's bedtime.

"Would you mind if I read to her?" my mom asks.

"Please," Dad says. "I could use a night off from reading *Green Eggs and Ham* for the five-thousandth time." Mom lifts Erin out of her high chair and goes upstairs while I load the dishwasher and Rose pulls a pan out of the oven.

In fifteen minutes, Mom still isn't back and Randall's regaling me with the financial intricacies of his current case at work. When Rose comes out of the kitchen, a peach cobbler held in oven mitts, her eyes go to my mom's empty chair, and she frowns. "Megan," she says, interrupting Randall's endless string of details. "Would you go upstairs and tell your mom dessert's ready?"

I shoot her a grateful look and escape into the hallway, passing the photo over the stairs from Dad and Rose's wedding. It's dark in Erin's bedroom, the door ajar. I push it open and find Erin's in her crib, already asleep. "Mom?" I whisper the moment before I see her in the rocking chair, the book closed on her lap.

She hurriedly wipes her eyes. "Hi, honey," she says softly. She forces a smile. "Is everyone having dessert?"

Searching for what to say, I watch her straighten her

blouse and set down the book, clearly intending to just go back downstairs. "You— Are you okay?" I get out.

"Completely," she reassures me. "There are . . . a lot of memories in this house. Nothing to worry about."

I follow her out into the hallway. The picture from Dad and Rose's wedding looks a little too big and a little too beautiful. I feel like I should say something more to Mom, but I decide not to press her further because I know what's upsetting her. There'd be no point in talking about it when there's nothing I can change, and she's obviously struggling enough without me dredging it up one more time.

I knew this trip would be a mistake. The thought burns into my heart like a brand. I knew it would hurt my mom. I knew it would remind her of her old life with my dad and of his new one. It wasn't enough for her to move out when they got divorced—she had to move from Oregon to the Southwest to escape everything that reminded her of the man she's still pining for.

Including me.

It's something she and I have in common. We're always looking backward for the people who've moved on without us.

TWENTY-THREE

FRIAR LAWRENCE: *Affliction is enamored of thy parts,*

And thou art wedded to calamity.

III.iii.2–3

I FLOAT THROUGH THE SCHOOL DAY IN a black cloud.

When afternoon rehearsal ends at 5:30 and the bus for Ashland pulls up outside, I find Anthony in the parking lot. He's drumming his fingers on his leg, and his lips twitch in the way I know means he's dying to run lines. Undoubtedly noticing my expression, he thoughtfully restrains himself and gives me a hug before hunting down Tybalt and Benvolio.

Eager to sit down and close my eyes, I join the line filing onto the bus a couple of people behind Tyler, who's wrapping Madeleine in his arms. Of course she came back to school to send him off. She's not coming to Ashland because she has her alumni interview this weekend for her early action app to Princeton, which obviously she's going to crush.

She and Tyler finally separate, and I glimpse tears in both of their eyes like the prospect of two days apart is nearly unbearable.

I shake my head, and then she turns and I see what she's holding. It's a tiny mountain of brownies on the same flower-shaped plate I remember her bringing to school for me during my parents' divorce. She hasn't brought it out in years—she hasn't needed to.

Her eyes find mine between the heads of our classmates. Without a word, she leaves Tyler and walks down the line to me.

"You didn't have to," I say, taking the plate from her.

"Of course I did," she replies matter-of-factly. "It sucks you're going to Ashland right now, but call me whenever. Seriously."

"I will," I promise. I called her last night about how I found my mom, and before I knew it two hours had gone by. I would've stayed up later talking to her, but sleeping on the couch with adults coming downstairs for trips to the bathroom and drinks of water didn't leave me much privacy.

We've shuffled forward in line, and it's my turn to get on the bus. But on the first step, I hesitate. "Hey," I call, halting her. "I feel like a sleepover's in order when I get home."

She smiles lightly. "Definitely." Giving me a final wave, she walks back toward campus.

I trudge to an empty row near the back and take a seat next to the window. People are beginning to fill the bus, and I catch a couple pairs of eyes checking out the seat beside mine. I place the plate of brownies on the empty cushion, declaring it off-limits. When Owen boards, I watch him in my peripheral vision while pointedly staring out the window.

Finally the bus rumbles to life, and I close my eyes. Just for good measure, I put in my earbuds, the universal sign for *don't talk to me*. For a while I listen to nothing, trying to go over my lines in my head. But I turn on an old playlist when I realize the only words ringing in my ears aren't Juliet's. They're my mom's—*There are a lot of memories in this house. Nothing to worry about.*

I don't open my eyes for forty-five minutes, until we park outside a Burger King for dinner. Between thirty high-school students ordering burgers and freaking out over the premiere, it's not hard for me to hide my nose in my script and avoid the conversation. In an hour, with night falling, we're under way again.

We pass sporting goods stores and strip malls on the way into Ashland, and then the wide street I take to SOTI. I watch coffee shops, bookstores, clothing boutiques go by in the window. We round a corner, and a compound of low buildings in Elizabethan style emerges on the right. And despite my horrible mood, my heart lifts a little when I see it.

The Oregon Shakespeare Festival isn't an event. It's a place, a collection of smaller theaters grouped around a main stage built to resemble Shakespeare's Globe. I don't know why they call it a festival, because they have plays year-round, but I do know the production of *Macbeth* I went to in sophomore year is the best piece of theater I've ever seen.

I've dreamed of having a production on one of those stages. I just never thought I'd be acting in it.

We drive on past a quaint, three-story inn with a picket fence and a gabled roof, and I begin to look forward to falling into bed with a view of the theater. But we keep driving, and two right turns later, we're parked outside a Springview Hotel. Despite the proprietor's meager efforts, including a couple of ceramic plates on the walls, it's charmless and corporate.

I grab my room key from Jody, who's watching me with concern, but she's busy with the thirty other students clamoring for their keys. I slip out to the stairs, not in the mood to bustle into the elevator with my giddy cast-mates.

My room is empty when I open the door. Feeling the irresistible urge to wash off the bus ride, I walk into the bathroom. When I turn on the shower I think I hear the beep and click of my roommate coming into the room, but I'm intent on relaxing in the steam before I'm forced to have a conversation. Under the hot water, half of the tensed muscles in my back unclench.

Once I've put my clothes back on, I open the bathroom door and come face-to-face with Alyssa.

"Unbelievable," I say under my breath at the precise moment she gives me a glare of ice. *Thank you, Jody. A night stuck in a room with Alyssa is exactly what I need right now.*

"Don't worry, I'm not staying," Alyssa says sharply from her seat at the edge of the bed. "I'm waiting for Will to text me, then I'm going to move my stuff to his room. I'll be sleeping there." She tosses her shiny black hair over her shoulder.

"Of course you will," I mutter. I expect the mention of Will to hurt, but it doesn't. I really don't care what he's doing tonight, or who he's doing it with.

But Alyssa's eyes have narrowed. "What's *that* supposed to mean?"

Something in me snaps. The combination of Owen, my parents, this stupid fucking play, and now Alyssa staring at me does *not* have me feeling like playing nice. "I get it now,"

I reply with false lightness. "I wouldn't sleep with him, and you will."

She stands up to her full height of five feet, four inches. "I'm not going to be shamed by a girl who's had ten boyfriends in three years. You go right ahead and tell yourself I'm the bad guy, but I won't feel guilty for *finally* getting with a boy I like."

"It's not that you got with a boy you liked. You got with a boy who had a girlfriend." I push away the memory of kissing Owen, feeling the cold of my wet hair down my back.

"You date everyone, Megan!" Alyssa's voice goes shrill.

"And? Because I've had a lot of boyfriends, my relationships don't matter?"

"No, I don't—" She looks away, and suddenly there's something besides indignation in her tone. Something like pain, or purpose. "I mean, you think you're the only girl who's had a crush on Tyler Dunning? Or Dean Singh? Or Will? Do you even know what it's like to want someone who will never notice you? I watched myself get overlooked for you time after time. Finally, a guy liked *me*, too."

I open my mouth, then close it. Of the ways I've understood my relationships over the years, usurper to Alyssa wasn't one of them. But with everything else pounding through my head right now, I can't deal with hearing her out.

"Whatever," I say with what I hope passes for finality. I walk to the door. "Enjoy your night," I say, the door closing behind me.

🐜

Without knowing where I'm going, I head toward the stairs. I only know I need something to occupy me, to keep me out of Alyssa's way, and to keep my thoughts from Owen and my family. I decide the lobby's the best bet. I'll run some lines until I figure it's safe to return.

Rounding the corner at the other end of the hall, I catch sight of Tyler in front of the vending machine. I pass him with my head down and shoulders squared, hoping to convey I don't want to talk.

"You don't want to go down to the lobby," I hear him say cheerfully before I reach the door to the stairs. "Jody's enlisted everyone in folding programs."

His words bring me to a halt. "Thanks," I mutter, realizing now I have nowhere to go. While I'm considering my dilemma, Tyler swears under his breath, and I turn to find him shaking the vending machine to what sounds like little effect.

"Fucking money-eating piece of . . ."

"Louder. I don't think it heard you," I tell him, unable to resist the urge to heckle Tyler.

He eyes me, and then he clears his throat and repeats himself in his grandest stage voice. "Fucking money-eating piece of vile, execrable filth."

I laugh, surprising myself. "Better. Imagine the vending machine sitting in the back row," I say, adopting my most directorial demeanor.

He's laughing, too, but he halfheartedly kicks the vending machine one final time. "Make fun all you want," he replies, grinning ruefully, "but I'm a man in a crisis right now."

I take two steps toward the vending machine, where I glimpse a bag of Skittles caught in the spindle and hanging half off the shelf. "A Skittles crisis," I elaborate, smiling inwardly at how perfectly Tyler Dunning the situation is.

He nods gravely. "The worst kind." I step up to the glass, scrutinizing the stuck spindle. "I tried shaking it," he explains. "I even reached my arm up through the door—"

I ram my shoulder into the glass, interrupting him. I hit harder than I intended, and the whole machine bounces against the wall with an echoing bang. The Skittles tumble into the bin at the bottom.

Tyler's watching me, mouth half-open. Before he says anything, a door opens across the hallway. Owen's head emerges. "What's going on?" he asks, his eyes round with concern. When they find me, it's like someone's switched off a light in an upstairs room.

"Our Juliet just beat up a vending machine," Tyler says behind me, sounding impressed.

"Oh," Owen replies flatly, his gaze shifting to Tyler. Without a word to me or so much as a glance in my direction, he withdraws and closes the door.

I stare at it after he's gone, feeling the laughter of a couple moments ago ebb away. Tyler nudges me. "Hey, slugger," he says, and I turn, putting Owen and his disinterest firmly behind me. "Do you need some ice? That looked like it hurt."

I rub my shoulder, considering. "It felt kind of good, actually."

Tyler looks at me for a long second before he shrugs, his expression relaxing. He tears open the Skittles and tips the bag in my direction without taking any for himself. "You want some? They never would have happened without you."

I feel myself smiling as I hold out my hand. He shakes the bag, and two purples and a green fall into my palm. We start to wander down the hall, not saying anything while we pass a group of juniors playing cards on the floor. "Final rehearsal tomorrow," Tyler says, slowing down and tipping more Skittles into my hand. "You feel prepared?"

I glance at him out of the corner of my eye. "That depends."

"On?"

"On if you remember to lift your leg before you roll over me in the bedroom scene." I wince, remembering a week of rehearsing the scene in November and the consequent bruises on my thigh.

"It looks good!" Tyler protests. "Jody said it looks good from the audience."

"I don't care! You knee me every time! I'm going to have nerve damage by the end of this play!" He laughs, and I point a finger in his face. "I'm serious. You do it in tomorrow's rehearsal, and I'm eating garlic before the premiere."

He pulls a look of horror. "You wouldn't."

I nod threateningly. "You think playing opposite me is hard *now*? I want to see you 'It was the lark, not the nightingale' me when I smell like ten servings of raw garlic."

"Actresses . . ." Tyler rolls his eyes. Then his voice softens. "But seriously, it's awesome starring with you. You're a great Juliet."

"Really?" I snort, keeping my eyes on the floor. "I feel like

I'm kind of stumbling through it. I still think I'm going to freeze up and forget my lines in front of a real audience." *An audience including members of the SOTI faculty.*

Tyler drifts to a halt in front of a door. "Everyone thinks that's going to happen. But it won't." He smiles reassuringly. "Not if you know it." He nods toward the door, and I realize it must be his room. "We could go over it one more time, if you want?"

Why not? I think to myself. Running lines with Tyler will definitely distract me from my empty room and the look on Owen's face before he closed his door. "That'd be great," I say, following Tyler into his room.

It's empty, but I quickly deduce Jeremy's his roommate from the backpack on one bed with *Jeremy* stitched on it. Walking over to the other bed, I briefly wonder if Cate's managed to sexile her roommate, and if anyone but me will actually sleep in their own room tonight.

I close my eyes, bringing to mind my lines and the staging for my first scene, and feel Tyler sit down on the bed next to me.

"How now—" I begin to recite.

The rest of the line is smothered by Tyler's lips crashing into mine. His hands grab my waist, his nose pressing into my eye. This isn't his Romeo kissing, gentle and thoughtful—this is Tyler, kissing me with the sloppy overenthusiasm I remember from a year ago. *What the fuck is he doing?*

I shove a hand into his chest, pushing him off me. "What the hell?" I gasp, wiping my lips.

"I thought it was obvious." His brow furrows, but his voice sounds impossibly reasonable.

"*What's* obvious?" I jump off the bed.

He gestures at the door, looking at me like I'm the one who's lost my mind. "I invited you into my bedroom to read lines . . ."

I don't believe what I'm hearing. "You think after complimenting my acting and giving me some Skittles, I'll just jump back into bed with you?"

"It doesn't have to be a big deal," he says easily, sending my head spinning all over again.

What doesn't have to be a big deal? I want to ask. Is it that his relationship with Madeleine means so little that he'd throw it away to cheat with me? Or if he really is in love with Madeleine, is hooking up with me so inconsequential he's not even considering what it would do to his relationship? I don't know which one is worse.

"A big deal?" I get out. "I thought you were in love with my best friend."

Tyler shrugs. "Madeleine doesn't have to know. Not if you don't tell her."

I'm stunned speechless for a second. Tyler is somehow a worse guy than I thought he was—than I *knew* he was. Even when he cheated on me and dumped me, I never expected he could be capable of something like this. Hurting Madeleine for no reason just to have something he's had and replaced.

"We did this, Tyler," I hear myself say. "Remember? You're the one who didn't want me anymore."

He tries to place a hand on my arm, but I twist away. "It's just, doing the play with you, being here with you," he begins, "I'm remembering what it was like when we first got together. We had something really great for a while."

"We did." I glare at him. "Until you chose Madeleine."

He holds his hands up in defense. "Okay, okay. Forget it, then." I watch him cross the room to his suitcase and pull out his script. "You want to run the lines?"

I stand there with shock written on my face, not believing anybody could possibly shrug this off. But there he is, already opening the play. "No, I don't want to *run lines*," I spit. Doubting he'll bother to reply, I leave his room and hurl the door closed behind me.

I don't get two steps before my heart sinks. Tomorrow, I'll have to do a lot more than run lines with Tyler. I'll have to run the entire play, in front of everyone. The thought makes me want to drink poison and lock myself in a sepulcher.

TWENTY-FOUR

ROMEO: *Is the day so young?*

BENVOLIO: *But new struck nine.*

ROMEO: *Ay me, sad hours seem long.*

I.i.164–6

I WAKE UP THE NEXT MORNING AT 10:14 a.m., having slept for ten hours. I'm pretty certain it's a personal record. I only woke up briefly before 7:30 room checks when Alyssa snuck back in. The next time I woke up, she was gone.

I reach to the nightstand to grab the schedule Jody passed out on the bus. I've missed breakfast, I discover. Rehearsal's supposed to start in an hour, which means I should get up. I should get ready to endure Owen ignoring me, to withstand Alyssa's scowls and face Tyler, to play the role of a beloved, lovestruck girl who I really, really hate.

I stay in bed instead.

I know I have to tell Madeleine, but I also know doing so will ruin her relationship, a relationship everyone thought was perfect. It's not fair, when I think about it. It'll be my words that hurt her, even though it's Tyler who did something wrong. I'm not up to giving her that call just yet.

If not for me, Madeleine wouldn't have anything to find

out about Tyler. And if not for me, Mom wouldn't have to be reminded of or talk to the person who broke her heart. She would've moved on the way she wanted when she moved out. She might've even been happy if I hadn't been there to reopen wounds she'd tried to forget. None of this is my fault, but it is *because* of me.

The thought hits me then, involuntarily, like it's come from somewhere outside me. Like someone else wrote it down and shoved it into my hand, the world's worst love note.

I'm the reason everyone close to me gets hurt.

Rehearsal time comes and passes. I don't budge, staring up at the ceiling from under the covers. It's six minutes into rehearsal when the texts start. The first three from Bridget Molloy, the stage manager, with increasing urgency culminating in a long string of exclamation points. One from Tyler, just u coming? A longer one from Jenna notifying me that Jody's freaking out and is going to send someone to my room in two minutes.

I wait ten minutes, refusing to get out of this bed until I'm dragged by the ankles. Nobody comes.

I'm dozing off when a final text lights up my phone.

WHERE ARE YOU?

Anthony's name on my screen stabs me with a sliver of guilt. I remember what this performance means to him. It'd destroy him if this show was ruined, and especially if his best friend let it happen.

It's not just Anthony, either. There's Jason Mitchum, who really learned to swordfight from YouTube tutorials to play Tybalt. Jenna, whom I overheard murmuring her lines to herself the entire bus ride. And then there's Owen, who loves every word of *Romeo and Juliet* with a deeper appreciation than any actor I've ever worked with.

This play is important to people other than Tyler Dunning. People who are important to me. Showing up and playing Juliet is one small opportunity I have *not* to hurt them. And am I really ready to throw away my chance to go to the college I've dreamt of since I was a kid? I launch myself out of bed, throw on a pair of jeans and a parka, and fly out the door.

I run the three blocks to the theater, the cold biting my lungs, and thread between bicyclists and coffee-carrying pedestrians. I'm out of breath by the time I hit Pioneer Street, which fortunately isn't crowded because it's the Oregon Shakespeare Festival's official off-season. The rounded back of the Elizabethan theater goes by on my left as I rush down the hill to the Angus Bowmer Theatre straight ahead.

Throwing open the door, I burst into the auditorium. Our monastery set is on the stage. No one is seated in the audience, unlike at school, except Bridget with her headset and Jody with her clipboard and a pencil pressed to her lips.

"I long to die if what thou speak'st speak not of remedy," I hear from the stage, and despite my parka and the overactive theater heating, I feel a chill run through me. That's my line . . . but I'm not on stage. I watch motionless as Alyssa walks to my mark while Owen gives Friar Lawrence's reply. She doesn't stumble over a single line, delivering Juliet's desperate dialogue flawlessly. Better than I would've.

"Take thou this vial, being then in bed—" Owen pauses in the middle of his monologue when he sees me. Jody follows his gaze, her eyes narrowing.

Without bothering to call the scene to a halt, she walks up the aisle toward me. Her face is red, her mouth pulled tight in something between irritation and disappointment. "Where have you been?" Her voice rises on the final word and echoes in the empty theater.

"I—I overslept," I mumble.

Her eyes widen. "You *overslept*? In the four years I've known you, Megan, you've never been less than ten minutes *early* to a rehearsal. I know you weren't thrilled to get the Juliet role, but I thought you were mature enough to handle it, or at least that you respected us enough to show up and try."

"I'm here now, aren't I?" I force impudence into my voice to push down the tears.

"You're here an hour late to the most important rehearsal of the entire production. You were off your game in class yesterday, obviously distracted. I'm tired of fighting you on this, Megan." Her expression softens, and she looks unfamiliarly sad. "I don't know what's going on with you, but you win. I'll give you what you've always wanted. You'll play Lady Montague, or nothing."

I don't answer. Alyssa watches me from the stage, and I realize what's happened. They don't need me. They never did. Jody waits for me to decide, but I turn and walk toward the door. Away from what I knew deep down to expect.

If they want to replace me, fine. It's probably better if they do.

I'm halfway to the hotel when I feel my phone vibrate. I pull it out, dreading a gloating text from Alyssa or one from Anthony telling me I'm the worst friend ever.

Instead, it's Owen.

What the hell was that?

Blinking back tears, I send him what I hope will end the conversation.

What should have happened a long time ago, Owen.
Just leave me alone.

It's the first time Owen's voluntarily talked to me in weeks, and under better circumstances I wouldn't pass up the possibility of figuring things out between us. But not today. Not now.

TWENTY-FIVE

I HAVEN'T LEFT MY ROOM IN SEVEN hours, except for the trip to
the vending machine to pick up what passed for dinner—
which hardly counts. I pretended to sleep when Alyssa returned to the room to be counted for nightly room checks
by a parent chaperone, and while my former understudy
unpacked noisily, probably wanting to wake me up in order
to brag about Juliet, I didn't budge until she left for Will's
again.

I'm flipping channels between two stations of Ashland
nighttime news when there's finally a knock on the door.
Three quick taps, light but deliberate. I've been expecting
Jody to try to talk to me, or maybe lecture me some more, ever
since rehearsal ended. I'm surprised she waited this long.

What if she waited this long because she's sending me home?
Worry constricts my chest. *What if she had to organize my
transportation, or whatever?* Knowing I can't ignore her, I drag
myself to the door.

But I crack it open to find Owen, clutching his notebook.

"What do you want?" I ask, holding the door open only a couple inches.

His expression is guarded but gentle. "I want to show you something."

I start to shut the door. "I'm really not in the mood, Owen."

"I finished it." He holds up his notebook, and in a moment I realize what he means. His play. It surprises me enough that I release my hold on the door, and he brushes by me into the room.

I collect myself, rounding on him. "You ignore me for weeks, and now you barge in here to show me your *play*? That's . . . great. I'm really happy for you," I say sarcastically.

"I wasn't ignoring you." His voice is quiet.

"We haven't talked since . . ." I can't bring myself to complete the sentence. To put a name to whatever happened between us in his room.

"What you said about Cosima and my play stung, and I know I said enough to make you hate me. I was ashamed and frustrated with myself, and I needed distance." He fervently flips the pages of his notebook. "But I couldn't ignore you. Not even if I tried." He looks up at me, a tentative smile curling his lips, and my heart does a familiar Owen-related leap. But it turns back into lead when I remind myself of everything that happened this weekend and everything that stands between us.

"Well, thanks," I say stiffly. "You can go now."

His smile disappears, but he doesn't move. "I won't go until you tell me what's wrong."

"Nothing's wrong."

"I know you better than that, Megan," he says, looking at me intently. "Your text had complete sentences and perfect punctuation. I know something's happened." I say nothing, knowing he'd see through whatever bullshit explanation I give him, and he continues. "What you said to me in my room, you were right."

I look up sharply. *About Cosima?*

"I was afraid to write because I was afraid I'd suck," he goes on, and I deflate a little. "I didn't want to hear it, but I needed to." He places the notebook on the bed. "I wanted to show you the play because it's entirely thanks to you. I thought you might need a reminder of how important you are."

File for future reference: Owen can crush me with a word.

"Owen . . ." I turn away, trying to hide the tears welling in my eyes.

He steps forward and places a hand on my arm. "Does it have something to do with Tyler? I saw you with him last night . . ."

I jerk back. "Did he say something?" On top of everything else today, I couldn't handle it if Tyler was spreading some story about us that didn't happen. Knowing what he's capable of, I wouldn't put it past him.

"No." Owen frowns. "Wait, what would he have said? I just meant that he tries to make you feel bad sometimes."

I sag against the dresser in relief. "No, it wasn't that. He . . . tried to hook up with me. Nothing happened," I rush to say, not wanting Owen to believe I'm the kind of person who could go behind my best friend's back like that. But he's still looking at me with concern, and there isn't a trace of judgment in his dark eyes. "It just changes everything I thought about him and me, and him and Madeleine," I continue.

Confusion traces a crease in his forehead. "Which was what?"

"I guess I could accept being dumped, or even being cheated on, when it meant Madeleine having something perfect." I drop my gaze, unable to meet his, and study his rumpled black sweater and the smudge of ink on his thumb. "But I don't understand why Tyler would break up with me if this is how he's going to treat her."

Owen pauses like he's searching for words. "It's not about you or Madeleine," he says slowly. "It's not about you being inadequate or her being perfect. It's Tyler. The guy's an asshole. He was *never* going to be a good boyfriend, to either of you. He's like every guy you date—" He stops, correcting himself. "I mean, they're not assholes, not every one of them. It's just, Will, even Anthony, who was obviously gay—you pick guys who will leave you, who will hurt you, who could never be what you deserve. You're trying to protect yourself from getting your hopes up."

Indignant, I flush. He's one to talk. He hurt me and deserted me just like the rest. "Who do you think you are?" I say, fire in my voice. "You've only known me for a few months. What gives you the right to come in here and tell me that my relationship history is some sort of fucked-up self-fulfilling prophecy—"

"Every prophecy is a self-fulfilling prophecy, Megan," he says seriously. "You taught me that. We *have* only known each other a few months, but you've seen me in a way nobody else ever has, and I think I might know you better than any-one, too." I feel myself softening, until he continues. "You tell yourself you deserve to be dumped, but you don't. You choose it."

"Wow," I say harshly. "Thanks, Owen."

"No, I—" he stutters, backing away from me and begin-ning to pace across the room. "This isn't coming out right. I mean—I know what you were thinking when you saw Alyssa on stage playing your role. You were thinking what you're always thinking. That you're replaceable."

He *does* know me better than anyone. The realization hits me like a blow, because despite him being here, despite how he's unfailingly loyal and passionately caring, he isn't mine.

"But you're not." He pauses in his pacing to look up at me, and there's an undeniable change in the air. "You're irreplace-able. To your family, to your friends—to me."

The ashes of everything I felt when he was kissing me weeks ago leap into a flame. He's standing in the middle of the room, watching me with his eyes unguarded, and I can read in them everything he wants. It's exactly what I want, too.

I walk forward like I'm being drawn to him, then stop, only inches away. He reaches out and takes my hand, and whatever was between us finally crumbles as I bring my lips to his. He kisses me back softly, still without stepping forward to meet me. Pressing his fingers into my palm, he pulls back.

With his free hand he traces the line of my cheek, and in his touch I feel a hesitation, like he's holding back hope. "How do I know this is for real?" he asks in a whisper.

"Doesn't it feel real?" I'm breathless, hardly able to form the words.

"Yes, but it's felt real to me before, even when you were just flirting for fun. How am I supposed to know you mean it? Especially considering I'm not exactly your type. You know . . . shy, *sweet*." He grimaces on the word.

I tilt my head to find his eyes, forcing him to meet mine. "Here's a hint. With you, it was never just for fun." He nearly smiles. "Besides, my type hasn't exactly worked for me, as you eloquently pointed out. And yes, you're sweet. I like that you're sweet. But you're not only sweet, you're witty, fascinating, charming . . ." I close the distance between us. "And we both know you're not shy." I raise an eyebrow.

He leans in, laughing, and kisses me once more. And this time, there's nothing hesitant about the way he grabs my waist and tugs me tightly against him. Without letting him go, I lead us toward the bed. I remember what I felt the last time we were in this position, how desperate I was to have as much of him as I could, but . . . it's different now. For the first time, I'm not focused on when it will end. I sit down on the sheets and wait for him to climb on top of me.

He doesn't. Instead, he reclines next to me, and with one unexpectedly quick motion he pulls me on top of him. I let out a surprised laugh and lower my face to his. But before our lips meet, I draw back suddenly.

"Wait," I say, leaning up while straddling his waist, my heart plummeting out of my chest and onto the floor. "We did this. You have a—"

Owen cuts me off. "I broke up with Cosima."

"What?" I stutter, reaching for my heart on the floor-boards. *"When?"*

He props himself up and strokes my side. "Pretty much the minute you left my room."

It takes a moment for the words to come together in my head—it's possible his hand on my side isn't helping. But when they do, I'm overwhelmed. Relief, indignation, and adoration fight for space inside me. It's all I can do to kiss him deeply before pulling back and peering at him admonishingly. "You really should have told me."

A smile spreads across his face, then slowly fades. "I thought you weren't interested."

I take his face in my hands and stare into his eyes, refusing to let him misunderstand me this time. "Sweet, witty, fascinating, charming," I say slowly, "and an idiot." He's laughing when I lean forward to pick up where we left off.

I lift my shirt over my head and take no little pleasure from the way his eyes widen. "Off," I order, pointedly nodding at his sweater. With boyish urgency, he pulls it off, and—

Owen has a six-pack.

Years of pursuing jock-bros like Wyatt Rhodes, and it's *Owen Okita* who's finally going to fulfill my high school goal of hooking up with a six-pack. The universe works in mysterious ways. They're not the most defined abs I've ever seen—he's not Zac Efron—but they're there. Isn't there some law of nature that the sensitive, writerly guys shouldn't be ripped?

"Owen!" I prod his stomach. "How did this happen? Explain yourself!"

He looks down, uncomprehending. I run a finger down

the line of his muscle, and his face lights up. "I don't know," he says with a lazy smile. "Just enjoy it, Megan."

Laughing, I get off him and walk to the door. But with my hand on the deadbolt, I pause.

I don't want to do what I've done in every one of my relationships before. I don't want to rush. With Owen, though, this doesn't feel like rushing. It feels exactly right, right now. I don't want to be with him in this way because I think I have to now, before he disappears. I'm not doing it under a deadline, under the expectation of everything falling to pieces—it's not rushing because it's not for the wrong reasons. If I know it's real, and Owen knows it's real, it doesn't matter how fast it is. I want to be with him because I *want* to.

I close the deadbolt and turn to face him. "Those too . . ." I point in the general direction of his gray corduroys. I'm expecting the Owen blush, but he only smiles.

"Okay, okay." While he undoes his belt, I step out of my jeans. Thankfully, I'm wearing more respectable underwear today. Nothing written on it.

I climb on top of him, and we kiss in the way people do when there's not a hint of doubt it'll progress to something else. I let my hands explore his chest and—yes, his six-pack. His fingers brush the skin of my back, skimming the lace at the bottom of my bra. I urge him on with my lips.

When I guide one of his hands lower, he pulls back. "I . . ." he starts. "I wasn't expecting anything like this to happen."

I'm thrown, and I tense up. "Do you not want it to?"

"No," he says quickly. "It's not that. It's just . . . I've never . . ." He trails off once more, this time with a vivid blush.

My eyes widen. For the first time I consider the possibility he's not feeling everything I am right now. "I'm sorry, I didn't— If this is too fast, or not special enough—" I move to get off him.

Owen's hand on my hip holds me in place. "It's not that. I just wanted you to know."

"Oh," I say, relieved. "Yeah. I understand. Well, I have," I add, not at all sure how to have this conversation.

"Yeah, Megan. I know. You told me in detail." The corners of his mouth twitch upward. I feel mine do the same.

"Never with Cosima?" I prod his chest. "You guys were at *camp*."

He grabs my hand. "I hadn't known Cosima for very long." His voice has gone hushed. "I wanted to wait for something meaningful, for someone I cared about so deeply I needed this to express it."

A tiny tremor runs through me. *I* feel everything he's saying, but it wouldn't be unreasonable if—

"I was waiting for this," he says. He pulls me down for a kiss, and for a while we just sink into each other. His hand in my hair, his breath on my cheek, I reach off the bed for my bag.

"I have the . . ." I say, my fingers catching the plastic wrapper.

Straightening up, I notice him watching me questioningly. "Not that I'm not grateful, but who were you planning—?" He stops, reconsidering. "You know what, it *really* doesn't matter." He reaches to kiss me again, but I place a hand on his chest.

"Nobody, for what it's worth." I smile sideways at him. Dropping my gaze, I bring his hand back to my thigh. "Nobody I'd rather ..." I finish the sentence with a kiss.

We don't rush. Each motion is a step onto uncertain ground, into an unexplored place. My hands find the back of his shoulders, and I clutch him close to me, our hearts pounding together. It's nothing like it was with Tyler. It's how it's supposed to be. From the way Owen's eyes hold mine, I know he feels it, too.

I've spent the day in this bed, in this room, committing to memory every detail of the paint on the walls and the kitschy pattern of the curtains. It's been empty, suffocating, but with Owen it's bursting with light. It doesn't matter the hotel is cheap and plain, the view out the window ordinary—it's perfect. I don't need skinny-dipping under the stars. I only need this.

Owen breathes my name, and I feel like the center of the universe.

We lie in bed for minutes that feel like seconds or hours, my head resting on the hollow of his shoulder.

"Wow," he whispers in the darkness. "No wonder you thought I was insane for having a girlfriend all the way in Italy."

I feel him smile, and I laugh softly. "Yeah, now you know what you've been missing out on."

"I was missing out on a lot before I met you."

I slide my hand up his chest. "To be fair, I didn't know it could be like this either."

"Really?" He tilts his head down.

I look up, meeting his eyes. "Really." I pause, a little nervous to ask the question in my head. "Do you want to stay?"

He hugs me tighter. "Of course I do."

I close my eyes, not bothering to wonder how long he means. Tomorrow, two weeks, it doesn't matter—right now is enough.

TWENTY-SIX

ROMEO: *I have more care to stay than will to go.*

Come death and welcome. Juliet wills it so.

How is 't, my soul? Let's talk. It is not day.

JULIET: *It is, it is. Hie hence, begone, away!*

III.v.23–6

WHEN I WAKE, OWEN'S NEXT TO ME.

I roll onto my side to find him already awake. He's lovingly tracing a finger down my arm, and when our eyes meet, he kisses me lightly on the shoulder.

My stomach growls. Owen looks startled, then amused, and I realize exactly how hungry I am. Madeleine's brownies and the two granola bars I had for dinner aren't holding me after the events of last night. How long *has* it been since I ate? I glance at the clock. "Shit!" I elbow Owen. "It's seven twenty!"

"Ow, Megan." He's rubbing his ribs when I turn back over, and in the morning light I'm given new appreciation of his shirtless chest.

"Sorry," I say, not really meaning it. "Seriously though, you're going to miss morning room checks if you don't leave."

In the back of my mind I notice Alyssa hasn't returned yet either. Whatever she's doing with Will, she's really cutting it close on time.

Owen props himself up on his elbow, blinking. "Oh. Right. Yeah." He tosses off the covers and begins searching for his clothes on the floor. Pulling on his pants, he pauses and faces me, concern in his eyes. "Hey, um," he says hesitantly, "everything's . . . okay, right?"

Touched, and noticing his ears have gone my favorite shade of red, I smile. "Oh my god. You're perfect."

"Um, thanks." A smile flickers on his face. "But you didn't exactly answer the question."

I leap out of bed and fling my arms around his neck. Tilting my head upward so our noses nearly touch, I smile shamelessly. *"Okay* would be putting it mildly." I crush my lips to his, spurred on by his adorableness. Without hesitation his arms encircle my waist, and—I feel him leading us toward the bed.

"Owen!" I say, chastising. Not that I blame him for his enthusiasm. I did just throw myself at him without a stitch of clothing on.

He looks taken aback. "But you just said it was—"

"You have nine minutes," I interrupt, picking up his shirt and halfheartedly offering it to him.

He only grins. "Nine minutes is so much time, Megan."

I laugh and shake the shirt. "No, really. I don't know why Jody didn't drop by yesterday, but she's definitely going to today, to lecture me or something before call time. Besides, do you want *Alyssa* to walk in on us? She'll be back any minute." Owen groans, and I have no choice but to toss the shirt in his face. "Out, Romeo!"

Morning room checks happen with no sign of Jody—or of Alyssa. Brian Anderson's mom, the chaperone, picks up my Juliet costume for quick alterations to fit Alyssa's petite height and measures me for the Lady Montague dress, and I realize Jody's given me the part whether I like it or not. I guess that's her style. I'm beginning to wonder whether she'll *ever* come talk to me or if she's written me off completely.

I've just returned to my room after running downstairs to grab a bowl of oatmeal—I wanted to hit the buffet before everyone else got there—when I hear a knock on the door. I know it's not Jody, who's discussing set placement with the stage crew for their scheduled meeting in the theater. It's probably Owen coming back to get his belt that he left when I kicked him out. I open the door, the belt in hand.

"Dad?"

I hurriedly toss the belt in the trash can behind the door while he strides past me into the room. He looks around without appearing to really take anything in. "We have to talk, Megan," he announces.

"Why are you here?" I ask haltingly.

He raises an incredulous eyebrow. "You disappeared from rehearsal on a school field trip."

"Yeah, but how do you—"

"Jody called me," he says, his voice suddenly lowering.

"She sounded angry, saying something about you no longer playing Juliet. Is that true?"

Now I understand why Jody hasn't come to see me. She brought in the big guns. "Yeah, it's true, but it's fine. I didn't want to be Juliet in the first place." I keep my voice steady despite how I'm still reeling from his intrusion. "I'm Lady Montague now, the part I should have had from the beginning. I have, like, two lines."

Dad perches on the edge of the bed and frowns. "I don't know what you're talking about, the part you should have had from the beginning," he says eventually. "I know you've put a lot of work into this play. It's why your mom flew home to watch you." I hate how innocuously he says *home*, like he doesn't know he forced Mom out of the place where she belongs. "Then we get an irate phone call from a teacher who's always loved you—your mom and I are worried."

"Don't pretend you care how Mom feels," I shoot back, surprising myself, and him. He recoils, confusion written in his eyes.

"What do you mean?" he asks.

I know I probably should take it back, but everything I've watched happen to my family over the past three years is boiling to the surface, and I charge on. "Weren't you paying attention when we had dinner at the house together? Or were you too busy with your new wife to even notice how upset *my* mom was?"

"Your mother's not upset," he says calmly, like I'm the one who has this wrong. "We went out to lunch yesterday, the four of us."

"She was crying, Dad. When she put Erin to bed, I found her in Erin's room crying, alone." I feel a tremor in my own voice. "She's heartbroken. She's always been heartbroken. It's why she shouldn't have even come here in the first place—it only makes her sadder. But what would you care, right?"

"That's not fair." Dad tries to interrupt, but everything I haven't said to him for years is rushing out of me.

"You're the one who divorced her, who stopped loving her. Then you jumped into bed with Rose, not even caring how hurt Mom was." I take a breath. I've run out of words for what I'm feeling.

"I wasn't *in* love with your mom anymore," he says gently, his shoulders sagging, "but I do still love her. I'll always love her. Your mom knows that. She understands why we couldn't be together anymore, but she knows how I feel about her."

"She obviously *doesn't*, Dad," I return. "If she did, I wouldn't have found her crying upstairs in her old home. Remember?"

"Just because your mother understands how I feel about her doesn't mean it won't hurt her sometimes. It hurts me, too." He rubs his face distractedly, his eyes desolate. "It's a hard thing, ending something that permanent. It's a pain that never goes away."

I try to reconcile his words with what I know. It doesn't work. "But you moved on. You moved on so quickly," I say weakly.

Dad straightens up, looking surprised. "I fell in love with Rose, but I haven't moved on," he amends carefully, uncertainly even. "I guess I never considered how it looked to you. How quickly I brought Rose into my life. But finding Rose has nothing to do with what I feel for your mother. Your mom is an invaluable part of my life, and no matter what, she always will be." From the vulnerability in his voice, I feel the truth of what he's saying. He pauses, something searching in his expression. "I hope you know, Megan, if you think Erin and the baby change your place in our family—nothing could ever change that."

I say nothing. I don't know how to tell him he's wrong. They *have* changed my place. It's impossible to admit out loud.

"Hey. Look at me," he says gently. I do, tears I wish I could banish brimming in my eyes. His voice is rough when he continues. "I'm sorry," he says. "I haven't been there for you the way you needed, the way you deserve. I'm trying to figure out how to be a new father *and* raise an intimidatingly smart, self-possessed teenager, and I know I haven't gotten it right every time. But us moving to New York isn't us leaving you behind." He pauses as if for permission, which I give by waiting. He goes on. "You're kind of scarily grown-up now, Megan," he says with a faint grin. "Next year you're going to college. You're going to be pursuing your own future. I want you to have that experience on your own—being the incredibly independent adult you already are."

I smile back, a tear stumbling over my eyelashes.

"That said," he continues, "if you ever need us, or want us, or you're tired of being grown-up for a while, then come home."

Home? I feel my smile fade. "New York's not my home," I say. "It won't be the same. You'll have your own life, and I won't belong."

"Where we are doesn't matter," he says with half a laugh,

as if he's surprised I could imagine otherwise. "Wherever we are, we're family."

His words dissolve the weight on my chest, the weight I hadn't fully realized had lain there for years. He stands up and walks across the room, placing his hands on my shoulders and looking down at me.

"Nothing could ever change how much I love you," he says, and I collapse into a hug against his chest. I'm crying into his shoulder without even realizing it, his hands stroking soothing circles on my back. We remain that way until I'm out of tears.

Finally, I pull back, noticing the ugly snot stain I've left on his shirt. He doesn't seem to mind. "So," I say, casting around for something to defuse the heavy emotion in the room, "how pissed *did* Jody seem on the phone?"

He laughs. "Pissed. Not pissed enough she wouldn't talk to you about the role, though."

"I'm fine with just being Lady Montague. I only need the acting credit for SOTI," I say, stepping away and picking up my new costume. "It doesn't matter what part I play."

"I don't believe that," Dad replies sharply, and I whip to face him, surprised at his sudden conviction. "For months, I've heard nothing but *Romeo and Juliet*. This role is yours. You earned it."

"It doesn't matter," I protest. "They found a new Juliet."

"So what if there's a new Juliet?" he asks, throwing the thought away with a wave of his hand. "I want to know that if you don't go on stage to do what you've worked for, you won't regret it tomorrow."

Still clutching the Lady Montague costume, I picture walking on stage in the Angus Bowmer Theatre just to say two lines. I could do it, but it'd hurt. I've put hours and hours into this play, I've made Juliet my own, and to just walk away . . . Then I picture standing on Juliet's balcony, delivering lines to Tyler Douchebag Dunning—and it doesn't feel impossible.

I thought I wasn't meant to be a main character, on stage or anywhere else. But I also thought Madeleine was perfect and she and Tyler were meant to be, that my dad didn't care about my mom and my place in our family was disappearing, and that Owen could never want someone like me. I thought I couldn't fall for someone absolutely and completely. I've been wrong before.

I look back up at Dad, and I know he sees the resolve in my eyes, because he's smiling. "Jody's in the lobby. I saw her returning when I got here," he says, taking the costume out of my hands. "Go."

In one step I've reached the door. But before I pull it open, I double back and throw my arms around him. "Thanks, Dad."

I enter the lobby, and I'm momentarily overwhelmed by the pre-performance chaos. The noblewomen of Verona have gathered in full costume around the brunch buffet and are chattering excitedly. Nearby, one of the prop masters explains to Anthony for the hundredth time how to use the blood squib for his death scene. The stage crew, Will included, have chosen the center of the room to go over the set changes one final time.

I pick out Jody by the front doors talking to a couple of parent chaperones, none of whom looks happy. Threading in between the costumed girls, I catch snippets of their conversation.

"Heard he was . . ."

"She just called . . ."

". . . Italian girlfriend."

Wait. I stop so abruptly that Jeremy crashes into my back. He mutters an apology and darts around me. I know there's only one person *Italian girlfriend* could refer to, but I have to be certain. I come up beside Courtney, ignoring the indignant looks I get from everyone I just cut in the buffet line.

"Megan! You're here!" Courtney doesn't bother hiding the curiosity in her voice.

"Uh, yeah. I wasn't feeling well," I lie, eager to dodge this conversation. I match their gossipy tone. "Hey, did I hear you talking about Cosima?"

Jenna cranes her head past Courtney. "Yeah, I think she *might* be real." She giggles.

"What—uh—makes you say?"

"Owen's roommate was telling everyone that Owen and Cosima were on the phone this morning," Courtney rushes to say. "They were talking for, like, an hour. Apparently it was . . . *intense.*" She raises her eyebrows suggestively.

"Intense how?" I force myself to ask.

"We heard he was doing a lot of apologizing and reassuring. Whatever Owen did . . . he regrets something." Courtney sounds obviously pleased with herself.

I don't know why I asked. I knew what I would hear. "Still doesn't prove she's real." I fake a laugh as my heart is ripped from my chest. "I'll see you guys later," I say while they're laughing.

Leaving the line, I pause by the stairs to catch my breath, my chest tight. I don't want to be the kind of person who jumps to conclusions based on gossip, but with my roman-tic history, it's pretty much impossible not to. When Owen left my room this morning, he probably realized he wants to be with Cosima and regrets being with me. He called her to apologize.

I thought I'd done something different when I fell for Owen. He said I'd repeatedly chosen the wrong guys—I thought he was the right one. Instead, I've done exactly what I did every time before. It's like I can't escape putting myself in a position to be discarded and replaced.

Out of the corner of my eye, I catch Jody walking toward the door.

Asking for the Juliet role might just be putting myself in the same position once again. Jody could say no, and I would have to watch Alyssa take everything I've earned. But I have to try. I'm happy I tried with Owen. I know deep down I am. Even if things with him are over without having hardly be-gun, I don't have time to fall apart right now. The play's too important.

I march up to Jody, sidestepping everyone in my way. Her

hand's on the door. I slide in front of her, stopping her from leaving, and her expression hardens.

"I'm *really* sorry about yesterday," I say in a single breath. "It was unprofessional and disrespectful to you and to everyone involved in the production."

"Yes, it was," she says, unwavering. "I don't have time for this. I'll deal with you after the performance."

"No, we have to talk now," I tell her. I've talked back to Jody before, but this degree of boldness startles even me. It definitely gets her attention—she drops her hand from the door and crosses her arms. "You need to give me the role back," I continue before she can reprimand me.

Surprise joins the sternness in her eyes. "Why's that?"

"I didn't think I could relate to Juliet before. I thought she was an idiot, giving up everything for a guy with mediocre flirting skills." Jody raises an eyebrow but doesn't smile. "But I understand her now." I pause, hoping she's willing to hear more.

"What do you understand, Megan?" she asks, sounding tired.

Encouraged, I go on. "Everyone's an idiot like Juliet sometimes. Or everyone should be. Juliet dares to care about something. It makes her do crazy things—crazy like confronting her director in the middle of a crowded hotel lobby to beg for something she probably doesn't deserve." Jody permits a small grin. "I'm ready to be like that. To care. I want to be Juliet, for you, for everyone in the play who I've worked with—and for me. *I* want this."

I finish my monologue, the most impassioned one I've ever given, and there's a horrible, quiet moment. Not quiet in the lobby, obviously, but between us, there's the silence of the empty stage before the curtain rises.

"Finally," she says at last. "I didn't come talk to you yesterday because I was hoping you'd come to me. You're a wonderful director, Megan. I've seen you break down and explain countless characters, all but delivering the lines yourself. I gave you the role of Juliet because I knew you could do it, but I wanted you to realize you could do it, too."

A grin spreads across my face. "Wait," I say hesitantly, "does this mean I have the role?"

"What do you think?" Jody gives me a wry smile. It's all the answer I need.

Relief races through me, followed by the thrill of this having actually worked. Then—"What about Alyssa?" I wonder aloud.

"That's the other reason I'm glad you came to talk to me." Jody shakes her head, sounding relieved herself. "One of our chaperones caught Alyssa trying to sneak back into her room this morning during room checks. I don't know where she went last night, but the conduct handbook requires I send her home, which would have meant forcing Jenna Cho to memorize the entire play in two hours. Now Jenna won't have to, and one of the stagehands will be reading Lady Montague."

She checks her watch. "Better get in costume, Juliet."

TWENTY-SEVEN

JULIET: *My bounty is as boundless as the sea,*
My love as deep. The more I give to thee,
The more I have, for both are infinite.

II.ii.140–2

I DO A THOUSAND THINGS IN THE next hour. I hurry up to my room, where my dad gives an honest-to-god cheer when I tell him I've got the part. I practically have to push him out the door before I take the world's fastest shower. Throwing on my sweats, I walk with wet hair dangling down my back to the parent chaperones' room, the Lady Montague dress wrapped in a ball under my arm. It takes reciting a portion of my final monologue to convince Jeremy's mom I need the Juliet costume back. I catch her grumbling about having to re-re-alter the dress.

Before I change, I drop by the dining room to grab an apple, which I've eaten by the time I've reached my room. I pull my costume on—no help from Owen this time, unfortunately—and text Anthony, who deserves an explanation, and Eric, who wants directions to the theater. If I survive the play, I'll try to corner him in the back and convince him to at least say hi to Anthony. I don't think that counts as meddling. Eric decided to come on his own, after all.

I do a good job not dwelling on Owen in the fifty-seven minutes it takes me to finish everything. I rush downstairs into the lobby, which I find has emptied out, unsurprisingly. Everyone's already on their way to the theater for an hour of makeup and mic checks before the performance.

I push open the front door, only now remembering I forgot my parka. Even with the sun streaming through the cloudless December sky, the air is eye-wateringly cold. But it's not the end of the world—Juliet's dress involves long sleeves and tights. I step out, hugging my arms to my chest. Only a few pedestrians cut me glances as I walk down Vista Street in full costume. I guess they're used to this sort of thing.

My dress fluttering in the wind, I march into the crosswalk on Fork Street. I'm in the middle of the road when, several steps in front of me, I spot a familiar friar's costume.

"Hey, Owen," I call to his back. How do I talk to someone who was heard having an "intense" conversation with his Italian ex hours after I took his virginity? I'll figure it out.

He turns in the middle of the street, his eyes lighting up when he sees me.

Whatever's going on with Cosima, I'm not going to be weird about it, I decide. I want to keep Owen as a friend, no matter how last night redefined everything for me.

"I heard about your epic speech to Jody," he says when I catch up to him. He's holding the schedule binder Jody handed out to everyone. "I'm really glad you're going to be Juliet."

"Thanks." I scramble to hold together everything his smile unravels in me.

318

"You look beautiful," he says, not doing me any favors.

The way he's looking at me—I can't help but remember him helping me when I was stuck in the dressing room, his hands brushing my back, his fingers lifting the hem up my body. And yesterday. *Yesterday.* But I play it cool. "You look chaste." I nod to his frock.

Owen steps up onto the sidewalk and twirls in place. "You know, appearances can be deceiving, Megan," he says, stunning me with a wry smile.

I blink. He's 100 percent flirting with me. I know it when I see it. I take a breath, walking beside him. "Hey, so, um, I heard you talked to Cosima this morning." I force myself to sound casual.

His eyes narrow quizzically. "Who told you that?"

"Just . . . some of the girls, you know."

He shoots me a sidewise glance like I've just claimed the Earl of Oxford wrote Shakespeare's plays. "No, I don't know. But, yeah, I did talk to Cosima. She just wanted to clear the air. We left things kind of ugly the last time we talked."

"Oh." I pause, replaying his words in my head and searching for clues. "And . . . ?" I finally ask.

"And . . . then we hung up?" he says like he has no idea what I could be implying. He looks over at me again, and he must notice the desperate curiosity in my expression. "Oh my god. Megan! I was reassuring her the breakup wasn't her fault." His eyes go wide. "Tell me you didn't think I was getting back together with her."

I feel my face redden. "I thought you might feel like last

night was a one-time thing—" I begin defensively. I hear how empty it sounds, how illogical. It's a reflex, born of breakup after breakup.

"I snuck out of my room after room checks," Owen cuts in, talking over me, "I told you you were irreplaceable, I showed you my play, and *then* we—" His face flushes spectacularly, and he gestures emptily in the air. "Which, remember, is something I'd never done before and something I'm desperately hoping is not a *one-time thing*."

We stop in front of the door to the back of the theater. When I look up at Owen, for the first time today I don't hold back what I'm feeling for everything about him, every part of him. Not for the crooked smile he's giving me this very moment. Not for the way he made me laugh while telling me exactly what my heart wanted to hear. Not for his intelligence or his humor. *Nor any other part belonging to a man*, I hear Juliet's voice in my head.

"I'm hoping it's not a one-time thing either," I say softly. "I kind of . . ." I feel a thought forming, and I follow where it leads. "I want to make this official. I don't know. What do you think?" I ask fumblingly.

Owen looks surprised, and then an uncontrolled laugh escapes him. "O, speak again, bright angel," he quotes, and I roll my eyes, recognizing Romeo's line. I move to shove him lightly, but he pins my hand to his chest. "I *really* want to make this official, Megan."

He kisses me, and I feel like call time might as well be in a million years, because I could do nothing but this forever. It's every bit the raging rush it was only hours ago in my hotel bed. His hair—ever too long—brushes my cheeks. My fingers, numb with cold only moments ago, tingle and trace burning lines over his shoulders. My pulse races.

I hear giggles behind me, and I realize what we look like to whoever's walking into the theater. Here I am, Juliet kissing a Romeo she never expected, who's dressed in the costume of a monk. Owen evidently notices them, too, because he holds up the binder to hide us from view, never once breaking our kiss.

I finally pull back and look up at Owen, arms still encircling his waist. "You're in luck, you know," I say. "Every one of my boyfriends finds the perfect girl right after we break up."

Owen kisses the top of my head. "Not every boyfriend," he murmurs into my hair. "I have her right here."

I don't have words for how this feels. I don't know that there are words. Not even in Shakespeare.

Heavy makeup coating my face, I wait in the wings for the curtain to rise. I didn't often force myself to imagine what this moment would feel like, but on the occasions I did, I didn't imagine this. There's no knot in my stomach, but I'm not giddy with excitement either. I feel calm. Centered. Each of my scenes lies before me in a lighted path to the final bows.

The curtain goes up. I peer into the audience, and even though it's dark, I feel my breath catch at the sheer number of people I can see. But I keep looking until I find them. Randall, Mom, Dad, and Rose sitting in the second row. Dad holds Rose's hand, but he leans into Mom's shoulder to whisper in her ear. I watch her smile at whatever he said while Courtney, the narrator, finds her mark.

"Two households, both alike in dignity . . ." I hear her begin.

I go on for my first scene with Romeo and realize it's the first time I've spoken to Tyler since Friday night. We exchange amorous glances across the Capulet Manor set, and I linger downstage before he strides to me and takes my hand. Waiting under the lights, I feel none of the revulsion I do for Tyler himself.

Because I'm not watching Tyler right now. I'm watching Romeo, and I'm Juliet.

He kisses my hand, and I snatch it away, playing the hard-to-get Juliet I've come to love. I exchange hushed dialogue with Nurse Jenna before I exit stage left for the end of Act I. Anthony's by the curtain, his eyes fixed on his mark, his lips moving imperceptibly. I put a hand on his shoulder and whisper, "Juilliard's going to love you." I catch his slight smile in the uneven backstage lighting.

In the wings, I watch a couple of freshmen diligently organizing the prop table. There's the dagger, the apothecary's bottles of poison, Owen's prayer book. The stage crew silently wheels the balcony set into position behind the curtains, and I catch a glimpse of Andrew Mehta and Bridget Molloy standing next to each other watching the narrator on stage, their hands inconspicuously entwined. I smile to myself. I guess *Romeo and Juliet* gets to everyone.

I turn and find Owen, who's helping Jenna with a quick-change from nurse to noblewoman near the wings stage right. And because I'm flushed from the Capulet Manor scene, because he's my *boyfriend*, because I'm ridiculously happy about that, because it's borderline pathetic how much I want to kiss him right now, I can't keep my eyes off him. He looks up, and he returns an unabashedly huge grin. We're *worse* than Romeo and Juliet.

Not taking my eyes off him, I walk backward, knowing I only have a minute to climb the stairs to the top of the balcony set. Mercutio and Benvolio are nearing the final lines of their scene on stage—

There's an enormous crash.

I whirl, restraining myself in the middle of the show from yelling at whoever's fault it was. I find Tyler in a heap on the floor, the wooden trellis in splinters surrounding him. Everyone's frozen, every head turned in our direction. Tyler begins to brush himself off, looking dazed if unhurt, when Bridget rushes over, her face ashen.

"Are—are you okay?" she stutters, clearly fearing the lead has just broken his leg. "What happened?"

"I was practicing the jump, and it just . . . collapsed." Tyler gestures to the trellis. His eyes clear, and a sudden fury fills them. He rounds on the stagehand nearest to him. "What the hell?" he hisses in the loudest whisper he can.

"It wasn't secured properly," Andrew Mehta offers weakly.

"Yeah, no shit." Tyler fixes his glare on Andrew in the dark. "What I want to know is whose fault it was."

"Tyler," I say sharply, stepping in to shield Andrew. "We don't have time for this. Anthony's on the final lines of the scene."

"If we don't have the trellis, we don't have the scene. I have to stop the show until we can fix it," Bridget murmurs in exasperation. She glances over her shoulder. "Where's Will? He's our only carpenter."

Nobody says anything. It's Andrew who finally speaks up. "He, um, left. He said he had to call Alyssa."

Bridget lets out a frustrated groan and begins muttering feverishly into her headset. It's exactly like Will, I realize. I don't know if he's trying to make the production, and by extension me, look bad because he's pissed I got the Juliet role back from Alyssa, or if he just doesn't care about the play anymore. Either way, he's screwed us over.

If we pause the play, it wouldn't be the worst thing ever. It'd just pull the audience out of the story, look unprofessional, reflect poorly on the Stillmont drama program—okay, it'd be the worst thing ever. But without Romeo climbing the trellis and kissing Juliet, I've never been able to pull off the scene. Owen walks up then, and his eyes meet mine.

And just like that, I know.

"However long it takes!" I hear Bridget say. "We need to drop the curtain, and tell the audience we're having technical difficulties—"

"Don't," I cut in. "We'll do the scene without the trellis." I give Tyler a quick look. "Just play it like it's written." He gives a short nod. Anthony comes off stage, and I turn to the stagehands while Bridget hurriedly calls off the curtain. "Roll the balcony on," I tell them as I step onto the set. I climb the staircase, the wooden boards creaking beneath my feet like they have in countless rehearsals.

I'm briefly blinded when the lights come up, and I watch Tyler from where I'm hidden on the set. Once again I'm impressed by how flawlessly he delivers his lines, this time because I know he's tempering his anger from hardly a minute ago.

When it's my cue, I walk onto the balcony and begin Juliet's monologue. Instead of waiting for Romeo to kiss me, I try to coax the love from Juliet's fearful heart. I find myself glancing at my family out of the corner of my eye. I remember Owen's steady heartbeat under my cheek while we drifted off to sleep. The way my dad held me this morning. With every line, I feel Juliet coming to life. I know what it is to love and to be loved.

I wonder breathlessly whether a rose by any other name would smell as sweet, I give Romeo my faithful vow, and when I tell him, "Parting is such sweet sorrow," I feel tears in my eyes.

I die tragically in Act V and come back to life once the curtains have closed. When I walk to the front and take Tyler's hand for my bow, the cheering gets louder, and I can't help it—I'm proud of myself.

I don't know if I'll ever act again. I won't write it off entirely. But I do know I'm glad I did it. Being in the spotlight's not terrible, and it taught me that losing yourself in a character might lead you to find something new in yourself. If I *do* return to acting, maybe I'll play someone without an all-consuming teenage romance.

Then again—where's the fun in that?

We file off the stage. The instant we're out of view, we're no longer noblemen and noblewomen, daughters and cousins, Montagues and Capulets. We're us, smearing stage makeup in a stupidly happy group hug.

I look for Owen and Anthony in the throng. But instead, I find Will waiting behind the crowd, looking uneasy. Out of the corner of my eye, I notice Tyler break off from the group and head directly for him.

"Look who showed up," Tyler says, his voice raised and edged in sarcasm. Everyone falls silent, and I know he's done restraining his anger.

Will doesn't flinch. "What's your problem, man?"

"You, *man*," Tyler returns. "Do you have any idea what could have happened? I could've broken my leg on stage, in front of everyone. You could've ruined the entire show!"

"Whatever. It went fine, didn't it?" Will tries to say. "You got your applause—" but before he finishes the sentence, Tyler steps up in his face.

I'm running toward them in the next moment, knowing their staring match could erupt in the blink of an eye. The excitement and pride and camaraderie of the room are ebbing fast, transforming into something ugly. "Tyler!" I force a hand between them.

"What? You're defending *him*?" Tyler rounds on me.

"It's so not about that," I fire back. "It was shitty"—I glare at Will—"but it doesn't warrant physical violence," I finish, turning back to Tyler.

"I deserve an apology. You do, too. It was your directing he ruined."

"Yeah, I do." For more than Tyler knows. I look back to Will and, surprisingly, from the guilt in his eyes, I know he knows what I mean. With Will in front of me, Tyler at my back, I tell the two guys who've hurt me worst what I know to be true. "If you beg for every apology you're owed, your throat will go dry," I say, noticing Owen watching by the back door. "You can't lose yourself over every problem, hurt, or wrong someone's committed you. Bad things happen. You fix your eyes on the future, and you move on."

I don't wait for Tyler or Will to say something. Without a backward glance, I walk to Owen.

"Ready?" he asks. There's an eager waver in his voice.

I nod, reaching into his heavy sleeve to take his hand. Instead of fighting our way through the crowded theater, we head to the back door behind the dressing rooms. We run into the night, the cold turning our cheeks and noses pink. It's a short sprint to the front foyer where our families and friends are waiting.

I search the room for my parents, and instead my eyes land on Anthony, fake blood staining his tunic. Out of the way of the crowd, Eric's handing him a bouquet of flowers— small, yet they look carefully chosen. Eric's eyes are eager, colored with a little nervousness. Anthony's are understanding, and appreciative. I don't know what's going on between them. But I feel like both of them know they'd be idiots to give up on each other.

Anthony catches my eye, noticing me. And though he gives me only the hint of a grin, he's glowing.

I nod at him and begin to walk away, wanting to give them their moment.

"Megan." I hear Anthony behind me, and I turn around. "You were an amazing Juliet."

"I was, wasn't I?" I say jokingly, but my smile is genuine.

My family's seated when Owen and I get to the restaurant, a white-tablecloth French bistro near the theater. My parents went ahead and got a table while Owen and I changed, scrubbed the stage makeup from our faces, and met Owen's family. His mom, a surprisingly short woman considering Owen's height, looked startled that Owen had a new girlfriend, while Sam tromped around the foyer boasting that his brother was dating Juliet. Owen didn't appear to mind.

When we sit down at the table next to my mom, Rose peers at Owen.

"I know you," she says, her face lighting up. "You're Biff Loman!"

"What?" Dad sits up and sets down his glass. "You've met Megan's new guy already?"

"*Dad . . .*" I say warningly, not liking the direction this conversation is heading or the way he clarified "*new* guy."

"I'm just really glad I have the chance to meet one of Megan's boyfriends," Mom chimes in while buttering her baguette.

I round on her, my eyes shouting *traitor*. "Mom, you're making it sound like there's one every week! I've only dated one other guy this year."

"School year or calendar year?" Randall asks, raising his eyebrow. Next to me, I hear Owen stifle a laugh. I jab an elbow into his ribs.

"He's handsome, this one," Rose whispers to me like she's finally finished her appraisal of him. "He's got nice eyes."

"Two sets of parents are *way* better than one," I grumble, reddening.

Dad leans in. "You're not afraid of heights, are you?"

"Dad!"

I feel Mom squeeze my hand under the table. "Let's let Owen be," she says reprovingly to my dad. "I'll bet Megan's given him enough trouble." She winks at me, and mercifully the discussion moves on to the new baby and Rose's birthing classes.

Two crepes later without further interrogation of Owen, we're in the middle of ordering dessert when my phone vibrates in my back pocket. I surreptitiously check it under the table, and my heart stops.

The email is from Professor Salsbury at SOTI. I open it with a shaking hand.

Dear Megan,

I'm terribly sorry I had to run after the play before we could chat, but I felt I couldn't let a performance as fine as yours go without prompt recognition. You played an outstanding Juliet.

I've been speaking to your teacher, Ms. Jody Hewitt, and she couldn't have had higher praise for your directing achievements. I think you'll be a wonderful addition to our directing program.

I look forward to seeing you on campus in the fall!

Michael Salsbury

I glance to the side, wondering if Owen's reading over my shoulder. But he's talking to my dad about *Snakes on a Plane*. I bring my phone up to the table, and I'm about to tell everyone the news until I notice Randall. Wiping sweat from his brow, he raises his knife to his wine glass and taps it once.

"If I could steal the spotlight for just a couple minutes," he begins, everyone's eyes on him. "I would like to say something to Catherine in front of all of you."

I'd almost forgotten. I hold my breath, knowing what's about to happen.

"This has been the greatest year of my life," he continues. "You, Catherine, are the most kind, caring, intelligent, creative, beautiful woman I've ever known."

I glance at Mom. Her eyes glitter with tears.

"You've given me innumerable gifts over the past year," Randall says, "including tonight, here with your family. I didn't have much of my own growing up. Since we met next to the Greek vases in the Blanton Museum—I had no idea what I was looking at, and you showed me everything— there's nothing I've wanted more than to be with you. But the more time I've spent with this family, the more I've realized it would be an equally great joy to be a part of it, too." He shifts his eyes to me. "I know you were joking, Megan, when you said 'two sets of parents,' but the truth is, I feel like we have become a family. And there's nothing I'd like more than to make that permanent."

He takes my mom's hand before he continues. "I never thought I'd be lucky enough to meet someone like you," he tells her, "let alone spend a year with her. If I could just have a little more luck—"

He kneels and pulls out a small black box. Mom gasps.

"Catherine, I love you more than anything. Will you marry me?" Randall asks.

Mom manages a yes through her torrential tears. The restaurant applauds while Randall slides the ring onto her finger and sweeps her into an embrace.

Owen puts his hand on my leg, and I feel him lean into me. He's looking at me questioningly, wondering how I'm handling this.

I watch my mom for my answer. She's staring into Randall's eyes, and I don't know why I ever doubted her feelings, because her gaze holds as much love as I've ever seen when she looked at Dad. I never expected Randall to earn it, but I felt tears in my own eyes when he knelt down with the ring. Randall isn't just an awkward accountant who's in a bowling league—he might be the love of my mom's life. My dad's words from this morning ring in my head. While Mom may never entirely move on from her past marriage, she *has* fallen in love. She's happy.

There's nothing holding my family together, not now, because there's nothing left broken. It doesn't matter where they'll be next year and where I'll be. They're *my* family. Complicated, messy, and mine.

I turn back to Owen. Placing my hand on top of his, I give him my answer in a smile.

I wouldn't change a thing.

TWENTY-EIGHT

ROMEO: *Did my heart love till now?*

I.v.59

THEY NAMED THE BABY JULIET.

I tried to dissuade them, but Rose insisted it's because of Juliet's wit and strong will, not the lovelorn-teenage-lunatic thing. She fell in love with the name after the performance, and I had no choice but to take that as a compliment.

"I don't think the name suits her, honestly," I say to Owen, who's hiking a couple of steps in front of me. I'm not a natural-born hiker, but today's the first day of spring, and I've been planning this since December. "She does nothing but sleep. Erin prepared me for the worst, but Juliet's, like, the most even-tempered baby I've ever heard of. I don't think she's really a Juliet."

"You never know." I hear the smile in Owen's voice. "I've seen Juliet-ish behavior come from the unlikeliest of people."

I roll my eyes even though he can't see me. "Well, I found her chewing on a copy of your play in the living room. Is that Juliet-ish behavior?" He laughs ahead of me. "It was my favorite scene, too. I think I'm going to need you to print me a whole new copy."

"You don't need to read it again, Megan," he says, sounding secretly pleased.

"Of course I do. My boyfriend wrote an amazing play, and I intend to read it every month until forever." We reach the top of the mountain, and I walk to the edge of the campground to take in the view. "Wow, you were right. This *is* nice." The forest opens in every direction below us. It's quiet, and the trees have grown in their new leaves, washing everything in bright green. I remember looking at the photos of this place, Bishop's Peak, on my phone with Owen months ago. It looked beautiful then. It looks nearly unreal now.

I take a quick picture and send it to Madeleine, who graciously lent me her hiking boots this morning. In the months since *Romeo and Juliet*, we've become even better friends. I told her about Tyler when I got home from Ashland, and she promptly broke up with him. She was upset for a couple of days—until she got into Princeton early, continuing her trend of being, well, perfect.

I turn to look for Owen and find him sitting on a log, notebook already out on his lap. I walk over and gently take it out of his hands, setting it down next to him. He glances up at me questioningly. "Owen, I didn't *really* bring you up here to write."

His eyebrows rise. "No?"

I climb into his lap, the bark rough under my knees. "Remember when you told me you hadn't gotten lucky up here, and I told you we should do something about that?"

His hands find the small of my back. "I have a vague memory of that, yes."

"Owen"—I lower my lips to his—"we should do something about that."

In the moment before our mouths meet, he laughs. "You know," he says, pulling back, "I had no idea what to do the first time you said that. I was utterly out of my depth."

"And now . . . ?" I whisper.

"Still utterly out of my depth," he replies, kissing my neck, "but I have an inkling."

This time it's he who moves to meet my lips. His hands tighten on my waist, pulling me closer. "Wait," I breathe, leaning back. "I want to say one thing first."

He nods, waiting with calm curiosity.

"I love you, like, really love you," I begin to ramble. "Like, a lot. Like, so much. So much that if you were to do something stupid like climb my nonexistent balcony in the middle of the night or compare your lips to two blushing pilgrims or something nonsensical like that—I'd still want to kiss your face off." Somehow I stop talking.

Owen brushes a hair from my face, his fingertips tracing the shell of my ear. "I love you, too."

"Wow." My face flares. "This is why you're the writer. Economy of words. I should have gone with that."

"Your way was perfect, Megan. And I would've elaborated, except you, on this mountain, with me, telling me everything you just told me, your hair looking the way it does and your beautiful eyes"—he stares right into them—"have me not at my most eloquent."

"Oh," I say, feeling even less eloquent myself.

His smile softening, Owen presses a long and deep kiss to

my lips, and I realize it was a terrible idea to haul myself to a place with Owen and thin oxygen and expect not to faint.

"Dost thou love me? I know thou wilt say 'Ay,' and I will take thy word," he whispers, catching my chin and tilting me closer.

"Owen," I say, recognizing Juliet's words. "That's my line."

Acknowledgments

THANK YOU, READER, FIRST AND FOREMOST, FOR picking up this book and following Megan's story. Imagining this in your hands is why we do what we do.

We'd be nowhere without the amazing Katie Shea Boutillier, our agent, who believed in this book from the beginning and who's given us incredible guidance in the form of keen editorial comments and an unwavering understanding of exactly what this story should be. We are endlessly grateful.

While we were utterly thrilled for this book to find a home with Puffin and the Penguin Young Readers group, we had no idea how lucky we'd be to work with the wonderful Dana Leydig, editor extraordinaire. For sharpening this story with commentary that consistently rang true, for finding depths where we didn't know to explore them—and for making us laugh in your line edits—thank you from the bottom of our hearts, Dana.

Thank you to Kristie Radwilowicz for capturing the perfect cover design we'd always hoped for and never could have imagined. And thank you to our publicist, Katie Quinn, and the entire Penguin Young Readers marketing and publicity team for getting the book into readers' hands.

To Julie Buxbaum, Huntley Fitzpatrick, Morgan Matson, and Micol Ostow, thank you for the blurbs of our dreams and for your encouragement and wisdom on the publishing journey!

To the Electric Eighteens, you guys rock. Thank you for making our debut year a hundred times better with your enthusiasm and your invaluable insight, and, of course, for giving us so many wonderful books to read!

We owe an enormous debt to our friends for reading our drafts, for following our trials and tribulations with a thoughtful ear and tireless encouragement, and for supporting us every step of the way.

Thank you to Mira Costa High School for introducing us to each other, without which many things would not have happened—this book included—and particularly to the English department for introducing us to Shakespeare.

Finally, we are eternally grateful to our families for, honestly, everything. The Bard said it best, as he often does: "I can no other answer make but thanks, and thanks, and ever thanks."

TURN THE PAGE FOR AN EXCLUSIVE,
NEVER-BEFORE-SEEN CHAPTER
FROM OWEN'S POINT OF VIEW!

YOUR FRIAR LAWRENCE

ROMEO: *Under love's heavy burden do I sink.*

I.iv.22

I SUCK AT ROMANTIC DECLARATIONS.

Everything else, I find—I won't say easy. It's not easy finding the perfect way to express your thoughts, to embody emotions honestly and affectingly. It's just not impossible.

I've been writing long enough to have gotten somewhat comfortable with crafting characters, detailing their worlds, figuring out how they would interact. Everything except goddamn romantic declarations. I do this every time, positioning my protagonists perfectly to fall for each other, then finding myself utterly incapable of giving voice to their feelings.

Granted, I could keep romance out of my plays entirely. But I don't. That probably says something about me.

I drop my eyes to the notebook open on my knees, the unfinished dialogue I'm working on taunting me. The hill outside the drama room is quiet, which is fortunate. In the hour since school ended, I've sat here writing exactly three and a half miserable lines of dialogue while members of the Romeo and Juliet cast rehearse inside. I can't walk home yet because

Friar Lawrence has a scene scheduled for today. For twenty minutes ago, to be exact. Jody is running late, per usual.

I'm not complaining. The delay gives me writing time, or would theoretically give me writing time if only I could figure out this scene. Nicolas, the character I've invented for Rosaline's love interest, is expressing his ardor to a disgruntled Benvolio. I reread the words I've written for the hundredth time, hoping irrationally that the end of Nicolas's declaration will jump out and finish itself.

NICOLAS
She wants with every fiber of her soul;
she rushes forth where others wander on.
Like fire in wind, her fearless joy o'erleaps
her hungry heart; it catches, every empty
room and roof alight, renewed in flames.
Her greatest gift is this, the way her lust
for life—for love, for hunger—passes fervent
into every soul she crosses. I could

Could . . . what? And here I wait, unable to write Nicolas's profession of love. I reach for the depth of detail, the feeling I need for the words to flow involuntarily and authentically onto the page. I find nothing. I scribble down one halfhearted effort. *I could only wish for* . . . Then I scratch it out. I scrawl something else—then scratch it out.

I'm writing another sentence, which I already know is shit without even finishing the line, when the drama door opens with the heavy clunk only school doors seem to have. I watch Megan Harper walk out. She shoves her hand through her long brown hair, her chipped green nail polish catching in the October sunlight. From where I'm sitting several yards away, she looks frustrated, the line I recognize from every rehearsal forming between her eyebrows.

She's forgotten the jean jacket she was wearing today, and she shivers slightly in her black dress, a turtleneck with long sleeves. With her black Doc Martens half laced and a tenacious concentration in her eyes, she's impossible to ignore.

She doesn't look in my direction. Instead, she leans back on the closed door, reciting words I know by heart. "'Romeo is banished'—to speak that word is father, mother, Tybalt, Romeo, Juliet, all slain, all dead." It's her monologue from Act III Scene ii. I find myself listening while she tries out a few different inflections. "All *dead*. All slain." She pauses. "All dead. All *slain*."

She lets her head fall back against the door in exasperation. I watch her. I know I ought to be writing. I don't have very much time in my day to put pen to paper, not with school, with Sam, with rehearsals and now the Senior Showcase scene I signed up for. Not with getting enough sleep to function like a normal human being. I need to use every minute I have.

But I don't. I'm unable to look away.

Megan straightens up, her eyes finding mine. She smirks. "Owen," she says. "You're staring."

I drop my eyes hurriedly to my notebook, my cheeks heating at her insinuation. Which is entirely off the mark. I collect myself, knowing if I stutter or flub, it'll just give her more to work with.

"I was not," I reply evenly. "It may shock you to know I came out here to be alone. If I wanted to stare at you, I could've stayed in rehearsal and watched you cry over Romeo on stage."

The response pleases her, I can tell from the coy gleam in her eyes. She saunters over—with Megan it's always a saunter, full of suggestions, possibilities, *implications*. Sitting down next to me, she brushes my leg with her bare knee. It's unmistakably intentional.

She's not embarrassed in the slightest that I caught her rehearsing. If there's a way to embarrass Megan Harper, I haven't come close to finding it. Me, on the other hand? The flush is only starting to fade from my cheeks. I was embarrassed she caught me staring, not to mention her suggestion I was checking her out. Which I wasn't. It's been months of this since the year started, Megan dispensing innuendos with staggering frequency and me calling on every ounce of wit and swagger I have to deflect them.

I gesture to my notebook. "Did you not just hear me say I came out here to be alone?" My voice carries none of the irritation I intended. Which, if I'm being honest with myself, is because I'm not irritated. I would be if it were anyone else interrupting me during a difficult, unproductive hour of writing. Megan is different. She's a part of this play I'm working on, after all.

"Are you asking me to leave?" Her question is genuine, not

offended. If I told her I wanted time to write, she'd return to rehearsing her lines, or she'd find Will to flirt with.

I close the notebook. "Why aren't you on stage, anyway?"

Megan grins. It's a grin I know well. It says, *you have fallen into a trap.* I brace myself. "Wow," she says, putting a hand on her chest. "First, he stares at me. Then, Owen Okita puts away his precious notebook for me. You know I have a boyfriend, right?"

I roll my eyes, even as my ears burn. "You do, don't you?" I reply, teasingly rhetorical. "I wonder, then, why you're out here flirting with me."

She elbows me, but I know she enjoys it whenever I challenge her. When we first started hanging out, I would spend nights pondering her inconsistent flirting, trying to figure out her intentions. Then I got to know her and realized it's just the way she treats everyone. It never means anything. Not that I'd know how to decipher when it's nothing and when it's *not* nothing. I guess if I were V-neck-wearing "Sexy Stagehand Owen," I would probably presume it's not nothing.

"I'm not on stage," Megan replies, "because Jody told me I have to rethink my monologue completely." I hear a hint of annoyance in her voice. "She gave me ten minutes to rehearse before we"—she nudges my knee with hers—"have to do Act II Scene vi."

I groan. This means my writing time for the day is up, unless I finish my homework fast enough after helping Sam with *his* homework. I could reschedule FaceTime with Cosima, except I've rescheduled more FaceTimes with Cosima in the past month than I'm proud of. Our calls often consist of me trying to follow her zero-context stories of classmates whose names I don't recognize. It's nice enough, though. I'm definitely hoping to return to the theater program where we met this coming summer. We're better in person.

It hits me every now and then how unlikely our relationship is. We're dating across 5,500 miles—I googled the distance once—because we spent one summer together at camp in New York. Then I remember how easy our days with each other were, and I don't question it. Our connection may not be one of sweeping passions, but such emotions are for the theater, not everyday life.

"I don't want Juliet to sound only distraught or lovesick," Megan says suddenly. "I want her resentful. Angry. She knows how little power she has in her own life, and she's using Romeo to express how horribly unfair it is. You know?"

It takes me a moment to realize she's talking about the monologue she was rehearsing. I nod, remembering the lines and how the scene ends. "What about when she says she wants to kill herself? Do you think it's out of anger?"

She pauses, pursing her lips. "I'll to my wedding-bed; and death, not Romeo take my maidenhead!" she recites. Her eyes sparkle like she's sharing an inside joke with her character. "My girl is pissed she didn't get to consummate her marriage. I'm not having a hard time with that part." She winks, then turns studious, her eyes drifting from mine and the line reforming between her brows.

I can't help liking this about Megan—the way she's flirty and flippant one moment and then deeply devoted to Shakespearean interpretation the next. Whatever she wants, whatever she's doing, she's one hundred percent.

"It's pretty bold, what Juliet's saying," Megan continues. "This teenage girl speaking openly about wanting to have sex. It's kind of progressive." I listen to her muse, understanding, not for the first time, why she's such a good director. "It's like she kills herself not entirely out of anger or lovesickness, but because it's the only way she can exert control over her own life."

She falls silent. I say nothing, wanting to hear whatever she's thinking.

"Waitwaitwait." She seizes my elbow, saying the three syllables in one exhilarated word. "Okay. I got it. Okay. What I'm missing is, like, revolutionary zeal. Underneath the anger, there's something almost hopeful. She's convinced she can reach the future she's entitled to if she just fights hard enough."

I mull over her words, impressed if not surprised. I could honestly listen to her talk Shakespeare all day.

"What do you think?" she asks earnestly.

"It's genius," I say, hoping she hears the decisiveness in my voice, the honesty.

Her lip curls softly in the sort of smile only meant for herself, full of quiet satisfaction, her eyes glowing with pride.

She's beautiful. The thought enters my mind without prologue or introduction, then flees equally inconspicuously. Guilt follows on its heels. *I have a girlfriend.* I shouldn't be noticing how beautiful someone else is, even for a brief, inconsequential moment.

The drama door clatters open, jolting me from my half-hearted remorse. Megan and I look up to find Anthony Jenson poking his head outside.

"Hey," he calls. "You two ready for some nuptials?"

Megan grimaces. She heaves a sigh, getting to her feet. While I'm shoving my notebook into my bag, she offers me an outstretched hand, which on any other day I'd take without a second thought. I place my hand in hers, trying to ignore how it feels, and pull myself to my feet. The instant I'm up, I release her hand. Which doesn't help—I feel the memory of her touch even when she's turned from me.

She jogs to the door, where Anthony waits. "Please tell me you were terrible and Jody's bar is really low," Megan says.

He snorts. "I'll have you know I received a standing ovation."

I follow them into the drama room, my head entirely elsewhere. While cast members stretch their legs between scenes, I find my thoughts returning to my earlier observation. *She's beautiful.* It's not the first time I've noticed it, obviously. But before, it only existed in the back of my head, like knowing the sky is blue. It's something I was consciously aware of, something I could picture if asked, yet haven't found myself thinking of often. Now? Now it's like I'm thirty thousand feet in the air and falling through nothing but blue.

Huh.

I can't concentrate on my lines. I'm onstage with Tyler, whose scenes we couldn't rehearse until he finished a makeup exam for extra credit. Romeo's failing calculus. He holds my arm, declaring his love for the offstage Juliet.

Instead of even pretending to listen, I continue dissecting whatever happened to me on the hill outside. I probably *should* call Cosima tonight. I'm probably only noticing Megan because I haven't talked to my girlfriend in too long. It's not because of Megan or her possible beauty. It's because I miss Cosima.

Yes, it's definitely that.

"Therefore love moderately," I remind Tyler, finishing Friar Lawrence's lines to Romeo. "Long love doth so; too swift arrives as tardy as too slow."

Megan enters, wearing Juliet's eager expression. I know Friar Lawrence has the next lines. I forget them immediately.

"Um," I say to Jody, who's sitting in the first row of chairs. "Sorry. Could I go again?"

Jody nods, frowning. Walking off the platform we use as a stage, Megan turns so only I can see the face she makes. Tongue out, eyes rolled up in zombie rictus. Then she winks, the goofy expression collapsing into a grin. She does this whenever we're on stage, sometimes even when she's watching me from the front rows of the audience. Whenever stage fright sets in, Megan finds a way to make me laugh.

Except this wasn't stage fright.

It was noticing the way her dress hugs her hips, the hem brushing her thighs. I've seen her in this dress before and never found myself this interested in the body beneath it. I'm dumbstruck, dizzy, my mouth dry.

I repeat my lines. This time, I'm speaking to myself. I listen to the Friar's warning not to rush this. *Love moderately*. It's ironic, of course. Friar Lawrence repeatedly tells Romeo and Juliet to take things slowly, yet he's eventually swept up in the lovers' impetuousness himself, because it's beautiful. It's irresistible, tinder to the fire.

When Megan enters, I somehow finish my lines without fumbling.

"Good even to my ghostly confessor," she replies, perfectly hitting the syllables of "confessor" for the iambic pentameter. Her gaze holds mine even while she clings to Tyler.

"Romeo shall thank thee, daughter, for us both," I say. Megan traces two fingers down Tyler's sleeve, doing provocative Juliet effortlessly. It is not hard to muster Friar Lawrence's discomfort.

"As much to him, else is his thanks too much." Now she drags her eyes to Tyler, letting them linger. I look away while they continue the scene, all smoldering stares and wandering hands. Jody has them rehearse the lines three times. I hang out uncomfortably on my side of the stage, waiting for them to finish, for rehearsal to end, for me to be back home and done overthinking everything I'm noticing for the first time.

Jody interrupts them, pencil to her lower lip. "Megan, you're *choosing* to play Juliet this overtly sexual, right?"

I hear snickering in the audience. Megan's cheeks don't color. "Yes. The text is pretty clear about Juliet's desires," she replies. "I want to be clear about them, too."

Jody pauses thoughtfully. "Complete mess," Alyssa whispers very not quietly to her friends surrounding her in the middle rows. They hide their laughter unsuccessfully. Megan stands up straighter, unflinching.

"All right," Jody says finally. "One more time."

Pride leaps into Megan's eyes, the way it did on the hill outside. In that instant, everything is different. I don't know what it is until it's upon me. My chest ignites. My stomach flips over. It's like my feelings for Megan were words in a foreign language I couldn't read, and now I know what they say.

I *like* Megan Harper. Not just as a friend, not just as someone I hang out with. I like her with a wanting I can't ignore, a wanting I feel in the pulse pounding in my ears, in the heat raging through me, the tingling in my fingertips and the tightening of my heart.

She brushes past me as she resets the scene. Catching my eyes on her, she raises an eyebrow. I know what she's saying with the look. *You're staring again.*

Yes, I am.

I'm sitting in my room hours later. Since I got out of rehearsal, I've walked home and cooked dinner and helped Sam with his homework and finished my own. Now I'm sitting at my desk, head in my hands. I didn't call Cosima. I didn't know what I would say.

The feelings that overcame me in rehearsal haven't disappeared. They haven't even dimmed. I'm helpless, caught up in infinite questions. When I'll see Megan again, what she's doing now, whether she's with Will, if she's thinking of me, too.

This, I realize, is missing someone. I saw Megan hours ago, and yet this wrenching, magnetic yearning pulls on me harder than months of separation from Cosima. What I'm feeling now is urgent. It's imperative. It couldn't be satisfied by intermittent FaceTime calls or hopes for the coming summer.

I rub my eyes. I should go to bed. It's nearly two in the morning, and I have a French test tomorrow. Or really, today.

Instead, I lean back in my chair. I have to be rational. I can't like Megan Harper. For—reasons. There's Will, for one thing. There's Cosima—whatever our relationship really means to me. But even if there weren't others caught between us, there's the very nature of *Megan* and *me*. She's larger than life. I'm distinctly life-sized. I might be fine to flirt with, but she could never consider me seriously.

The feelings will fade. They have to. If I try harder with Cosima, they'll vanish on their own. It's the only way to protect myself.

I pull out my notebook, needing a distraction and knowing sleep isn't a possibility with the fever of these thoughts. I reread the words I wrote today, focusing on the rhythm, the imagery, even the way my blue-inked handwriting looks on the page. Returning to the end of Nicolas's declaration of love, I pick up where I couldn't finish earlier today.

Now the words come easily. Verses and verses.

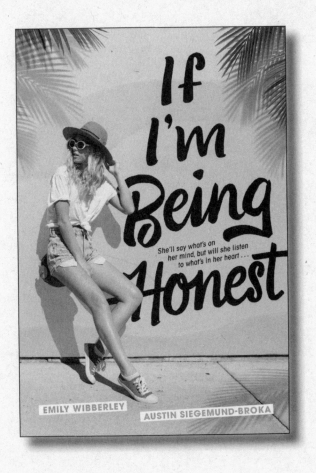

One

"*BITCH.*"

I hear the word under Autumn Carey's breath behind me. I guess I earned it by daring to walk ahead of her to reach the dining hall door. I cut her off while she was examining her reflection in her phone's camera, trying to decide if her new bangs were a bad choice. Which they were. Part of me wants to whirl around and tell Autumn I don't have the *entirety of lunch* to walk behind her, but I don't.

Instead, I tilt my head just enough to tell Autumn I heard her, but I don't care enough to respond. I have things to do. Autumn's not remarkable enough in any way to hold my attention, and I've been called that name often enough, under enough breaths, for it not to hurt. Not from a girl like her. It's hardly an uncommon thought here. *Cameron Bright's a bitch.*

I throw open the door and walk outside. The sun sparkles on the fountain in the heart of the courtyard, encircled by low hedges and lunch tables. It's about a billion degrees out because it's September, when Los Angeles gets apocalyptically hot. I head for the stairway to the second-story patio, under the red-tiled roofs and cream-colored arches of the school's mission architecture.

1

I notice heads turn in my direction. The girls watch me with half worship and half resentment, the boys with intrigue. In their defense, I do realize I'm . . . well, hot. I'm a natural blonde, and I have the body that comes with running six miles a day.

A sophomore girl stares from the railing with the undisguised interest of someone who doesn't realize she's been noticed. I give her a *what?* glance, and she drops her eyes, her cheeks reddening.

I'm popular. I don't entirely know why. I'm hardly our school's only hot girl, and it's not like I'm rich. I'm not. My dad is, but he's lived in Philadelphia since the year I was born, which is not a coincidence. He sends a check for my tuition and my mom's rent, and nothing else. And I'm not popular because my parents have won Oscars or played for sold-out stadiums or were groupies for Steven Tyler. My mom could be considered an actress, but strictly of the washed-up, C-list variety. She had roles in a couple of commercials and stage plays when I was in elementary school. From there, it's been a downward trajectory to watching daytime soaps on the couch and job searching on the internet.

I'm uninteresting among my classmates, honestly. Beaumont Prep—the top-ranked, priciest private school on the West Coast—is full of the children of the rich and famous. Actresses, entrepreneurs, athletes, musicians.

Then there's me. I live forty minutes away in Koreatown. I drive a Toyota I'm pretty certain predates the Clinton presidency. I don't set trends or post photos of myself on Instagram that get thousands of likes around the world.

2

Yet I'm popular. Undeniably and unquestionably.

I find our usual table overlooking the courtyard. Everyone knows the second-story patio is ours, the best view to see and be seen. No one's here yet, which gives me the opportunity to pull my notebook from my bag and write down a quick list, organizing my thoughts.

To Do 9/8
1. Pick up peer-reviewed Wharton essay
2. Conditioning run
3. Econ homework

I know there's a fourth item. I'm itching to remember it, and it's not coming. I use lists to unwind because I get edgy when things feel disorganized and out of my control. The way I feel right now, trying to remember the final thing I have to do today—

"You could come over tonight . . ." croons an obnoxious male voice, unmistakably Jeff Mitchel's. Two bags drop to the ground at the table behind me. I roll my eyes as a female voice replies.

"You're not going to Rebecca's party?" The girl's tone is bashful and obviously flirtatious. I wince. Jeff Mitchel is the worst. Rich, spoiled, and just attractive enough to make him insufferably entitled. He gets straight Ds, smokes pot instead of going to class, and enjoys impressing girls by "treating" them to five-hundred-dollar dinners at Daddy's restaurant.

"Not if you're coming over," Jeff replies. I hear fabric rustling, telling me there's been physical contact. Of what form, I don't want to know. But I have a list to finish, which won't happen with *this* playing out behind me.

Gritting my teeth, I round on the two of them.

I find Jeff in his popped-collar glory, one hand on the white-jeaned knee of Bethany Bishop. Bethany, who's had her heart broken by nearly every one of Beaumont's dumbasses of record, a string of careless rich guys and philandering athletes. I have neither the time nor the inclination to watch this one cross the starting line.

"Really?" I drag my eyes to Bethany. "You're flirting with *him* now?"

Bethany flushes, glaring indignantly. "No one asked your opinion."

"You just got dumped." I ignore her. "The whole school knew. You ugly-cried by your locker for *weeks*. I'm not interested in having to walk past that again on my way to Ethics every day, and Jeff's a worse guy than your ex—"

"Hey," Jeff cuts in.

I fire him a glare. "Don't get me started on *you*." I turn back to Bethany. "Honestly, you're decently attractive. I mean, your wardrobe needs updating, and you have a really annoying laugh. But all things considered, you're a six-point-five for Beaumont. Jeff"—I fling my hand in his direction—"is a two. You could be doing way better," I tell her encouragingly.

Bethany grabs her bag. "Screw you, Cameron." She walks off in a huff, not realizing the huge favor I've done her.

Nobody ever does. When they're not calling me *bitch*, people have told me I'm overly honest. I know. I know I am.

When you grow up with a dad like mine, whose unwaveringly direct commentary came with every one of the rare visits and phone calls we've had throughout my childhood, it's just an instinct. He's never wrong, either, even when his words hurt. Which they do—I know he's a jerk. But he's a successful jerk, with Fortune 500 profiles and penthouses on two continents. With every critique he's given me, I could wither under his words and feel inferior or I could rise to them and become a better version of myself. I've always appreciated his honesty for that.

Bethany clearly sees things differently.

"What the hell?" Jeff asks, irritated. "Bethany was one hundred percent going to put out. You owe me."

"Please. *You* owe *me* the ten minutes of my life I'll never get back."

He eyes me, his expression changing. His raised eyebrow makes me gag. "I could give you ten minutes," he says in a voice he must imagine is seductive.

"I'd rather die."

"Damn, Cameron," he says. "You need to loosen up. Do the world a favor and get yourself laid. If you keep up this ice-queen routine, eventually there won't be a guy left who'd do the job."

"As long as you're first on that list." I'm ready for this conversation to be over.

"You don't mean that. Come on, you're coming to Skāra tonight, right? I'll be there. We could—"

But I don't hear whatever it is Jeff Mitchel wishes we could do tonight, because his offer, while thoroughly disgusting, reminds me of the missing item on my list. I return to my notebook and start writing.

4. Find out if soccer team is going to Skära

I may be a renowned "ice queen" on campus, but I won't be for much longer. Not if a certain member of the soccer team comes to the North Hollywood nightclub where one of the cheerleaders is having a huge party tonight.

"Are you even listening to me?" Jeff whines, demanding my attention.

"Of course not." I look up in time to see my two best friends approaching. Elle Li levels Jeff a look of such pure disgust she doesn't even have to utter a word. Jeff picks up his backpack and *finally* gets out of my sight. I swear, she has a gift.

"Permission to rant?" I hear characteristic exasperation in Elle's voice. She drops down across from me, Jeff entirely forgotten. I close my notebook as she and Morgan place their lunches on the table.

Morgan has her brilliantly blonde hair in an elaborate braid. She's wearing a Dolce & Gabbana dress, but Morgan LeClaire could wear sweatpants and she'd look like a movie star. Because she pretty much is one. Her mom's a record executive, and Morgan's hung out with the Donald Glovers and Demi Lovatos of the world her whole life. She decided she wanted to act when she was ten, and a year ago her agent began booking her roles in local indies. On the bench next to Elle, she looks bored, and I get the feeling she heard the first half of Elle's rant on the walk over from the dining hall.

Elle flits a perfectly manicured hand through her short, shiny black hair. She's five foot two, and yet everyone—teachers included—agree she's the most imposing person on campus.

Which is why I'm not about to interrupt her. "Permission granted," I say, waving a hand grandly.

"MissMelanie got the Sephora sponsorship," Elle fumes, her British accent coming out. She grew up in Hong Kong until she was ten and learned English at expensive private schools. "I made multiple videos featuring their lip liner. I even did a haul video where I spent seven hundred dollars of my own money on makeup I don't need. I wrote kiss-ass-y emails to their head of digital promotions—for nothing. For them to go with an idiot like MissMelanie, who mixes up 'your' and 'you're' in her comments."

Ellen Li, or Elli to her 15 million YouTube subscribers, is one of the highest-viewed makeup artists for her online weekly tutorials. Every week she creates and models looks for everything from New Year's Eve parties to funerals. She's been on *Forbes*'s Highest-Paid YouTube Stars list twice.

Despite my complete and utter lack of interest in makeup or internet stardom, Elle and I are remarkably alike. She's the only other person I know who understands how desperate and careless 99 percent of this school is. Elle's unflinchingly honest, and she'll do anything to achieve her goals. It's why we're inseparable.

And it's why I know she can handle a little attitude in return. I cut her a dry look. "You know you're acting incredibly entitled, right?"

Elle hardly even glances in my direction. "Obviously," she says, hiding a smile. "I'm *entitled* to the Sephora sponsorship because of my hard work, just like I'm *entitled* to have you listen to me unload without complaining because I've come to every one of your interminable cross-country races."

To be fair, this is true. Elle and Morgan have come to pretty much every race I can remember. They're often the only people in the bleachers for me. They first came when I was a freshman, when I'd invited my dad because he happened to be in town for the week to woo investors for an upcoming stock offering. I'd gotten my hopes up he'd come and see me win. When I crossed the finish line, he wasn't there—but Elle and Morgan were. They surprised me by coming, and it was the only thing that kept me from being crushed.

"You two are terrible," Morgan says, shaking her head. "I don't know why I'm even friends with either of you."

Elle and I don't have to exchange a look. We round on Morgan in unison. "You're an honor student, you're nice, you have cool, rich parents," I start.

"You're an actress, and you're gorgeous," Elle continues.

"You're too perfect," I say.

"No one *but* us could handle being friends with you," Elle finishes flatly.

Morgan rolls her eyes, blushing. "You guys really are the worst."

I shrug. "But you love us."

"Debatable," she delivers with a wink. She pulls out her phone, probably to text her boyfriend, Brad.

I catch the time on her screen. *Shit.* There's only ten min-

8

utes left in lunch. I have to drop off the essay I peer-reviewed and pick up mine from the College and Career Center. I shove my notebook into my bag and stand. "Morgan," I say, remembering the final item on my list. "Would you ask Brad if he knows if the soccer team's coming to Skāra tonight?"

Two pairs of eyes fix on me immediately. It's a reaction I knew well enough to expect. "What do you care about the soccer team?" Elle inquires. "You're not considering ending your two-year streak of lonely Friday nights with a hookup, are you?"

"What's wrong with a little window shopping?" I reply lightly. I throw my bag over my shoulder and leave, eager not to be interrogated.

I head in the direction of the College and Career Center. Passing the courtyard fountain, I pointedly ignore Autumn Carey and her friends glaring in my direction. I could not care less. If every glare I earned, or didn't earn but received nonetheless, bothered me, I'd drown in the judgment.

I quicken my steps to cross campus in time to pick up my essay. The College and Career Center pairs up seniors to read and review each other's college essays. It's mandatory, unfortunately, given the utter disinterest I have in my classmates' opinions on my college prospects. I was paired with Paige Rosenfeld, who's outstandingly weird, but luckily I don't have to talk to her. Her essay was about feeling like she couldn't help a classmate who was being bullied, and I gave her only a couple comments. Learning about Paige's personal life isn't exactly item number one on my priority list.

I have *my* essay to worry about. It needs to be perfect. I

worked for the entire summer on the draft I submitted to the CCC. Writing, rewriting, reviewing. I even had Morgan's boyfriend, Brad, who's on track to follow in his dad's footsteps to Harvard, edit it with permission to be harsh, or as harsh as Brad's capable of.

Because I need it ready, polished, and perfect by November 1. The deadline for the Early Decision application for the University of Pennsylvania's Wharton School.

It's my dad's alma mater. Even though we've never lived together, even though our relationship is admittedly dysfunctional, I've long wanted to go where he went. If I got in, he'd know I could. If I got in, we'd have Penn to share.

I walk into the College and Career Center with minutes left in lunch. It's empty, and I cross the carpeted, overly clean room to the student mailboxes. I drop Paige's essay off, then head to my box. The envelope with Paige's comments on my essay sits on top. Hurriedly, I slide the pages loose and start scanning the red ink in the margins.

Which . . . there's plenty of. I feel my heart drop, then race. I didn't plan on particularly caring what Paige Rosenfeld had to say about my essay, but faced with this treatment, it's hard to ignore.

I flip to the final page, where I find Paige has written a closing note. I force myself to focus on each sentence, even when I want to ignore every word.

This just reads as really, really inauthentic. Anyone could write this with a couple Google searches on UPenn. There's no "you" in here. Whatever reason you want to go there, tell them. Try to find a little passion—and then start over.

I frown. Who is *Paige* to tell me what's "authentic"? She doesn't know me. It's not like her essay was brilliant either. If I'd cared, I could have written her a note criticizing her trite choice of topic and overdramatic descriptions. Beaumont hardly has a bullying problem.

It's embarrassing, reading feedback like this on writing I was proud of. The worst thing is, though, I know she's right. I was so wrapped up in being professional that I didn't get to anything personal.

But I refuse to be discouraged. I'm not like Bethany. If I could be broken by harsh words, I would have given up a long time ago. I *will* rewrite this essay, and I *will* get in to UPenn.

Inside my bag, my phone buzzes. I pull it out on reflex and find a text from Morgan.

> The soccer team will be there. Looking forward to whatever you're planning . . .

With half a grin, I flip my essay closed. I drop it into my bag, my thoughts turning to tonight.

Two

I'M LATE TO SKĀRA BECAUSE FRIDAY-NIGHT TRAFFIC on Highland is horrendous, and I had to hunt for half an hour for parking because I didn't want to pay seventeen dollars for the garage. The club is on the top floor of a huge mall on Hollywood Boulevard, between tall apartment complexes and art deco movie theaters. I have to dodge tourists clogging the curb chatting in languages I don't recognize and taking photos of the Hollywood Walk of Fame.

I finally reach the door, and the bouncer waves me in. The club is typically twenty-one and up, but tonight Rebecca Dorsey's dad rented the place out for her birthday. They won't serve us drinks, obviously, but people find creative ways to raise their blood alcohol content.

Under the erratic lighting, I spot him immediately.

He's leaning on the velvet couch near the edge of the dance floor, laughing with the rest of the soccer team. He's the picture of perfect carelessness. The picture of perfect hotness, too. He's tall, built like the varsity athlete he is, and his smile stands out in his corner of the club. I watch him reach up with one arm to rub the back of his neck, pulling up the hem of his Beaumont soccer polo, exposing the strip of dark skin above his belt. It's a nice strip, a really inviting strip.

This is my moment. I just have to walk up to him, join the conversation, and then lead him to a place where it's just the two of us.

But I can't.

The music pounds uncomfortably in my ears. I can't even walk past the kitschy sculpture by the door.

I've wanted this for a year. I've planned for it. Why can't I do this? It's possible I've forgotten how to flirt. I've been rejecting guys for two years while developing this crush in secret. What if I've forgotten how this particular game is played?

I watch him roll his eyes at whatever idiotic thing Patrick Todd's saying, and I know what's coming next. His eyebrows twitch the way they do every time he's preparing one of his effortless comebacks. He's wonderfully no-bullshit.

It's the first thing I ever loved about Andrew Richmond. Even when he was new to Beaumont, I noticed his quick and imperturbable humor. Our friendship deepened because we both felt out of place among our wealthy, glamorous class-mates. Andrew had the added difficulty of being black in our predominately white school. For one reason or other, we both entered Beaumont feeling like outsiders.

I've talked to him countless times, but never in this con-text. Not even crappy pickup lines are coming to mind. I need help.

Feeling my heart race with frustration, I sweep the dance floor for my friends. People I know and people I don't fill the crowded, darkened room. Morgan, dressed like a hipster on a Beverly Hills budget in a strappy gold dress with a beaded headband, perches on one of the L-shaped white couches near the balcony. She's eyeing Brad with that eagerness I've learned to recognize—and avoid. I know where their night's headed, and I won't be interrupting *that*.

But in front of the bar, Elle's running a finger down the arm of Jason Reid. Ugh. I have no problem interrupting Elle's completely indefensible hookup plans. Before she can pull Jason into a dark corner, I cross the room and grab her by the elbow.

"Cameron!" she protests.

I ignore her and usher us both into the ladies' restroom. I close the door, and Elle walks past me. I give the restroom a once-over. It's filthy, and the dimmed lights don't hide the spilled drinks and littered tissues on the floor. In one stall a girl in a sequined dress holds her friend's hair while she dry-heaves over the toilet.

"I hope there's a very good reason you pulled me away from Jason," Elle says, raising an expectant eyebrow.

"Other than the obvious?" I reply, my goal momentarily forgotten. I've explained to Elle a dozen times why I disapprove of Jason. He's an annoying, airheaded actor who adores nothing more than his own reflection. He has a girlfriend, who I'm guessing isn't here—and who I have to hang out with every day during cross-country after school. "You know I don't condone this."

"If I wanted your opinion I would have asked for it," she replies. "Why'd you pull me in here?"

My nerves catch fire. Andrew's out there only feet away. I

14

pace the disgusting restroom floor, running a hand through my hair in frustration. "Do you have a shade of lipstick that's, like, seductive?"

Understanding dawns in Elle's eyes. "You *are* interested in one of the soccer players. Tell me who."

"Andrew."

"Andrew *Richmond*?" Elle starts to smile.

"Do you have any lipstick or not?" I ask loudly, crossing my arms.

Elle's watching me with skepticism and a hint of humor. "For your information, I don't just carry around a complete color palette wherever I go. If you're going to borrow my makeup, you're going to need to text me beforehand what you're wearing and how much sun you've gotten that day. I don't just *have* lipstick for you."

"Fine." I level my gaze with hers. "I'll go borrow Morgan's. I have plans for the night, and if you won't—"

Elle sighs. "Come here," she orders. "You'd look awful in what Morgan's wearing."

With a swell of satisfaction, I lean on the counter, facing away from the mirror, and watch Elle pull out no fewer than four shades of lipsticks from her purse. She proceeds to mix them on her hand and then dab the color on my lips with one finger. Elle's a professional and a perfectionist. I knew she'd have something.

"For years you have me do the dirty work of discouraging every guy interested in you," she says, holding my chin while she paints my lips. "Now you're chasing Andrew Richmond. Would you care to explain?"

"No, I would not," I reply shortly. I could explain if I wanted to. For months I've had a list of reasons to break my no-dating rule for Andrew. *He makes me laugh. He's objectively gorgeous. We're both runners. He's committed. He's proven he has goals and works hard. I don't want to die a virgin.*

"It's because he's new blood, isn't it?" she goes on, ignoring me. "He's new to the popular crowd. He just made varsity soccer, he's the only guy here who hasn't dated every blonde within reach—he's exciting. And you haven't had enough time with him yet to know he's as lame as every other guy."

"I've known Andrew for years," I fire back. "I'd know if he was lame. Like I know with Jason." I cut her a pointed look, which she brushes off. "Andrew's . . . different."

"*How* different?" Elle presses, her voice heavy with skepticism.

I don't reply right away, because I'm remembering a rainy afternoon in December of junior year. We were in my bedroom because our moms were having dinner downstairs, but we couldn't go for a run with buckets pouring from the sky. We'd been working on homework, and I was panicking about a group project on which I'd been paired with none other than Abby Fleischman, who'd unacceptably decided dressing in a ridiculous costume and going to a comic book convention was a worthwhile use of her weekend. Which it obviously wasn't, and we'd gotten nothing done on the project. I was five minutes into a world-class rant about Abby's objectionable life choices when Andrew glanced up from his history textbook.

"People are starving, Cameron," he said dryly. "You'll survive."

I blinked, too thrown to be angry, and burst out laughing. And then Andrew was laughing, and the panic in my chest eased. I noticed he was cute when he laughed. I noticed the dimple in his right cheek. I noticed the way his eyes lit up, and the whole room with them.

"We work. We just do," I tell Elle.

She doesn't reply. "If I'm going to finish your lipstick," she says after a moment, "you'll have to stop smiling like an idiot."

I can't help it. I smile wider.

Elle flicks my nose in return. "Okay." She steps back to scrutinize her work. "You're ready."

Every memory of Andrew and me dances through my head—every conversation, every run, every laugh. Every private, perfect moment. Why was I nervous? Tonight isn't about looking perfect or saying the perfect flirtatious thing. It's about him and me.

"I am," I say, not bothering to check my reflection in the mirror. Andrew knows me better than everyone except my closest friends. All I need is to be myself.

LOOK FOR EMILY AND AUSTIN'S NEXT NOVEL

As We Go Forth